THE MARK OF GOLD

SISTER SEEKERS BOOK 6

BY
A.S. ETASKI

Published by Corpus Nexus Press
ISBN: 978-1-949552-11-9

www.etaski.com
miurag.etaski.com
www.patreon.com/etaski
www.goodreads.com/etaski
www.bookbub.com/authors/a-s-etaski
www.facebook.com/asetaski
www.twitter.com/asetaski

Cover Design by Eris Adderly
Book design by Guido Henkel

*Dedicated to the unsuspecting GM tasked to read
my first 50K-word character backstory,
whose enjoyment in reading it reignited my drive to write.*

For dear Hubs and an old youth gaining wisdom and vision.

CHAPTER 1

THE TREES WERE BENDING.

It was subtle, but I was spooked despite guiding an undead horse in the dark, her tepid muscles rolling without cease.

"What do you sense?" Gavin asked.

"Mm. The forest."

"Vague."

I motioned to our right. "Do you see it?"

"No. It is dark. Describe it to me."

I tried.

In a broad view of continual forest and worsening road, it appeared close to what I'd studied for months at night. Yet in the smaller view, some of these Surface mainstays leaned uphill while some listed down along the very same grade. Older trees possessed bulges and crooks with bark split or stretched like the scars upon Gavin's back, as if these bits might have swelled in the last fortnight instead of gradually adding girth every spring. Next to one, I believed I spotted a sapling with its newest leaves growing underside-up.

There had been birds and insects at sunset, and the rustlings of burrowers in the brush or squirrels in the trees, but I expected those soon to alter their tone. Or disappear altogether.

As I fell quiet, the mare's hooves thudding the ground, Gavin said, "Let us stop soon for a short rest."

The road was deserted. We had passed no one and could camp in the middle without obstructing travel, although resting in the open was not my habit. I smirked, looking ahead for a likely spot to hide on one side. "Are you tired?"

"Some, yes."

"Do you need sleep? Or food?"

"Yes."

I was surprised. *Finally.*

"And guidance," he added.

One brow lifted but I let it be. "Then I shall guard."

The death mage and I had been traveling North from Troshin Bend for two days and a night since our escape from Brom's Inn. We'd stopped thus far only for me, about four hours in midafternoon as I collapsed into a troubled Reverie on solid ground.

Gavin and his brown mare had waited patiently, neither needing sleep. He'd gathered a surplus of wild roots, eggs, and berries to take with us, while I used Callitro's ring to make certain I obtained fresh meat. Unable to preserve my catches for long, I had eaten all which was edible, and Gavin took the rest; we wasted nothing.

Not deep into this second night away from Brom and the Ma'ab, I slowed the horse by mental command alone, clutching the bone talisman tucked beneath my glove into my palm. There were no signs of recent travel, no camps along the path despite the Witch Hunters' earlier claims of passing through twice.

As we moved off the road, I fretted about eating anything here if the woody giants showed me something might be wrong with the soil. Supplies stored in the saddlebags would last about a week if I rationed it, but how long would we be here? How large was the spread of warp rot in this forest, and where would we come out of it?

Will *we come out of it?*

I kept watch while Gavin ate an egg and a handful of berries—too little, indeed, for his tall frame—before he laid down, draping a blanket over his head and torso with his boots sticking out. The pale man had said nothing to me, and I knew the plan well enough not to delay him seeking "guidance" with more chatter.

Although, in truth, I tended to speak to Gavin so the red rune dagger wouldn't speak to me when my mind wandered. I could ignore that gleeful, bare whisper if I wasn't touching it.

You're a curious one. You will use me again.

Carefully, I brought out my three guardian spiders for company. The Dwarven eve witch, Osgrid, had been correct that the magical bubble trapping them within would fade on its own with distance from the sorcerer who'd made it. Not a perpetual spell, thank goddess. Familiar, black arachnids crawled up my arm opposite the dagger to settle on my shoulder and at my nape. They weren't hungry. I was lucky to have them.

I could have lost you.

I kept watch over Gavin as I'd promised, although I sank into a heavier mood as the final events at the town to the South dragged at me.

My spiders hadn't been able to help me.

I was caught with my pants down.

Why hadn't I used the same poison on Kurn which took the Chief Warrant Bictrius? Why had it been the slow fever paste?

Because I grabbed the wrong jar. No sense or time to swap.

What would have happened if I had killed Kurn quickly as he chased me around the kitchen table? I wasn't sure the outcome would have been better. I would not have yielded my netherhole, perhaps, but both Castis and Brom could have done something even harsher to neutralize me, to wrench my will away and press me down. Amelda may have surprised me, for she'd been faking part of her tranquilized sleep.

They still underestimated me.

There was a reason for that. Why *hadn't* I killed the Ma'ab before leaving, surviving such threat? Especially Kurn, drugged again with his own dagger up his ass. I thought on this and hesitated to hear my own answer.

Because Soul Drinker wanted me to, and I refused.

That same moment, Osgrid had been urging me to get out, and Gavin needed me. My baby needed me to escape, and Gaelan was waiting for me. I had little but confusion in the time I made my choices.

And now that it is quiet?

I looked around the forest, listening. I wasn't sure either Rithal or Mathias would or *could* catch up to us. Gavin had gone two days without sleep and his horse wasn't alive anymore; she did not need rest, food, or water. This was a concern as she slowly decayed, moving without healing, feeling neither pain nor caution if she tore a muscle or cracked a bone. Her maker was working on a solution to make her last longer.

Or so he said.

If my allies, the Dwarf and the skin hunter, could not catch up then perhaps neither could my enemies, the Ma'ab and Zauyrian sorcerer. I needed none of them. *I have Gavin and both of Sarilis's vials.*

According to the Zauyrian *and* the Deathwalker, that might be enough to purge the warp rot. Once we found its source.

Soul Drinker chuckled. *I know the source, Davrin. Ask me.*

My ear twitched, and I flicked my hand as if a bug harried it. I made a face to realize my other hand lightly touched the pommel. That was why the voice was so clear.

~*Why would you know?*~ I asked.

We existed long before these chaos pockets began bursting through the material crust. We were there when they began in earnest.

Leading my curiosities. How like a Priestess.

The voice sounded neither male nor female but hissed far less than when I'd been struggling for my life and my mind at the inn. I frowned as the forest around me seemed to waver.

~*Where were you made?*~

★*Oo!*★ The demon sounded surprised. Delighted. ★*North.*★

~*North?*~ I recalled the Zauyrian's story of recruiting the Ma'ab to find the dagger again. ~*The Empire?*~

★*Even farther. Older.* **Colder.** *The Ascended are children compared to what lives at Ice Heart.*★

I eschewed the obvious path, knowing this game. ~*How will you help me when we find the source of the warp rot?*~

Soul Drinker abruptly grew excited, squealing and hissing as it had at our first meeting. ★*Eee-hee-hee! Yesss! Yes, you are determined. And touched. Are all Davrin touched by a broken god? Your Father will be displeased, oh, he will.*★

My face scrunched. ~*The source of warp rot, dagger. I'm asking you.*~

The demon settled down. ★*Cris-ri-phon ended the Desert war. Cris-ri-phon lost the Desert war. Thus, the warp rot spreads where he's not looking. It's all the Sorcerer-General's doing. Why your kind fled ancestral lands.*★

I shook my head. The entity answered to meander and tease but didn't answer straight in the here and now. I asked something else.

~*Do you 'drink' Vis? Or Vitas?*~

I saw red strokes slide around my periphery like a tainted paw caressing a canvas, and the demon snickered. ★*Both. I relish it, gorge on it. And I can share with you. We already have. You've seen her, the Queen's Vis.*★

I swallowed, not daring to ask how her own dagger turned on her.

★*You may feel the Vitas with me, but you must feed me first. Use me, and I shall share.*★

~*Why would I want to share the Vitas of those we've slain?*~

You accepted our aid. I heard you. If you're weak, we can make you strong. If you're hungry, we can satisfy. If you're bleeding, we can heal. Use me. Feed me, and what you lack, you shall have.

I pursed my lips. ~Do you know what a Deathwalker is?~

Hrm? Curiosity. No annoyance at the change of topic. *No. Not truly.*

~How can that be? Cris-ri-phon could have chosen to become one.~

A path denied long before he quested to find me. I hate them. They steal Vis from me, and their souls are… unpalatable.

I glanced at Gavin sleeping. He made occasional grunts beneath the blanket as if he might be dreaming something as uncomfortable as the ground upon which he lay. At the same time, my spiders came into view on my forearm, creeping closer to where I tightly grasped the hilt of the black dagger.

~Who is Braqth to you?~ I asked.

Soul Drinker cackled then shrieked. I flinched like in an outward attack.

Nothing at all, it hissed.

Despite that claim, my guardians eased onto my wrist, chiming softly in their protective way. The heavy air seemed to clear, and my hand relaxed. I drew it away from the relic while I could.

Awww, hehehe…!

~Rest, now. All of us.~

I ignored that fading laugh, cradling my recently freed babies in both hands. I decided not to ask what the demon wanted from joining my journey, for it would taunt me with that knowledge eventually. My Sisters would be in danger after I found them, though, and I could not imagine the potential destruction of carrying it into Sivaraus.

A mental image returned, of Osgrid holding out her hand.

I'll bury it for ye.

Perhaps. After I learned the Queen's full story.

Should I discover where Osgrid or any of her kin had gone.

GAVIN WOKE IN THE COLDEST PART OF THE NIGHT WHILE I walked the perimeter to keep warm. Without warning he sat up, the rough blanket falling from his scowling face, his black eyes glowing an icy blue in the center, his face a misty white. I was accustomed to this new face even as it could never be comforting or forgettable. In that way, the Deathwalker offered insight to how some others might be startled by my appearance.

And I don't have red eyes. No race up here does.

The death mage's gaze was unfocused, floating, seeking that anchor to the waking world. Anxious as I was to hear him speak, I stood still, easy to see but silent, waiting until he spoke first.

Finally, he recognized me. "Sirana."

I smiled a little. "No change here. Far as I can sense."

Gavin nodded slightly and leaned forward, his veiny hands out to push himself up, unfurling like a rapidly rising shoot of grey grass. He looked North and West, lifting a finger.

"Another ten leagues that direction," he said. "The forest will change rapidly."

I frowned. Leagues, again. "That was how far *you* can walk in an hour? Not your horse?"

"Correct."

"Midday by horse, if we do not stop?"

"Indeed, good timing."

I grimaced. "You say. To challenge the warp rot at the brightest of day when my headache is worst?"

"I'd rather not attempt to face it in deepest night," the death mage countered. "I see you by your life aura, remember."

Yet he was clear in every detail to me. I sighed, spotting the large moon on its rise. The last of the night would not be dark, the day ever warmer as sunlight grew so intense as to obliterate the moons. Such were my days, weeks, and months on the Surface.

My stomach growled, and I ate slowly from the saddlebags draped on a standing corpse while Gavin took a brief time to write in his book. My patience lasted only until the end of my meal and the moment his ink had dried.

"So, did you receive 'guidance'?" I asked.

"Warnings," he replied.

"We have no shortage of those while awake."

Gavin glanced up as he firmly stoppered his ink bottle and wiped off the tip of his stylus. "Have you spoken much with the relic?"

I shifted my feet, making effort to keep my eyes on my ally. "Just after you laid down."

"Did it suggest how it harmed the Deathless?"

"No, I did not ask."

I heard a whisper but ignored it, waiting for Gavin to inquire what Soul Drinker had spoken of instead. The Deathwalker did not ask; he continued packing.

"Let us ride and talk. We are fortunate nothing found us."

Nodding, I turned my ear toward the forest. The constant sounds of small and tiny creatures hadn't ceased, though they were quieter than they had been anywhere else thus far. Waiting until he had his pack secured, I observed Gavin delay us a bit longer.

The death mage cut his arm with the eating knife on his belt and offered the blood to his mare. She lapped at it with a wide, dry tongue, the lips of her muzzle stiff as they remained drawn up afterward, exposing her blunt, dully gleaming teeth.

Suppressing a small shudder, I mounted up when Gavin covered his arm and signaled to me. Soon I was guiding the mare onto the overgrown road.

"What warnings has your Greylord offered?"

Gavin paused. "I've never spoke of her thus. Where did you hear this?"

"Amelda. She said your worshipping the Grave Mother of long ago meant you were a traitor to the Ascended, because of your Ma'ab blood."

He grunted. "She would view it as such. I do not. The enslavers of Ennikar do not own the blood in my veins, and almost every deity I've heard whispers about is older than them."

What Soul Drinker had claimed. *Farther North. Older. Colder... Your Father will be displeased...*

"What warnings, then?" I asked.

"Curiously, that the Ma'ab close faster behind us than we expected."

I cursed. "The Deathless as well?"

"Not yet. Left behind, though his daughter rides with the men. Why I asked you what the rune dagger had done to him."

"You *want* me to ask?"

Gavin grunted. "It is not urgent."

I rolled my eyes. "The dagger suggested the same as your dream at the inn. The wrap rot spreads because of the Deathless."

"It did?"

"Beginning in the Desert when the war was lost. It keeps 'bursting' through the material."

"Hm. How?"

"I don't know. It teases answers."

"Unsurprising—"

Our mount stepped in a rut rounding a bend; I didn't see it until it was too late. We jolted forward in a stumble which threw Gavin against my back and me against her neck.

~Stay on your feet! Run!~

The horse caught herself and continued loping without breath. Fortunately, the leg bone didn't snap although any other horse would have pitched us off and collapsed in a squealing heap. Instead, Gavin had kept us mounted by gripping the front of the saddle until I could guide her stable again.

I took a deep breath, attempting to straighten, only to realize how dense he was. As bad as Kurn or Brom, yet he was without their bulk.

"Off!" I grunted. "Heavy."

Gavin rapidly made space between us. "Apologies."

I exhaled in relief. "Where was I?"

"A war lost and somehow causing the warp rot, following the Deathless."

"Yes," I agreed, "but just that."

"Anything else of note?"

"It doesn't know Deathwalkers well, too new. It knows enough not to like them."

"Oh?"

"Yes, the relic drinks both Vis and Vitas, thus its name, Soul Drinker. Sometimes it shares that essence with the wielder, feeding strength or healing. But Deathwalkers 'steal' Vis while being 'unpalatable' in Vitas. It didn't like those death mages in the Desert."

"Ah." Gavin considered. "Interesting."

My ally fell silent, and I gave him time to ponder as I kept close study upon the moon-shadowed road so we would not stumble again.

"If this is true," he said in time, "this relic is your best defense should you be confronted by a natural creature infected by warp rot."

I arched my eyebrow. "You *recommend* I use it against them?"

"In defense, yes."

I made a face he couldn't see but he could hear the rise in my tone. "Sharing warp-tainted souls with this demon blade would *corrupt* me, would it not?"

"No," Gavin replied. "Souls can't be 'tainted' by warp rot."

"Oh? How so?"

"Vis and Vitas are immaterial essences, neutral in power. This essence follows the ebb and flow of Existence. Those who study or feed on it may use it for any purpose, for currency or vitality, yet none corrupt the order of things even if they may imbalance resources around them."

I scowled at the passing ground, prompting my scholar to continue. "What is corrupted, then?"

"It is *how* Vis and Vitas are re-bonded with the material of a single plane. It ignores natural processes as we know them. If you could pluck a sliver of light from a bolt of lightning and use it to weave a cat to a candle—"

Weave a cat to a candle?

"—the result is illogical and mad. But due to the corruption of the very rules by which we are, it works. At the same time, it isn't sustainable without constantly changing and feeding those altered processes, an escalating imbalance seeking to correct itself. Thus warp rot grows and eventually alters things beyond sustainable function, beyond where the cat or candle should exist. The cat should have rotted away, and the candle melted and guttered out. Yet they remain as something that may be neither and both."

The image in my head spread to the trees around me. Shaking off a shiver, I huffed. "What happens if I stab this 'cat-candle' with the rune dagger to take the essence?"

"The mal-bonded threads of lightning would sunder. The mad process and cycle are interrupted, forcing the transition."

"Transition? If that is so, how can any but death mages and relics accomplish this?"

"Mages perform similar effects with other talents. The importance is not life or death, but altering the essence *using* the rules of our home. Resetting them. With corrupted bonds cut, these chaos bodies self-destruct to become their simplest parts again, accessible to the material and no longer warp rot."

I took a slow breath. "That... does not sound like a beautiful process."

"Indeed, it may be terrifying. Pure madness for the weak of will. Generally, a trained mage has the will to withstand it."

"Noted." I scowled to think only a cursed dagger might put me on a level like Gaelan or Gavin, to accomplish something like this. "So, why will Sarilis's vials work as well?"

"Its design is a catalyst, inducing a surge in a well-known Ley site, potentially making it unresponsive or unfamiliar to the Bishops who have controlled it for three centuries. What I did not know then but could guess is how far this surge may reach along the Ley Lines, and what it may disturb in doing so. If the Deathless warned you that we would not get the chance to find out, then he likely has some idea what would happen."

Another frown. "But? He is well with using it on the warp rot, even though he's causing it somehow?"

"A catalyst," Gavin repeated, "and a surge of power using the known rules of magic. Yes, I agree with Brom that it would sweep clear a lot of corruption in one or two waves. Perhaps all of it if we release the vials near the center of its influence."

"I see."

In contrast, I had stolen a method to stab my way closer to that center and undo the same corruption. To think how *useless* I would be otherwise because I was not a mage.

Unless 'mind mage' counts.

I did not see how. Everything my Elders had said, everything I'd experienced in fighting the Ornilleth and the Tragar, *everything* Phaelous had said about my saphgar pendant...

These do not seem to follow the 'known' rules of magic.

Did that mean psions were corrupt by their very nature? Is that why so many Davrin mistrusted them? If mages were crucial to "re-setting" these boils of warp in our home plane, then where did a psion fit? If one were present amid warp rot, would this fact make it worse or neutral? I did not see making it *better*. All the psions I knew were hidden far, far below.

Perhaps they didn't have a place on the Surface.

Should I tell him? Try to explain what he's seen? What I've done?

My mind blanked, at a loss how to begin, especially as we were so close to our goal, with the warning of pursuers catching up.

The sky had brightened considerably while I'd been brooding, the dawn rapidly turning blue. I noted continuing, cross-growing trees along the slopes and sickly green bits growing like toadstools through brown leaves. The birdsong was weak and mournful. Uneven and unsettled.

I thought someone weeping.

Or laughing.

~Slow.~

She responded, dropping from a canter to a trot.

"Sirana?"

~Stop.~

From a walk, the mare obeyed, holding in place with her ribs unmoving. Gavin was looking around us.

"Did you hear anything?" I murmured.

"No. What was it?"

"A voice. I could not tell if—"

The abrupt cry came again, and my eyes snapped left where the road's bank swelled up and disappeared over a crest. I waited to see if anything would come sprinting over the hill, leaping down from the high ground.

~Walk forward.~

The mare carried us around a bend to where we could see more of the forest floor on either side of us. I felt marginally better.

"Did you hear it that time?" I asked.

Gavin hesitated but answered true. "No."

Great.

17

"Am I hearing tricks of the wind?"

"Perhaps not. Your hearing is keener, and you are sensitive to sleeping thoughts."

"Only when *I'm* sleeping."

"Up here. You said you were injured below. Was this different before?"

I didn't respond. I couldn't say then *how* it was below. I'd never fully discovered what it was...

For a moment, I couldn't remember anything before Kerse.

Nothing before Reishel.

"Sirana. Your aura is warping. Be calm."

~*Easy for you to say.*~

"We needn't discuss it."

"Thank you," I croaked.

The Sun was full in the sky, and Gavin's hands had shifted tar black as my eyes began to ache. I gave up resistance and donned my sunblind, unable to tolerate intense light with the increasing rustling around us, the distant crying, and the disturbing cessation of insects and birds.

It helped me that Gavin's mare could not be startled, that none of my tension transferred to her, that she would not rear up or bolt unless I commanded it. My companions' cool bodies and calm supported my lead, kept my actions deliberate, my impulses numbed. If any predator here smelled my fear, sensed my spiking body heat, perhaps my not-living companions muffled it.

Mere months ago, that would have seemed strange.

Nothing approached as we climbed the fading road. The forest merely... watched us.

Something watches us.

"Do you see the green auras?" Gavin asked.

"I see nothing," I replied irritably. "Even without the Sun. I am not a mage."

18

"Very well. Shall we trade places for the day? I would prefer you focus on what you hear."

This exchange was normal between us; the one with the better eyesight guided the mare. Still, I regretted giving up the task, reluctant to trade it for the vaporous wails and incorporeal laughter, sounds better suited inside the Sathoet chamber of the Sanctuary than a vast forest upon the Surface.

We stopped, I swung one leg forward and over the mare's neck, turning to slide and drop off the side. I noticed how much weed and grass lay beneath my boots, how the colors were off through my blind, and the abundancy devouring the dirt road. The sky was visible, but I wondered how far before the shade deepened and the contorted trees closed in.

I clasped the grey mage's hand and the saddle pack, springing up to drape myself across the wide rump and eventually wriggle upright moments before Gavin silently urged our mount to a brisk walk.

"We expect to approach 'the center' by midday?" I asked.

"Unless something delays us. Will you pass me one vial?"

Carefully, I withdrew the wrapping which contained Sarilis's vials and passed Gavin one. "Where do we drop these? What do we seek?"

"I do not know its form. I will recognize it by its aura."

Something unseen tickled along my ear, and I shivered, scratching the itch. "Do you imagine there will be resistance?"

"Probably. Unpredictable to say what or when, however."

"Brom said warp rot mimics fears."

"That may not be deliberate. A frightened sentient offers many possible shapes once the cycle of corruption has begun."

My hands clenched where they rested on my thighs. "Hmph. It still bothers me I have not seen evidence of eighteen horsemen having come this way in the last week."

Gavin shrugged. "The massive storm which caught us was moving North. The downpour would have erased it for leagues."

"And any sign of Gaelan. I do not know where to begin looking for her here."

The Deathwalker turned his head somewhat. "Help me purge the warp rot first, and the field will be clearer afterward. We will have time then to seek what became of her."

"Will we? Your mistress warned of the Ma'ab closing in on us. Say we accomplish this cleansing quickly. We may be forced into a hit and run game of chase."

Gavin did not speak for a while. "Do you suggest we somehow search for her first?"

I grumbled, "No. Seeing her mission complete is wiser. I am only… regretful."

"Regretful of what?"

"That I did not kill them and be done with that filth."

"Hm. I assumed you prioritized escape."

My mouth tightened. "Hm. What did you 'prioritize'? It wasn't escape until Jacob was dead."

Gavin grunted as well. He may have been pondering an answer, but I had no patience for anything cryptic.

"What of Rithal and Mathias?" I asked instead. "They said they would meet us later."

"They did, but I find it unlikely. I think they will turn around if they run across the Ma'ab, or once they see this place. Neither had goals this far North nor are they mages, so their help is doubtful anyway."

Just the two of us, then.

Us and those who stalked us.

Gentle breezes began to pass by my ears in odd ways, not brushing past but bending to collide with us like we were the heaviest boulder on the mattress. With them came moaning and giggling, snarling, and screaming. Tremors rippled through the air as the sounds grew loud enough for Gavin to hear as well.

"Closer," he confirmed.

The road had disappeared as shade deepened, and I removed my blind to free my periphery as chills spread over me. I saw yellowish haze collecting in several copses of trees, always positioned near the top of a hill, with bluish hazes unreliably flowing into dips and depressions on the forest floor. Gavin was sure to guide us in a wide berth around them.

Had the Witch Hunters reached this far? Or were we in the unexplored region no one sane had seen in however long?

"Do you see a situation where we would retreat?" I murmured. "Perhaps recruit mages at Augran, as Brom suggested?"

Gavin was silent long enough to give me his answer. I waited for him to collect his thoughts and speak.

"No," he began flatly. "The Ma'ab siege at Manalar will be in full rush by the time we travel to Augran and return here. The corruption will only be worse. I have died once; I've lost that fear. I will not retreat."

"Fortunate for you."

"We'll see. You did not have to come with me, but you *are* capable of aiding this task. Our trade was my effort to find your sister in this region before the Ma'ab or Deathless might, correct?"

"That has not changed."

"Indeed."

I paused to observe the twisting forest in despair before bursting out in frustration, "*Why* hasn't anyone done anything before now?! Why did an ancient sorcerer ignore it on his own border for over a season? Why not Osgrid or... or anyone?!"

The death mage shook his head. "I do not know. But we are here now. As an Elf, you may feel this threat more invasively than I do, but we agree it cannot be overlooked any longer. If anything, your Queen assured this before you came to the Surface."

I sneered. *Yes, at Gaelan's expense.*

And Jael's, with her standing in the path of that coming siege. How much did she know about what she sought? If her contact with the Valsharess was like mine, it wasn't enough to survive without resisting at every turn. My hope for her there lay in knowing that resisting was all she'd ever done.

My arms had tightened around the death man's waist; I did not realize it until he leaned forward. I let him go, felt my face flush in irritation that I'd been clinging at all.

As if he can shield me from my doubts.

I summoned a deep, deep breath, releasing it with my hands on my stomach.

You are capable of aiding this task.

I will not retreat.

"*We are here,*" I spoke in Davrin. "*No demons but us.*"

"Hm?" Gavin asked.

I smiled. "Nothing. I will not run, Gavin. We shall reach the center."

The Deathwalker nodded, guiding his unshakeable steed deeper into the trees.

"*…Sirana…!*"

With nothing in front, cautiously, I looked behind.

Nothing.

The horse breathlessly heaved her way up a steep slope and then another. The clouds had thickened while the trees thinned, and for a moment I could see a glimpse of the old road not yet overgrown wending its way South. I should not have been able to see so far in the day, and yet I glimpsed a large, black horse and a man riding it. A few others who could be Castis and Amelda followed.

"*…Sirana…*"

"*…coming for her…!*"

"…kus…"

I looked away, taking a drink with my waterskin once the ground levelled out and my glimpse of road vanished. "Do you hear shouting behind us?"

"No," Gavin answered without hesitation. "I see something ahead of us."

What?

I leaned around his long torso, familiar by now, as we slowed and stopped by silent command. At first, I could not tell if what sat on its haunches by a stream was a massive dog or a giant frog.

The mottled green-black hide was speckled with warts and blisters, patches of fur sprouted but failed to make a coat. The long, sticky tongue panted, dripping a gooey mucous which floated in the water. Bulbous eyes were void black, staring across the way, not at us. It grunted, the bloated body bearing down, and expelled pearly green beads from a rear orifice. These spread across the soil in a fishy froth I could smell before blackening and become sludge before our eyes.

"Let me," Gavin whispered. "Be ready."

I pressed my palm briefly to his back for acknowledgement, unable to see what motions or focus helped him prepare.

Better to watch the rest of the forest.

A gravid frog could be solitary, but a mother dog may be part of a pack. Or it may follow no such logic at all, and we could only react as things arrived.

I was certain I saw shadows of movement in the brush as Gavin murmured in the dead tongue, and we clopped a few steps closer. A strange buzz settled in my ear when Gavin lifted his hand in a similar arcane gesture to when he'd blocked Castis's fire spell. The frog-dog jerked its body in a laborious hop, turning on slimy mud to face us; its tongue whipped out of the water and lashed out at us, crossing an impossible distance.

"Ussgreyn!" Gavin barked, completing his motions, pitching his focus and his aura at one target.

Black fire caught the bulbous end of the creature's tongue and raced toward the demented wielder like its spit was an accelerant to real fire. The egg-layer gulped and bellowed a baying croak that sent every leaf to quake as it dove into the stream.

"*Sillhyenis!*" the death mage added, intensifying his gestures with arm outstretched.

The black fire did not turn to steam upon touching the water. Indeed, it wasn't burning at all as it consumed the wailing warp rot. As any reality I'd been sure of crumbled before my eyes, I looked away in time to see the smaller, yellow-black version of this thing not five paces away.

The creature lashed its tongue out and caught Gavin's forearm in a sizzling loop. The death mage's dark skin turned grey where the tongue held him, something oozing out. It started bawling, equal chance in pain or victory.

I dropped off the horse, drew the red rune dagger, and launched straight at the canine amphibian, punching the tip through center mass as that familiar voice shrieked in joyful surprise.

Yesss! Yesss!

Staring at bulging, swirling eyes, I expected the unnatural body to explode and cover me with gooey filth. Instead, it shriveled and charred like a vegetable on a spear over a campfire. I choked and coughed, drawing back, gripping the handle of the dagger as if it kept me from falling a cliff. Surreal warmth swept up my arm to my chest and immediately my lungs cleared. I took a full breath.

I felt well.

Looked around for another target.

Nothing.

"Gavin?" I asked, looking to him.

He'd rolled up his sleeve to inspect the black blood cooked into a crusty ring around his grey-dappled arm.

"Hm," he grunted.

Uhhh-ohhh. Hehehe!

I kept watch, shifting my weight nervously. "Does that hurt?"

"Yes. Though not... how I remember pain."

New pain is a bad sign.

I cleared my throat. "Will it... grow worse?"

Gavin arched a brow. "Am I infected, do you mean?"

I shrugged.

Yesss, you do. Say it!

I kept my mouth closed as Gavin's icy eyes shifted over to the shriveled corpse I'd stabbed turning to a grey ash or powder. He held out his wounded arm, pulling the long sleeve back. I was at a loss.

"You said Soul Drinker once found Deathwalkers 'unpalatable,'" he began.

Ohhh, nooo... The dagger groaned like it covered a face.

"Perhaps it would like to suck out the 'maggots' of Vitas which this corrupted tongue left behind?"

Bah! Best friends, his maggots!

"What should I do?" I asked.

"Press the flat of the blade against my skin."

Hah! What a hideous palate!

"What if..." I waved with my free hand. "It turns the edge on you."

Gavin shrugged. "Then we shall find out if Soul Drinker would attempt to steal from the Grave Mother. That would be interesting to see."

Grrrrr.

One corner of my mouth lifted as I checked around us again and approached Gavin's arm, taking firm hold of his wrist to lay the naked blade against the wound blistering my ally's skin. I heard grumbling; it wasn't Gavin.

~There will be many more of these things, dagger. Keep us both strong, and you'll feed well today.~

Several of the runes flashed red as the poison-scorched blisters dried up. *You'd best find full sentient offerings, Davrin. This is demeaning to my true power.*

~You want it all the same, I notice. Drink.~

Grey flakes began falling from Gavin's skin, and while a fresh rise of black blood concerned me, I could also see the Deathwalker's skin healing.

Or, closing, at least. Renewing, somehow.

Hsssss...

"That is good," Gavin said.

Lifting the black metal from his skin felt like trying to pull an eager lizard away from his meal too soon. I took a step away for added assurance, watching as the man's long fingers prodded and traced over new pale skin, quickly turning dark and smooth in the daylight.

He nodded in satisfaction. "It worked."

I breathed out in relief.

"However, I would not recommend this remedy for anyone not sworn beyond death to a higher being."

Pfeh.

I smiled dryly. "Noted."

"Do you need a hand up?"

I turned to look at the deepening forest beyond the stream and shook my head. "I will walk beside you. Fastest way to act with a dagger."

Gavin dismounted. "Then let us both walk and use the mare as a shield."

"Good idea."

The mare's flesh was breaking down, anyway. If Gavin did not come up with a way to mend or preserve her, then acting as moving cover would be her final service in our journey. This thought would dismay Tamuril, for this wasn't much different from Sarilis's grinding down of animal corpses.

Even our present task echoes from decades ago. Sarilis and Rausery. Gavin and me.

Though the black dagger had suggested longer. Deathwalkers, Desert Queens, and lost wars were why we'd come here.

Still cleaning up someone's mess.

CHAPTER 2

SOUL DRINKER STAYED NAKED IN MY HAND, NOT ONLY TO IMPROVE my response to threat but because we discovered the dagger detected concentrated Vitas somewhat like Gavin's eyes. My arm moved without conscious effort as the tip of the blade pointed at living creatures like ferrous shards drawn to a lodestone.

The dagger did not control the hand which held it; I could resist and override it for now. However, its voiceless tug provided spare moments for me to react to the plethora of mindless tendrils and viny pseudopods quickly thickening the forest, so I gave the red rune dagger this slack.

Gavin had noticed these instants of warning which spared him having to speak; he did not protest and focused on casting to undo the warped creatures accosting us. Like me, he accepted the aid of the relic despite shared misgivings that its feeding on this simple essence soon wouldn't be enough.

You'd best find sentient offerings, Davrin.

At the same time, Soul Drinker was generous in sharing what it drew off the environment. After confronting the amphibious canines, I *had* been growing hungry. Now, I wasn't, despite not having eaten. No sharp pangs, no light-headedness or weakness in my limbs as I kept moving. No distraction.

Not like when I'd been running from Gavin's killers.

As we climbed, the scent of the darkening forest shifted to something foreign and upsetting. Sour, bitter, sweet, and unnamed. All at once. I'd expected "rot" but knew well the scent of bodies and plants decomposing, and this was not it. As Gavin had explained, this was not happening; change was unchanging, its escalation worrisome for anything living.

Interrupt the cycle.

The warp rot had enfolded us completely, and I tightened the strings on my spiders' pouch, despite their protesting chimes. *~No. Be still.~*

I did not want to discover what warp rot would do with venom like theirs on compromised creatures, or how their little bodies would change. Tree limbs swayed like long slugs, dripping mucous and weaving in a nonexistent wind. We stabbed or engulfed these in magic, creating a path out as the writhing branches dropped off, but left the tree standing.

Constant yips and cries sounded within a purpling brush while we worked, sometimes fleeing, sometimes charging us. Gavin's ethereal fire flowed along the ground in waves, leaving barren dirt and chirping roaches in little piles of ash. It was slow going for a long time; estimating that we'd reach our goal by midday was a useless measure. I lost track of time as the light filtering in was sickly green and greyish blue. Leaves turned shades of red and purple but unlike what Rausery had described in the falling season.

"Must we stab every tree in the forest, I wonder?" I muttered aloud.

"No lasting good there," Gavin answered. "We must purge the center."

We still didn't know what that looked like. I wanted to ask why there *was* a "center," how it began or how he knew it existed, but these curiosities were only to distract from my dread.

In truth, I feared what we would see. I hoped Gaelan had somehow resisted the Queen's curse and escaped from here after the Witch Hunters saw her. She clearly hadn't succeeded in her mission before I arrived.

If we find her, and she is corrupted, whispered the blade, *we can cleanse her. Free her essence from warp rot.*

I swallowed. ~Liar.~

A menacing hiss. *Not one bit, you arrogant Elf.*

I weighed that. Indeed, freeing her essence from warp rot was true regardless of what happened next. My stomach roiled at the thought of communing with Innathi and Gaelan at the same time, born millennia apart but somehow dead in the same time.

Hehehe! We like this thought!

~Quiet.~

Maybe? No. No, I think not.

I went out of our way to stab another snail-limb, for Soul Drinker tended to talk the longer it waited for the next feeding. It rumbled with contentment as Gavin watched me curiously, his pale hand resting on the horse's neck. I returned on the path we were making as branches fell off, landing in a black poof on yellow-red grass.

"Relic speaking again?" he asked.

"Nothing helpful. Continue."

We used Gavin's mare for the first time to slow a pack of bare-backed wolf-rabbits covered in warty pustules, so we could take them one or two at a time. The undead mare made no sound, but we saw afterward that she had numerous bites. As with Gavin's arm, Soul Drinker grudgingly sucked the Vitas "maggots" out of the bitemarks while the death mage again let her lap at his blood.

The relic stopped the moment it encountered whatever strength Gavin's blood extended to the horse. *Yech! Tough as Orc hide!*

I smirked, absently patting the torn animal's withers as if she could feel it. ~Good sign for us.~

Pfeh.

Deeper into the hills we went. Gavin and I had long since pulled our hoods up against frequent drips of slime from high in the branches. Neither of us dared look up to confirm, but the sky could have been overcast or we could have entered a greenish fog bank that nestled in the upper canopy.

Either way, it was dark enough that Gavin tripped over a tendril or arching root in the deeper shadows. The lighting began to remind me of wild, glow worm caves in the Deepearth.

Ahead, it was growing stronger.

Sssirana...

I frowned but focused, wary of what might lay over the next hill.

Sssirana?

~Quiet, dagger.~

I ignored my name a third time.

Heh. Should I stop shielding you, then, from what's been trying to gain your attention?

The dagger's handle cooled in my palm to an extent I could feel it through my glove. At the same time, a will and endurance I had thought was mine was instead leeched from my limbs. My armor felt... *thinner* in body and mind. The cries and laughter were loud, no longer muffled. I choked on the scents of decadent madness tumbling past me. Unseen threats enveloped me, closer to getting through my clothes, into my very *skin!*

~No!~

"Sirana!"

I spun around to hear a female voice, keeping the mare at my back. Gavin stopped.

"Don't," I pleaded aloud.

"Don't what?" he asked, preparing to anyway.

I might have been speaking to him, not to the imposter mimicking Gaelan.

Her smile was frightful. "Sirana. You came here."

Goddess. It's not her. It's not.

"Sirana?"

"Gavin!" I yelped, pointing with the black dagger. "What is that?"

He paused. "I see a corrupted corpse."

"What kind of corpse?" I snapped. "What race?!"

"Human. Paxian."

Gaelan's three-eyed face wrinkled with disapproval, her head shaking in disappointment as one ear curled in on itself like a bark worm. Her black boot took a step closer in the slimy muck. And another. Uncoordinated, jerky and without grace.

"Kiss me," she said, holding out her arms.

Frozen in place, I felt Shyntre's pendant warm up as the gap between us closed.

Shhhall we, Red Sisster?

My arm lifted, brandishing the weapon in defense as a broad, skewed grin split Gaelan's face in half.

Then Gavin's shadowy fire flew past me, engulfing the first two-legged warp victim we'd seen, and sending Soul Drinker into a whirl of demonic insults about the Deathwalker's private pastimes. I didn't repeat them, only watched Gaelan's face peeling off, falling like the dull flakes of an extinguished fire. My vision blurred before the body crumpled, bones click-clacking against the ground.

*That was **mine!*** Soul Drinker roared.

"Sirana?" Gavin asked.

I took a breath to speak, coughing on the thick, sickening haze.

"What pains you?"

I hunched over, hacking up a glob of spit. ~Everything!~

"That wasn't a Davrin. I assure you."

Tell him we get the next one! Me! Tell him!

~Argh...~

"Th-the relic," I choked out, "wants the next two-legged one."

"Only if it doesn't waste time," Gavin replied with indifference. "Act quickly, and it may have all it can take."

★*Good! I shall beat you to the horde, I will!*★

"Alright, yes!" I answered, and my next breath was easier.

And the next.

My limbs no longer shook, and my head cleared as the incessant crying and face-clogging scents dampened into the background once again. I felt strong. Glancing over, I saw the bones turning into black mulch. Gavin was right about it being Human. The skull, rib cage, pelvis, and femurs were far too thick to be a Dark Elf.

It was not Gaelan, and I was seeing things.

My heart hammered inside my chest when we took up opening the path again. No twisted vision of Gaelan popped out from the brush, though a cluster of naked, screaming Humans did.

Former Humans.

The dagger and I quickly acted this time. Using the horse as a spacer, we took three down with only one stab each to the chest, regardless if I hit the heart or not. Gavin destroyed the fourth one coming too close. Thankfully, the relic didn't have another fit over this "theft," but hummed with delight following each body dropping, ultimately content with the Priestess's share.

Meanwhile, the ice blue of Gavin's irises disappeared as he stared ahead. A trick of the shade could suggest he had no eyes, those sockets empty as a skull.

No, no, of course he can see.

Probably more than I ever wanted to.

The Deathwalker put a long finger perpendicular to his lips, suggesting no talk, before he motioned to me but put his palm out toward the horse. I wanted to sign to agree on the farthest distance we'd go from her, but that was too complex for his crude sign language.

Very well.

Hunched over, we took the next crest with caution, stepping over writhing roots and crushing yellow plants like they were made of glass. While I grimaced at the unavoidable noise, there was enough wailing and shrieking ahead to cover it as we reached the top. Below us there was movement, but we couldn't see detail from here.

Black blade out, mottled hood up and lightly glistening with yellow sap, I used cover to descend, peering through trees bleeding violet and red from carvings made beneath their bark. I stopped in a low crouch with a better view, and my eyes widened.

Ohhhh… shit.

Gavin joined me in a similar position, his shoulders higher than mine and sloped forward. Soul Drinker pointed down the glistening slope, I tapped Gavin's shoulder with my free hand and mouthed with eyebrows high, *"Center?"*

The death mage nodded solemnly.

We had found it, but I didn't know how to *begin* this, much less where to end it. Below us, several hundred running paces away, was a fresh scar of the earth filled with wandering and rolling bodies, mostly Human and forest animals. They numbered in the hundreds, drifting, knocking into each other, attempting to keep in the orbit of a crude, mildewy quartz pillar which had broken through the raw earth.

After I stared at it longer than three ticks, it resembled a stocky, Dwarvish torso with four arms and too many curled fingers shredding the flesh-like moss from its face.

I whispered, *"Gavin."*

He didn't answer at first, void-black eyes staring at the source of the warp rot. I tugged on his robe sleeve, and his neck popped when he turned it to me. All that time riding to Troshin Bend, and I hadn't thought to suggest learning some Davrin sign as he had taught me Trade with a Manalari accent.

"Overwhelming," I whispered.

No-o-o-o, Soul Drinker cooed sinisterly. *A valley of plenty! Go on.*

"Must have drawn whole villages," Gavin replied, pondering.

I held still, without ideas for the moment. We couldn't pitch the vials from here, and I would not wade my way down there only to be overborne, no matter how hungry the black dagger was. The Witch Hunters had been right; this needed as many mages as one could conscript.

According to Gavin, there had been two mages following us.

Maybe three.

I glanced behind me, confirming that the forest had not re-claimed or hidden the trail we'd made this far. It was easy both to follow the powder-grey line of trees to the road, and for someone to follow us in.

"Gavin," I whispered, tugging on his sleeve again and motion-ing away from the crest. "Must talk."

He shook his head. "Must observe. See if any leave."

"If Ma'ab behind us, could get caught here. Need a plan."

A swelling chorus of agony erupted among those dancing wild-ly around the warped quartz, and for an instant I thought we'd been noticed. It settled quickly, however, and for the moment we were undetected, but it was enough to spook Gavin. He agreed to with-draw for now.

CAUTIOUSLY, WE MADE OUR WAY TO THE HORSE, BUT I HEARD too many creatures where we were. They would be drawn to us eventually, so we mounted up on the mare with me guiding in the shadow and strange light. We walked calmly at first, only to dis-mount in a hurry to take care of a skittering clutch of ducks with pointed teeth.

"Even the demons make more sense than this!" I barked once.

"Good to know," said Gavin dryly.

Once we were mounted again, I urged our horse to a brisk trot along the clear grey path, eager to be some place we could relax a little. The next time we were accosted, we'd kicked up to a gallop before I could properly see what they were. We flat outran them.

Aww. Coward.

~Innathi wants her story told. I can't do that if I fight without plan or heed.~

By your touch upon her soul, I'd protect you amid that festering pocket, warrior.

~You didn't before when I saw something not there. I don't trust you.~

You doubted me. That was only a taste of how strong I can be for my wielder. You are the fool if you see only punishment.

"Gavin," I said aloud, my voice uneven from rolling with the horse's gait as I worked to sheath a grumbling relic.

"Yes?"

"Talk, please."

"About what?"

"Pick something. Um. Who taught you Ma'ab in the Greylands?"

"That is difficult to describe. A scholar and keeper of tongues for my Lady."

"No name?"

"I wasn't provided one, nor did I ask."

I exhaled, guiding the mare along a lumpy stream, somewhat slowed as we loped beside it. It was enough to take hold of the black hilt again so it could eavesdrop as I formed my next thoughts.

"Very well. Your thoughts on backtracking to seek Castis and Amelda instead of waiting to be cornered? We could bargain for their service."

Gavin was silent.

Then, "Kurn will be with them."

Soul Drinker chuckled; it was listening intently. My mouth stretched; I wasn't sure if it was a smile, a grimace, or a sneer.

"I know," I said. "This is too big for us, and we have no time to hire mages from Augran before the siege. There are two other mages close by, and we know what they want. Kurn may draw out a third."

"What do you mean? The Deathless?"

"No, the aura you sensed in the canyon. It hasn't followed me here. It must be the Hellhound it wants."

My ally sounded deeply skeptical. "How *would* you bargain with them?"

"I have the red ruby, the vials, *and* the relic. The men must have the former, yes? They cannot return home without it."

"Hm, I'd forgotten."

"And Amelda will not want me to keep Soul Drinker, stolen from her sire. Yet as with you, she cannot command alliance. The relic chooses, not her."

So true…

Gavin grunted. "And you say there is no evasion. Only delay and pursuit."

"Correct. If we cannot purge the warp rot alone, we are flanked by dangerous foes and insanity. There is no truce. Only victory for the boldest of us."

I hadn't been ready to claim that stance until I witnessed the true scale of the warp rot, but the red rune blade squealed in delight to hear me say it. The death mage made a noise of acknowledgement but not agreement, so I added to my argument.

"The Ma'ab want us intact. We want them dead. I have my guardians back, and you have your black blood. Meanwhile, they lack their will-bender stone or anything to trap your Vis for their masters. We have the advantage."

"I imagine they have thunderstones," Gavin countered. "What is your proposed response should they surprise us with one?"

I scowled. I hated those things, and I didn't have a convincing answer.

Prevent it, Soul Drinker suggested. *Use the ruby on the fire mage who makes them. Compel him not to. It's only fair, broken one. He tried to rape your mind as the others raped your body. Hold the stone in your bared hand, and I can show you how to use it.*

My heart was pounding in my ears while an ill trickle of interest and excitement entered my thoughts.

"Sirana?"

"I'm thinking," I said. "What would happen if they use blade or fire on you?"

"The same as if you were struck with such methods," Gavin replied with a tight tone. "I recover from injuries faster, but I will still be injured before that with all the consequences of such."

So I'd witnessed when he cut himself. "What would it take to trap your Vis for the Ascended?"

"You say this twice now. Where did you hear it?"

"Cris-ri-phon. He said Amelda had nothing she could use against you in such a way, so it was better to keep us both in Troshin Bend while Kurn and Castis sought the warp rot with the vials."

"He spoke this in front of you?"

"No. I was listening outside with Osgrid. He was waiting for me."

Gavin grunted and answered my question. "She is not a death mage, so she would need an object of power designed for this exact thing. Aside from the rune dagger, I did not sense anything else in my time inside his office, nor as I walked about the town."

"That is good. You sensed Soul Drinker?"

"Yes. It is a Vis trap. A strong one, and the only object she could have used against me."

"Huh." My thoughts on her motives for chasing us shifted. "Then it is for more than her sire's pride she wants it back."

"I imagine so."

"The dagger claims even the Ascended can't speak to the dead taken by it."

"Boastful. I would not believe that on its word alone."

Soul Drinker snickered, enjoying this conversation, but nudged me again. *The red stone. Tell him. Unless you have a better idea?*

I tried to think of one. Those damned thunderstones. Other than demanding that the Ma'ab hand them over before we entered the forest—?

Come now, broken one, that won't work. You cannot win if you do not use your greatest weapons.

~That would be you and the ruby?~

Much more. The mind magic that is your own. I've not enjoyed such clear banter and resistance in a long time. Most minds are like mashed dung wrapped in fog compared to yours, Blue Eyes. We'd enjoy learning how you came to be this way. You are a worthy wielder. We will help you. It hissed. *Tell him.*

"For the thunderstones, I could…"

Gavin waited after I stopped. "Yes?"

"Assuming we make a bargain," I added, "then I could use the ruby to compel Castis to give them to me and not make anymore."

"Can you?"

"The dagger claims it can teach me."

My ally considered. "Hm. Kurn and Amelda would protest."

"I'd not *ask* their permission," I griped. "They did not ask mine."

"True."

Gavin was quiet for some time as Soul Drinker and I waited with me guiding the horse. It was then we exited the last line of brush and arrived at the beginnings of the road heading South. Most of the senseless noises I'd been blocking from my thoughts had retreated into the depths of the warp rot forest behind us, and the overcast had returned to a familiar grey turning to its darkest shadow as the day was ending.

"Very well," Gavin agreed. "Let us follow the road. We will meet them head on by dawn."

IN THE MIDDLE OF THE NIGHT, WE TOOK A BRIEF BREAK. I HAD TO stretch; I needed to eat and drink, not having done so since late morning. This had been the longest I'd gone without since reaching Sarilis's Tower. I could not help but worry, had I hurt my unborn going so long?

Wouldn't the Deathless be disappointed about that? Soul Drinker remarked snidely. *And, no, warrior. I have been feeding what you need to maintain your body as you are. Your Deathwalker does the same with his horse. Such as it is with those who understand the intimacy of transference. You should rest in Reverie, however. While you can.*

~You can't 'feed' me sleep as well?~

Indeed not. Sleep is the only base need of mortals not based in their immortal essence, their Vis or Vitas. I call it the mortal essence, for it cannot be captured or kept before shriveling like a collapsing thought. A curious state of suspension. Every mortal mind of this world needs sleep. Some serve beyond themselves by doing so.

The demon was in a conversational mood. I glanced up from where I leaned against a slightly unusual tree, grinding my last mouthful of nuts and fruit for the night as I took a swig from my waterskin. Gavin was writing in his grimoire, his focus wholly inward.

~An example of one who serves many?~

Desert Elves, for certain. But you know this, yes?

I rolled my eyes. ~Fell straight into that ditch.~

Soul Drinker chuckled. *Go on, Davrin. Take Reverie. We'll attune you to the ruby after you wake. We'll be waiting.*

Gavin glanced up as I removed my belt and laid it beside me, so the relic would not be in direct contact with me or lying on top and visible. My spiders returned from their hunting then and gathered under my hair at my nape.

"Wake me if *anything* concerns you," I said, waiting until the man nodded before settling down, tucking my arm beneath my head, and closed my eyes.

I dropped into Reverie suddenly, as fast as if someone waited for me and I knew I was tardy. In vain I tried to steer where I landed, braced against ever-tightening walls, helpless to slow the relentless pull of the world. A scattering of glowing, red runes swept by and around me; at first, I wondered if I had fallen "into" Soul Drinker again.

Then I spotted the altar in the center and struggled to keep my last meal.

The Forming Pit. No!

The hidden room in the Sanctuary where the Conceiver had dragged me with her two sons, her Sathoet and her tainted Consort, after magically paralyzing me. The latter had been intended to impregnate me while Kerse watched as punishment.

But he rebelled.

I backed onto the path lined with scarlet-lit carvings, the only shield against the Abyss, trembling as I wished fervently to wake again.

~I don't want to sleep!~

Someone shifted behind me. I whirled in place, slapping my waist for nonexistent weapons. I saw three cages with iron bars, unreasonably tight and narrow against the stone wall. Facing the center one from the outside, a long-haired, entirely blond bua grasped the black metal as if his hands were melded to it. He was naked and shaking, head bowed in despair.

Phaelous?

No. He was shorter and too young. He didn't know I was here, and I watched him uncurl the fingers of his left hand and reach through the bar to touch the stone wall inside. His fingers sank in as if rock had become the softest clay, a shimmer of gold light surrounding them like a glove. With effort, he reached deeper into the stone, turning his slim body to the side to wedge it between the bars and extend his touch.

I watched in open-mouthed silence until his hand submerged to the wrist. Every muscle from neck to calf strained before I saw the effect: a magical aura pressed outward, creating an uneven hole in the Deepearth by sheer will.

Beyond on the other side, I saw stars in a night sky, and the glimpse of a too-familiar firebird flying by.

Goddess…

The voices began talking again; I knew the words that would come, although the naked bua wasn't shouting just yet.

"Help me, Uncle! Please!"

"I can't stay. I must return later with aid."

"Take me with you or you won't find me again!"

"What are her plans?"

"Free me, Uncle, and I'll tell you…"

"How do you claim this? I never knew you existed…"

I stepped closer, peering through the glimmering opening, wondering if I would see my face as I remembered this dream, or…

Black hair and beard, a much younger face, and a foreign uniform.

It was him. The Human General of the Desert Queen.

~Cris-ri-phon.~

The Davrin bua was startled as he seemed to hear me. The gold light vanished as he pulled his hand away before the stone would have crushed it. The hole closed, and he looked over his shoulder, one golden eye peering at me like a reptilian predator about to defend its lair.

I stepped back, my hands out and forward. He blinked, turning around to where I could see his bare chest and taut belly. My gaze had drifted to his naked haunches and white thatch crowning his penis before I looked up again.

The bua's eyes had changed to a normal color, a lovely scarlet which calmed me in an instant. Instead of yellow eyes and hair, he had only one blond streak leading from his temple.

I *knew* him.

"Auslan," I whispered.

His smile captivated me. *"Sirana."*

I followed the path of protective runes to approach him, unsure what I would do when I got there, and he pushed stiffly up from scraped knees to stand. He opened his arms first, showing me what he wanted, and I swept him into my embrace as tight as I could maintain, astonished at how *good* this felt. It wasn't simply that he was naked, that he felt and smelled like peace and pleasure.

The last time we'd seen each other, the iron bars had prevented this.

Now I didn't want to wake up. *Not yet.*

"I am glad to see you." He sighed in relief. "It has been dark lately."

I replied dryly. "It's the Deepearth."

Quietly he laughed, his nose buried in my neck, and all was quiet in the Forming Pit where he'd been made. We both ignored the altar to the Abyss standing like a barren stump behind us.

"I haven't seen you in the sun market," I said.

He clung harder to me. "I am sorry. I... stopped dreaming."

"But I've seen Toushek again," I continued. "After you warned me."

He leaned back, his palms resting light on my shoulders, blinking. "Be careful, Sirana."

"Who is he?"

Auslan shook his head. "I do not know. He watches me sleep. Now he is watching you."

"Hm."

I tried to ask something else. Anything else.

About the Valsharess.

Nothing came.

Absently, I ran my gloved hands along his flanks, and he shivered, his eyes half closed. His drifting expression made me smile, and I leaned forward to kiss him. He groaned in welcome, returning it, arms sliding around my shoulders again as I held him close, dropping one hand to cup his rump. He grew hot and erect against me, only my black uniform separating us. Inviting him to merge with me still seemed possible without letting him go to undress.

"I know you cannot speak of Her," he murmured after our lips reluctantly drew apart. "Of how you are to serve. You come to me now… This is enough. This is clean, even if it is *here*."

I stroked my hands down his back, massaging, tightening my arms as he exhaled because I was unsure what to say.

Clean.

Not where I'd last fallen to rest. It was corrupted.

"I seek my Sisters where the Sun touches," I said, testing if I could. "I must know what they are tasked to do. If they die trying. I can't… turn my back now. I am too close to one of them."

Auslan nodded, leaning to meet my eyes again. "I am glad, yes. Seek the Sisters. That is what you must do." His gaze drifted sideways again. "The strain builds again and where it bends next, I cannot see yet. But many ancient eyes are… rising. Waking."

"What do you mean?" I asked.

My Consort's bright eyes blinked and focused on me as concern etched his face. He looked toward the jump circle, his fingers digging into my biceps. He whispered earnestly, peeling away from me.

"Sirana, escape! Hide!"

The Forming Pit grew quite cold, and I listened to a mortal Gavin as he'd warned me, just before he died: *For the sake of your unborn, hide!*

I obeyed without question, skimming along the walls to enter the shadows. Behind me the familiar, magical suck of air signaled the arrival of another in the Pit. The Abyssal hiss told me whom to expect the moment I discovered a passage through which I could escape, a last shimmer disappearing though the stone remained open.

"Ahhh, a pleasssure to find you here, Shhyntre."

Shyntre?

Before climbing out, I glanced behind me.

There, dressed in blue mage's robes, his hair cut short and uneven, was my wizard facing the Drider Keeper in her wild Davrin form. Hands fisted, shoulders squared, every line screamed his stubbornness to resist whatever happened next.

Meanwhile, my Consort was gone.

"We knew you would come here eventually."

"Throttle yourself in your own web, Auranka."

"Ohhh. You first. Deliciousss bua."

Stay.

Help him.

"She's alive up top, isn't she?" Shyntre taunted loudly. "The Valsharess won't do anything about that. And I know why."

Auranka cackled like Soul Drinker. "Only a matter of time, bua. There isss no escape from the web we've woven. You know that. How often you've tried."

Escape.

Prove her wrong.

I turned and dove into the passage left open for me.

I SAT UP IN A RUSH, MY BREATH HITCHING FROM STABBING soreness in my shoulder and hip. I massaged the former, took a deep breath and knew I was surrounded by plants of the Surface, catching the scent of night air. No painful light, no headache.

"Hm," Gavin grunted from several body lengths away.

"What?" I croaked, blinking to bring him into focus.

"Dreaming?" he asked. "Or some connection like you've described with the Deathless? It was not with me."

The former monk was glad for that, no doubt.

"I, uh…"

I paused, comforted and apologetic as my guardians crept cautiously out of my hair with a quiet chime. They'd hung on to me tightly as Auslan had down below. Had that been a portent in any way, not merely all my fears from this turn lumped together?

It felt real.

I glanced where the red rune dagger lay hidden beneath my equipment, quiet for the moment but I recalled what it had said of my "greatest" weapons.

The mind magic that is your own. We'd enjoy learning how you came to be this way.

"Dreaming, yes," I answered Gavin. "A connection. Someone I left behind."

The Deathwalker was unhurried, meticulously packing up his things. "What sort of connection?"

I shrugged, my face warming. "The sire."

Gavin nodded, cinching up his pack and getting to his feet while I donned my belt and weapons. "Frequent?"

"No, not that often. But I was… glad to see him."

He turned his inverted eyes on me. "Why?"

I blinked, baffled. "He is alive."

"Interesting." Gavin moved over to the mare to secure his pack. "Was he in danger of death when you left?"

"Yes. Much. Maybe worse than death."

"From what threat?"

"The same... events which sent me here."

Finishing up, Gavin tilted his head toward me. "Sounds like exile."

"Or a trial."

"Ah, yes. Your offer to return with me to challenge Sarilis for the Ley Tower. You intend to head that way at some point."

"Before winter, yes." I considered. "I suppose my offer is still viable."

Perhaps he and I even stood a better chance, now.

"Very good." One corner of his mouth quirked. "I wager your pregnancy is somehow unsanctioned yet was allowed to continue, though you were sent away for some unfathomable service."

I folded my arms to cover the discomfort in my middle and stared at him. Gavin was *almost* smiling, as if he were genuinely amused.

"Hm. That explains your interest in my mother." He paused. "And my Lady's mention of you."

I squinted. "Mention?"

"Opaque and sibylline, I assure you."

I didn't know what the second word meant, but he looked away before I could ask, his manner evasive now. He waved at our mount.

"If you will, guide the mare. It is still dark."

I moved forward. "And we shall encounter the Ma'ab by dawn."

"Roughly."

Gavin didn't speak after we got on our way; as usual, he had a feast of thoughts to choose from to keep himself occupied. I did as well, but I envied him his apparent admiration for his "Lady" and the proof of an active education. He had learned to understand the

Ma'ab language while he was *dead*, for Goddess's sake! I envied that purpose he drew from whatever "sibylline" direction she provided in his dreams, which somehow involved me.

He could ask her for guidance. He knew how far the warp rot valley was, he was right.

This appeared opposite of my relation to my Valsharess, who compelled me with fear and illness, who let me stumble around following the vaguest of trails. Any oblique warning She may have shown me was useless as I fell into dangerous pits of unawareness, lacking any understanding of past events which brought me where I was. I could not trust or rely on Her, as I'd not any elder female in my life.

Sent away for some unfathomable service. To return below for more of the same. Kept ignorant, indeed.

Touching Auslan in Reverie had been the most rewarding moment in this entire sojourn. He was still alive, I was certain. Under strain but unbroken.

Like me.

While we embraced, I only knew that I wanted to protect him, to reassure him that I wouldn't treat him like the other Matrons. As a trained Consort, he hadn't asked as to the health of the womb he'd helped to quicken, for that was not his place. In hindsight, I wished he had, for my effort thus far proved that it mattered to me.

Perhaps a healer-by-touch could tell without asking.

The Reverie had shifted to one of abject danger; it had become Shyntre facing off with Auranka. The need to escape, to not be seen, had clashed with that same impulse to protect him. Shyntre, whose temper I had pushed because I always got a reaction. He was entertaining. Challenging.

Bold as any cait, shouting at the Drider Keeper like that.

Admirable, if foolish. If it had been real.

The Valsharess had believed Shyntre was the sire of my unborn; why She did not execute or condemn me.

And I know why.

Seek the Sisters. That is what you must do.

We cantered toward our enemies in silence, and I found myself smiling and calm. I may not have a wiser female guiding me on my mission, but I did have a purpose and two remarkable buas who admired me somehow, who wanted me to return. I couldn't protect them where they were, but I could draw a new strength from their memory.

It was a feeling I liked, because Troshin Bend loomed smaller on the horizon. If Shyntre could show that much spine to an Abyssal abomination, I anticipated this chance to do the same with a self-serving group of Ma'ab nobility.

We entered a stretch of road where Gavin's night mare did not need constant direction, and I tugged off the glove which did not hold her talisman. Tugging out the Ma'ab's ruby, I also touched Soul Drinker with the same hand.

~You awake?~ I jested.

It sniggered. **Always. Sleep well, did you?**

~I did. As you promised, show me the most effective way to use this gem.~

Certainly, Blue Eyes, but promise me at least one Ma'ab kill in exchange. Without question or hesitation.

~One kill, yes. I've already decided who.~

Excellent. Hehe! This will be fun.

CHAPTER 3

I COMMANDED THE MARE TO STOP, TURNING MY EAR AHEAD OF us without speaking.

Gavin spoke in a whisper. "You hear them?"

"Yes. They wake early."

"With the forest changing, as I'd expect."

I smelled the smoke of a campfire—something neither Gavin nor I had risked—and hoped we were far enough away that they had not heard the clop of hooves. I first donned the ruby pendant, leaving it out where it could be seen while the saphgar remained hidden. I also opened my pouch to release my guardians. They scrambled out and up to my nape, alert and ready. Gavin waited patiently while I double-checked the poison in which I dipped my bolt this time.

The one that killed Bictrius quickly, not the fever.

Satisfied, I inspected my hand crossbow for serious flaws, noted minor ones, and loaded it before hooking it to a loop on the saddle. I wouldn't be gripping and aiming it in threat first thing, but Callitro's ring would assure I could snatch it and hit what I aimed for.

Finally, controlling and slowing my breath, I urged the horse forward down the road.

Calm. Confident. Show no fear.

I wasn't alone. I had two strange and magically powerful allies plus a nonreactive horse, but I *was* leading this. It was my idea.

I wish Jaunda were here.

The mare's walk was steady, and there was no way to be quiet. We merely waited to see how long it would take them to notice and who would sound the alarm first. I pursed my mouth when I recognized Mathias was that one. He had been sitting on a log farther from the Ma'ab, unbound and close enough to be considered on watch voluntarily. He stood up.

"Oi!" he shouted, lifting his arm high, his hand empty. "Who goes there?"

He couldn't see details, and neither could the other three as they scrambled to their feet to make ready. At this distance, I recognized Kurn, Castis, and Amelda easily by their shape, size, and color, though their pale faces blurred some against clear expression.

I also saw someone else move. Short, stocky, wrists bound in front.

Red beard.

"Rithal, captive," I whispered. "Mathias, free."

"Hm," Gavin acknowledged.

I sought another, Osgrid, but did not see her or any Humans from Troshin Bend. Just our old traveling companions.

"Mathias!" I called out.

He sounded baffled. "Sirana?"

"Forest trickery!" Castis barked, raising his hands, ready to cast. "Be wary!"

Indeed, I'd have thought the same thing in their place.

"We found the warp rot center," I said plainly. "It's too big for one mage. We come to—"

Kurn hauled his bulk onto his stallion with an aggressive yell which could have been enhanced by a sore netherhole.

"*I have Soul Drinker!*" I bellowed. "Charge us, and your fate shall be worse than death!"

"Tacuf, aljaheem!" Amelda cried angrily at Kurn.

"Stop, Hellhound," Gavin translated near my left ear.

"Aful ma'aqit!"

"Do as I say."

I offered no indication I'd heard him but his confirmation of Amelda strongarming the dog's leash was useful. An order, not a bribe or beseechment. Nonetheless, the large man bristled at her as his black horse pranced in nervous confusion, and I believed he might kick the beast forward regardless. There was not a moon to see by nor the first grey of dawn.

"Dabh," Castis agreed, lifting his right hand and summoning light to the end of a walking staff which looked borrowed. Glaring with nostrils curled, he added, "You saw the center?"

I squinted against the light as it revealed shades of green both sick and healthy. Mathias remained where he was for now, his back to the forest as he watched us on each side. Rithal's focus was on anyone moving, though he sat like a rock. Now that Kurn could see and I couldn't, he held back; his stallion continued to stamp.

"We saw it," I answered, lifting my voice, speaking slow. "Gavin cannot purge the corruption. We need mages. Will you negotiate?"

Castis and Amelda glanced at each other then, curiously, at Kurn, who trotted his mount around in a circle, heavy blowing and burring raising tension in the other three horses and Rithal's pony. Gavin's mare remained still as a tree.

"Negotiate with a thief and a coward?" snarled the Hellhound.

"And a clumsy rutter," I said. "Distasteful, yes, but so I must."

"Kadh'a!" he spat.

Gavin didn't bother translating, and my smile was brief. "We must stop this spread, Ma'ab. That is the greater threat for which you followed us North."

"Return the dagger," Amelda spoke before Kurn could, stepping forward. "And the ruby you've stolen, and you shall have our aid."

I chuckled. "I am not stupid. You must be motivated. *Earn* them back."

"One item returned now," she countered. "The ruby. The dagger when the forest is cleansed, and we part ways."

Soul Drinker began to laugh maniacally.

~Shhh. Stop it.~

Alas, a giggle slipped from me as well. "Hm! Part ways? Were you not hungry to drag both of us to your Ascended?"

"*You* may go, Elf," Amelda clarified. "The *maknuut* will be enough."

Bodiless laughter drifted around me, through me, though I resisted making the same face both Kurn and Castis did. The female Noble made such great effort to avoid speaking to Gavin or acknowledging him unless it contained demands for others to act upon his fate. It was as if she thought he had no ears or will.

Although her revulsion went beyond Castis's dismissive spitting while traveling, Gavin did not speak out either way, and I understood why. It was both a statement of intent and a useless challenge. I had no binding power with the Deathwalker or his mistress, and neither the Ma'ab nor I believed we would simply "part ways."

I addressed Mathias instead. "And you? I thought you ran from the town's mob. These Ma'ab were in no shape to stop you."

The skin hunter offered a lax smile and a shrug. "Turns out I forgot something."

I waited, expecting a mention of the Dwarf, but Mathias added nothing. *Not good.*

Tilting my chin up, I prompted, "And Rithal?"

As Mathias repeated his shrug, Castis stated, "The fool followed us. We caught him recently."

So the skin hunter had left Troshin Bend with the Ma'ab. I sensed the hard fingers of the governor on this.

"You did not kill him," I noted.

"We may correct this," Kurn growled, turning his stallion's haunches toward the Dwarf.

Rithal's eyes grew so wide I could see it past Castis's torch, and he rolled backwards off his perch in time to evade the horse's powerful hind kick.

"Saeid yusbik!" Amelda barked. *"Murkib!"*

"Ascended hold you," Gavin whispered. "Self-control."

"They are very tense," I replied.

"The warp rot will engage them first. Offer to trade me and one vial for Rithal, instead of either object."

Trade one of Sarilis's vials? I kept my face still. "If they injure you for spite?"

"What are you saying?" Castis called loudly, closing distance with Mathias, who took a few steps closer to the Ma'ab. "Do we negotiate or not?"

"We discuss," I replied tartly, ignoring him and his bright light.

"There will be consequence," Gavin murmured. "If I suffer, so shall they. I only ask you to use the moment well."

I offered a slight nod before speaking out to the smaller female. "I shall not give you the ruby now, and Soul Drinker politely declines your company—"

Hehehe!

"—but let us trade like for like. The mak-noo-uht for the Dwarf—"

Amelda grimaced at my pronunciation then looked briefly concerned about my address of the relic. It was clear that Kurn, Mathias, and Rithal were confused while Castis had a dawning realization.

"—and the return of the old man's vial as defense from warp rot," I finished, drawing one out where they could see.

Both mages couldn't hide their interest while Kurn's brow lowered enough to obscure his eyes. *A good sign.*

"If you keep both ruby and relic," the noblewoman countered, "we keep both the Dwarf and maknuut. Only then shall the vial be enough."

"No," I said. "Gavin is worth five Rithals."

The Dwarf chuckled audibly, unoffended, as Gavin decisively dismounted, leaving his pack and belongings strapped to the mount. He drew off the spade in a long pull.

"Oh, no," Castis protested, pointing. "You put that back!"

"Care to contest wills again?" Gavin asked, brandishing the digging tool in his grasp. "I was fully mortal before and quelled you."

I saw a narrowing of the noble mage's eyes and a glance at Kurn, who sneered and looked away from both. Mathias had decided to get out of the middle and moved to the far side of Amelda where he was on the fringe.

No withdrawing now. I dismounted as well, removing my crossbow from the saddle and attaching it to its holster. I beckoned with one hand. "Come, Rithal. You ride with me."

The redbeard crouched behind a rock, wary of Kurn's huffing stallion, as Gavin walked closer to Amelda and Kurn than he did Castis, forcing a divide visible to me. I moved forward, toward Castis but motioning past him.

"Come, Rithal!" I said loudly.

"I got a pony, Elf."

Amelda sneered as she backed up from Gavin's approach. "We keep your pony. This one will ride it with his legs dragging!"

Nuance broke down as we repositioned. Castis tried to keep an eye on me but Amelda and Kurn gave way for Gavin, who must be baiting the woman as he showed his back.

She raised her hands, unable to resist. *"Kun mithl ajalid!"*

"Uthkariss," Gavin answered, swirling on her.

"Ah, shit!" Mathias cried between them.

Ice and black fire met in proximity, back-blowing on them and causing Kurn's stallion to scream and rear up. Castis's magical torch went out as he turned, and I lunged forward, seizing him in the sudden dark.

"*Hrk—!*"

I found the Ma'ab's throat and dug in my fingers, my other hand seizing the pain point under his arm. His open mouth made no sound as I caught his eyes, dragged his will down where he stood. My intent was to penetrate, as Soul Drinker showed me, as both had tried against me.

As before, the ruby had the delicacy of a bull's prick up the ass.

Castis went rigid, his eyes wide in shock. I could see him better than he could see me. I wasted no time as Soul Drinker squealed around me and my spiders guarded my body.

~*Pass me every thunderstone you have,*~ I ordered.

Fingers fumbled at a pouch on his belt. I released his throat and let him breathe, loosened the pouch by feel, without blinking.

~*You cannot make more, Castis, even with components. You are incapable. You have forgotten how.*~

He nodded.

~*Given the opportunity to steal Kurn's and Amelda's thunderstones, you will do so without them seeing and pass them to me intact. If they try to use one, you will do everything in your power to stop them. You cannot speak of my demands. Understand?*~

His eyes rolled up, snapped back, trying to focus. *Y-yes...*

I hid his pouch and stepped away from the mage to survey the scene. Any abruptly severed connection was disorienting, but I had no choice.

You are fiiiine, Soul Drinker cooed. *It was but an instant and your ssspiders did not leap.*

Yet what I feared most in that instant, when I'd looked into Castis's eyes, was that Gavin had been decapitated by Kurn and set afire, as Amelda wanted.

No.

Gavin was upright, his head attached and robes unscorched, indeed, still walking in the dark. Amelda had clambered into the forest on the far side of the road. Kurn was trotting to and fro, indecisive on what to do, snarling and snapping in his tongue. Mathias was out of sight.

In silence, I called Gavin's mare closer while glimpsing the redbeard finally coming toward me, dragging his pony by the bridle with neck outstretched. The sky had begun to lighten. Gasping, Castis blinked as I held up one of Sarilis's vials.

"Here, as agreed," I said. "Take this."

He did, darting in Kurn's direction but nearly ran into the tall Deathwalker.

"*Gagk!*" he cried, recoiling as Gavin turned his head to peer at him.

Castis swiftly joined Kurn and Amelda on the far end of the camp while Gavin stood between them and the rest of us. I sought signs of black blood or something else but only saw a broad, lanky, robed monk.

"I shall ride behind you, and Sirana in front," Gavin said. "Though I'll not be gagged or bound."

"Then that is no trade!" Kurn barked, but Castis held up his vial.

"We have this," he said, and Amelda held out her hand but Castis drew away. "If Sirana can lead us to the center, it is all we truly need, not the Dwarf."

For now.

That practically hung in the air.

"Are we ready to leave?" someone said.

All looked over as Mathias emerged, leading his horse toward Rithal; the skin hunter drew a knife, offering to cut the rope from his wrists. The Dwarf accepted, clutching his reins but holding his arms forward.

"Why th' fuck ye want tah go?" Rithal demanded as he was set free.

"Hey, I was in the shed, too, remember?" said the skin hunter loud enough for the three Ma'ab to hear. "I want to see what else this 'apprentice' has up his sleeve."

In the shed. What happened in the shed with Jacob? It sounded like a deflection.

With no one making a move to try to bind Gavin, Kurn finally steered the stallion over to sweep Amelda up and onto his saddle, not dissimilar to what he'd done with me at the Ley Tower except she wasn't fighting him.

"Get the horses and packs," commanded the Hellhound without using Castis's name. "Let the *maknuut* ride the extra mount while the black witch rides the rotting one."

"W-was it bitten by anything when you saw the center?" Amelda asked.

"She was," Gavin answered too honestly. "Sirana's command of Soul Drinker, however, drew out the corruption before it could spread. She can do the same for any of you."

Several pairs of dark eyes bore into me, and I grinned, shifting my left hip forward to show off the red rune sheath and dagger at my hip. The thunderstones were out of sight on my right.

"Demons abetting demons," Kurn growled with a spit.

I rolled my eyes and mounted Gavin's mare alone, once again the caretaker of his possessions. I noticed Castis pull another pouch from the saddle bags of the extra horse before he gave the reins to the Deathwalker, then he glanced at me.

Well done, the dagger cooed as I straightened and placed my gloved hand on its pommel. *He will find a way to do your bidding, Davrin. Be patient.*

Skeptical and wary that it had been so easy, I thought, ~We'll see.~

Its cackle lingered until all of us mounted and, with the sun rising, were on our way along a road which was fast disappearing into a collapsing forest.

RITHAL STOUTLY WATCHED MY BACK, MAINTAINING HIS PONY'S position between me and Kurn and Amelda sharing the stallion, and Castis on his own gelding. Gavin was behind them and a good distance from me, with Mathias bringing up the rear.

The Ma'ab muttered in their tongue; I could hear them clearly though they did not realize. It was good that Gavin was behind them, as their words would trail back, and they did not know he understood them now.

Given the good pace of our travel with little delay from familiar infighting, I reflected that we'd found the only balance that might allow us to function as a group for a time. The one wild growth that worried me was Mathias.

I had to assume he was here at Brom's command, or Amelda's in his name. The skin hunter made no motion to negotiate with me now; he had obtained what he wanted much earlier than he thought. Something had changed in his desires, but he would not state what. He had been in the shed with Gavin and offered that as a reason, but it did not explain if he was ally or foe.

I'd long known Court Nobles who played sides as he did. Pincer worms waiting to strike. Had I been any greater threat than a lone Thalluen coaxing buas into bed, I would have been on the receiving end of all I'd witnessed.

We reached the end of the road at midmorning, the sky overcast, and I did my best to tolerate the brighter light with only my hood up, rather than cut my peripheral warnings with the sun blind. The grey pathway Gavin and I had carved into the wilderness was still visible to me but not as pronounced; it had narrowed since yesterday.

Peering around us, feeling the wrongness of the place, the Humans and Dwarf muttered low and beneath their breaths. Gavin opted to speak.

"A mage will be greatly reliant on auras to judge one's surroundings," he said. "Non-mages with a magically imbued item may have some protection from false images but, regardless, you will face madness. If Mathias, Rithal, or Kurn do not have a magical anchor upon which to focus, I would not advise that they enter. Likewise, the living horses are likely to bolt and be attacked. One could tie them here. If they eat the grass, you may have to put them down."

No one made a peep, at first, as Gavin dismounted and demonstrated, tying up his borrowed horse. I smiled that he sounded like such the indifferent scholar sharing wisdom best not ignored. I waited to see if anyone would.

Mathias turned his head to Rithal. "Thoughts?"

"Goin' in," came the flat reply as he dismounted from his pony and led her to a bending tree.

"You have a magic anchor, Dwarf?" Castis asked acidly. "We must put you down if you are taken by visions and become a liability."

The redbeard turned and spat in his direction. "Shut it, mule. Watch yer own backside."

I hoped that was an affirmative rather than foolish stubbornness, for Castis was not wrong about what may happen.

Mathias peered around. "There's a fair amount of grass."

The Dwarf shrugged. "I noticed she don' want tah eat anything the last day, her stomach's rumblin'. She's smart an' can last a bit longer."

Mathias and Castis followed suit although without the same vote of confidence for their mounts' intelligence about eating the grass.

Kurn held his chin high and adjusted Amelda in his lap. "If the *maknuut* nag enters with us, so does my warhorse."

"Kurn," Castis protested, but was cut off.

"If either try to escape, I will run them down!" barked the Hellhound.

"Ain't wise," Rithal grumbled, "but ain't new."

Mathias grinned and shrugged in agreement. "Alright, then. Let's walk."

Were magically imbued items so common among us, then? I'd seen no sign of anything powerful except for the ruby while traveling, and the three mundane males did not prove their protection now. Perhaps Amelda had aided the men; Soul Drinker was far from Brom's only possession. Osgrid could have helped Rithal.

The dagger cooed eagerly. *We're about to find out.*

Kurn's stallion didn't rebel immediately upon entering the forest. Indeed, the beast at last settled somewhat, trotting ahead while I walked the mare beside Gavin and Rithal, with Castis and Mathias staying close in front.

I watched their expressions and body language, silently drawing the relic to accept its help anticipating the warp rot creatures we knew would accost us eventually. Castis craned his neck around when I did, focused on me and my aura for a moment. I wasn't sure what he saw, but he shifted over to the far side of Gavin's mare.

"You're as clear as the day," he remarked, holding out the pouch he'd taken from Amelda's saddlebag. "While so much else is in a green haze."

"If you say," I said, accepting the pouch as subtly as I could, though Rithal and Mathias were no doubt aware. It felt to have three stones in it.

"The rune dagger is proven effective against the warp rot," Gavin said, drawing their eyes from me. "Although I understand it has a will of its own and chooses its wielder."

I smiled. "It likes me."

Indeed, I do, Davrin. Indeed, I do.

Castis's dark eyes widened as he stared at the dagger then he moved away from my mount. "I will catch up to Kurn and Amelda lest they go too far."

The Dwarf and skin hunter looked confused at this behavior but didn't call it out. It was far easier going this time with a pathway carved out, as the many small things which once challenged our every step were avoiding the grey path.

Rithal remarked, "I see th' creep an' feel sick, but me mind is clear."

"Proximity to Sirana may be helping," Gavin remarked.

"Eh? Why?"

My Deathwalker's answer was blunt as usual. "The Davrin has talents amplified by a relic once linked to her people. Sirana and Soul Drinker act as a consecrated sanctuary within the corruption. She is the one most likely to get close to the center to toss in Sarilis's vial."

~I am?~

Ohh, yesss, didn't you know? Hehehe!

"If you aren't certain what action to take," Gavin continued, "defending her also defends your sanity, if you wish to look at it that way."

As Rithal and Mathias evaluated me anew, I smiled with enigmatic confidence, as if I'd known this before now.

"Huh," Mathias said. "Alright. In that case, maybe we should catch up to the three Ma'ab?"

"Castis be comin' back," Rithal pointed out.

Indeed, and he held his head like it ached. Kurn's stallion had stopped to wait for us, scraping a front hoof against the ground. The Hellhound held the small Ma'ab woman like she was a child's comfort. Both seemed alert but not paranoid for now.

The first creature large enough to dare cross the threshold into purged land was a hunched, burrowing deer with short, strong forelimbs and spindly hindquarters intended for dashing. It was in a continual charging posture.

Kurn kicked the stallion forward first. Shoving Amelda forward onto the thick neck, the Hellhound drew his sword and pierced the wailing creature through the neck, sending it into seizure. The swift break down of the mutated body and shedding of grey ash proved what object was keeping the big man sane.

Castis used this distraction to pass me a third pouch of thunderstones he'd retrieved earlier from the stallion's saddlebag. Despite his haunting look of muzzled silence that I recognized too well, I felt relief. *That is all of them.*

For several hours I did little except maintain that "sanctuary" for Rithal and Mathias while they, Castis, Gavin, Kurn, and Amelda all challenged the encroaching warp rot. Their continual cleansing broadened our pathway where it had begun closing. Soul Drinker hissed in continuous disappointment as I held us back from all but the closest prey.

So be it, Davrin, they can have the animals. Promise me the corrupted sentients in the center. You said as many as I could glut! Promise me!

~Yes, yes. We conserve strength and wait for the best opportunity.~

And give me the Ma'ab. All of them.

~At least one, we agreed.~

All!

~If there's opportunity.~

You lie. You do not want to kill the woman despite the danger she poses to you and your grey servant. You will hesitate. Fool!

I frowned. ~I will get you at least one. You're irritable because you're hungry.~

Oh, so? Then show your strength, Red Sister, and feed me!

I shook my head, knowing better than to respond to such Courtly goading.

Weak fool, it pressed. *You must impress me to be worthy.*

~You said I am, and Queen Innathi promised I had your aid. If you discard me as your wielder so quickly, how will she discover what became of her Queendom?~

The impatient dagger didn't respond and pouted in silence; thus I had some sign this agreement upon the blue sands held a benefit for the demon. Admittedly, I was not certain what it was. I didn't know if Innathi was separate from this lipless voice or part of it.

"Yer mighty calm, Elf," Rithal said with a slightly shaking voice, his axe covered in green slime slowly flaking off as black ash, his leather-bound shield colliding with things that ran faster than him. "Never seen anything like this."

"Calm is good," I replied. "And I was here yesterday."

Mathias wielded an unfamiliar dirk which proved effective, but he had no shield and had to stay light on his feet. "All the kid tales I've heard about not leaving the path in a fey forest are as real as I could imagine." He laughed. "Just like demons being real, eh, Sirana?"

I smirked. "Just like."

Castis favored fire spells, which covered a wide area before being quenched. While most of the fire became yellowish steam as the corruption instantly turned to ash, if he repeated the treatment, it would catch fire for real. He sneered after the third time Rithal griped at him about having to stamp out the embers.

"Jus' once'll do!"

"Well, there is your proof it is cleansed!"

"Yeah. Now stop wastin' yer strength on branches that ain't gonna bite ye!"

Kurn ignored the bickering as he and Amelda led the way down into a darkening valley. With the big man as her devoted bodyguard, her many icy mist spells seemed to work as well as the spread of flames, be they of elemental light or ethereal shadow. Gavin's theory had become truth before my eyes.

Our group was charged by further warped wolves and a gigantic, fat-muzzled deer with a rack made of freshly chipped flint.

There appeared to be no pattern or rhythm to when we would be attacked; it seemed not to matter if we made more noise or less. Jubilant voices rose behind the hills and within deep shadows but spoke no sensical tongue any of us could make out.

The morning had long since passed, and I still wasn't hungry. Or thirsty.

Ahead, around a bend in the slope, Kurn's horse screamed. It was soon followed by Amelda crying out, then the Hellhound shouting.

"What in—!"

Castis and Mathias sprinted forward, slowly followed by Rithal. Gavin lengthened his stride significantly but did not run, and I remained next to him, seated astride the mare undeniably showing her wear and tear.

Once we got into view, I saw the big horse struggling to pull a thick foreleg out of a narrow muck hole. It had plummeted so deep that it painted the horse's powerful chest in green mud. Kurn had dropped his sword near where Amelda had toppled into the grass from the saddle. He was attempting to brace his mount and help him out by plunging his entire arm into the liquid earth to grip beneath the chest.

"Rithal, give me your aid, now!" barked the Hellhound as the horse whinnied and squealed in panic above his dark head.

The Dwarf's bushy red eyebrows lifted in utter surprise. He folded his strong arms as Gavin stepped forward and to the side, casting his black fire to the left of the struggle, pushing against the corruption which had overtaken this part of the path. Castis took the hint and cast his fire on the right side, and Amelda moved to where a goop spattered Kurn could see her.

"Kati alhif!" she insisted, rapidly explaining something about the ground as she waved her arms about and motioned him away.

He didn't want to leave his stallion; for a moment, he argued, resisted. Something large and dark moved in my periphery, and I snapped my focus to my right. Green haze swirled, leaving a vague wake as the commotion filled my ears.

No warp rot close, Soul Drinker reassured me. *Although if the brute doesn't pick up his sword soon, you may have... difficulties.*

Rithal and Mathias stayed near me while the mages worked, and I watched warily as Amelda had no choice but to cast ice on Kurn and the horse, hurting them both in all appearances. Still, this altered the nature of the liquid earth; at last, the stallion rolled and pulled his leg out, hooves kicking the air as the huge body struggled to right himself.

Meanwhile, Kurn huffed loudly as he limped away from the lanced boil in our pathway, his hands shaking as he reached for his fallen sword. I spotted movement around the edges of his bracer and gauntlet. The wriggling looked at first like leeches trying to dig beneath the hardened leather and metal, but then I realized that *was* his armor.

The small hairs at my nape stood up, and my guardians grew alert as I slowly dismounted to stand next to Rithal. Mathias reached for something at his belt as the Dwarf adjusted his grip on his axe.

"Kurn?" Amelda asked in a smaller voice than before, and Gavin and Castis paused to pay attention.

The Hellhound straightened up, holding his naked blade with a scowl on his pale face. Wordlessly, he walked to his stallion and mounted up, motioning us forward with his sword.

When we hesitated, he barked, "Let us go!"

Although his horse limped forward several paces, no one moved to catch him as Castis glanced at Gavin. "You... you said Sirana's blade could draw out corruption before it spreads?"

The Deathwalker did not reply but turned to me.

~Will you?~ I asked.

Would you want me to? We were both there when his cock was wallowing in your back hole.

A hot flush of humiliation flared but I tamped it down. *~He got his next. But now he becomes even worse.~*

*★Then you should have followed your training and killed him when you had the chance. Do you really want to get near him only to **help** him?★*

I knew the answer to that.

"Kurn," said the fire mage without awaiting my answer. "Let Sirana cleanse *Mikhaob*. His leg, look—"

"She won't touch him!" the big Ma'ab roared.

The black stallion left a black and green hoofprint in the grey dirt as he pranced. I saw his eye roll and show white.

★Put him down,★ Soul Drinker whispered. *★It's too late.★*

~Which one?~

★Either. Or both.★

"Kurn, dismount!" Amelda tried, staying in Trade for once. "We must tend to wounds before we continue."

"I am not hurt," he growled brandishing his long sword. "And if the black *kus* nears my horse with that blade, I'll chop her hand off at the wrist and jam her cold fingers down her throat!"

Rithal glanced at me as I withdrew my hand crossbow from my side. The bolt remained dry-coated with the quick-kill toxin, though I did not know how long it would take to overcome a horse of that size.

~Maybe it would be better to hit Kurn with it, instead.~

★Don't you dare,★ the dagger hissed. *★You give him to me, or I leave you exposed at the very core of this corruption.★*

Kurn's arm continued to tremble, the armor writhing against tightening straps; the black stallion's agitation was spiking. Amelda backed up quickly, seeking refuge behind Mathias, and Kurn focused on her.

"Woman," he said, his tone sounding off. "Come, get on my saddle."

"No need, I shall walk," she replied proudly though failing to hide her fear as she glanced at me, her dark eyes pleading.

~*What do you expect me to do?*~

Claim him for me.

"Castis!" the Hellhound bellowed, baring teeth in a smile I hadn't seen before. "Bring your tight *alibat* here! The *shareth* proclaims herself untouchable. Let us use the ruby on her, together. Hold her down, like before. If you don't want a turn, I know others who do."

Amelda sputtered, and Castis trembled as he stared at his fast-declining partner. The nobleman shook his head in disbelief and anguish at what he saw then he pointed at me.

"Sh-she has the ruby."

"What?"

"Remember, Kurn? Sirana has it."

"*Sohn o'a fargith*," Rithal muttered, going two-handed with his axe.

"Don't you remember where we are?" the whelp continued. "We're in a warp rot nest! We need you!"

I saw green froth dripping from the stallion's mouth as his ears flattened against his skull. The burr of protest which came out of the muzzle held a high-pitched laugh within it as it half reared. The foreleg which had dropped into the earth continued to leak fluids of ever-changing colors.

The stallion whinnied, and the forest howled in answer.

~*It's too late.*~

Kurn paced his mount, their bodies twitching together in uncontrolled spasms, and I raised my arm straight once the horse's broad side was to me. The Hellhound focused on me as I aimed behind the stallion's shoulder and in front of the saddle; Callitro's ring must assure I didn't miss the animal's lung. I squeezed the trigger, and the bolt launched, striking at close range with a thump.

The air filled first with twin calls of rage, and then Mathias pitched something. There was a crack of sound and a burst of light at the rearing horse's feet, blinding me as I stumbled from the shockwave with my ears ringing.

Fuck!!

My spiders' feet tickled as they skittered in confusion; I sensed movement around me but couldn't determine imminent threat where I crouched. How far was I from Gavin's mare? I squeezed the talisman beneath my glove.

~Come to me. Stand in front.~

Clever! But let me use your eyes, I shall guide you.

I shivered as a large, decaying body loomed above me and stopped. ~No.~

Stubborn! Useless! You must give him to me, you promised!

~Better done as if underground.~

Fool—

That split instant later, I felt the impact rather than heard it, muted squalls and babble closed in underneath the high pitch in my ears. Something pushed my mount with force, and I scuttled toward the center of the path, hoping I didn't trip over the Dwarf. The mare's head brushed my shoulder as she stumbled and fell without audible protest, and my spiders left my neck, leaping away behind me.

I panicked. ~No, wait! Return! Return to me!~

Their launch was the best warning I had of how close Kurn really was. A large, strong hand seized my ankle, pulling me prone and dragging me to him as I curled up and stabbed blind with the relic. The grip released me at the first graze, the Ma'ab threats furious and slurred, his reflexes so fast they did not seem Human.

Rithal bellowed not far from me as the flickering blind spots in my vision began to clear. "Mathias, ye bastard! Where are ye?!"

There, your senses are healing, Soul Drinker snarled. *Give him to me! He is close!*

Indeed, he hulked over and above me, and a second chill darted through me when I spotted the large, familiar black arrow sticking out of the Hellhound's neck. He didn't seem to feel it. The whites of his eyes had turned putrid green as he foamed at the mouth with his gums bleeding red. Behind him, the wailing stallion bucked madly, kicking out at invisible targets.

"Cleanse him, Sirana!" Castis shouted, preparing to cast; what, I didn't know. "Cleanse him now, or I'll—!"

Another black arrow sliced the air and cut him off, lodging in the mage's chest. The Ma'ab collapsed without another word.

Oh, no.

"Gavin, the creature from the canyon!" I blurted.

★Kill him! It'll be too late! Killll! Give him to MEEEE!★

The relic would not be denied. Against all better judgment, I lunged forward as Kurn's big hands reached for my neck, my arm outstretched like a battering ram. Powerful hands closed around my throat as the point of the dagger touched the armor covering his gut—

My eyes remained open as he cut off my air. The black metal sank in as though he were naked, yet I strained to push it deeper. The demon shrieked in astonished delight, my ears popped, and suddenly the blade seemed caught in solid stone instead of flesh.

★Yyyyeeessss!!★

Kurn released my neck, his arms dropping like severed ropes. I shook as his greenish-white face stared at me, his eyes madly wide and face erupting in gruesome contortions. The enormous body began to convulse as invisible fire engulfed my hand gripping the blade's etched handle, heat racing up my arm like molten lava. I could not release the weapon if I tried.

★Miiiine!★ Soul Drinker crowed.

Violent images flashed behind my eyes; the scent of snow and sweat filled my nose as pale men bellowed around me. The weight of a chain wrapped around my right arm; I tested the swing, imagining it to be magic. I tasted bitterness that the chain had no spikes to pierce my skin, that it would not move through the air at my will. I had no markings, no spells, which could have prevented dying with an enemy's dagger in the gut.

She took it all away.

The small woman had an old, wrinkled face, and she appraised me with disdain. *"Divigna says you failed for the last time, Habod Kurn. Report to the Slum Guard Captain. Such an immense disappointment for one with your blood."*

I shook with rage. I couldn't see straight, could barely stay on my feet as I braced against a frosty, stone wall. I would make them pay.

I would make *her* pay.

Writhing, blind, I screamed as the voices surrounded me.

…Hold her down, Castis! Hah! Look at her…!

Use the poison, that's it.

Now grab the Ridhian! Let us go!

"Are you sure?"

Far too late for the noble to be asking that, but the ass licker still hoped for more. He would follow me to the ends of all lands.

We shall meet them at Manalar with anything we can find to break down the walls. We'll be champions greater than the Hellhound infiltrators.

I will be rewarded.

An urgent chime sounded once and held as a sustained, united call. Slowly, the fog in my mind cleared, the heat in my arm dissipated, and I once again felt the tickle of my guardians around my neck. My vision cleared, and I realized it had only been gone an instant.

I was on the ground, dead center of the grey path cut through the warp rot forest. Before me, Kurn had slumped to his knees, his eyes returned to normal though they were empty of any presence at all. His armor had stopped wriggling, and his skin was as pale as ever, the spittle at the corners of his mouth clear. The black arrow in his neck was starting to dissolve.

Cold with fear and confusion, I withdrew the relic without resistance now. Its red runes were obscured with blood, and my arm seemed the only thing holding the corpse upright. The big Ma'ab toppled to one side, landing as a sack of bones and meat with no signs of corruption.

The forest, however, was anything but quiet as it witnessed what Soul Drinker had done. A swell of voiceless calls hurled themselves at the threat.

We'rrrre commminnng!

Commminnggg…!

Fffforrr youuuu.

Know where! Know how!

Commminnnng!

Tear! Rip you freeeeee!

My heart slammed against my sternum as my eyes swept the skirmish ground. Mathias and Amelda were gone. Rithal stood in front of Gavin and his severely damaged mare, Dwarven axe at the ready. The redbeard stared at the black stallion, which had collapsed, trembling from the poisoned bolt, wailing piteously as it continued to change. My death mage's eyes turned void black as he searched the forest.

There were too many problems upon which to focus.

~Pick one.~

The archer was closest.

I jumped to my feet and issued a challenge to what I desperately hoped wasn't a Sathoet. "Show yourself, hunter! You were at the canyon, at the town while it burned! You are here now! Come forward!"

No response but for the distant, approaching screams.

I continued, "The center of the warp rot heads this way. I hear it! We are down two mages; you killed one and let the other escape! Help us purge the center if you would ever leave this forest again!"

More silence from the archer. No derisive laughter, at least, and for once, Soul Drinker was silent. No taunts or distractions. Was this good or bad?

The multitude of voices one valley over swelled above the dripping treetops, sending shivers up mine and Rithal's spine. Gavin did not tremble but gripped his spade with readable concern. The impulse to run, to try and escape this forest swept me, but all three of us couldn't sit on the mare.

Either we leave someone behind to run, or—

Gavin's black gaze snapped to the treeline to my right as the lightest of steps exited the corrupted foliage, a stealth unsettling for a creature of greater height than Gavin and larger bulk than Kurn. I saw rough-skinned shoulders, muscular arms wearing only a pair of bracers decorated with metal knots. His skin was the color of purple onyx, oddly pebbled in places but smooth in others.

Black hair formed a brow peak just visible within a heavy hood, the rest of the cloak pushed out of the way. Within the hood were yellow eyes, a bestial mouth, and flash of fang which threatened to make me heave. For certain, it was male. My body froze while precious time to run drained away.

Soul Drinker hissed.

~*What is he? A Sathoet?*~

Ha! No.

~*Another demon?*~

Yesss. Do not bargain with him, and by your soul, do not let him take me!

Not a Sathoet, though his bare, tough feet were large and sported ivory talons, and the ankle and leg joints were like that of a Priestess's Son but without the coarse tufts of hair. Further pebbly skin—*Scales?*—roughened the appearance of the tops of his feet, disappearing beneath a pair of loose pants, which covered his genitals.

He has a tail.

He was also armed to the tips. A harness instead of a belt held countless items, covering a chest thrice as broad as mine. His clawed hands were empty; I didn't see the bow and arrows he'd used. Instead, he bore a pair of long, naked blades, one secured vertically at each shoulder. My eyes traced them swiftly.

Double-ended. Two weapons, four blades.

I imagined them all too easily cutting us into meat. It took an enormous effort to project my voice through a tight throat. "Battle mage, help us purge the warp rot. We have little time."

I expected him to draw those blades while saying nothing; I waited to learn if his intent remained to kill. My spiders were ready; so was Soul Drinker.

Instead, the cloaked fighter tilted his head curiously. "A large and dangerous task. What payment do you offer?"

Of all the Surfacers and their Trade accents, his was disturbingly familiar.

Before I thought of a price, the mercenary's glinting eyes offered a suggestion, dropping to the relic in my hand then the ruby around my neck. Unlike a Sathoet, he had pupils. They were vertical and black like a serpent's, expanding to reveal his interest in my possessions.

I will kill you if you try to give me away!

The wailing crested and spilled into our valley.

Ffffuck.

CHAPTER 4

I CAN'T.

I couldn't offer him the payment he wanted. The relic was non-negotiable, and I could *not* hand over to a fourth, powerful male this goddess-damned red stone which had been used so many times against me.

Yet I had nothing else of worth to a mercenary. Neither did Gavin. Did Rithal have coin? Could it be enough to shift that avaricious stare away from these dangerous, stolen items?

*Do **not** bargain with him,* hissed the demon. *His words are binding!*

"I-I, uh," I stammered, as the large beast chanced to look away from me, estimating how much time we had before being overrun.

The creature's eyes weren't demonic yellow as was familiar to me. They were metallic gold, their sheen as I'd seen recently. Like...

Auslan's eyes.

I doubted my last Reverie had been Auslan in truth. Cris-ri-phon had seen it before; my dream somehow mixed with his.

~*What do I see now?*~

Nothing. He is nothing.

~*A far cry from 'binding' a moment ago. Are you afraid, demon?*~

As you should be!

~I see no way to make him leave and survive the warp rot.~

Hssss!

The fighter looked at me, his hood bowing open enough to glimpse a large, pointed ear.

I blinked. *Are they Elven?* "Take down your hood, mercenary."

The hunter smirked at me, his gaze steady and unblinking. He glanced at Gavin, who was searching Castis's corpse, then rumbled, "The corrupted come now, Baenar. I can lead two of you to the center and help purge it. Again, what will you pay?"

Two of us?

Was he saying Rithal should run? I dared a glance his way. The Dwarf was visibly shaking, his face flushed bright red; he did not look well.

Now I reached for the ruby.

Do not trade the Ridhian! He will turn it against you! I shall lead you to the center unharmed, we do not need him!

My hand froze in place, aching for no apparent reason until I hastily pulled the cord of Shyntre's pendant, tugging the blue stone out where the fighter could see it. The saphgar clacked against the ruby, creating an odd, white spark.

A forked, lavender tongue slid out from between the fighter's dark lips as I read his interest or curiosity. "What is that?"

"*Tragar sapphire,*" I said in the Queen's tongue, "*tempered by our most powerful Davrin wizards to turn it this shade of blue. Extremely rare below. Unique on the Surface.*"

The creature arched the dark ridge of his brow but displayed no confusion.

~Damn the web, he understands me.~

We warned you!

Unexpectedly, the mercenary reached to drop his hood where we could see his face. Without drawing attention to them, he displayed the long and tapered ears convincingly Davrin, even above a Sathoet.

Half-blood.

The iron grasp of the Valsharess's geas clamped down on me like a prison chain. I grimaced as the pain and illness swept through me. Despite the dagger's warning, I couldn't *fail* to reach a bargain with him now.

"Defend two of us to reach the center of the warp rot," I agreed hoarsely, glancing toward the unseen source of desperate wails. "Do not stop cleansing until the forest is fully purged. Every bit of it. Do this, and my unique treasure is yours."

The mercenary considered for mere ticks before holding out his hand for my pendant. "Done."

No deal!

Ignoring the dagger and the ache in my chest, I pulled the necklace over my head and tossed it to him. The mercenary caught it without effort. His serpentine tongue flicked out, not quite licking it, before he stashed the blue stone in a pouch on his harness. He raised his voice above the nerve-shredding chaos closing fast on us, sounding neither afraid nor hurried.

"I suggest the Dwarf escape while he can. He lacks sufficient defense. And that puppet mare cannot stand the coming assault."

Gavin and I both knew that.

"Rithal, mount up!" I said, my irritability leaking into my tone as Soul Drinker spewed a slew of insults at me. "Take the mare and get out of here!"

The redbeard sounded like he was hearing voices of his own. "Lass, I don'… 'm sorry…"

"Get on the horse, Rithal," Gavin agreed, approaching his mare's muzzle, and removed a scalpel to place against his pale wrist. "She will return to the road and stay there. You need not wait, especially if it grows dangerous."

Rithal's eyes were fevered and fearful as Gavin smeared his blood across the horse's mouth, his pupils winking out for a moment. As she shifted to present her broad side to the Dwarf, Rithal stowed his axe on his back.

"I-I'll head tah Augran wit' Osgrid," he said, "in case I keep hearin' 'bout this an' it keeps spreadin'."

I watched as Rithal made a supreme effort to mount the taller animal, jumping from a standstill farther than I thought he could. He got firm hold of her saddle and mane, which held, but his boot missed the stirrup, and his legs flailed a moment. The mercenary glided in before either Gavin or I could act, catching the stout boot with one large hand before guiding and tucking it into the loop of hard leather.

"Good idea, Rithal," said the merc. "Now go."

The redbeard yanked on the reins and kicked Gavin's mare out of habit, but she didn't respond. He looked baffled.

"Hold a moment," the Deathwalker said as he secured his spade to the packs with his other belongings. "Do not take anything, Dwarf."

"Nah, won't, swear," Rithal agreed. "J-just wanna leave."

With a nod and flick of Gavin's left hand, the mare turned around and began a steady trot down the clean path like it was a pleasure trip. The mercenary chuckled watching the Dwarf cling to his way out and pulled out a length of material. I watched as he covered his nose and mouth, tied it behind his head. Given the spray of liquids coming our way, that was a good idea.

I struggled to sheath the irritable weapon, but once I did, I felt naked, instantly hungry, and so thirsty. My stomach growled as I hurried to tighten the makeshift mask across my dry mouth, and to coax my reluctant spiders into the safety of their pouch.

~*You can't bite anything here. Sorry. Thank you for your help against Kurn.*~

I also thought about my unborn for the first time that day, shocked that I'd forgotten. Knowing what was coming, I wondered if I would still carry Auslan's spark by tomorrow morning.

Don't. Seeing tomorrow at all means success.

Tomorrow held the possibility to search for Gaelan and Jael.

Soul Drinker laughed when I drew it again, louder than before. The void inside seemed bigger, emptier, though my hunger and thirst vanished the moment the rune-etched handle settled into my palm.

A price, Davrin. Always a price. But there is something to balance your foolish bargain. The Ridhian you kept shall add to our power. We may grow so that we can stun the beast the moment you must escape him, destroy him as you didn't the Deathless. We will protect you from yourself.

The ache spread in my chest; my jaw clenched hard enough to be painful. My gut clenched down. ~Don't, demon. Stop. I **can't** harm him. My Valsharess——~

Ha! Coward. You can. You'll prove it. Wait until we are better attuned, you and I.

I blinked to see the half-blood was watching me carefully, and I wiped all expression from my face. "What?"

The mercenary shrugged, looking to the biggest threat I had been deaf to for long instants. "We prepare now. We have three minutes."

Imaginary ticks tapped away inside my head as the fighter reached for both blades at once, grasping behind him at his shoulders. The swords detached readily from his harness, letting his cloak drop full around him. I was certain he deliberately blocked my full view.

Next, he jammed both blades into the ground and began dragging them as he took off into a sprint, scoring the earth in a double line with him in between, sending up clean clouds of dust. His lips were moving, words tumbling in a growling purr underneath the imminent howling.

He was half-finished before I realized he drew a massive, oblong circle around us.

"Sirana," Gavin said. "I need your aid."

I ripped my eyes from the half-blood's progress to where my death mage crouched next to another dead horse. "Of course. Tell me."

"Interrupt the corruption for the stallion, as you did Kurn. I shall use their bodies to defend us."

That thought was more unsettling than the Witch Hunters arriving outside the shed, but I acted without hesitation. Sulkily, the dagger sucked out the festering Vitas after I laid it naked upon the bulky, cooling flesh.

"Castis's vial?" I asked.

"I have it," Gavin replied, glancing where Kurn's sword had fallen. "Retrieve that. His corpse can wield it."

Sucking spinnerets.

The moment the dagger had finished its snack, I withdrew to give the Deathwalker space to work and picked up Kurn's long sword. It was heavier than it looked, especially compared to the relic. The tip dipped down to the ground and, since I couldn't hold it with both hands, I didn't fight it.

"*Uunshoa prienatyi,*" Gavin uttered behind me.

I glanced back. The pale man had opened his vein again and was dripping a steady stream of viscous blood onto the corpses of Castis, Kurn, and the stallion, focusing on the eyes, mouth, and the holes left behind by those black, vanishing arrows.

Looking at those wounds, I wondered where the merc had dropped his bow and quiver, tensely waiting for the inevitable combat with my short but powerful weapon. My attention cycled between Gavin raising his new bodyguards, the Davrin-beast pacing his circle around us, Soul Drinker's eager giggling, and the reckless charge shaking the brush and snapping any wood that hadn't turned to something else.

Hurry, you two...

My ears popped on a suck of magic when the circle was closed. The golden-eyed fighter stood inside with us as Gavin calmly instructed three familiar corpses to heave themselves stiffly to their feet. I handed Kurn's sword to Gavin, who presented it to the undead Ma'ab, laid flat across both palms. It was surreal how Kurn accepted it without word or sneer to the *maknuut*.

~Hellhound's not so ugly when he is quiet like this.~

The relic cackled in agreement.

"What happens, death mage," asked the merc with a test twirl of one blade, "when the cannibals bite these servants?"

"The rot collides with my magic and will unravel," Gavin answered simply.

The half-blood nodded, again gauging our remaining time as my nerves pulled drawstring tight. "A shifting barricade while you cast a wider net from behind them?"

"That is the plan."

"Good."

I listened the best I could but thought my breath through the cloth was too quick. With Kurn's and Castis's dark eyes as empty as an Ornilleth thrall preparing for battle; with innumerable cries heralding the incoming onslaught over the next hill; with the forest transforming into a lake of sickly-sweet flesh and waves upon waves bearing down on us before my eyes, I might have vomited from fear alone were it not for Soul Drinker as my anchor.

★Claim my share, Red Sister, all I can consume, and you will be well.★

So be it.

"Watch my space, Baenar," growled the half-blood, displaying his massive reach.

Surprised, I stepped back, resisting the urge to fold my arms in front of me. *~Baenar? What is a Baenar?~*

★Something else your queen has forgotten?★ the dagger cooed. *★He's insulting you, what else?★*

"The circle will slow them, not stop them," the half-blood continued, giving me orders. "Take any cannibal pushing against the second boundary. Above all, keep them from reaching your mage. It is crucial that you cover his blind sides."

"Understood," I said tensely. *Elder Rausery taught us that.*

Gavin glanced at me. "Use the thunderstones if you must. They can be as effective as anything I can do clearing out an area."

"They didn't work against Kurn or his horse," I challenged.

"They were intact," he returned brusquely.

Implying all these naked bodies I spotted weaving through the green-white haze were not.

The mercenary narrowed his eyes at us, disliking this idea as much as I did, but he did not protest.

"How many stones?" he demanded instead.

I tried not to look straight at what was coming for us. "Nine."

I think.

He nodded. "Try to wait. Call a count for each you throw."

That was Jaunda's advice, too.

Helps you think, Blue Eyes. When things get noisy, don't stay quiet.

Not even the flayers' thralls in superior numbers had been this loud.

The cannibals spilled into the small clearing, stumbling and climbing over each other without heed. Once pale-skinned Humans, they'd become emaciated, greenish, and outright putrid; their eyes were universally fogged over. Their yawning, lipless mouths revealed teeth either broken, missing, or growing like antlers jutting in blatantly wrong ways from their jaws. Their limbs were mismatched; some clawed the air with filthy, overgrown fingers, waved and grasped with constricting, boneless tentacles, or kicked and punched with hardened nubs or hooves in any color.

I refused to see remnants of Gaelan among them.

★*Trust what you see is real,*★ the relic cooed.

My nostril curled. *Like last time one of these things charged me.*

Before we would see if the ritual of protection had worked, the merc crossed his blades in front of him, lifting them close to his mouth. The rumble pouring from his lips carried well despite the crescendo of screams.

"*Kayo pabixen.*"

A ball of orange light formed where the two blades met, swelling large and becoming opaque. Meanwhile, Gavin chose his first targets as a black, ethereal chain appeared beyond the border and wrapped two cannibals together, dragging them within range of Kurn's sword. He skewered them as one, dropped then writhing on the ground, turning to dust as further feet, hooves, and coils trampled them.

The masses had reached the boundary.

The mercenary pulled his crossed blades apart with great force, his arms thrown wide, grip on each sword tight as he stepped forward in a lunge. The orange ball followed the edges as they slid against each other, gaining momentum as the caster made a motion like a swordsvrin flinging blood or water from her weapons onto whomever was in front.

The magical glob struck the first misshapen body then *splattered* over the nearest five pressing at the circle; it stuck like tar and set them ablaze. The magical fire on decaying flesh was effective but horrible to breathe; I was glad for the cloth mask.

The fighter-mage did not wait for the full effects to play out before he spun both weapons thrice and took two low swipes at the masses, severing what passed for legs on no less than twelve attackers. This hampered them severely as grey flakes began dropping off their undeterred stumps.

The half-blood let them crumble, aimed at another cluster, and barked another word of magic. Something invisible knocked five of them backward, and he followed up by opening his mouth wide, spraying them with a clear liquid from beneath his tongue. Their hideous faces instantly melted before sending them to ash.

My eyes were stuck at their widest to witness all this. The beast-Elf was *full* of magic within his full control. Wherever this dark-skinned half-blood had come from, whoever had *made* him, and for whatever reason he roamed the Surface, I could guess his Mothers had considered the consequences as carefully as the Priestesses did with their demon-sons or the tainted Consorts.

That was to say, not very much.

I'm waaaiting! the hungry dagger bawled.

I flinched and growled in my throat. ~I'm not crowding the mages, but there are too many. They'll surround the circle soon enough.~

Better be soon.

It would be. I hoped.

The corrupted bodies piled on each other ten deep and were beginning to slide along the curve drawn in the ground. As they did, Kurn's corpse was covering Gavin's left flank while Castis and the stallion were on the right. Under the Deathwalker's control, each effectively shored up the strain on several spots of the magic circle while Gavin continued casting spells. I sought signs of exhaustion in him, for no mage could focus and set one's body under such strain indefinitely, but I wasn't sure where the weakness was for him in this new form.

Meanwhile, I *knew* that I should be exhausted and light-headed now. I should have eaten long ago and drained my waterskin. But no, I felt strong, and I waited for the best opportunity to come to me.

For an instant, I focused on the broad back of the stranger, and my arm lifted the dagger, my hand turning it, prepared to throw.

I stopped in place.

Now I was sick, and I dropped to the ground.

Aww.

I gasped for air behind the mask, swallowing down bile as one arm crossed over my gut. ~Now who's the fool, Soul Drinker? You will only kill your carrier if you go against my Queen.~

Curse your Queen! To the ice pit with Braqth!

"Sirana?" Gavin asked. He'd noticed me on my knees.

I scrambled to my feet. "I'm well! Focus!"

He did not question while the two Ma'ab corpses and the horse were slowly torn apart by the roiling chaos upon the border. The wait was excruciating from there. I stood dead center of the circle as hundreds of warp thralls arrived seeking a weakness around the circle, and the dagger and I were out of reach of every single one of them.

The death mage and the mysterious half-Elf cut down over half of the things quickly, their corruption untangled before they got halfway around the circle. Eventually, I realized this was because the two mages shared one half of the circle and I was at the center. There was nothing to draw them behind us; the chaos creatures displayed no strategy at all.

So draw them back! Move away from the mercenary and lure them to the other side!

~Bad idea. Their approach is controlled, and the circle holds.~

And he takes all the glory! He makes you look weak! Act! Fight! Step back!

I stepped back, then stopped only with supreme effort as I imagined Rausery would give this same order. I grasped the tactics, and I watched the carnage, listening to Soul Drinker complaining, taunting me, and berating me.

Clearly, the weakest here is you, Red Sister! Without me, you are as helpless as your pitiful sister you seek!

A stabbing pain entered the left side of my head and lingered as my eyes watered. I couldn't shut out the voice, couldn't muffle it as I had before. I was no longer certain I could sheath it. ~You act like a First Daughter.~

Good! You need guidance! You waste the strength I'm offering you!

No escape from this cursed blade.

I took that ground I'd given then held myself in place to keep the attack coming from one side. The warp creatures climbed upon each other's backs, three bodies tall and somehow beginning to meld together, focused on and looming over the mercenary, who revealed yet another trick about his exotic weapons.

The half-blood moved three steps away from Gavin and fearlessly close to the wriggling wall of warp rot, and something clicked on each of his weapons. He continued to swing and twirl them about himself, and I witnessed how far his arc of attack extended even beyond where it had been.

The hilts were no longer static; these were not merely a set of double-ended swords. The grips each slid freely along a single-piece blade long as the merc's arm. The flared tips on each end prevented the hilt from separating from the sword as he used them.

While his motions were fluid and constant, he could adjust for either an exceptionally long reach or a shorter one, dancing smoothly from his first move to his second. A practiced opponent would've been hard pressed to predict exactly how far the cutting edge would reach during any singular swing.

Undeterred by the change, the tower of cannibals was cut into four pieces in short order. Several in the rear were beheaded without having reached the double line, and the number of bodies landing at once increased two-fold. They steamed and sizzled in collapse, and the piles of grey ash and dust gradually became a third line, then a mound which might become a bank with fewer feet to scatter it. A grey cloud had since lifted into the air, drifting through the woods and obscuring distance.

With the surge demolished, I heard the same two clicks again, and the twin blades seized in place, ceasing to slide, once again the balanced, double-ended swords with which he'd begun.

Envious? sneered the demon.

~Not really, cunt.~

It squealed in glee. *Plenty use yours whether you will it or no! Use me and do your part!*

The mercenary kept going as I watched Gavin's meat shield at last break down, as Kurn and Castis became pieces and lumps under clawing, twisted limbs, gnawed on by broken sentients with inhuman teeth. The Deathwalker darted in to snatch Kurn's sword from the border and retreated, his balance unsteady before he caught himself.

I stepped toward him. "Gavin?"

"Take over," he said, his muscles tired although he didn't gasp for breath as I did. "I must rest. We're almost done…for now."

I scanned the forest. He was right. Almost.

Now?!

~Now.~

Soul Drinker screamed as loud as the cannibals as I sprinted forward to fill the gap in defense. My reach could not extend beyond the first line, but I quickly learned it did not matter where I punctured or slashed them; anywhere would do, and the unraveling began the instant after.

Although I had feared these once-sentients would pass their memories through me on their way out, as Kurn had, I experienced nothing stronger than an ethereal wail fading seconds after the physical one. Some collapsed and laid over either one line or both, still shuddering as they broke down.

"Be wary, it's weakening," the merc ground out.

Yes, bua, I can see that.

The chaos force was shrinking fast. The merc and I had less distance to stay out of each other's draw while avoiding a trip over fast-decaying limbs and torsos. We were breathing hard through our face masks spattered with gore and foul-smelling fluids; my muscles burned from the sudden and intense effort, but I was not even close to finished.

More! the relic cried joyously. *More, oh, yes, my wielder, you are worthy!*

I rolled my eyes and kept stabbing, letting the frustration and fears collect at the point of my blade. My vision blurred as I took another and another, and I continuously blinked to clear it. Up close like this, I didn't see anything that looked like Gaelan.

Tear them up. Put them down. Dig up the roots so this can't keep growing.

The chorus of threats was dampened, and as the last bodies broke the circle to scramble into protected ground at the end of the battle, Gavin was there with Kurn's sword to run through those I couldn't catch. The relic complained bitterly about this, but its fever-pitched railing could not make my heart race any faster at this point.

Finally, the last body fell face first into the dust and broke down. My ears felt numb in the following quiet. I didn't believe it was real.

Shaking and gasping, I tilted my head at the long sword in Gavin's hands. "Surprised... you can lift that."

"Only with both hands," Gavin agreed. "Effective only against opponents as untrained as I am."

"Mm-hm. Beyond what I could do."

Just wait! Hehehe!

To our right, the mercenary turned his ears in various directions before securing his filthy blades on his back and using a rough, bare foot to break the circles and wipe out part of them. I took that as a good sign we were safe for the moment.

In fact, the more I studied, the wider the sane path seemed to be, extending far beyond any spell Gavin or Castis had flung into the trees. The corrupted pit Kurn's mount had fallen into was not only gone, but I could not see where it had been. Looking up, I could see a glimpse of grey sky through the thick branches.

"Catch your breath," said the merc. "We cannot stay long, but we can withdraw again to this point if we must."

I nodded in vague agreement, looking twice before grasping that Gavin was staring at me. I growled at him, "What?"

"Your aura is changing," he said bluntly. "I cannot tell if it is the forest alone, but there is less..."

"Less what?"

"Less contrast between them. Greater similarity."

A bizarre feeling spread from the back of my neck, and I noticed the half-blood was paying focused attention to the death mage and what he'd said.

Ohh, the buas think you're unstable! Hehe!

I snarled, "So? That's good. You said I would be the one best suited to throw the vials at the quartz center! I will complete my Sister's mission. You can stay back, monk."

"On the contrary," the ugly man countered without blinking, "it's not 'good' if your aura attunes to chaos now when it was not before."

I mocked his expression but hesitated at his wording. *Attunes…*

Not to worry, the Deathwalker is wrong again. That is you, me, and the Ridhian strengthening together. He fears you becoming powerful. But you shall soon be free of your compulsion and do as you wish! You can look for your sisters without needing to follow this half-breed!

When I didn't respond aloud, Gavin looked at the mercenary. "Would you trade the sapphire for the ruby? It is of greater aid to her than you."

Heh heh heh.

"Gavin, shut up," I growled. "That's not yours to say."

Yet the creature considered it as if it were, his tail sweeping a small pile of grey dust to one side. "Potentially, I would."

"Liar," I accused. "You wanted the ruby first!"

A shrug. "And you would not give it up."

"I still won't. Not to *any* male."

He tilted his head, the forked tongue flicking out briefly. "Why not, Davrin?"

So, he did know what I called myself. Yet as both males focused on me expectantly, I found I couldn't answer.

Because he who holds the ruby can paralyze you? Soul Drinker whispered snidely. *Or make you spread your ass while he mounts up? Come, see how the big one reacts to that. Describe what happened in the kitchen.*

I couldn't speak. I hated them all.

"Let's go," I said, turning down the path. "My breath is caught up."

I anticipated one of them attempting to stop me, but they followed without speaking. The progress toward the center slowed tremendously as the pathway Gavin and I had made was overtaken again. We returned to stabbing, cutting, and casting our way through the slime-ridden foliage as the forest darkened to evening colors.

The way ahead lit by the haunting light of the center, and the forest continued to speak to me, any real distance fading away as I walked among stars.

Fffforward, baaaackward, enter and ssseeee…

Motherrr is anngry, she is highhh, up and low…

Crushhh, mashhh, form growth, grow and growwww…

Ahead, and close, something crunched. I stopped, as did my males behind me. The air crackled.

"Big," I whispered, not for anyone to hear me.

The pounding steps accelerated, and something monstrous and deformed pushed over the weeping, violet trees to make room. The roots ripped out of the blackened soil, soft and wet as blood vessels.

"Behind me!" the merc snarled, coming forward, reaching for my shoulder.

Fuck off! I sprinted ahead, Soul Drinker in one hand, a thunderstone in the other. "ONE!"

"Uh-oh," Gavin said.

I pitched the first of Castis's cache at the golem's feet, my eyes closed, ears covered with the heels of my palms against the expected flash and boom which sent the forest to jiggling anew.

The rising roar came down upon us like a storm surge. I raised my fist.

★Bring it!★ Soul Drinker bellowed.

The merc and I sprinted ahead at the same time. I doubted his eyes had recovered yet, and I wagered the relic would heal me first. What I saw ahead when it did, well, I could barely make sense of what formed it.

It appeared as if a score of bodies had all been melted together in a pot and hardened into something that could barely walk on two "legs." Its crotch was smooth as a rock archway, but the protruding, tightly distended gut above it was something I hesitated to slice open, despite Soul Drinker cheering me on. It had a disproportionately large mouth, enough to clamp down on my head and snap it off at the neck if I let it. Its arms were the size and rough shape of Human bodies, able to both crush and grapple us between them at once.

"Keep it away from the mage!" the half-blood shouted.

Easier said than done, though the mercenary began by engaging the chaos giant as directly as he had the horde, slicing its legs with his powerful sliders. Unfortunately, it appeared like he had drawn a knife through a warm pudding as green goop dropped into the cuts, molding putrid flesh together, only a few grey ashes fluttering away with each hit. The giant swiped at him and stumbled down the hill toward Gavin, who had shifted to the left, cleansing enough forest to make space for himself.

"Go right!" the merc barked, and we dove off the path, successfully drawing it our way.

Tohhhvaaaaahhhh! rumbled the mass of mouths, somehow conveying actual *sense* within the madness!

"You've made it angry!" I shouted, pulling another thunderstone. "The cannibals weren't angry!"

"Put that away, Baenar!" he barked. "This way!"

If he'd showed me his back instead of pacing me, I might have thrown it at him. Terror at the realization seized my arm and thoughts.

★Pah. You'll survive without him.★

I doubted it. The powerful fighter's aura was creating a safe if narrow path as we ran through the corrupt forest. I couldn't do that.

With enough distance, the half-blood spun around and engaged again while I took cover. Blades spinning then crossing in flowing motion, he barked the same spell I'd heard earlier and threw a fireball from his blades. The burst of light hit the giant directly in the chest and sizzled, creating a small dent as black ash plummeted to the ground.

The unraveling of chaos at the edges of the wound, however, slowed then vanished before our eyes.

"Shuiblith." The mercenary quickly shouldered one blade and stretched out his arm, his voice rumbling loudly. *"Thrae, ternesj!"*

I watched the half-Davrin make the motion of lifting and pitching something at the abomination, and an actual boulder that had been farther up the hill launched from the soft soil, snapped the tops of two trees, and smashed into the thing's head. It shrieked, blinking five swelling eyes at different rates but caught itself before it could stumble.

The merc shook his head with an audible growl, seeing the minimal effect, and I detected a quiver of effort in his muscles as he drew the second sword again.

He's finally getting tired.

Hehehe!

I sensed when his yellow eyes shifted to the straining gut, targeting the softest and most vulnerable part in front of him.

"No, don't!" I cried in panic. "It's gravid!"

He held the easy strike and retreated defensively as he led it right into a recovering tree.

"It's concentrated defense and learned to overcome my weapons," he said when he joined me again, "while spell fire and boulders are an annoyance! Any ideas?"

He's asking me?

I *wanted* to be able to stab it with Soul Drinker, it was all I could think about and the dagger let me. But I did not have the mercenary's reach and couldn't make myself charge while it could swat me to the side like an insect.

~We need his aid.~

★*Pah!*★ The red rune dagger grumbled but didn't disagree.

"The thing has emotion," I panted aloud as we moved.

"Fear," he agreed.

"And a will?"

"Rudimentary at best."

"I must get behind it. Onto its back."

He glanced at my relic. "Keep up then, Baenar, I will get you there."

Despite the blade whispering otherwise, I could not keep up. The mercenary was holding himself back, matching my limit, while his long blades cleared the worst of the waving branches before us. We raced down the slope then up again, circling around near to where we started. My lungs burned with my muscles, and I coughed from the rank scents and lack of good air in my dry throat.

"Onto the ledge!" he ordered.

I scrambled into place, thunderstone finally put away, but too late. My target was turning to face us; I did not have enough time. The mercenary pointed his clawed hand at the largest tree near the creature.

"*Jikmada!*"

The wood at the base ruptured into splinters and began to fall straight for the giant. The noise and imminent threat caused the servant of the warp rot to turn away from us long enough.

"Ready?" the mercenary panted, lifting his hand toward me like I was another boulder.

I was *not*.

"*Thrae—*"

My feet left the ground. ~*Fuck.*~

"— *ternesj!*"

"*Fuck!!*"

The half-blood tossed me into the air, long-dragging instants passing me through the slapping branches before my body slammed into the spongy, slick flesh. I collided high enough to expect a shoulder blade which wasn't there, and there were no real hand holds. Instead of a deliberate stab, I used Soul Drinker to gain purchase, ramming it deep, angling it down, hoping desperately that it would hold my weight for a few flicks.

I planned nothing else. The relic pulsed and felt again to have fused with stone as my hand cramped and seized. The demon howled with its legendary hunger, thrashing and tearing at the roiling cloud of souls within, like a lake monster generating froth.

I cried out and hung helplessly high off the ground. It felt like Thena and her squad catching me, dominating, biting, and shoving me down, combined with the fetid, revolting scent of the monster to which I clung.

~*Soul Drinker, stop! It hurts!*~

The demon heard nothing in its frenzy.

I tucked my knees up as if I could curl into a ball in midair, groaning in abject misery, enduring, waiting for it to stop. The warp giant's willpower, abstract and conglomerate, broke at last, and my too-intelligent weapon sucked in all Vis and Vitas provided, feeding until the gravid belly collapsed and shriveled in upon itself like a dried fruit.

In this whirling insanity, I glimpsed a possibility, something real and not; a vision where the blade singer had cut the belly open.

Opening a tear in the world which would summon a defense we would not survive...

Suddenly, the black blade released the shrinking flesh, slipping out of the oozing wound before I could see straight. My senses overwhelmed, my head threatening to burst, my body went limp as the chaos giant began to tilt. I could not tell which way was up as we separated from the target.

Something warm grabbed me, hauled me away, and set me down. Big and dark, his body covered me. My eyes made out the splintered trunk of a fresh-fallen tree while, beyond it, an avalanche of mulch dropped in an enormous pile, coating the entire hillside. The choking scent of natural decay billowed out and surrounded us.

I touched my brow to the firm ground, attempting to stop the world spinning as I fought rising bile, my stomach heaving with futility. There was nothing to expel anyway. Meanwhile, the large male was alert and looking around, braced on one arm, his heavy body shifting against my thigh.

"G-get off me," I uttered on another heave.

The half-blood raised himself up and shifted to one side. I expected him to stand up and away, but his large, warm hand rested on my cloak between my shoulders while I got my nausea under control. I should have told him to stop touching me, but… it helped.

"Can you stand?" he asked.

"In a moment," I grumbled.

"Hm. Well done."

I shook my head slightly. "D-demon did it, not me."

I checked my hand, confirming I still gripped the relic and hearing a bloated, languid sigh.

"I know." The half-blood paused. "I *am* impressed you can determine the difference."

I squinted and nudged, *~Do you know each other, dagger?~*

It murmured back, *We do not. But I know his kind.*

~His kind?~

"Will you trade the sapphire for the ruby?" the mercenary asked suddenly, and I snapped aware.

"No," I growled. "Keep your payment, merc."

Without further response, he finally climbed to his feet and called out, "Deathwalker?"

When the death mage didn't answer at once, I scrambled up as well, the ruby shimmering at my chest. *Oh, Goddess, Gavin!*

In the dark, eerily quiet forest, the relic chuckled indulgently, and then—

"Hurry," a familiar voice called from my right.

Turning with relief, I spotted the pale man in grey robes waving to us through the mottled, partially cleansed trees. He held Sarilis's vial in one hand, Kurn's sword in the other.

"The center is unguarded," he said, "but not for long."

CHAPTER 5

"Plan?" the merc asked before we had crested the final hill. He motioned toward the vial in Gavin's hand.

"Sirana and I each have one," the death mage answered, showing care where he placed his feet among the remnants of the giant. "We must break one or both vials against the source."

A pause.

"Exit strategy?"

Gavin looked at me, and I showed my teeth in a dry grin lacking humor. "You scattered it, assassin."

The mercenary grunted. "Fortunate I followed you, then."

This struck deep as questions tainted with regret flooded my thoughts.

*Who were you following all this time, me or the Ma'ab? When did you start? Why didn't you kill Kurn when you had so many opportunities? Why did you **stop** me? Where were you the night I escaped Troshin Bend? Why do you want my ruby? What do you want?*

Soul Drinker was listening, snickering, then cooing with sympathy. *What, indeed?*

I bit down on the questions and returned the figurative mark to the hybrid's side of the map. "I'll listen to a replacement strategy."

The massive, bootless fighter stopped moving forward, lowered his sliders, and looked between us with metallic eyes glinting. "If you give to me the vials, I will throw them in the center for you. If you stay farther away, you'll better endure what's sure to be a strong disruption which may harm or kill you."

"What about you?"

"Magic shield."

Gavin was either easily convinced or had been ready if the creature made such an offer. He handed out his vial collected from Castis. "I must bear witness, and I have protection from the surge, but I need not be the one to throw this."

The fighter accepted the vial, his tongue flicking out like it did when he claimed Shyntre's pendant. When they each looked at me expectantly, pure fright and chill streaked up my spine to my head.

I wasn't ready.

Wise. They will gradually convince you to hand over everything, including me. Just watch.

I shook my head once in refusal.

"Sirana," Gavin began, his pale blue pupils lowering to my middle.

~He'll give it away.~

*Indeed! And you've seen how these big Surface males react to secrets like that. As if they own it. And **you**.*

"I have protection," I cut them off gruffly. "And I *will* finish my sister's mission whether she survived or not!"

I turned and led the way, within moments feeling stupid and glad they couldn't see my face. How many questions about my home and my Queen had I placed into the half-breed's hands? Where did he come from? His accent was strange but not like Crisri-phon's ancient one. Was he "new" Desert perhaps? Or Deepearth, somehow? How could Sivaraus never have heard even a whisper of a creature like this?

There were so many threads, now. Too many, too fast, binding me. I blinked away tears, despair threatening to hollow out my chest.

~*I should have stayed out of sight of every Human.*~

Aww, I'm glad you didn't, warrior. I would still be in that cursed box. Your suffering always serves a purpose.

I sneered, tasting the sour tang of the air. ~*Never a good one where the Abyss is involved.*~

Hehehe!

I crested the final hill as swiftly as I could, listening to Gavin and the merc keeping pace behind but not overtaking me. Ahead, the corruption was thickest yet, and I froze in place to realize the ground was not truly solid. I waited for them, having no option but to allow Gavin and the tail-waving hybrid to lead the way from here. At best, I could only stab a few slime-dripping trees, and did so to release stress.

They made no remarks of my lack of reach while their dense, combined magic slashed and burned a new pathway through this last, slipperiest of slopes down to the break in the earth below. The ground became firm with their passing. I watched them step on it first and followed Gavin's stride easier than the half-blood.

Below was the source of the warp rot. It looked somewhat different from last time, if only due to the lack of hundreds of bodies seizing and undulating around the jutting rise of rotting stone. It still resembled an armless, Dwarven torso to me, quartz-like but suspended on the edge of crumbling, streaked through with veins of frayed mold.

The face I'd thought I'd seen before wasn't there.

"Sirana."

I looked.

Familiar garnet eyes peered out from beneath a weeping willow, nearly collapsing my chest. They were the right shape and number, and the body and hair were as she had been the final night I saw her on the mountain.

~S-Soul Drinker? Is that… illusion?~

I've not withdrawn my protection, warrior. It is as you see. Might be a lure, but warp rot has no motive easily recognized. We can tell you that taking form like this is exceedingly difficult for the source to do.

I swallowed. ~…And?~

And we think it has something to tell you.

About Gaelan? Could I survive hearing it, whatever it was? Why else had I come if I could not?

I approached the visible border between us, one side of solid ground and the other a hazy morass. Time seemed gently bound, cradled in a cocoon. Gaelan—her form—attempted to walk and meet me. She pretended to walk. It was a close mimic.

"Broken One," she said.

I flinched. A greeting? An insult? I couldn't tell.

"Dreamers split around the Firstborn," she continued. Her lips did not match her words. "As they split around the Thought. There are not enough to hold her again. Absence is the way open as the Great Work seeks the source of the River."

Incomprehensible.

Gaelan reached out her hand. "Touch the Mother of All, Broken One. Be One. Defy time, undo the All. It is the Mother's Gift to know All as One and Always."

Her "voice" was level and not the least agitated.

She did not *appear* mad.

But she was.

The fear within me grew up and down, becoming so profound that I could not sense my body anymore. Was I reaching out to touch her? Was I shrinking back in mortal terror? All but my thoughts were numb as everything appeared like black quartz, spreading all around me, closing me in forever. I was the foundation upon which the crystals would build, where roots would spread unseen for some time…

Until they burst through, breaking the sky itself into shattered fragments.

There are not enough to hold her again.

I spun around but could not escape; there was no distance to gain. I imagined pounding against a black mirror, that it was a door.

A way out.

~Stop, stop! Let me out! Let me go!~

"—*ana.*"

Distantly...

A voice. Calling me.

I knew him.

"Sirana!"

~Help! Gavin, where am I? Let me out, please!~

Long, cold fingers took hold of my arm but I slipped; I was free-floating for an instant. Then they grabbed hold again, dug in hard, and dragged me firmly through a cool, quiet mist.

My body slumped sideways, shaking and unbearably heavy. I might have fallen down the slope or against Gavin, but someone bigger caught me, holding tightly to my right wrist to keep Soul Drinker pointed away from us. I coughed, dragged air through an aching throat, and my empty stomach clenched down as I froze upon the mere thought that this deadly point might aim toward the mercenary.

~He has no idea how safe he is.~

★Rrrr!★

"What did you see?" the death mage asked me, his tone that familiar, irrepressible curiosity.

"G-Gaelan," I gasped. My mouth moved, but no other words escaped; I could not describe it.

★Don't disappear like that again, Davrin! How dare you!★

Was... was the demon unnerved by what happened as well?

"Mirages are common with warp rot," rumbled the merc. "The unknown and the known are the same. It draws out both with no boundaries or care how it affects mortals."

I glanced up at him skeptically. "You've s-seen this before?"

He nodded once before his attention went to the break in the world. My teeth ground down on the thought that he might have fought the warp rot without any payment at all, but the forest drew all our attention again. The light from the source was shifting from green to purple.

Gavin grunted. "Hm. We must cleanse it now."

Agreed! Soul Drinker squalled. *Get up, warrior! Break it down! I will shield you to the end. Run, hurry! The color you see is only a hint of the Change about to erupt!*

Seized with urgency, I scrambled to my feet, spotting the second vial in the merc's hand. Without thinking, I snatched it at the same moment I freed my wrist from his loose grip. I launched myself at the source of the warp rot, following the pathway the two had created for me.

The merc seemed oddly slow in trying to catch me.

"Baenar, wait!"

The pull of the world tilted severely, the closer I got to the center. The way my feet touched the ground grew inconsistent, sometimes slowing just before I could spring my full height off the ground, other times slamming down so hard after a single stride that I thought I fractured my ankle. Nothing hurt, though.

In one hand were both of Sarilis's vials; in the other was the relic's eternal presence. The vials became warm, and the wax seals began melting down my gloves with corks ready to pop. The black blade's aura shone visibly even to me, encasing my body within a blood-red glow. The valley shifted to a terrifying sublimation, the wounded earth venting like a spring, becoming violet-green air...

And a cloud of light into which I plunged.

Worse.

Into which all that struggled was undone.

As if it had never been.

Throw it! Do it!

Supreme focus guided my pitch of the rupturing vials. The bones of my arm bent like reeds, catapulting my attack with a snap, far beyond my best throw in a century. This assumed distance meant anything at all.

I stared at the progress, waiting, willing the disintegrating vials to land dead center of the headless torso. It arched back, faceless yet screaming into empty space.

Baenar, run!

An arm of stone hooked my waist, dragged me against a solid anchor.

~NO! I must see it—!~

My boots left the ground, floating before me as we accelerated.

Drawing away from the center.

Fleeing as timelessness faded and gravity resumed once again.

I clung to the merc's front like an infant bat to its mother, the ground speeding beneath us, the pressure put upon my form at last recognizable.

We were almost *home!*

A man in a grey robe appeared, and the large male grabbed him, too, mashing long ribs against my left arm, pinning it in place. Forcibly hauled together, we crested the hill, made it just over the top—

"Fethos troth!"

The merc collapsed forward, I fell beneath him, and Gavin partially so. A shimmering force spell covered us like a bell.

"Close your eyes!"

"Close your mind" would have been a better demand as the sky above exploded in utter madness. Seized with terror, I waited for the ground to unravel, for the void to sweep in wide and swallow us up. I grasped at him, at them; I grasped for *some*thing, anything solid.

Anything *real.*

"ARE YOU TRULY FINISHED NOW?"

The dead tone drifted out from within his grey hood while crows cawed louder outside the shed.

Mathias was drinking water he'd scooped from the barrel. Lowering the wooden cup, the skin hunter sighed with regret then grinned. "I suppose."

"There is no stopping once I begin."

"So?"

"So, I must hear a firm answer. I may have all of him?"

Mathias made a wry face. "Not sure I want to watch that."

Gavin rolled those new eyes in an old gesture, which was a delight. I smiled, and his glance toward me was so brief that I dismissed it as a tic.

"Poking fun, monk," the nobleman said. "Of course, you can have 'all' of him. I've taken what I wanted."

The death mage gave a solemn nod and turned to Rithal. "His mortality can be used against the Bishops. You may find it interesting if you will stay and help. But do not interrupt, no matter what."

Rithal reaffirmed a stout nod.

"I require a bucket of clean water and a cloth," he said to the Dwarf.

"Got it."

Rithal grabbed an available bucket filled with soiled water from earlier and used it to flush the small middens trench leading outside. He refilled it from the barrel using the clean cup rather than dunking the filthy waste bucket directly, rinsed it out, and tossed the water again. Mathias sorted out some used cloths as the Dwarf filled it for the third time.

Meanwhile, the naked and gagged Witch Hunter struggled, bound upon the same table which had supported Gavin's corpse.

He shouted to the ceiling with a ravaged voice, the muffled accusations no doubt wild and creative, but imaginary.

Gavin finally lowered his hood and approached the table, offering Jacob a long look at his pale, gaunt face, and dry, leathery skin. He peered down at the condemned man with his sullen ugliness, the unsettling, inverted colors of his eyes, and his black teeth and fingernails unhidden. Looming, he spoke to Jacob in fluent Manalari, yet it had none of the righteous bluster I was accustomed to hearing from those shouting the language.

"This began within your soul, crusader. The Sun God planted the seeds of this imbalance long ago, shaped by you and your brethren. Those who challenge it will manifest at the next conflict at Mount Sonai, and I've accepted the task to see it through. You shall help your brothers bear witness to the inevitable transition, Jacob, come what may, but your Vis shall not return again to Musanlo."

This threat and warning were at once too clear and too nebulous for the Witch Hunter to reconcile. He went temporarily, fiercely mad against his restraints. We had always intended to kill Jacob; there was no releasing him for any reason, any advantage. He had known that, claiming to me that he was ready for death and that it would serve a higher purpose.

How prescient the statement had been.

During a pause in which his thoughts seemed interrupted, Gavin once again seemed to glance at me, making eye contact for the beat of a moth's wing before Rithal set down the full bucket of clean water and offered the cleanest cloth, and the risen mage looked away.

"Thank you," Gavin said flatly, rolled up his sleeves, and got to work. Dipping the rough cloth in the water, he began wiping the dirt, sweat, and stains from the struggling Jacob's skin as efficiently as he groomed his mare when she was sidestepping. He removed the gag to clean around the neck and mouth; it was both thorough and galling for the Witch Hunter.

Mathias leaned toward Rithal. "Cleaning the slate?"

The Dwarf only shrugged. It clearly surprised them all when Gavin disrobed after dropping the cloth in the bucket. Not only did Mathias make a face as the Deathwalker removed his robe, but Jacob went dreadfully silent as they watched the worn, leather armor and his long shirt follow the robe. With deliberation and care, Gavin set them far aside.

Mathias exhaled in quiet relief when Gavin kept his hands away from his braies and his feet stayed in his boots. Jacob stared at the apprentice's ribs showing on a hairless torso, at his ropey muscles visibly attached to the long bones of his gaunt frame. Given the disgust and judgement, I had to think it was purely practical that the death mage removed any clothing at all.

Next, the death mage withdrew his surgical kit from within his pack to set on the chair then gathered a few other items. I recognized some from his buying list with Rithal the morning after our arrival at Troshin Bend. His whole focus was on his motions; he thoroughly ignored everyone. When he turned to reposition the chair closer and begin spreading out his tools, we all saw his back.

"Aw, shit," Rithal hissed within his beard.

"Oof," Mathias agreed.

"Dyos karta," Jacob whispered.

No response from Gavin, who possessed scars from more scourging than Jacob. Several marks were much older with the way they stretched at the edges as if the skin had grown a lot since they formed.

However, something else drew Jacob's attention, and his voice broke on a blurt of surprise. *"Archimandrite!"*

"Hm?" At last, Gavin reacted.

The Witch Hunter pulled on Mathias's excellent knots. *"Y-you were once ordained, cleric? Impossible!"*

I waited eagerly for Gavin's response, if any, and studied the raised brand of a stylized Sun. It was high in between his shoulder blades and branded into his skin with white-hot metal half his lifetime ago. I'd only seen a glimpse before, but it matched the symbol on the Witch Hunters' saddle blankets and gear.

"This is no mark of a cleric, fool," Gavin murmured, choosing to answer in Manalari, though Mathias and Rithal probably understood most of it. *"I never made an oath to Musanlo to betray him."*

"Only oath-takers have this mark," Jacob barked like a wounded dog. *"Proudly worn where the praying man's dawn touches him first!"*

"Indeed, so it did, many times."

"Betrayer! Corrupter!"

Gavin turned toward the table with a small vial in his hand and smiled without showing his teeth. *"I refused any oath of consequence that would betray my Lady. The branding was forced, a desperate act for a father to cleanse his son of his heretic dreams and his mother's Ma'ab blood."*

Jacob looked twice in quick succession. *"Archimandrites do not have children. They do not wed; they are celibate."*

Gavin shrugged, adjusting a few implements resting upon his cloth roll. *"I am sure many of them lie with others even as they lie to God."*

"Your father was bewitched after the whore dropped you!" Jacob drew breath to continue but stopped as something struck him. He began to quake. *"Y-you must be the well-fouler of Chirtu Cloister... you poisoned them all, killing the Archimandrite! Confess! We found you!"*

Gavin's icy blue pupils glimmered. *"Indeed, I confess. My intent."*

The cool lack of remorse unnerved the Witch Hunter. *"A-and we executed you, as you were sentenced in absentia! Sworn upon the Temple Pisc'sagrad! There was nowhere you could hide from God's Warriors, for Musanlo himself led us to you!"*

The Deathwalker sighed. *"Correct, again."*

"Now you've made an unholy pact to get revenge upon us. You sacrifice Musanlo's battle-blooded crusader for power!"

"In a manner of speaking."

"Who is she?! Who is your devil's slut!"

Gavin showed his teeth this time. *"Were your soul's resonance not in such harmony with your Bishops, mage, I would not be able to use you in Her name. Remember this when the Veil finally lifts."*

Motioning to Rithal, my Deathwalker requested his help to force Jacob to swallow what was in his vial. This was a small show on its own, for the resistance was impressive, but the redbeard eventually overcame teeth and jaw and gag reflex with a flexible pipe produced from his gear and pushed down his throat.

I pondered the possible effects, watching the Witch Hunter gag and cough and curse, then seem to itch all over, quite badly, demanding again and again to know who Gavin's Lady was. Jacob grew quieter, and I watched his eyes lose focus, his tongue become heavy as his speech slurred.

Soon, the Witch Hunter stopped trying to speak.

With that welcome rest upon the ears, Gavin's final preparations in the quiet shed, coupled with the encouraging caws outside, seemed to calm him. He unrolled his kit, took a moment to study their cleanliness, arrangement, and distance from the quick-breathing body on the table. All smirk and satisfaction had vanished from body and mind before Gavin selected the first tool: a small scalpel.

The death mage turned and, with careful, long-fingered hands, without hesitation or expression, drew precise cuts in Jacob's skin at multiple points on his light brown body. Rithal and Mathias were absolutely quiet, watching. Though the drugged captive flinched and moaned, the skin hunter did not seem discomforted in the least, while the Dwarf's expression was hard and numb to any visible suffering of a Witch Hunter.

I waited for a pattern to emerge, listening above the roof to the feathers flutter and beaks clacking like Osgrid's pet. Gavin avoided the largest vessels or cutting too deeply, any action which might lose control of the blood flow. I could not read the marks, but they resembled runes or glyphs as I'd seen the Davrin wizards and Priestesses use. I was thankful they didn't easily match what I'd seen on the walls of the Forming Pit, or in what lay upon Soul Drinker's blade and hilt.

When Gavin was finished with his scalpel, he traded it for a tiny, hand-held basting brush which looked new. Or maybe it was a paint brush. The fact that he could trade for his tools at many crafters' stalls left me to wonder if the intended use had been culinary or not. Regardless, he dipped the new brush into the blood welling in one glyph before painting a mirrored glyph in the same location on his own pale body before moving onto the next: shoulders, forearms, chest, pits, stomach. Gavin needed to push his own braies down a little to draw the groin glyph. There were none on Jacob's legs.

An unsettling whisper bounced strangely off the wall, and I jerked my head toward the door before realizing it was from Gavin. He intoned exceptionally low, his words in the death tongue; for the Dwarf and the man, the crows obscured them but, for once, I understood what he said.

"My Lady Nyx, Citadel Prophet among Greylords, I am ready. Pain until birth, pain until death, each I've endured to see beyond the veil, as it must be. Grant me witness as I guide and know them in one, within this pinnacle soul of the Sun, as you know and have seen him. Grant me witness I may prove I can serve you in walking upon this world, through ages if your need be there."

While he chanted, Gavin's hand become incorporeal before my eyes, the fingertips slipping into Jacob's chest, deep in to the knuckles, his pale skin surrounded by bloody glyphs. Gradually, the black-eyed death mage began withdrawing his hand with a firm grasp on something which might be all or part of Jacob's soul.

It was like a vapor which possessed all manner of vibrant colors, intense and in no danger of fading. Also within was an oddly harsh, serpentine void that lacked any color at all; it moved within the rest like a worm in loose sludge.

A chill seeped into the room, flowing through the barred door as if it were wide open and foggy outside. Mathias drew in a breath, his tired body shuddering though he kept his eyes on Jacob. Rithal fixed blue eyes upon the secure entrance; I wasn't sure what he saw but it made him curse beneath his beard.

Jacob seemed to come awake as Gavin drew his hand back, his mouth opening in a silent scream. His body seized in violent fits; the restraints fortunately strong enough to keep him in place. His eyes were open, but he did not seem to see anything around him.

Mathias made sounds of utter fascination as bright red blood from Jacob's glyph incisions flowed toward the clutch of colors that Gavin held in his palm. At the same time, my risen mage's own black blood seeped out through the mirror-glyphs on his skin. The dark flow glinted as it flowed toward Jacob's soul-light, appearing to contain innumerable, tiny shards of glass. It mixed with the red fluid and tainted light cradled within pale, curled fingers, and the two souls became connected as if by a birth cord.

It was here I saw the pain in the death mage's eyes, the subtle tremor in his body, a slow-rising agony apparent in his voice as he continued to pray.

"My Lady Nyx, Grey Maiden of Manalar, I give of my bones and blood to weave the immaculate prison and crown gem of the Brother's journeyman. As his pleasure and his pain have become a singular edge of flint in life, let this stone heart hold that sharpest edge in death, and slash the Veil in transition when the reckoning is at hand."

A low shudder passed through the floorboards, below the ground, and the two males seemed to shake out of their stupor and look around. They did not know what Gavin had said, though the fear on their faces revealed their first impulse to leave mid-ritual.

No. Not yet.

"Rithal," Gavin rasped, his black trance complete. "Have you any grief left to share?"

At first, the Dwarf couldn't speak. He tried.

Then, "Plenny."

I saw Gavin's slight nod of acknowledgment. "Let your offering seal this prison behind his soul. Cut the threads, and the Bishops shall have no defense against their own corruption."

Uncertain of the specifics but understanding the sentiment, Rithal moved slowly toward the quaking body, soon standing on the other side of the table. The air grew colder inside the shed, and the black-streaked vapor in Gavin's trembling hand had begun to take the shape of a man. I saw Jacob's likeness which pleaded for pity as tiny impressions of hands reached out.

He would find none in an elder survivor willing to stand exactly where he stood now.

"Fer Brenna," Rithal said, pulling off a glove. "Gone this last century an' ten but still loved at night. Fer li'l Hancet an' Pitrel, ne'er seein' their craft come tah their hands. Fer Nabrin an' Shoana, Deacon, an' Quir. Bridges burned an' sheep slaughtered, stone walls an' garrisons built on yer graves. M'sorry I couldn't do more, or sooner." The redbeard wiped his weeping eyes with his thick hand, collecting his tears as his voice broke. "M'sorry for bein' worse an' them a time 'r two, but if the Grey Maiden's lad can see the leash-holders broken, so be it."

Rithal reached out toward the gossamer light clinging so tenuously to the body. "Take 'em all, *Tirgeu-hreik*, those bitter tears I got left, an' let God's Warriors get what they've earned."

The Dwarf waved his wetted hand in the space between the body and Gavin's grasp. His tears ate away at the very spirit of the man, the first threads snapping like spider's silk. Jacob's struggling body went slack as the last of them were cut, the face frozen in a terrified death mask, and at last, Gavin held Jacob's soul wholly in his grasp.

The colors turned chaotic as the essence writhed anchorless, twisting like an animal to escape the jaws of a predator. I could well imagine Jacob's threats as a rising black sheen seemed to grow from the middle, washing out all color until Jacob's soul was pure black, darker than the space between stars. It seemed to me that it fought and refused the inevitable, railing against its fate, blurring and roiling as Gavin's glowing, blue eyes stared unafraid into that darkness.

"For you, my Lady," he said in the death tongue, *"through this righteous soul, you shall be heard again."*

The movements of the dark essence had become sharp and punctuated, restrained, as if it were throwing itself against an invisible wall. One time, it had darted out directly toward me but again stopped abruptly, its space seeming to shrink, to fold in on itself, as every attempt left it less and less slack to try again. The colorless black bubbled and swirled in a way I could see; soon, the boundaries of the Witch Hunter's soul were defined.

Gavin held a black, glossy stone in his palm, a flint shard as long as his hand was wide. It was sharp on both ends, and the Deathwalker used one end to slice deeply into the flesh just below Jacob's sternum, reaching with his other hand inside the man's body cavity.

There was nothing ethereal about his hand going in this time. It was quite visceral, familiar as Gavin jerked, twisted, and finally removed Jacob's heart through the gash. He brought the organ to his mouth, as unhesitant to bite into it as he'd been on his last mortal night alive.

In the time it took for the black flint to form, the small room had become frigid. Rithal's breath escaped in huge puffs, and frost formed on the tips of Mathias's damp hair as he wrapped his cloak tighter around himself, looking toward the door. Meanwhile, Gavin ate about half the heart, quickly, and the moment he finished, the ritual ended as the chill rapidly left the room.

In the empty silence, we heard the first villagers shouting for Brom outside the inn, and Gavin hurried, kneeling by the bucket to clean off the black shard and his hands, face, and torso before dressing and collecting his tools. He rolled the shard into a scrap of leather and slipped it into a pocket in his robe.

"Cut Jacob free," he said. "Let his corpse stand with us."

It struck me then, as he picked up his spade to face the mob, that I had just been attacked and raped in the kitchen.

I'm outside with Osgrid. Right now.

In my desperation, I'd drawn Soul Drinker. In my anger and humiliation, I'd punished Kurn, though without succumbing to the relic's hunger. I'd sheathed it, showing Osgrid that I could. She had found and returned my guardians spiders to me.

I lifted my empty hands, baffled. *Where am I?*

"The better question, life flower," whispered the shrouded woman in the far corner, *"is when."*

I jumped in surprise. ~*W-when?*~

"Indeed. When shall we become what we are?"

Rithal and Mathias not only didn't hear her but also vanished from the shed like smoke. The cawing of crows and the threats of the villagers outside ceased as well. Only Gavin remained, puzzled for a mere instant before he focused and—

Saw me.

He narrowed his eyes suspiciously. "Sirana."

I glanced toward the whispering woman, but she was gone.

Gavin took a step toward me, his face resentful. "I asked you not to play in my dreams."

The punch in the gut was worse than when Cris-ri-phon had accused me of the same.

"I am sorry," I said. "I-It was safe here."

One dark eyebrow raised. "Be that as it may. I asked you. You've seen enough."

I backed away, pinched myself hard as I could.

~*Wake up!*~

CHAPTER 6

MOVING AT ANY SPEED WAS A MISTAKE, BUT WHEN I OPENED MY eyes, I was breathing in Gavin's face.

And about to puke.

Roll away!

Flat on my stomach, a moan slipped out of me before I was overtaken in a fit of brutal dry heaves. My back burned and my belly ached in the effort; my hands shook where I dug fingers into solid, mundane dirt. My vision repeatedly skidded to one side regardless of how I tried to focus dead center.

Beside me, Gavin sat up with far less noise and theatrics, maybe only a joint or two popped. "Hm. Horrifying enough to induce vomiting on sight. Noted."

"Ugh…" I wheezed. "'S'not you…"

My body seized again, expelling only bile. *Hork-hork!*

"Well. You are clearly not well."

Gasping, I shook my head. The misery and illness felt marrow deep.

"Can you stand?"

I doubted it. Still, I tried pushing against the earth. My arms quivered while cold sweat and nausea muted all sensation. I could not rise; I utterly lacked strength.

"N-not yet..." I admitted grudgingly.

"Hm. Rest, then. We seem safe enough."

Are we?

My last memories were a barrage of strange colors and constant motion, yet I noticed the gradual, predictable shift of pink and orange light across a blue and purple sky.

It is... dawn.

The night had come and gone. How long had we been here? What happened? How did we survive? I lay still, noticing my hands were empty. Cautiously and despite the stubborn threat of the world tilting, I peered around.

Soul Drinker?

My middle grew cold as I became certain it had been stolen from me. Then, a cautious relief as I spotted the dark, naked blade not far away. It lay quietly in the center of a ring drawn in the dirt. The circle was filled with white crystals, decorated with four silver coins placed equidistant from each other.

What in the Abyss?

"Gavin?" I asked, staring at the relic.

"I see it," he answered.

But he hadn't done it, I could tell.

The forest was too quiet. No insects, no birds.

Nothing but us.

Again, I tried to push myself up. With dizzying effort, I got as far as an elbow, enough leverage to fumble at the relic's empty scabbard and then, nearby, my spider pouch. Holding my breath, I tugged the knot on the latter and opened it.

Slowly, my guardians crept out, and I exhaled. Though I'd trained myself never to land upon my right side or roll that way without releasing them, I didn't recall how we'd landed before, or what had thrown us.

Then the answer appeared from out of the tilting trees.

The muscular half-blood with Elven ears and metallic gold eyes walked into my view. He had just finished a patrol, perhaps, as he had his bow and quiver out and constantly scanned the landscape.

The memories of the warp battle returned in a rush. Worse, the previous day's insanity upon the Surface blended with those deepest roots in my mind; my bonds and chains to Sivaraus held fast as all else rampaged over me like a maelstrom.

I studied the portrait of the placid, gold-eyed bua, standing in a hall of the Sanctuary. I wondered who had painted it. The young male sat so straight, holding still and beautiful through centuries, until the frame began to splinter and wear away.

He moved then, his filthy face and shining eyes taken over with desperation and despair, the scabbed knuckles on his hands visible as he gripped the iron bars in the Desert canyon. Begging to be let out.

My chest ached to soothe us both, and I kneeled to touch him through the bars in Solitary, leaned to kiss him through the iron barrier. Promising I would return for him. That I would find him again.

When I leaned back, however, there was only the accusing, tawny eyes of the Valsharess. Her voice in my head. Her hand laid possessively over my womb.

"He has not sparked a new gift in centuries. He has been spiteful."

Auranka cornered him inside the Forming Pit, forcing him away from me, keeping herself between us. I dodged to the side, remained blocked. I protested.

"Shyntre!"

"He cannot hear you. Lissten! Listen to storiess of Elven origin…"

Suddenly, I couldn't move.

"Listen to rumors of half-bloods."

My compulsion.

"And if you find any, bring them to Us."

"Sirana? What do you see?"

The world upended. I tumbled into darkness, numb to my weakened body as it slumped onto the ground.

THE PULSE IN MY THROAT BATTERED ITSELF AGAINST A FIRM touch like a rabid bat beneath a dome. My skull threatened to crack open like an egg, and I whimpered as I wished my eyes were blind in truth, never to be bothered by the cursed Sun again.

Someone jostled me, sat my useless body up where my tender head flopped against too much leather and metal. That someone pressed cool, soggy cloth upon my bottom lip. Reflexively, I swallowed.

Water.

My lips clamped on to it and sucked hard. Too soon, the liquid ran out. I bit down in frustration when someone tried to pull it away.

"Whoa."

With another firm tug, he took the cloth away, adjusting his arm around me. "Alright, here."

A waterskin's spout.

I craned my neck, drank what flushed my mouth, moaning after it flowed soothing down my throat. Too soon, he tilted the spout away. My teeth snapped, but I missed this time.

"Slower. Not too fast."

Fuck you.

If I could have raised my arms, I'd have snatched the skin and served myself, but panic plunged deep into my gut to realize I could not.

I was paralyzed.

"Easy. You are safe."

I'd heard that before. I didn't believe him. Why was he doing this?

I gasped erratically, overtaken with panic but still couldn't move.

~Oh, Goddess, my babies, where are you?!~

Three little chimes answered, and I knew instantly where they were: one on my chest resting near the ruby, one on my crown and tickling my scalp, and another crawling along the large muscle of a violet-black arm wrapped around me. I couldn't believe it. They were free and crawling around, and they hadn't bitten him?

What have you done to them, merc?

I could move my head well enough, and I could flex my fingers. I *wasn't* paralyzed, just… weak. I dared not look into the eyes of the arm's owner; I couldn't, regardless, as the sky grew too bright. But when he offered more water, and I gulped it, my throat ready to work again.

I couldn't wait any longer. I coughed, "G-Gavin?"

"I am here."

I turned my stiff neck to my left. The death mage's hood had been pulled up against the early morning light, and I was envious. He observed me as calmly as my spiders did, sitting cross-legged on the ground with Kurn's sword and scuffed scabbard together and laid across his lap.

"And he is correct," Gavin added. "You are safe for now."

For now. No wonder I hesitated to relax. "Soul Drinker?"

Gavin's eyes slid to focus behind the merc who cradled me. "Still within the circle of salt and silver."

I made a face. "Why?"

The half-blood spoke. "Keeps it quiet."

I had felt the vibrations passing from his chest to my arm when he spoke. Squinting, I finally tried to look him in the eyes. He had the advantage, looking down with a hood also protecting his face from the light. My head continued to pound, and I closed my eyes, squeezing them against the light. I gave up for the moment.

The hybrid hummed in thought. "Will you answer a question honestly, Baenar?"

I sighed. "What?"

"Are you with child? Do you carry right now?"

I didn't know how to answer that question, and the collision of terror and irritation hit me like a stone. I flung pure accusation at Gavin as he watched me without remorse. "Damn you, Gavin!" I snarled.

"It is relevant," the mage said. "You can't regain your feet, Sirana."

"I was asleep!"

"You fainted."

"The relic has been starving you," the mercenary interjected, his tail shifting behind him. "Now that you no longer hold it, what you lack catches you all at once. You *are* ill, young fighter."

"It's only been a day," I said through gritted teeth.

"Two," Gavin corrected.

I growled back, snapping, "I have a healing potion!"

The mercenary interjected. "You do?"

"Yes!" I fumbled for my belt but heard a wary rumble in his throat as I indicated the vial.

"Can you also check its integrity?" asked the half-blood. "In my experience, objects imbued with magic can be neutralized or destabilized by massive surges such as we saw. Potions and powders are most vulnerable."

Fucking web guts...

That meant I couldn't be certain about Shyntre's pellets, either.

"I'm not a mage," I said plainly. "No, I cannot."

He nodded once. "Regardless, you've not had enough water, made worse that you carry and have not eaten. A healing potion cannot feed you. You *must* eat if you would live, and you need time to recover your strength. The damage done cannot be reversed with a sip."

I swallowed twice, taking a long, slow breath in, desperate to keep the water in my belly.

You are ill... The damage done cannot be reversed...

It felt that way, too much to recognize an appetite. Starving such that it was difficult to lift my arms. Was it too late for my baby?

Should I... Should I let it go?

How? I no longer had the vial to make it safe and quick. Avoiding their eyes, I tested the crotch of my leathers with trembling fingers. *Dry.*

"I smell no blood," the merc added. "You may still have time."

He spoke in a careful, neutral tone.

"All the food was on Gavin's mare," I murmured, "several valleys away." I paused. "Assuming Rithal did not take it with him."

"There is no food here," said the merc with complete certainty. "The corruption is only just cleared. It will take multiple seasons to revive the land with life patterns again."

I let that sink in. The corruption was cleared. We did it, then. Gaelan's mission by the Valsharess was done. My gaze lingered as one of my damned spiders crawled back and forth on the half-blood's pebbly skin. At least she wasn't swatted for her trouble.

I wiggled a lethargic finger at his arm. "Do you feel that?"

"Yes."

He knew exactly what I meant.

"What have you done to her?"

"Nothing. I acknowledged her guardianship so I could give you water."

I didn't respond at first. He could have trapped them like he had Soul Drinker, or as Cris-ri-phon had in his sphere to make sure they didn't bite. I glanced at Gavin, and he nodded simple confirmation like a witness.

Maybe the half-blood was immune to the venom and knew it. Either way, he wasn't afraid of them.

"So." My eyes closed again; I turned my head away from the rising sun as my pulse throbbed in my temple. "What next?"

Gavin watched us expectantly, and the half-blood's big chest expanded in a deep, crowding breath before he let it out. Turning his hooded eyes North, he said, "We must get clear of the barren area and hunt for food."

Hunt. More difficult than foraging. I pursed my mouth. "But I cannot stand. You think to carry me the whole way?"

"I can carry you to the mare, if you prefer to ride."

"If you can stay on her back," Gavin added.

My nostril curled up. "Thanks, scholar. And the dagger?"

"It must come with us," the mercenary said. "I will help to sheath it, but you must not draw it again. Starvation is one of the easiest ways it can break its bearer's will."

I growled, "Why not take it yourself then, if I can't control it?"

He paused. "A discussion for another time. I'll not steal from you, Baenar, nor harm your guardians. I ask the same from you. Let us start there."

I didn't reply at first. Slumped sullen and pouting, I grew ever aware of my aching, empty middle.

It was too quiet.

"What?" I asked.

The big male exhaled. "Do not steal from me. I will not steal from you."

Oh.

"I will not take anything if you don't," I agreed.

"I would add for you to consider," Gavin spoke, "that the relic does not seem to want competition for your attention. Not one once dead, nor one born, nor one unborn."

I stared at him in genuine shock, yet the insidious possibility gradually soaked in. *It was starving me on purpose? Starving us...*

"The Deathwalker recommends you, Baenar," the merc said. "He stated that you are normally a reasonable and curious Elf. You prefer to speak or negotiate, and are far less reckless when not listening to demons."

I made a face at them. That sounded like Gavin.

"High praise, indeed," I grumbled, fumbling for the empty sheath at my side, unsure how we would get the wild dagger back in. "So... we look for bountiful ground. How do we call you, mercenary?"

He paused as if to think, to choose something. *"Quell'dalik."*

I blinked. "That's not a name, half-blood."

"Isn't it?" Gavin asked, plainly curious.

"No," I said irritably. "It means 'house son.' An abandoned or orphaned *bua*. Unbelievable that this one would be overlooked by his mother, and I will not call him 'unclaimed boy.'"

Gavin tilted his head. "Ah. The rough equivalent in Trade would be 'bastard'."

The merc chuckled with a subtle cynicism to it, laying me down on my side and gently scooting my one guardian off his forearm. She went willingly.

"Hm. I shall think on a better name. For now, may I have the sheath?" He pointed an ivory-white talon at my belt.

"No!" I barked, instantly regretting that as my head swam. "Uhh... G-Gavin may."

"Why?"

"I don't know you, while he..." I glanced at him. "Gavin has made an oath to walk again. It is so strong, the dagger will not challenge it. I have witnessed it."

If Gavin was irritated at my sharing something private about him in exchange for the "relevancy" of my pregnancy, he didn't show it but simply set Kurn's sword aside and got to his feet.

"Hm, very well, Deathwalker. Let me show you what to do."

After helping Gavin detach the relic's sheath from my belt, I lay on my back, my spiders settled on my chest protecting me and the ruby. I could only turn my head to watch, disgusted with myself as neither drive nor strength tempted me to try again to sit.

The two males approached Soul Drinker with as much caution as one might a sleeping bear in the woods. The big mercenary could have blocked my view by standing with his back turned, but he moved to the far side, facing me, and allowing me to see what they were doing.

Gavin held the red rune sheath in one hand, positioning himself so he was aligned with the point of the dagger; he held the flint shard he'd created inside the shed at Brom's Inn in his other hand. Having something tangible that he had consecrated himself in the name of his Lady *would* protect his will, I did not doubt.

Idly, I wondered whether Jacob's claim that Gavin was "ordained" made any sense. It would make him like a Priestess, wouldn't it? Except he rejected it.

"This is no mark of a cleric, fool," he said.

Meanwhile, the half-blood withdrew a small, matte black rod from his harness and gave the uncomely man a nod, confirming they were each ready before releasing his spell with care. I flinched at the swell of the relic's aura as the circle of silver and salt was broken, and the blade jerked to point toward me.

Neither spoke as the bigger male used that rod to press the dagger to the ground, stopping its willful spinning. Gavin wasted no time fitting the tip into the scabbard and, together, they pushed the two pieces together. I imagined Soul Drinker screaming in defiance the whole time and wondered if they heard anything at all. If so, it wasn't apparent.

The mercenary retrieved from beneath his cloak a thick leather wrap with extra threads for binding. Soon enough, the relic was rolled and cinched up tight, and Gavin took possession of it, not the merc.

It was out of my sight. Still and quiet.

...*I'm so hungry.*

Mortified, I could not stop tears from flooding my eyes and dripping down my temples into my hair. My throat ached from holding in sound. How had it become so destructive, so fast?

★The Ridhian you kept shall add to our power.★

As opposed to the blue stone that I'd tossed away in an impulsive bargain. That was when my will had eroded. When I couldn't think and it began getting bad, like Jilrina had hold of me again.

The vivid memory seized me, the image of an aggravating, stubborn wizard running out of the Headmaster's Tower to give me something. He'd showed no fear of the massive Drider constructs which kept most other buas from leaving the place. *Shyntre...*

Regret and renewed fear followed on its heels, for I *still* could not trade the gems, red for blue. I did not know why he wanted it, how he might use it...

Large, bare feet came beside me. I was granted a remarkably close look at the dirt-tipped talons and real texture of his skin. Scales, like a lizard or a snake. It explained his tongue.

What have the Priestesses fucked this time?

The half-blood kneeled, his tail instinctively providing balance, and slowly gathered me up to lift me and my guardians off the ground. He noticed my damp cheeks and hairline.

"Does anything hurt as I lift you?" he asked.

Yeah. Lots.

I shook my head. "I am...just need food."

"Ah."

"Let us return to the road," Gavin agreed.

He turned around on a long stride easily matched by the hybrid. The pace was not leisurely as we retraced our path through the forest. The Deathwalker did not grow winded while the large bua carrying me possessed obvious and impressive endurance.

If I hadn't felt small and useless enough until then, the embarrassment and resentment grew as we passed the scuffed circle and piles and piles of ash where we'd faced hundreds of cannibals.

"Can someone pull up my hood?" I griped.

The merc's hands were full, so Gavin turned around and tugged it up for me. It was as great a relief as Soul Drinker not baiting in my ear.

I'D DRIFTED OFF WITHIN IN THE SHADE OF MY CLOAK, CRADLED against a warm body and listening to deep, regular breath and the naked pads of bestial feet trekking on solid ground. When the breath changed and the footsteps halted, I snapped awake in shock at having fallen asleep so soon after "fainting."

Not good.

"Where?" I whispered with habitual underground caution.

"Where you left the horses," he answered.

I sniffed and peeked out from under the hem of my hood. It was far too quiet for there to be any animals left besides Gavin's worn and rotting mare, but there she stood, alone and untethered, the spade and saddlebags strapped to her rump. Her death mage approached to circle her, inspecting.

"Any food in the bags?" the mercenary prompted, not entering the small clearing yet, though I didn't know why.

Gavin glanced our way and left off his study of the risen mount to check inside one of them. I was certain it was empty, watching him feel around with one long-fingered hand, then he moved to the other side to search the second.

"Rithal left half." Gavin pulled out several small wrappings from inside.

I exhaled. *Better than nothing.*

The mercenary cautiously left the brush and set me down to lean against the nearest tree to the mare. As he began investigating the area, I spotted innumerable hoofprints and several tethers which had been either sawed or chewed through. I wondered if Amelda and Mathias obtained their mounts to escape after running on foot, or if the horses had gone mad and left before they returned.

Either way, wouldn't Rithal have overtaken them on Gavin's mare and reached his pony first?

I didn't see the remains of one tether, implying the Dwarf had untied it and taken it with him. If he deliberately left half the food, then the skin hunter and Ma'ab mage could have seen Gavin's mount after Rithal left. I didn't know if either would touch her, or mess with anything in the bags. They hadn't taken the shovel.

My head pounded thinking this through.

"Can you... check the food?" I asked, light-headed and unable to hide it. "The Ma'ab may have... been here after Rithal left."

His tail swished along the ground. He was somewhere near Gavin.

"I can detect and recognize many poisons and toxins, Baenar. I offer to check all your food as you regain strength if you like."

"Wise to accept," my Human ally weighed in. "One naturally spoiled meal might be all it takes to miscarry."

I made a face within my hood. "Thank you, Gavin."

Their feet were pointed toward me. They were waiting for an answer.

I sighed, waiting for a wave of nausea to pass. "Yes, help me check the food before I eat it."

I peeked up again, squinting in the painful morning. I remained dizzy and unsure I could stay upright even with the tree propping me up, but at least I saw the mercenary unwrapping the rations taken from Troshin Bend and...

Licking them?

No, his forked tongue didn't touch it that I could tell. As with my saphgar when I'd thrown it to him in payment, he flicked his tongue in the air around the food. Was that all it took for him to tell if something was safe to eat?

He wrapped up all but one and returned them to the saddlebag. "They are unfouled."

So easy.

He brought one and crouched in front of me, breaking off a small piece and handing it out. I narrowed my eyes at him.

"Eat that slowly, first," he said. "If you keep it down, we shall repeat."

He liked being in control, for certain. And if he claimed no name from his mother's culture...

What is a Baenar?

I took the pressed travel bar of nuts, fruit, and fat and bit off a small piece, grinding it between my teeth, taken at once by twin impulses to ravenously shove the rest into my mouth and spit it out immediately. It took intense concentration to swallow it and try another bite. Gavin handed me a waterskin from his mount, guessing my mouth was too dry to chew, and I was annoyed how heavy it seemed when I lifted it to drink.

I hate this...

The two males said nothing as I gradually fed and watered myself, for which I was glad. I kept it slow to prove I wouldn't lose what I had, sipping water constantly, as my appetite gradually awoke over the illness. It took time, but after circling the area, the half-blood seemed convinced there was no urgent reason to leave.

"So," I said when he'd come closer. "A name?"

He turned to me. "What is yours?"

"I am certain you've heard Gavin say it."

He smirked. "We haven't been formally introduced."

"You care about formality?"

"When conducting business, always."

I rubbed my face, which had greater feeling than earlier. The talisman to guide the mare lay beneath my glove within my sweaty palm. I sipped again, looking up from beneath my hood to hold focus on his face as I answered.

"I am Sirana of *Vloszia Dalnanin*. Formerly of *Thalluen Qu'ellar*. And you?"

He tilted his head curiously at "former." He wanted to ask but didn't evade the simplest question this time. "I am *Morixxyleth*."

I blinked at the precision of his tone and the air moving around his non-Elf tongue. This was not a Davrin name. Was it demonic? No, no. True demonic names could be used to bind and control demonbloods, I knew this much.

Then again, hadn't Soul Drinker been shouting something like that?

Do not bargain with him. His words are binding. ...I know his kind.

"What origin of name is this?" Gavin asked. "Or what language?"

His curiosity had outpaced mine, unanchored by wariness. I needed only to wait as the mercenary acknowledged the question.

"It is *To'vah*."

"I do not know this word," Gavin said simply.

Granting a nod, the hybrid glanced at me. "Do you know 'Dragon'?"

My Deathwalker and I stilled with surprise.

"*Tagni'zurenor?*" I clarified, flatly disbelieving.

Not *the* Black Dragon?

The hybrid for once showed me his fangs in a dark-faced smile. "*Melthra'vlos.*"

That strange accent again, but it *was* Davrin. He was not claiming the Dragon's title nor being full grown. He was a young Dragon's blood.

Fucking Goddess...

This time, Gavin simply waited on my response. It took time to grapple for one.

"A spider cleric below mated with the under Dragon?"

His body language conveyed he didn't like that assumption. "She wasn't a cleric at all."

"She was someone in Sivaraus?" I asked blatantly, tumbling into my native tongue. *"Or the Fringe? The Deep Traders?"*

He enjoyed his next answer in Trade. "None of those."

I was taken by a bout of dizziness, reminding me to sip water, but I had no food to nibble. The half-blood noticed and broke off another piece of rations, stepping forward to hand it out to me.

I took it. "Then where are you from, Mori...ahm...?"

"Morixxyleth," he repeated.

With as many subtleties that crossed my ears, I knew I would butcher it each time.

"From *Vuthra'turn.*"

Uh-oh.

Gavin watched me carefully while I froze, and the mercenary's soft exhale somehow conveyed amusement.

"I've not heard of *Vuthra'turn,*" I said.

"I know. That is deliberate."

"Deliberate for whom?"

The hybrid straightened up. *"Your Valsharess, I am sure. Also, the Priestesses of Braqth who run the city."*

Gavin showed his annoyance when the mercenary slipped into Davrin again. I could feel only cold shock in my center.

Another... another Davrin Elf city in the Deepearth?

Well, why not? I hadn't known about V'Gedra and the Desert until I fell into Cris-ri-phon's dreams, unprepared, and straight into a trap.

"There... is a second city of Dark Elves underground?" I repeated for Gavin's benefit, and his shoulders lowered.

The larger male grunted. "Assuming it has not disintegrated since I left."

"How long since you left?"

He paused, his golden eyes narrowing in thought. "Four hundred-forty years."

Gavin and I didn't speak. I imagined the Deathwalker, despite what he'd witnessed while dead, could not imagine this time passing or count so precisely.

Neither could I, in truth. Anyone back home would have waved at the question with their hand and a vague "mid-four hundreds" or "not yet five centuries" answer. No wonder he was so practiced with his weapons and spells. A valuable mercenary, indeed.

He's older than Jaunda.

Maybe closer to my Elders, depending on his age when he left the underground. Like Kerse but without his Priestess chains. Either was unsettling, but I had so few older male Elves to which to liken this.

Why was he following me? Or had it been Kurn, and I was in his way?

I'd finished the next bit of food without realizing it, and Morixxyleth handed me the last of that first ration before I'd thought to look at it.

"Good sign," he said. "Keep eating and sipping water. If you need reverie before riding, we can afford to wait."

I did feel drowsy, but I did not want to miss any information shared between Gavin and the merc while I slept. I didn't know what else the death mage might count as "relevant."

"N-no," I managed. "I would like some help onto the horse, but please leave now for greater bounty."

"Mm. Very well."

MY SPIDERS HAD REPOSITIONED AT MY NAPE, THE RUBY HANGING from my neck as I lay forward atop Gavin's mare. We headed North over a vague path that once might have been a road. I couldn't sit up for long, and there was enough length to the animal for me to settle down instead. My hood was up but I resisted donning the sun blind despite the discomfort as the Sun strengthened in the sky.

Gavin had taken the lead, walking in front of his mount and me so I didn't have to concentrate on the talisman. The half-Dragon walked on the left side, his large hand reaching out to steady me whenever the ground tilted enough that I could slide off if I weren't paying attention.

Which happened too often for my liking.

A dry hum from the merc, possibly a chuckle.

"What?" I asked. *Are you laughing at me?*

"This is the first and only walking horse who will tolerate me so close," he said.

My irritation eased. "You have never ridden one?"

"No. They catch one whiff of me and often panic. Remaining aware of the wind shifts is critical to following any mark on horse-back."

It was a perfect opening. I drew breath to speak.

"She has no mind to tolerate you," my scholar pointed out.

"Yes, why it is funny," the bestial male replied.

I buried my eyes in the dark, ratty mane. *Damnit, Gavin!*

"I have often said I can only get close to a horse that is dead. This is still true, but I've not walked beside one before now."

"Often said to whom?"

I cracked an eye open. That was a good question.

The merc noticed and easily turned it aside with a shrug.

Fine.

"Who was your 'mark'?" I asked bluntly.

"Why do you ask?"

My fast-emptying stomach tightened. "Because you interfered in my challenges with Kurn at least twice yet pulled your strike and did not kill him yourself. In doing so, you left me vulnerable to men wanting to enslave me, which I did not understand until it was almost too late. Now, you position yourself to 'tend' me when I am too weak to refuse. Was that your purpose all along, motherless one?"

The large male glanced at me. "You are from Sivaraus for certain."

Helpless fury swept through me. "Do not belittle me, *bua!* Soul Drinker is in my possession because of that very chain of events! You and Gavin both suggest the dagger *wanted* to starve me to expel my baby, and I *mourn* that you are right, and now I am responsible for what it does next because I stole it from the Sorcerer-General in the first place!"

"Wait," he said, lifting a clawed finger. "Sorcerer-General?"

"The Deathless," Gavin replied, calmly leading the horse to keep us moving. "Also the innkeeper and governor of Troshin Bend up until a few nights ago." A shrug. "Or perhaps he remains so. My understanding is Sirana did not kill his body but left it bleeding after stabbing him with his own relic."

The expression of concern and surprise on the half-blood's face was unsettling, but I didn't understand why.

Unless...

"Wait," I mimicked lifting a finger, "do you *not* know what happened? You were there the night of the fires when the Witch Hunters killed Gavin. The black arrows, the chain-wielder illusion that scared off the Ma'ab. You were watching *and* acting. Do not deny."

"I do not, but...hm," he began, using the pause to flick his long tongue out and peer around. "I left that night to scout farther out. As you say, the death mage did not escape and was killed, and the innkeeper wanted to keep a close eye on you, seeing him ignore the Ma'ab and his entire posse to find and follow you."

I waited. "And?"

"And I thought, without Sarilis's apprentice, that you would either sneak out alone or would leave with the Hill Dwarf in a few days."

"Or I'd be forced to stay until you wandered that way again."

"Or that."

Gavin turned his grey-hooded head. "You thought you had more time."

"Correct," the merc confirmed. "I did not know you would return in such a spectacular way, Deathwalker. I am sorry I missed it." He paused. "Will you tell me what *did* happen?"

I cut in before my scholar to respond. "Only with even exchange, like for like."

Those golden eyes narrowed at me. "I can put together some of it from meeting you now."

I showed him my teeth in a feral grin. "The details design the web, *Melthra'vlos*."

"This truth, I know. But I cannot answer *anything* you want in exchange. You should consider with care the details you want in return."

"One question first," Gavin asked. "Are you a devil rather than a demon?"

"No," came a ready and unresisting reply. "I am *To'vah-krav*. I claim no admiration for either the Abyss or the Hells, though I know their methods and may use such tactics against them."

Does he meet them so often?

"Why would a demon claim your words are 'binding'?" I pressed. "And to be wary of making bargains with 'your kind.' Is that true?"

"Who claimed that?"

"The dagger, of course."

"Hmph." Morixxyleth smirked. "That comes from demons aggravated that a Dragonblood never forgets the details of his bargains. It would be to the Abyss's advantage if we did."

I scowled but listened. Forgetting one's bargains certainly seemed true for the Abyssal-touched Davrin, from the Valsharess down to the scavengers.

Unless it is a compulsion which forces us to keep it.

Which were outlawed in Sivaraus, except when the Queen used it.

"How many Dragonbloods are there to bargain with?" Gavin asked.

"Not many," the hybrid replied easily enough. "Few and far in between."

"You've met another?"

"Two in over three hundred years."

"What happened?" I asked, and the merc smiled at me without showing his sharp teeth. I could hear him repeat himself.

You should consider the details you want in return.

Gavin waited, and I hid my eyes from the light again until the throbbing lessened.

"More food?" the merc asked.

"Yes," I replied.

He retrieved another pressed ration from the saddle bag, unwrapped it, and gave me the bar whole without breaking it up. I nibbled on it and pondered our exchange.

"I must know who your real target was," I said, "and why you interfered between me and the Ma'ab. In exchange, I will tell you what happened after you left to 'scout around.'"

The half-blood nodded, no longer smiling as he glanced at the ruby swinging from my neck. "That is balanced, Sirana. What about you, scholar?"

Gavin grunted, nodding in his hood. "You have said that you wagered Sirana would leave Troshin Bend after I died, and this was enough for you to leave after the Witch Hunter attack without staying to confirm. This does not confirm your real target, but regardless seems premature and hurried. What drew you out of town?"

"Indeed, that is a different exchange, Deathwalker. What will you offer in return?"

"What do you want to know?"

"If you have any intention to travel to Manalar this year, and if so, why."

That's direct.

And, thanks to our recent mindlink, I knew enough to bargain if Gavin wouldn't answer. The mage seemed to recall that as he glanced at me mid-stride.

"The intention is likely but negotiable."

Was Gavin lying? I wondered. Either way, it was enough to interest the big male nodding in contemplation. After a lengthy silence, he went first.

"My original marks were Kurn Divigna and Castis Orlien. I was tracking them to the Ley Tower." Golden eyes looked at me. "Then you appeared, *Vloszia Dalna*, and I knew a lot had changed at the sight of you."

He did not overwhelm me with details but allowed time for this to sink in. I returned, for an instant, to the moment Tamuril had run from me. The Pale Elf had been afraid for someone.

For the "Godblood," the Captain at Manalar.

Fucking Goddess, someone had stopped me from tackling her then, too.

"That was your spell that interfered," I muttered. "The noise that sent me to the ground, the fear spell to make me run to the tower instead of chasing the Druid."

"Correct," said the Dragon's son without remorse.

"Why?"

"You were acting strangely. The Druid has been hurt enough by the Baenar."

"What is that word?" I demanded. "Baenar. This is not what we call ourselves. Is it an insult, as we call a Witch Hunter instead of *Dyos Guerrimos*?"

Morixxyleth looked at me with surprise, as if a little impressed. "No. The word is what Dragons call you."

"You are half 'Baenar.'"

"I am."

"Half *Davrin*."

"Perhaps."

My head hurt.

In the shade with my nose against the mare's musty mane, I struggled to get my thoughts on point. "You followed me from that moment?"

"Oddly, yes, because you traveled willingly with my marks. I watched Kurn run you down on his mount and seize you, take you to the courtyard. You did not kill him, so…"

Because I couldn't… I grimaced inside my hood as a sharp ache erupted inside my head.

"I assumed you were allies somehow. I would wait and watch."

A pained laugh escaped my lips. *We were not allies!*

Yet I could not explain my actions with the damned brute the same as I could not say why a fearful Soul Drinker failed to use me to stab this Dragonblood.

"It was clear he attacked you in the canyon, intending rape," the mercenary continued, "but you lead him on a dance of some sort. Intriguing but strange. I could not tell your purpose, *Vloszia Dalna*."

I growled. "What was *your* purpose in stopping me from stabbing him with his own dagger? That falling boulder which startled me, and again that wave of fear!"

He didn't deny this. "The Ma'ab was *my* mark, and he was vulnerable to submit to part of my contract."

"Part of your...?"

He showed the point of one fang. "The price on the loner's head included torment where possible. You offered perfect arrangement, Sirana, and I'd seen you hesitate to kill him yourself. I would not let it go to waste."

Hesitate.

This geas was going to get me killed.

"That is why he was so panicked in the morning," Gavin said.

"Indeed. He had a difficult night."

That should have made me feel better, but it didn't.

"And the chain illusion that made him run at Troshin Bend?" I asked. "More torment?"

"Correct."

"What did he see?"

"His father. The one who authorized the contract."

"Divigna, the century-old Hellhound," I said.

Again, the merc seemed impressed. "Correct, again. Kreshel Divigna is infamous in the cold North."

While Kurn was barely a quarter century.

"How is a Human that old breeding?" I grumbled.

"I do not know. Something the Ascended have done to extend his life."

"And... you were not helping with the Hellhound training, correct?"

The expression on the To'vah-krav's face was genuine, even with my hazy sight in the sunlight. He was baffled and disgusted. "Why would I?"

They still have the Sathoet. And maybe the Priestess.

Helplessly, I shook my head, lips pursed in the next wave of discomfort.

"Kurn told you something like that?" he pressed me. "What did he say?"

"Different bargain, Dragonblood," I replied.

"Then I've completed my part. I've told you why I interfered in you killing the Ma'ab. Now, complete yours. Tell me what happened that you possess both the sorcerer's relic and the Ma'ab's ruby, and reportedly stabbed the innkeeper of Troshin Bend but did not kill him. Why is this, Davrin? Any female I knew below would have finished it, especially if she was pregnant."

Hearing his tone, the pain moved beyond my head; now my entire body ached, and my vision blurred with tears. I felt their hands on me, their cocks jammed inside. I couldn't escape. I'd kissed the ancient one, sucked on his tongue as his wife had, determined to *outlast* them, to lull both men long enough to reach for the nearest weapon. The weapon calling to me. And after I was free…?

Like-for-like.

I'd confirmed this mercenary's existence from Kurn's own lips, relished his wail of disbelief with a blunt object jammed up his rear. Then I'd flat-out *denied* the demon as it shrieked for me to *kill them all…!*

No. Denying them all what they wanted from me, escaping as soon as I could, had been of greater importance than "finishing it." Or it had been when I didn't know what might happen after, or when Gavin needed time to complete his ritual, or when Osgrid looked at me like I might be insane.

Meanwhile, my Valsharess held most of my threads, and I knew I had run out of time.

How did I fail my Elders' training so badly?

The forest path tilted again, and my body began sliding. The large half-blood caught me before I could catch myself, pushing me onto the rotting cart horse who did not react at all. His palm rested on my back to hold me steady.

"Well?" he prompted. "What happened?"

I gritted teeth, watching the ground pass by. "The Deathless and the Ma'ab were fighting over me like dogs on a piece of meat, mercenary, trying to break me for 'service'. If the Druid was hurt enough by the Baenar then I've had enough of the same by Human men, and at least my sergeant dragged the pale one out of the dark and *let* her escape after she finished."

The mercenary fell quiet, asking no details. It appeared I'd answered just enough to fulfill our first bargain.

For now.

CHAPTER 7

MY THOUGHTS WENT DARK FOR A WHILE. QUIET. I WOKE TO someone shaking me, and the horse had stopped moving.

"You're sweating," rumbled a low voice. "Sit up. You need water."

My lids lifted the barest crack before I squeezed them shut. *Bad idea.*

Sensing my guardians nestled at my nape, I made the solid effort to lift myself up to drink. Strong hands took my shoulders, assisting me up, and one supported me once I got there. The other hand left to retrieve and raise a waterskin; his, again. Wordlessly, I accepted and drank deeply.

When I stopped, he asked, "Have you need to relieve your bladder?"

At first, I wasn't yet aware enough of my body to say but... by the time I lowered the skin, I knew. My head shook in the negative. He grunted.

"Very well. Finish the skin if you can. Better we discover now how long it takes before you need another break."

I sighed and drank the skin empty, handing it back with my empty stomach bloated. "How can we tell a trusted source?"

The half-blood turned a thick neck, looking North again, his tongue flicking out. "I can smell it. We are perhaps a day away."

I didn't know whether to believe him. The distance was reasonable, but *smelling* it from that far away?

"Indeed," Gavin offered. "The few hills we've crested, it looks about half a day before we are out of the barren forest."

That reminded me, and I forced myself to open one eye for a peek, looking at the closest area around. There were a lot of shadows because there were a lot of trees still standing. They lacked half their leaves, and the ground was thickly carpeted in grey and brown leaves in the wrong season. Many remained in the twisted shapes of before, but some displayed a new burst of spring green.

"Question," I said.

Both males made noises of acknowledgement. My mouth twitched in vague amusement.

"Why hasn't the entire corrupted forest turned to grey dust like near the source? Why do I see new leaves? And is there truly nothing we dare eat or drink here?"

Gavin tilted his head and passed that one off to the Dragonblood with a wave of a walking stick he'd found somewhere. The large male exhaled slowly as he peered around.

"The trees are woven together through their roots in a forest as thick as this," he said. "If you can imagine this, they resisted corruption for as long as they could, entwined together, sharing water and defenses, though some were overwhelmed anyway. The trees which turned to dust were the same as the cannibals who attacked us; they could not be saved but their bodies can be returned to the cycle. Those that stand farther from the center could purge themselves through the Sun and the magic surge, and live."

"You speak as if they can think," I remarked.

His broad shoulders lifted in a shrug. "Maybe they can despite having no mouths. It is not unheard of, is it, Baenar?"

I didn't reply.

Gavin pointed his finger, which immediately shifted grey to black in the light. "Are those green leaves safe to eat for an animal who wants them?"

"A first attempt at healing, yes. They need the spores clinging to their roots to hatch and begin again. They need the insects and birds and animals to venture back, to provide their dung and seeds to the soil. They need the rain to fall from the clouds. It will take time, and you and I best not strip what few resources remain for them to survive this final struggle. They are in a fragile state."

Before either of us could respond, the To'vah-krav focused metallic, eerily familiar eyes on me. "The trees are like you, Red Sister, in resisting corruption from the dagger for as long as you could. You have survived the danger and threat around you for months since approaching the Ley Tower, but you are spent and cling to your last strength. You need food, water, and a safe place to rest. I will see that you have this."

I narrowed pained eyes at him. "For what price, mercenary?"

He lifted a talon. "This once, no price. And I told you my name if you will use it."

"Well, it is a difficult name to speak under pressure," I admitted, "and I do not want to insult you by doing poorly. Is 'Morix' acceptable?"

"No, it is not."

"Why?"

"Because you insult me by breaking it."

I rubbed my eyes and adjusted my hood, sensing my ever-re-silient spiders creep out of the heat of my hair. They chimed clear as a bell to me. As often as the Dragon's son had rested his hand on me to prevent falling off the horse on steep grades, my magic-touched guardians never reacted as if we were under threat, nor were they lethargic as if affected by a spell. As far as I knew, they were at ease around this one, and I could not ignore that while my instincts were so scrambled.

"Until I can grasp the nuance of your full name," I said, "is there a simpler one you would accept instead?"

"Why should I accept that?"

"It is reasonable, bargain-maker. I do not require you to use my full Elven name every time you address me."

"Which is?"

I smiled and wetted my lips. *"Sirana d' Vloszia Dalnanin draeval uz'Thalluensareci."*

Gavin sighed so I could hear him. "Surely you are inventing that to add to your banter."

"I am not!" I replied, sounding offended.

"She is a noble," said the half-blood as if that explained it all.

Perhaps it did as Gavin glanced at me, reflected briefly, and nodded.

"Do you claim not to be the son of a noble, fighter?" I challenged my stalker. "Who *but* a noble or a cleric could have bargained with your sire to conceive and birth you? You disliked my assuming she was a cleric, so a noble she must be! What is your Elven name, the one given by your mother?"

His expression heralded an answer I regretted before he said it, like swallowing a cold, hard stone to sit in my gut.

"It was *Tighrabalt Mal'rak Ilharess'Dalninil,*" he answered, a tense and deep bass underlying his words. "And my mother did *not* give it to me. The matron did."

After that, the gold-eyed hybrid didn't blink but waited for my response as I stared at him, speechless.

Once again, my scholar's curiosity offered a way to slide out from where I was pinned. "What does the title mean, if I may ask?"

The To'vah-krav looked to the Human between us. "Roughly, 'Mourn Forever the Sister to the Grand-Mother.' I was called '*Tighra*' for short, but that is a *dead* name, Baenar. Let it stay so."

Gavin's brow furrowed further, his face quite homely as he concentrated on these new sounds. "Mourn, um, hm. The grand... mother?"

"Uh," I stammered. "I-it means you two have something in common, Gavin."

The Deathwalker's pale blue pupils lifted from his contemplation. "Oh?"

"Yes. His mother died birthing him. His mother's sister... the, um, noble ruler would not allow him or anyone to forget this. She held him responsible for keeping her memory."

Gavin grunted on a nod.

The mercenary lifted a nostril. "It is less gratifying that you grasp the nuance of this slave name and not my true one, Baenar."

"I... apologize," I said, having no strength to contest it. "I am where I was born. I have only left home once."

A pause, then the half-blood reluctantly offered a slow nod in peace if not acceptance. I glimpsed the bump in his throat move as he swallowed, then his tongue slithered out as if to scan the forest with this sense as well.

Eventually, the Dragon's son said, "If this is easier to grasp, Sirana, then you may call me Mourn. I will bear it in the Trade tongue only. Better I do this than you."

I showed my bafflement. "What? Me?"

"Yes. I ask no price for my assistance and protection *only* until you are recovered and your unborn is out of danger. I do not want to watch young *mata* grieve without need, especially when I do not know why she walks the Surface at all. Do understand, I will not entertain another bargain with you until you are of stronger mind and body again."

My stomach gurgled audibly as if in response; I cursed under my breath. The half-blood chuckled, crossing his arms to wait with a mature patience while I forced my mouth to work.

"Very well... Mourn. Um. Thank you, I accept your aid. No bargains for now."

Both males took it as a signal to refocus on our journey; my mare began walking again with Gavin guiding in front and Mourn to my left, ready to steady me as necessary.

I sniffed. The mount was becoming smelly in the Sun, every mark obtained since she'd stood up in the barn unchanged or worsened. For whatever odd reason, it was while I stared at the horse's unhealing wounds that I remembered my Sister: the whole reason I'd fled North at all.

I sucked in breath of alarm.

"What is it?" Mourn asked.

I glanced with guilt his way. "You said no bargains, but—"

"No," he said sternly. "All I have seen and heard thus far, Sirana, you have endured much abuse recently, and there is a conflict within you which concerns me. I do not expect you would remember or keep a bargain if I were to place you under that pressure now. My time is better spent not enforcing ill-made agreements with blurry boundaries, which only breeds resentment on both sides."

This consideration made sense, yet I gained no relief from it. "What if I told you another Davrin may be in this forest? What if she was sent to purge the warp rot, and we know she failed but may still be alive?"

Mourn frowned skeptically.

"The Witch Hunters saw her!" I insisted, my head beginning to pound. "That is why we rode North when we escaped Troshin Bend!"

He shook his head. "If she was on a mission and did not complete it, she is either dead or fled far away to escape punishment for failing. She would not be hiding here alive. It is a waste of time to search, and you must focus on your own recovery."

"You cannot know it's a waste to look!"

"Perhaps not but tell me this. How does your Valshuress assure young fighters like you do not walk any direction you will if there are no elders to watch you?"

An abrupt, high pitch assaulted my ears. Rising sickness hurled up from my middle. I turned away and promptly vomited up my last meal and most of my water on the far side of the horse. It splattered on the ground, but the hooves never broke stride. Slumped over her withers, my hood blessedly protecting me from the Sun, I moaned.

Stupid, stupid waste... At least, if the Dragonblood was right, what I lost might feed trees as fragile as me.

Mourn exhaled slowly. "Save your strength, Red Sister. If the Witch Hunters saw your squadmate several days ago, and the warp rot only grew worse since, then take comfort that she is cleansed as well by what you accomplished in her stead."

But she never said farewell!

I bit my lip hard enough to water my eyes, pulling my hood over my face. Unfortunately, once begun, the pain did not stop. Nor did the tears.

The Sun slowly descended as I sobbed on and off through the afternoon, as quietly as I could in between fumbled eating or drinking. I was unable to speak anymore, but neither male required me to. They pretended to give me privacy to grieve the loss I hadn't wanted to accept. They did so for longer than I pretended they wasted their effort doing so.

Weakened beyond hope, I wept at the memory of her face, and seeing the grief for her own Daughter when last we spoke in the flesh.

Although I ate everything in the saddlebag over the next day and ran out of water in the two skins long before that, I remained ill, lacking any strength. Now and then, Gavin would walk beside me and request that I speak, prove that I was "cognizant."

My reply was always, "Can you see my baby's life aura."

"I can see it."

His responses thus far had weighed in favor of both of us, his tone as close to objective and without apparent sympathy.

"The aura has diminished some, as has yours. You are both weakened and closer to death than you were days ago."

I stifled a flinch. "S-still have the dagger?"

"I do."

Good.

I thought about the Desert Queen I'd spoken to so briefly, "communing" with the dagger the first time. Was there any truth to her, or had that been a demon's trick?

In his office, Cris-ri-phon held the dagger laid flat in both palms. "It began here. Tell me how you know this blade. Was it spoken of by your Queen?"

No. I had seen it first not one span after I'd attacked Auslan on that small farm. The dream had seemed connected to nothing in the Void except for him.

But he doesn't have golden eyes. Mourn does. All gold.

That was not all. Shyntre and his sire, Phaelous, both possessed the color as well, subtle flecks of metallic gold in dark red eyes.

I always admired the beauty of Shyntre's eyes...

"Careful."

Strong hands on my shoulders. I'd almost slipped off the horse again. The sky grew dark.

The Dragonchild breathed out with the subtle hiss of his serpentine tongue. "I will carry her the rest of the way. We are nearly there."

"Indeed," Gavin said, "I was about to suggest you aim for a predetermined location."

"I have a cache nearby. There is food and clean water."

The large male removed my tool belt, and I couldn't protest as he secured it around the night mare's neck. My limp body was dragged off my mount and resettled against the broad chest. Three black spiders exited my hood and settled on my chest where I could at least reassure them I still breathed.

"I can't see in the dark as you can," the death mage said simply.

Mourn grunted. "Follow the ridge and keep the moon on your left. I will return to lead you there."

Gavin made no protest I could hear, not a mutter under his breath, then my carrier was moving quickly through the dusky forest. I attempted to hold his shoulders for stability but had too weak a grip for his pace. His response was only to squeeze me tighter.

I hate this…!

The last time I was this weak and defenseless, teetering on an edge of a terror and consequence I could not yet face, Gaelan was hovering above me beside a hidden altar in an outbuilding, speaking a spell after draining a healing potion down my throat. Behind her attempt to aid me was my eternally hungry eldest sister, threatening the potion maker.

Behind this half-blood's aid was the relic which had done much to harm me in such a short time. The dagger had not simply numbed my sense of hunger and thirst to delay it but had taken more than I had to give.

Damned Abyss. I *knew* this dance.

Never again.

I would get on my feet. *I will.*

I smelled the water, heard the gentle gurgling before the half-blood set me down on soft ground, surrounded by the lush, healthy plants of late spring. I breathed deeply; not since first emerging from the underground were their interwoven multitudes so sharp and overwhelming, touching my skin, sliding into my nose and mouth. These plants didn't struggle against warp rot.

We made it out.

Mourn kneeled beside me and put a metal cup to my lips. I wondered less about where it had come from, but rather how he'd found the perfect, chilled spring in all the wilderness.

"Slower," he said. "Do not shock your body. It is cold."

I agreed. Deliciously so. The purity and the sheer will to live woke me from my stupor, and I lifted my hands to take the cup after he refilled it. I settled like a suckling child, sipping, swallowing tiny amounts one after another, never taking my lips from the edge.

The gold-eyed bua watched me for a while and nodded in satisfaction. "Wait here."

I watched his tail trail away to one side and felt the urge to giggle.

As if I can do anything else?

When he returned, gently tugging my empty cup out of my hands, he replaced it with a large leaf serving as the plate for something impossible. I sniffed the scent rising off six white chunks of meat with char marks at the ends.

Bites of roasted fowl?

"Grubs," he admitted, reading my face. "Cooked. Safe."

Huh. Looking at his Dragon's teeth, I'd imagined he preferred everything raw and bleeding. In truth, I wouldn't have complained about raw; I'd eaten it before.

At the same time, he can summon fire on command...

I managed a nod and put one in my mouth without hesitation though not without a tremor in my hand. The warm and fat larvae was as delicious as the water, and I received a third cup to wash it down.

"Will you wait here while I return to guide the death mage?"

More alert now, I agreed. I *wanted* Gavin here. If he was writing in his book by dawn, things might feel somewhat normal for the Surface again.

The Dragon's son left while I stayed hidden in the brush, finishing my meager meal with silent gratitude.

ALTHOUGH I DID NOT SLIDE INTO FULL REVERIE WHILE I WAS alone, I drifted quite far. My thoughts began as a hazy blend of studying the empty metal cup in my gloved hands and Gavin's soul shard ritual in the shed. Then I thought, maybe, while I was unconscious or sobbing for Gaelan, the two males had made that one exchange I'd wanted to hear.

What drew you out of Troshin Bend the night of the fires?

What are your intentions toward Manalar this year?

Perhaps they spoke it on their way here. Maybe they negotiated another bargain, while Mourn had said he would not bargain with me until I was of sounder mind and body.

Damnit.

Gavin may have been reticent with a creature like this if he were mortal, as he had been with me at Sarilis's Tower. Now, he'd died—something I still sought to avoid—and had "walked" elsewhere. Walked in a place I could not imagine and no longer hid his clear motive for knowledge. The Ma'ab-Manalari man possessed a longer view of his future but hadn't learned subtlety, and I had been in no condition at all to teach him in this first instance.

Bluntness seems to work with the Dragonblood, anyway.

For now.

Gavin *had* been cryptic when speaking with Brom, though. In hindsight, I might guess that his "Lady" had warned him about what we faced in that inn.

The Deathless sorcerer, whom Queen Innathi told me was "many."

"My Sorcerer-General from V'Gedra is but one face of the Deathless… and you will come to know them all if you do not escape and take me with you. The world eater wants to bring me back to life… You will give birth to his new Queen if you stay."

Had it been the ancient, trapped soul of my Valsharess's sister, or only a demon's trick?

"He wants you to draw Soul Drinker… He will try everything to hold on to you now."

I jolted alert, my ears pricking up at the first rustle of leaves. My heart was racing, and sweat sprang up on my brow as my guardians rushed to my shoulders, preparing to leap at the first threat.

"It is us, Sirana," said Gavin from a good distance away.

I couldn't see them yet but relaxed so that my spiders calmed down. I realized that Gavin could not have seen or heard *me* and had been prompted so they could get closer without a spider bite. Did that mean Mourn *was* vulnerable but an excellent bluff?

Gavin and the mare appeared, the latter with my belt of weapons around her neck. Next came the beast-Elf carrying a rabbit and a pair of ground rodents in his fist. My eyes lingered on the catches.

"I've not yet scouted the area," Mourn said, "to know whether a cookfire is a good idea."

I pointed. My voice was lethargic and slurring, "If those are for me, I'll take them as they are."

Although I didn't ask it, he withdrew a small knife to swiftly skin and dress the animals, handing me only the meat on bone.

I smirked and started chewing on the rabbit. "Gavin might want the organs and skins. If not, save them for me."

Amused, Mourn refilled my cup from the spring without remark before offering the death mage three hides wrapped around tiny organs. Enough moonlight came through the trees that Gavin noticed the outreach.

"Yes, I can use them."

He sounded like he had an idea. With deliberate, inquisitive chewing, I watched him accept the blood-stained bundle from the mercenary, unwrap, and inspect it.

"Hm," he grunted.

Out came his scalpel from a makeshift sheath on his belt, made of scrap leather. Whenever I saw this tool now, I expected the pale man to cut his skin and prepare his magic, as he had needed to do so several times to keep his mare walking in one piece.

Sure enough, Gavin cut his forearm deeply and dripped black fluid over the fresh bits of flesh, whispering in the dead tongue. My spiders reacted in a brief skitter, though I did not in truth see or feel any change.

Still, I watched him place the pieces beneath his mount's muzzle and touch her nose. Stiff horse's lips quivered moments before she gobbled the pieces as she used to consume chunks of sugar roots we'd find. With a hollow echo of that same eagerness, she ground and swallowed the glazed organs under Gavin's touch. Next, she went for the hides, chewing and consuming those like they were hay.

The Deathwalker was nodding to himself, checking her teeth by feel after she'd finished without concern that she might bite him. She still had my belt of weapons and pouches around her neck. I dared to imagine Mourn speechless and hid my smile behind the generous cup of water.

"So, we camp here for tonight?" Gavin asked.

"For longer," Mourn replied. "As needed."

"We've arrived at your 'cache'?"

"We have."

"Hm." The pale man peered around at yet another hillside within another stretch of forest then up at the stars through the branches. "What of when the weather turns?"

"A moment, I will show you."

Mourn took, refilled, and handed a full cup to me as I switched to the fattier ground rat—the rabbit was a little lean—then paced along the sharp rise in the earth to my left. With the spring water I drank, I was not surprised that the hill had complexity.

The mercenary whispered to himself, and I *felt* something. Familiar.

A ward?

I leaned forward to see and hear better, careful not to spill my water, though drowsiness crept up to join my exhaustion. Determinedly, I watched as Gavin did, while this long-time shadow of ours crouched by a moss-covered boulder, tucking his large hands beneath it, and lifting. His arms bulged as his tail stiffened to brace against the ground.

Stone ground against itself as Mourn stood up, revealing what I'd anticipated: the mouth of a cave tall enough for the half-blood. If it were deep enough, the mare could enter as well.

"I see," Gavin said.

The boulder rolled to one side was one round piece, and so large that I couldn't imagine many physically capable of disturbing this "cache."

Not even Kurn could have lifted that.

It would take a stronger mage of the right talent to move it with magic, especially if there was a ward in place.

I breathed pure relief. *A secure cave to hide underground against the daylight.*

How long since I'd had this protection to rest in truth? Not since training with Elder Rausery. In retrospect, those had been the *easy* days. My eyes ached and head throbbed merely from the memory of every day since the tower, where I'd had the branches of thick trees for shade at best. Upon the Midway, for many sunrises in a row, I'd had not even that bit of relief.

The Human-built shelters—the inn and the barn—had too many windows and cracks where light leaked through to pretend it was a cave. While the buildings themselves had been better than being exposed, I'd been in one of the most dangerous places in my life because of who was inside, and there was no true rest to be had.

I was grinning while gazing at the cave but didn't realize it until the mercenary chuckled.

"There is a roll of cured hide inside," he said. "We can use it to cover the entrance without moving the stone. Block wind, rain, and light. It also faces North and East, so this entrance is in shade most of the time but curbs the colder winds. It rarely warms up as a result, but I stashed blankets wrapped in oiled hide a few years ago. They should still be good."

Bliss.

"Remarkable," Gavin said with a hint of suspicion.

He was right to wonder, but it was clear to me the merc knew how to survive wilderness in a state less than misery, rather like Rausery. I wanted to crawl inside, spin a cocoon from those blankets, and sleep until tomorrow night.

I want to be safe for just a little while.

To do this, I had to assume this large male's stocked den was somehow safer than Cris-ri-phon's bedchamber. I would start by *not* sleeping naked. I didn't have to remove any clothing, not even my cloak.

I looked at my empty cup. *Oh, shit.* Then sighed. *Make that piss.*

"Sirana?" Mourn asked.

Determinedly, I rolled forward onto my palms. "My bladder is full."

He nodded. "Good sign. Do you need help?"

Fuck, no!

My arms quivered, threatening to collapse and send my face to the dirt instead of helping me to stand up. I went to my elbows, instead, hissing curses in Davrin. My spiders moved with me, and the ruby swung and brushed the grass.

Goddess damnit, why am I so weak?!

"Maybe," I grumbled.

Without gloat or chortle, Mourn stepped up to gently take one arm beneath my pit. "Knees first. Then we can try standing."

Gavin kept his mouth closed as I eventually struggled to my feet. My legs, which hadn't been used for an entire day, shot through with needles and aches and cried to collapse. The mercenary's hands slipped beneath my pits before that point, and he held me up with such little effort that my face heated in annoyed humiliation. Meanwhile, my spiders inspected his fingers near my sore tits but didn't bite.

"Do not touch the ruby," I warned.

"We agreed not to steal from each other, remember, Baenar?"

Right. Damned Dragonblood.

I glanced to each side. "Where's the best place?"

"This way."

He steered me to the brush on the West side of the hill, where rainfall would wash any middens down and away from both the underground spring and the cave entrance, and it was unlikely we'd walk here while milling about.

"Can you set me against a tree?" I asked in Davrin.

"Your legs may not hold you. It would be faster and cleaner if I drape your cloak over one arm and squat with you."

I made a face he couldn't see. *"Have some debauched desire to watch? Or smell it?"*

"No." He sounded insulted and uncomfortable. *"I have experience aiding squadmates unable to care for themselves."*

Squadmate. He'd called Gaelan this.

"You don't look like a healer," I grumbled, tugging at the ties of one hip.

"I am practical. Your death mage avoids touch, and likely for good reason. I will do this if you allow." He leaned to one side. *"Do you need help pushing down your leathers?"*

"No. I can do this much."

Mourn waited, patiently supporting me as I got this done, then draped my cloak out of the way as promised. On a count, we squatted low to the ground, and I tried to relax enough to begin.

At first, nothing.

Damnit.

I thought I'd needed to go. Since when did I get performance fright?

"Take your time," he rumbled. *"I am in no hurry."*

I exhaled slowly, trying with deliberation to relax. Then, stupidly, and out of nowhere, I asked, *"What if Brom recovers enough to come after me, tracks me here, and you are in the way?"*

Mourn was quiet for a moment. Perhaps he was surprised. *"Are you warning me?"*

I thought about it. *"Yes. I awoke something... old. And dangerous. From the Red Desert."*

He was silent.

"I was ignorant, given no warning." I swallowed, too aware of the cool, night air on my bare slit. *"I am not sure how I would escape him again without Soul Drinker."*

The large male shifted his large, bare feet and his stance, adjusting his hold on me. Somehow, it was comfortable as we waited for my bladder to cooperate.

"I have seen the sorcerer as a possible threat for long before you surfaced but know better than to cull without necessity and leave a power void. I have taken precautions to hide this place, but I will keep guard all the same. If he becomes a threat in truth while you recover, I will respond accordingly to defend my den."

If this conflict were anything like his practices defending that circle against the horde of warped cannibals, perhaps the sorcerer could be rebuffed from me and the dagger. But could the Deathless be killed by a Dragon's son?

"You must rest and believe," he continued, *"that your first line of defense is not the relic. It is the Deathwalker and me. Leave the dagger as a last resort, lest the demon succeed in purging your child so it may have you to itself."*

My surge of fear in hearing that plain truth brought the strong urge to piss.

I didn't fight it. I let it come.

Finally.

CHAPTER 8

MOURN'S CACHE WAS DRY, DARK, AND STOCKED IN A WAY THAT required planning not too long ago. The blankets were present, whole, and only a little dusty; there were no creatures eating holes in them. Several layers of moisture-resistant leather contained separated pouches of dried, edible plants, mushrooms, and seeds, and there were a couple metal containers safely stored against corrosion, which could be used for heating spring water or cooking over a fire.

Removing only my dirty boots and cloak, I'd used the latter to cover my belt retrieved from Gavin's mount, and rolled up within three blankets in the dark cave. My spiders were free to explore as they would while I plummeted into darkness without dreams of any kind.

I'd woken shortly before sunrise to eat and pass waste again with Mourn's silent assistance. Gavin had been awake and well, though we exchanged no greeting as my stomach rumbled in its demand, and I'd climbed straight into the nest.

Before returning to sleep, I'd sat inside chewing busily through many of the preserves as the daylight grew stronger. Mourn had motioned his hand in silent invitation before he left, and I'd accepted it at face value.

Take what you need.

I'd recognized the Davrin silent tongue, though like his speech, the signs held unfamiliar accents.

After repeating this cycle twice more, I managed my first squat without the half-blood's help late the next night. I could hold on to a branch at the right level with both hands and keep myself upright. Breathing a sigh of relief, my sweating brow resting on my bicep, I closed my eyes.

I have never slept so much in a century.

Maybe that only showed how draining the Surface was the longer one stayed on it. Or that this was merely the first sign of how difficult being pregnant on the Surface would inevitably become for me.

Shit. Other matas aren't this weak, are they? I never paid attention...

I recalled yet again that I had no safe way to end it. I didn't know what methods I could use in this foreign land which would not leave me worse off than this. Cris-ri-phon would have wanted me dependent on him the same way I was dependent on Mourn to recover from the warp rot, but for much longer.

*Rausery was right. To catch something in your womb as a Red Sister is a two-year sentence of **not** being one.*

This was true whether I was kept by a Priestess, a Sorcerer-General, the Ma'ab, or a Dragon's son.

Ohh, I am in trouble.

Sullenly, I slinked into the cave for another dry meal and large swigs of spring water before settling down for the fifth time. Before losing consciousness, however, I turned over a few quiet thoughts on my present. I studied the cave, considered that there were enough supplies here for greater numbers than one.

I did not want to believe this mercenary had anticipated needing to bring me and Gavin here; that was too unnerving and paranoid to cling to. Mourn stated he had been following Kurn and Castis, and I'd stumbled in his way, travelling the same direction as them.

I wanted to believe this, as badly as this had gone for me. The simpler answer for this cache was then the half-blood was neither a loner nor recluse but traveled through here on other missions with enough regularity to mark its worth.

"I have often said I can only get close to a horse that is dead...."

"Often said to whom?"

He'd shrugged, declining to answer.

Who hires you, merc? How do you gain your "contracts" and, presumably, your reward?

Mourn also knew about "the Druid." Somehow, he knew Tamuril had been hurt by Jaunda. Did the Pale Elf know him by name, or did he watch her, too? Who on the Surface knew of this escaped Davrin son? Worked with him? Did it have anything to do with "squadmates" and his willingness to loan his own efforts to help one recover when weak or injured?

I kept my eyes on the blankets lest he read my face from across the cave and sense how I studied him. *He called the Matron's name for him a "slave" name... A dead one.*

How did she get her claws on him in the first place? I'd heard of one Black Dragon down below but never recognized a sign of him until now. If there were others, it would be as concerning as knowing there was another Davrin city besides Sivaraus.

Had a real, lurking mystery quickened a son for one of us half a millennium ago? One possibly greater in magic than any Sathoet given the freedom from his Priestess.

"You are kept ignorant, that is clear."

I turned over as it grew light once again and, outside, Mourn dropped the weighted hide to block the Sun.

Ahhh, thank you...

I slipped gently into Reverie and sensed when I shifted toward a strange dreaming. I was too numb to fear or fight but resolved that I would not take further punches unaware. I could expect the fist and try to dodge.

Come what may.

"THIS WAY," TOUSHEK WHISPERED, BECKONING UP THE SHEER, narrow split in the red rock.

The Davrin trader carried a shield of gold on his left arm which would have been blinding in the Sun. I stopped and peered straight up at the stars, recognizing the cluster which looked like a scorpion's tail.

He turned around and frowned at me. "We do not have much time."

"Why do you carry that here?" I asked, pointing at the shield. "Where did you trade for it, merchant?"

The bua narrowed dark red eyes. "It is yours, Godblood, if you come. If you find something for me, I might trade."

"Find what?"

Toushek beckoned again, taking steps backward. He refused to say more until I followed him. I went along because I recognized this narrow fissure which led to the prison where the golden-eyed bua was kept beyond iron bars.

Maybe I would see him again. *Maybe I can help the poor, pretty lad, as I promised.*

Far in we went but no barred window materialized near the rock floor. Only an empty, gaping door lay ahead, and the dead end beyond it.

"He is gone," said Toushek without pity.

"Already?"

"You are too late. The Everlasting Pit has him. But he may have left something behind which is important."

I swallowed. "Oh?"

"Yes. Something for which the Desert Guard may Bargain with us regardless of the circumstances, General. You will need much more than you have to prevent the Realms from coming apart."

The Desert Guard... The Realms?

"What of the Desert Queendom?" I asked.

The merchant shook his head, long, white hair waving. "Not within your power to save, Godblood. That survival is on the Sisters, and it does not look likely despite your many gifts. Focus on your own men and women. After this long, after this many decades beyond which you should have known nothing and had no say, let the Dark Elves face the fate which their best Seers have foretold."

No!

Imagining the Red Desert without the Davrin Elves terrified me, yet I was struck by how Toushek spoke as if he wasn't one of them despite his appearance. I remembered him showing up at odd times, always appealing in what he offered in knowledge or objects. I'd never questioned it before, but now I was here.

How many centuries had this creature been watching me, among so many others? I slowed, stopping outside the open, black door, staring suspiciously at him. "What lies within, informer? Or is it *betrayer* now? Are you a face-shifter?"

The Davrin bua smiled with amusement. "If I am, you are quite comfortable with those, General. Or have you forgotten Nalara already? Oh!" He lifted a finger as if catching his own error. "Forgive me. We call it Manalar now, yes?"

My chest seized in panic. *It... it cannot be.*

I had not thought of the blonde Druid in centuries. The Naulor companion had been a dalliance, a distraction from missing my Qu'eesan, my true desire, and long before the births of my children with Innathi.

"What do you imply?" I rumbled. "Who are you?"

Toushek waved his hand in smooth dismissal toward the cave. "Enter, General. Let your men carry the torches. Keep your hands free."

My...men?

A gradual, ethereal rise of flickering flames threw dancing shadows upon the red wall. Behind me were eleven of my most trusted men, all Human, all blind and deaf to Toushek's presence except for one at the back, my current Court Deathwalker. Oskar said nothing but occasionally focused his dark eyes on the smiling Davrin. He did not react to the mention of Nalara.

Perhaps he can see it but not hear the words.

"General?" the closest man asked, noting my hesitation. "Where are we? How did you find this place, and why are we here?"

I swallowed. "We... seek to save the Realms, warrior. Enter. Carry the torches forward while I keep my hands free."

A smirking Toushek entered the empty prison with me as the soldiers spread out, illuminating the scorched walls and fine dust and ash making the stone floor oddly soft. There was a large main chamber with living spaces and shelves gouged into the walls. The rock went deeper, closing in and leading to a tunnel which was barred by an iron gate.

"General!" my men cried in unison.

We froze in place, even Toushek to my left, to see a small woman's skeleton wearing a pale, lace dress. She sat with knees up, skeletal hands draped elegantly off the caps. Her back pressed to the gate; she blocked the way.

As if able to hear us, the skull lifted as silent and smooth as if it had flesh and muscle, though empty eye sockets peered at us. The death grin parted, and an eerie whisper escaped.

"Leave, now. This grave is under my protection."

A few men soiled their armor where they stood.

Toushek stepped forward. *"The Sorcerer-General needs something here, law keeper. We shall not be long."*

"Time matters not. I do not keep law if I bend it for you, deal broker."

"Trade, then. What do you want?"

Unmoved, the skull twisted upon her neck. *"Nothing. You shall not defile and rob from the grave of your kin, by your own hand or that of a puppet."*

The Davrin bua snarled, *"Obstinate fool! I am not defiling. We brought a Deathwalker to perform the correct rites."*

We had?

On this, I waved Oskar closer, but the ugly death mage didn't notice while he gazed at the skeleton woman. Then, spotting me, he approached. "General?"

"Can you hear her?" I demanded.

"Yes, sir," he said calmly, his eyes sliding toward the iron gate, "but I do not understand. I see her, but she does not speak the dead tongue. I do not think she is dead."

What? How could that be?

Her jaw flapped without tongue or lips. *"Your ears should bleed to understand me, deathless one, were it not for the 'dalliance' which gave you your heart's desire. Now, the appetite only grows and grows, and the motive no longer matters. I told you so. We always tell you, and no one seems to listen."*

"Until you make them," the merchant quipped, his tone snide. *"Thus, they never learn as you decide for them."*

The skeleton sat in silence, guarding her post, as we weighed the cost of attempting to pick her up and move her to one side. A few moments later, a deep rumble passed through the red stone, shifting grit loose into our heads.

"What are you doing, law keeper?" Toushek demanded, lifting his golden shield above his head like it might keep the ceiling from coming down upon him.

The skull turned to trail the ceiling as if she had eyes. *"I do nothing, deal broker. There is another who may be called to action if you disturb this grave."*

"That is what we want."

"Is it?"

I was already tired of their bickering, reminded too strongly of my decades at Nalara. The rumbling began again, the ground shook, and my men were afraid, barely holding their places.

Oskar pointed into the darkness behind the bones before the bars. He didn't have a chance to speak when a set of enormous eyes opened, metallic gold and floating in darkness. It wasn't the bua's eyes. These were enraged, maddened; its stare pierced us as a blast of hot air and sand erupted from the tunnel behind the gate.

ENOUGH.

The ceiling cracked, then the ground beside the skeleton. She scrambled toward a wide-eyed Toushek and hid behind his shield. Outside, the wind howled as a sudden sandstorm arrived.

If a mere five turns are all that is to be granted before thieves seek to rob from me, then the Desert will claim these men as new guards instead! You are not welcome here again! Get out!

"General!"

"Run!!"

The cave collapsed in pieces. The fissure was filling with sand as the windstorm battered at the cliffs.

Only the Deathwalker and I made it out.

Toushek and the woman's skeleton had fled, taking the shield with them.

"*AUGH!*"

I catapulted upright, ripped the cord from my neck hard enough to burn my skin, and pitched the ruby at the wall.

The Dragonchild ducked as the gem narrowly missed him, first clacking above his head then thudding into the dirt beside him. We stared at each other in heavy shadow, only a thin line of Sun leaking in at the bottom of the door cover. The cave filled with the sound of gasping and my racing heart.

"*Still mine,*" I said, expecting some dry remark, at least a raised eyebrow to comment on my volatile behavior. I didn't care for one fuck what he thought about it.

Mourn snaked his tongue out at the red pendant then used the tip of his tail to flick it in my direction. It was a good shot; I wasn't required to lean far to reclaim what I'd thrown. He wasn't smirking and said not a word about trading gems again.

The fighting mage wore his harness, bracers, and loose, black bottoms, but I didn't see where he'd placed his massive double blades. His hood was down, his long, tapered ears exposed, and his black hair was longer than I realized but bound up in a short, thick loop at his nape. Something pale and sharp poked up through that hair, closer to his brow. *Horns?*

"I need the trench again," I muttered, proving for the second time I could make it to my feet without falling.

Mourn nodded, watching as I tucked the ruby into the same pouch on my belt from which I withdrew my sunblind. Donning it, I exited through the weighted cover, walking barefoot to the middens side of the hill.

Gavin wasn't within my short-ranged view, though the mare was. The only movement was her tail in the breeze and, somehow, I thought her hide appeared darker. Being downwind, I thought she probably smelled less than I did right now.

Is she less damaged as well, or is that my sight? Bah…

I was familiar with my squatting spot by now, grabbing the branch with both hands so I didn't fall over. I did not linger this time because it was hot and bright out, flies were buzzing annoyingly, and I was hungry again.

Around and around, we go…

When I returned inside the cave, my spiders were calm and high on the wall, and my belongings hadn't been disturbed that I could tell. Maybe it was a test leaving it all with him alone in the cave; maybe I was fatigued being on lookout after months of doing nothing but that.

Or maybe the dream lingered like a lead ball in my gut. As I gingerly slid down the wall to sit on the blankets, my bones seemed heavier than Gavin's, and my mood and appetite sank like stones in water.

Why?

Why had I dreamt again of Cris-ri-phon and Toushek in the Desert when I was far outside of Troshin Bend? Had the two traveled together, to the same place where I had seen the golden-eyed bua? Or was that my fevered, hungry mind looking for sense where there was none?

Was this a warning? Was Cris-ri-phon somehow tracking me now, perhaps through the ruby, and he was too close?

I shivered. What were they after, and who was that skeleton woman blocking them? If Oskar was a Deathwalker, why didn't he have Gavin's eyes? And some creature had been angered so greatly as to force the collapse of that place, trapping those men. Killing them.

If that was my mind seeking "sense," then it made very little to me.

Could there be a single grain of truth, anything tangible to my waking world? Or was it all vapor as my mind disappeared somehow when I slept and became a mere cart for other minds more powerful than mine.

Is this what Kain did to me? Will I forget myself in time, living the dreams of others, from which I cannot escape?

Gavin's words from the Midway returned. *"I have seen mage abilities 'injured'… Becoming less controlled by conscious choice. Sometimes slipping into madness."*

"Sirana."

I blinked, surprised my cheeks were wet, and looked up. *"What?"*

Mourn's tail slid in a curve along the ground as he watched me. Whatever he'd been about to say, he reconsidered. He spoke in Trade. "You are safe here. I see you growing stronger. Let the healing continue, bad dreams are to be expected."

So, he could tell.

My eyes sliding away, I sniffed at my pit. "I could use a wash. My clothes as well. It has been…" I paused. *Goddess. Two weeks?*

The half-blood smiled without showing teeth. "I agree, a good idea. You will feel better. There is a riverbank not too far from here. You may ride, or walk, or I offer to carry you."

He was neutral about the method, leaving me to decide. *Bah.*

"I will walk," I said, using the wall to regain my feet, coaxing my spiders to me.

He joined me in getting up. "What of the mare? You could summon her to follow if you become tired before we get there."

I narrowed my eyes. Not so neutral, then. "How far is this river, exactly?"

"You haven't heard it, yes?"

"I might have smelled it."

"Mm-hm. It is two hills over. East."

"Current point of day?"

"Late afternoon."

So the Sun is behind us, at least.

Mourn watched me deliberate then added, "The Deathwalker is there, working. I scouted around and there is nothing close. He is safe but has a means to signal if that changes."

I sighed. Gavin had left the mare behind on purpose. For me. "Very well. Let me find the knucklebone and gather my things. I will ride the night mare to the river."

Mourn paused as if I'd said something odd then chuckled. "I will wait outside."

Both our hoods were up against the Sun, my spiders tucked safely beneath mine, and we had all our gear and what food was left from the cave. It might appear we were leaving without expectation to return but for the blankets inside, the weighted cover, and protection ward left in place.

It was hot enough and I was achy all over from so long lying on the ground that I imagined, if I had the endurance, I might stay up and spend the evening and early night beside the river. I had a great deal of inspection, repair, and cleaning of all my clothing and possessions. There were stains from the hailstorm on the Midway, for Goddess's sake. The Humans hadn't given me much chance to recuperate.

Abruptly, I recalled riding into the smelly town in the dark and downpour. I'd been riding with Mathias instead of Gavin. Little did I know then what to expect from the skin hunter, even after the teasing in the tall grasses.

"Just before you shot Kurn and Castis," I began.

Mourn turned his head. "Hm?"

"Mathias threw a thunderstone I did not know he had."

He nodded.

"I couldn't see or hear," I continued. "Could you?"

"Some. What do you want to know?"

"What were Mathias and Amelda doing?"

"He grabbed her by the arm and hauled her away at a sprint. His actions were one of a bodyguard getting his charge out of harm's way as fast as possible. Whatever she wanted in being there had been aborted. She *did* protest but not for long."

Mathias said he forgot something when I asked why he was there…

A compulsion of his own, maybe?

I considered further. "Do you know anything of Rithal from before the Ley Tower?"

Serpentine pupils slid my way and paused. That was a yes, but I waited for what he'd offer. No bargains yet, after all.

"He was a guide passing through Troshin Bend regularly enough. Unsurprising, given the pay and tetherless comforts optioned for one as lonely as him."

"He mentioned heading to Augran after Troshin Bend, but we found him bound beneath Ma'ab eyes."

Mourn shook his head once. "I know nothing of that. I came from the opposite direction."

"Yes, about that. Have you answered Gavin's question? What drew you that far out of the town he and I were at?"

I saw a flash of fang. "Not your bargain, Baenar."

My gut heated in irritation. "Gavin's intentions for Manalar are more 'relevant' to me than his volunteering my pregnancy to you."

"If that is so, then ask him. I am sure the Deathwalker will tell you without a trade."

Grrrr.

I scowled most of the way up the second hill then tried another angle. "Why do you call him Deathwalker? Does the title have significance to you?"

"That is how he identified himself. And, no, not really."

"You know of no others who claim to be Deathwalkers."

"Correct."

Hmm.

Mourn glanced at me. "Do you?"

I froze, grappling for an answer. "N-no, but Brom, er... the Deathless knew. From the Desert a long time ago."

"Hmm." A pause, then, "How did the apprentice change so drastically from when I saw him executed? I truly thought he was another Human slain by his own kind."

I nearly tossed the same answer he'd given me—*Ask him!*—but, in truth, I knew more about what happened around Gavin's body than the scholar did himself.

"What he told me," I said slowly, "was he planned it. Only that he had not the courage to suffer the 'pain before death' until he was given no choice."

I didn't mention that sucking Mathias had set that rockslide into motion. "Bictrius's dagger was made of silver. For some reason this 'blocked' his soul's path back to his body for some time, until I removed it."

"Why did you do that?"

I shrugged. "Because Brom and Amelda tried to keep me from doing it. The Ma'ab witch wanted to mess with his body herself. I challenged her for his body and the dagger."

Unexpectedly, Mourn smiled. "Huh."

"Much happened until then," I clarified. "The black blood, for example. And the crows."

"Crows?"

"I take it they are seen where one worships Nyx, the Grey Maiden?"

Shimmering eyes blinked within the shade of his hood and Mourn looked around us. I noted at least two of the black birds as we descended the final hill to the wide, glittering river below.

"There are no places I know of openly worshipping Nyx," said the half-blood, "so I could not confirm."

"There were *many* crows hovering around his body while he was dead."

"Noted. He is of greater note than I had judged at first."

"A challenger for Sarilis, perhaps?" I gauged him, squinting. I saw a small smile.

"Perhaps."

"You don't like Sarilis."

"Not in his place, no. If Gavin could oust him, I might be interested in aiding the effort for a price."

Still the mercenary.

"No leaving behind a 'power void,' hm?"

"No. That tower being empty is not good for the land, but neither is Sarilis, only to a lesser degree."

"Not if you ask Tamuril." I patted my mount, who indeed didn't smell as much as a few days ago. "The Druid mourns the animals he kills and uses until they are dust."

Now he squinted at me, glancing at my glove on the mare's withers. "You consider more than I would guess from mistakes you've made. The Deathwalker must be correct in that you prefer negotiation to zero sum tactics."

Zero sum? I shrugged, quelling the rise of irritation. "Of all *buas*, I enjoyed the *faern* the most. They had such curious things to talk about. They lived in a tower, too, like Gavin."

Mourn nodded. "Is that who made that gold ring for you? A *faern?*"

I was unsurprised he knew it was there. "Yes, though different mage made the blue pendant, plus several things on my belt. Smart *buas* are aggravating but often worth it for what they can do with their hands and minds."

He heard my tone. Sharp teeth showed in a smile both reluctant and sly. "Heh. Hm. Until one escapes his leash."

There is that.

I bit the inside of my cheek to consider the *other* yellow-eyed half-blood who slipped his shackles. My brow broke into a sudden, cold sweat as I held a steady tone despite the leap of my stomach. "Indeed, that does cause problems for some of us."

Mourn inhaled through his nostrils; his tongue flicked out. "Some of you?"

I focused ahead and ignored his question. We had reached the flats leading to the riverbank, the stone becoming large and uneven. Gavin's mare required all my concentration to navigate without both of us tumbling head over hooves.

The grey scholar saw us coming and, whether he welcomed the interruption or not, began moving a few things to consolidate his belongings closer to his tiny fire where he could keep better eye on them. One of them I recognized; it was the wrap holding Soul Drinker. I exhaled, taking cover to slide off the horse and hold the saddle blanket at each end while my booted feet grew accustomed to stony ground.

I sniffed. *Goddess, I stink.*

I hadn't performed any appreciable body scrub since... *Well.* Sometime before the kitchen. I still had dirt on me from fighting with Kurn and semen stains inside my leathers from Cris-ri-phon, although this was no doubt caked over from almost drowning in warp rot.

Knucklebone beneath my glove, I tried guiding the horse over the extremely rough terrain. Gavin called to me.

"Just leave her there."

Relieved, I grabbed all my stuff plus the food and stepped carefully over the stones toward the edge of the water. I looked forward to a long cleaning and mending session, but I also didn't. I must strip down to clean and mend everything, and working naked was simply the best way to begin. This wasn't even unusual as I had done it many times. I was a Red Sister; my training hadn't changed where it came to equipment maintenance.

The unusual part was how two, large Surface males who had watched me work this way, independently, had also attacked me like other Sisters in the sluicer. Behind me now watched a third, enormous male who'd rejected being owned by his Priestess-Matron as surely as Kerse had.

I didn't want this third male to watch, but admitting it was...

Showing fear.

I hadn't asked how the Dragon's son had escaped his "leash" because I knew it could not have been peaceful. Either he had bolted and escaped his pursuers in a lax moment, or he had killed whomever controlled him first.

The same as I killed Jilrina to be free of her. The same as Kerse beating Wilsira unconscious and leaving her to feel what happened next...

"Do you need help?" Mourn asked, noting my hesitation at the edge of the river.

I breathed deep, trying to slow my heart. "No, thank you. I am... stronger."

"Very well. Good sign."

I'll take any I can get.

I sat on a boulder, tugging my gloves and boots off first, eyes drifting over Gavin's spread. His tools shone clean and sharpened upon their cloth wraps; his pouches were rethreaded, mended, and sorted. I saw a lot of shriveled fleshy bits from small animals which seemed new, drying in the Sun. There were his grimoire and writing supplies, and a lean-to to cut the breeze or light. His robes were clean and dry, noticeably so, and his boots had been scoured of mud.

I bet *he* felt better.

Collecting what slivers of soap I had left plus some dried, scented sweetgrass, I shed everything except for my guardians resting at my nape and walked with determination toward the river. I was prepared to be scrubbing and spot-cleaning on rocks far into the evening, but first, while it was warmer, I would cleanse my body of these past filthy weeks, and try to begin fresh. To "feel better," as my stalker suggested.

I checked. *Yep. He's watching.*

Although, not with desire. This big male knew I was pregnant, had made many choices to aid my condition, and thus far hadn't tried to intimidate me while I was ill nor taken advantage while I was sleeping, or not so I could tell. He'd even helped me piss without soiling my bed or myself.

My crotch probably smelled rank enough to quell any interest in a rut.

I entered the cold water, smelled Gavin's fire as the wind shifted, welcomed these strong sensations which brought me firm into my body. I paid close attention to the position of my feet, to the growing current, and the stability of my spiders. I went slow because of them, mapping the river bottom with my toes. I needed to find the depth to dunk my head eventually but could not lose contact with the ground.

There. We are steady. Get scrubbing.

My guardians moved with me to stay above the surface as I lathered, scraped, and rinsed from feet to shoulders. Then, they shifted into one damp palm while I one-handed my neck, face, and hair. I was becoming chilly but stayed longer to wash between my legs and buttocks a second time—satisfied the soreness was gone, not just numb—and did a second cleansing of my head, shaking the water from my ears.

Ahhh. That is better.

Abruptly, her face came out of the dark ether; my chest ached, and my knees weakened. *Oh, Gaelan.*

It wasn't all better. I'd left her behind, somewhere, after trying so many weeks to catch up.

My eyes drifted in the hypnotic flow of the river over and around stone, but the reflections from the Sun caught me unaware, stabbing my eyes whenever I grew melancholic. Finally, I looked away to the bank, seeking Gavin. The setting Sun was still in my way, but his outline was sitting near his fire, flipping through his book, and clothed from head to foot with only his Sun-blackened hands showing.

The bigger, purple-black male nearby faced the water in a balanced crouch. His leg bones were shaped like a Sathoet's, they didn't bend like mine, so I wagered Mourn could keep that position for hours. He looked ready to do just that; wrists crossed, elbows propped on his thighs, his hood was down with face and ears exposed. He was aware of me in his periphery but not blatantly staring as I was at him.

In fact, he was so still, I was convinced that he listened elsewhere. Slowly, his head tilted as a wolf might attempt to pinpoint a sound, then turned his neck to listen with his other ear. His long, lavender tongue snaked out the greatest length I'd seen yet, then his tail moved in a long, slow wave, coiling up at the end, writhing in a way I couldn't read, yet my body's response baffled me. I became convinced that I was under imminent threat and must get out of the water.

Right now!

Gavin's hooded face lifted to see me rejoin with my dirty clothing and equipment, but I watched Mourn with utter confusion as he lifted one hand to wave with a soft bark of a word. I peered around for something different, spotting the thread of smoke from Gavin's fire shift direction. Instead of drifting out over the water, it flowed lazily toward our cave. It was against the wind.

Mourn reached up with both hands, dropped his cloak where he crouched, then began removing his harness. It remained a mystery where he stored his large bow and quiver of oversized arrows, or the massive, double-sliding swords I'd first seen attached on his harness at his shoulders. I watched as he carefully laid this corded web of useful items and tools upon his cloak then slowly rise out of his crouch to slide his loose, black pants down his thighs and tail. Once he pulled all three limbs out, he was nude but for his metal bracers.

I rubbed my damp forehead as my heart galloped in my chest. *Huh, bua, why…?*

The Dragon's son returned to his crouch and, for the first time, I got a good look at the overall shape of this hybrid's body. Most visible and noteworthy were the handful of ivory-colored, defensive spikes along his spine; they laid flat for now but appeared able to extend straight out. With his horns, teeth, talons, heel spurs, and now these spikes on his back, Mourn had something sharp on every side of him except for the tip of his tail and his underbelly.

Unless his cock is like Kerse's and has spikes as well.

The harsh clash of thought and sensation was difficult to sort in that moment, but it helped me stay perfectly still. After moving, Mourn hadn't turned that intense gaze on me, and I was glad. I might have screamed.

Metallic eyes remained focused out across the river while I sat comforting my chiming arachnids. I glanced out that way, trying to spot whatever it was. The banks were empty but for us, on both sides. Gavin noticed this display, too, and quietly closed his book, setting it aside. He watched the fire behaving against the natural order.

Finally, Mourn leaned forward onto his arms and crawled low across the rocks, holding his body straight above them, and headed straight for the water. His claws somehow avoided clicking the stone; the barest drip of drops trailed after his steps as he entered the shallows. He slipped through the water without rushing or making it splash, settling his belly down into the current to swim a few strokes before he submerged out of sight, his tail a dark shadow curving behind him.

If I hadn't been watching him, I wouldn't have known he'd gone into the water. *A creature that large should have left more ripples.*

A few moments later, I heard them. What must have drawn the hunter's attention to the far bank. *Pigs.*

A drove of eight or so were coming to drink from the river. My stomach gurgled, and I covered it in a vain attempt to muffle the sound. I remained seated and quiet, as did Gavin so as not to startle the prey. Although I did not know how much Mourn *wasn't* eating on account of me, giving away several smaller kills already, I still hoped he might share a wild pig if he caught one.

Otherwise, I must think about adding to Gavin's snare traps.

It felt like a long wait before the first, fuzzy blobs of pinkish-brown foragers gathered in a clump on the bank. Despite their clear grunting reaching my ears as they cautiously approached the water, Mourn did not resurface. Hooves paced and contented oinking interrupted their swallows as they drank. I could not think they would be lingering long after slaking their thirst; they hardly stopped moving.

Where is he? How long before he needs air? My stomach growled in comment from behind my hands, and I bit down the urge to shush it aloud. *Demanding infant.*

A deep whorl of sound barely preceded the terrified squealing of the pigs as the water exploded faster than I could swallow. I inhaled and coughed on my spit, holding my eyes stubbornly on the strike despite making an embarrassing amount of noise myself.

The hybrid's lunge had snared one of the larger beasts from the sounds of the struggle. One strong hand had clamped beneath the jaw, claws buried in its throat, and the dark body shifted parallel with his prey. His black tail wrapped once around the barrel ribs of the hog and tightened down such that its panicked squeals weakened instantly.

Mourn hauled the pig into the water with him, held it under until I must be sure the beast had drowned. Meanwhile, the rest of the pigs had fled, their shrieks of alarm and the snapping of brush echoing as they trampled through the forest.

"He learned to ambush first," Gavin commented from rather far away.

I nodded, coughing one last time to make sure my throat was clear. "Well, he ambushed *us*."

"Indeed, he did."

"And this is common for hunting the underground, anyway."

"Yes, I wanted to ask what you knew of a Dragon underground."

Oh, that. I grimaced. "Nothing. Maybe some legends of our queen fighting him, depicted in tapestries at court. But I think those are symbols, not recorded events."

Gavin's stringy, dark hair fell forward as he picked up his fallen quill. "Do you say his claim to be sired by one is possibly false? Is there no Dragon?"

"Well…" I considered. "I do not know. If it is not a Dragon, it is a demon which looks like one."

Gavin grunted, smoothing the ruffled feather. "And your spiders are at ease around him. As spiders are the symbol of your demonic goddess, might this be considered evidence?"

Again, I hesitated to accept that which seemed reasonable. "No. My spiders were not made by a cleric of that goddess but by a mage who hates them. She does not use that magic, as far as I know."

"Interesting."

Mourn interrupted us, surfacing in a noisy burst compared to when he'd gone in. He was dragging his massive pig nearer to the shore, beaching it slightly downstream from us. It was much larger than it had appeared from afar and for certain drowned. I could also see that the beast-Elf had refrained from taking any bites out of it on the way across the river. Unless he intended to gloat and eat it in front of us raw, I dared to assume he would share.

"Should you both be up for roasted pork, Deathwalker," Mourn said, huffing deeply for breath, his body dripping streams of water as he stood up, "I should like to have some as well."

Gavin nodded, slowly rising from his seat. "I will build the fire higher."

"Thank you."

Suddenly, I was *very* aware that I was naked and sitting on a rock. Mourn's genitals matched his size, and his scrotum seemed of tougher skin than a typical Davrin. His phallus had no obvious spines or ridges in its flaccid state, though the head flared and came to a point rather like Kerse. There was a small bit of wiry, black hair around the groin, but patches of scales around his thighs prevented growth anywhere else.

What is—

He rumbled in his throat, and my thoughts froze, my face and chest flushing hot enough only the fading Sun might have kept him from seeing it. He'd caught me staring. Studying his natural equipment.

Fucking Goddess.

I stood up on my feet before he could say anything, fully nude with my tits, mons, and white bush showing. His reptilian eyes *did* inspect me, down and up again, but without a hint of lust; most likely judging my strength, perhaps my unborn's well-being.

Quickly. Something practical.

"How can I help with the food?" I asked.

Mourn's shoulders lowered as he let the awkwardness go. "Will you help me skin and butcher enough for meals for three?"

"I do not require that much," the Deathwalker said. "Enough to rest in my palm."

"Very well. We will keep the rest wrapped for the morning when the Sun can help me dry it out."

I smirked to imagine what spell could mean the Sun merely "helped" with the drying and nodded. "Sure."

Retrieving my shorter blades, I quickly honed the edges. With spiders riding my naked shoulders, I assisted the half-blood with his catch. The work went quickly without any but the most necessary words, for Mourn didn't doubt my ability to dress an animal.

While working, I was struck by how different the exchange had been between Gavin and Mourn, contrasted with the Ma'ab hauling that grass-feeder from the Midway and wanting the apprentice to cook it. The simple and unassuming manners without contempt or bullying was enough to gain the apprentice's help with the cooking. It made me wonder if Mourn had watched that exchange and knew from the scents wafting his way that Gavin possessed skill in making wilderness meals flavorful.

Was the claim of his sire false? Was there no Dragon underground? Gavin and I had reason to be skeptical. However, if Mourn's blood was of any demonic heritage, then it was of a patient and observant nature to which I had no previous exposure to in connection with the Abyss.

The Daughters of Braqth consumed what they wanted with regular torment of those weaker. The Sathoet were controlled by their appetites only until they grew unstable and had to be destroyed. Soul Drinker, whose hunger was not patient or easily contained, who disliked all "competition" for its bearer's attention, was much more convincing as a demon than Mourn.

I was inclined to believe the half-blood was what he said.

Perhaps he might simply tell us about his Mother and his sire underground. How he came to be born.

CHAPTER 9

WE STAYED BY THE RIVER WITH THE CAMPFIRE GLOWING DURING a calm and warm night. My belly was full of further, tasty abundance, and Reverie did not beckon me for once. I washed my clothing first. Mourn offered a minor magical spell which would mend and dry my clothing so I could wear it sooner.

"Trade?" I checked.

"No. Now that you are clean, the odors on them are obvious."

I smirked. "Yes, and thank you."

Again, he rumbled those words in a language I had never heard, motioning with one clawed hand. Bumps spread over my naked skin in their wake.

Draconic? Or... what had he called it?

To'vah.

After dressing, genuinely refreshed, I got started inspecting my filthy and damaged gear, sorting it for either destruction or cleaning and repair. I did not hurry, expecting this to take until dawn, though Mourn said he would expedite it with another spell after I knew what could be salvaged.

As after the storm on the Midway, items had been compromised by the warp rot, pastes and powders discolored or smelled funny. Both Mourn and Gavin could tell with a glance if a component held any magical imbuement at all. Disappointingly, I had to discard all those once enhanced by magic, such as the slow-acting fever inducer I'd used on Kurn. The warp rot had spoiled them all.

This left only a single, natural toxin potent enough to use on its own—the one that had killed Bictrius. Between my spiders and this last paste, I only had two options, and both were to kill quickly. *Could be worse.*

I left the inspection of Shyntre's pellets until last, peering inside the pouch at the little brown dirtballs. I counted twenty in decent shape, pursing my mouth. What should I do with them?

At this expression, Gavin silently offered to inspect them, his pale hand outstretched. I handed the bag over and said, "A last-moment gift from a mage before I left. But I never knew if they were imbued."

"Why not?" Mourn asked. "You knew if all the others were."

I folded my arms across my lap. "My leader is not a mage but passed the maker's request with this pouch. They were intended only for me. I accepted the advice and didn't share."

"Why only for you?"

I shrugged with discomfort. "He knew I carried."

Gavin had peered inside but not for long before tipping one out into his palm with care. He studied it by firelight. "Their purpose?"

"Fester-shield and fever-breaker," I said. "To be taken after bleeding injury or during illness. Based on a mushroom, *genethsa*, which I also gave as a gift to Osgrid for her wisdom about Gavin's state after his death."

Mourn tilted his head curiously as my scholar said, "Interesting. Dosage, and how much time to tell if they are helping?"

"One or two a day. I could tell improvement in that time."

Gavin returned the pellet to the pouch and cinched it closed. "If they were magical, they aren't now. Or they may never have been and are potent like the toxin."

"My thoughts as well." I accepted the pouch. "If I could be sure, I might have taken them the last few days and recovered in the cave faster."

"I am glad you did not," Mourn said. "Should your body's response prove worse than neutral…"

I cocked an eyebrow, and he stopped talking.

Yes, I got it. I would be that young *mata* in mourning he didn't want to watch. A fate evaded both with a sigh of relief and some pinch in the back of my mind. I wondered if I'd missed a window of opportunity to miscarry and be safe enough to recover from it. I wondered if it would be better "after."

Less worry or vulnerability.

The fear of inevitability clung to me, that being pregnant required too many resources while I was also compelled to travel. That it would kill us both in time, and I feared that pain before death Gavin had described. His reason for delaying his "transition," despite wanting to serve his Lady in a greater capacity than a mortal Human could, was the same reason as mine.

How did I get here? Did the Valsharess See this coming? Perhaps that was why She had been shouting at me in the sandstorm, insisting that I look, as well. Had this Deathwalker been that unrecognized smudge of grey I'd seen on the red horizon?

Gavin and the Grey Maiden.

"How many knew you carried when you left Sivaraus?" Mourn asked, startling me out of my thoughts. "Is this common for the *Vloszia Dalnanin?*"

"The what?" Gavin interjected pointedly.

"Blood Sisters. But it speaks more the color of blood. *Red* Sisters."

The Sisterhood.

Should I answer this? The Prime would not like me discussing this, but Elder Rausery had told Sarilis about the Red Sisters, and the Queen's geas wasn't preventing me from doing the same with these Surfacers. I also wanted to know what this mercenary knew of Sivaraus, since he'd blurted out the name like that in front of my scholar.

"Hm." Gavin glanced at me, noting my all-black uniform. "Why are they called this?"

I smirked. I could give him that. "The uniform is blood red below, and we use light to its best effect in the great cavern."

He paused as if imagining that, and Mourn prodded me again, "Do Red Sisters often gain the Surface while pregnant?"

"Rare," I confessed, my chest and throat aching with the unspoken threat of saying too much. "Few knew. Less than five. My leader figured it out after watching for weeks, my younger sisters did not."

The hybrid nodded. "Is the mage who made those shield pellets also the sire?"

I shook my head, relieved he did not try to ask of my mission. "No. His… brother made them."

Yes, that feels better. I could speak about Shyntre and Auslan.

Mourn's tail curved slowly along the ground; he settled, relaxing as if this made utter sense to him. "I have known brothers who will look after each other's offspring if it is known to them. Sometimes even if they were not sure who was the sire, but the female had shared them."

I blinked at this unexpected, voluntary insight. "You, *uhm*, have?"

"Yes. And I have known brothers who defend each other where they could. Most were wary of *me*, for good reason, but I observed *buas* who made small sacrifices for the other." He paused. "Sometimes large ones."

Was it so common? I shook my head. Although this seemed to fit my wizard and Consort, they felt like the exception in Sivaraus. "I saw mostly currying favor with females for protection and gifts, often betraying each other in this ambition, making the other look foolish or weak."

Mourn gave me a look. "Noble brothers, yes. They will stab each other as readily as sisters will for that status."

Didn't I know this?

"I speak of house guard and common born," he continued.

Was he army, once? Is this why he claimed to have been a slave despite his clear blood-relation to the Matron in his name? It could explain his weapons training, unless he discovered it on the Surface somewhere.

"The sire isn't house guard," I admitted, touching my womb. "He is as far from melee as a male can be in the city."

"What do you mean?" Gavin asked.

A smile tugged at me. "He is a trained companion."

"Trained how?"

"A pleasure slave," Mourn translated too accurately. "Or perhaps, prostitute?"

Gavin blinked and looked at me. When I didn't protest, he nodded. "Interesting to hear how the roles are so fully flipped between Manalar and this... Sivaraus?"

I wrinkled my nose to recall Jacob and Mathias in the shed. "We are *not* like the Witch Hunters."

Mourn cocked a brow. "Aren't you?"

"No! We do not do what those men d—"

I stopped. The purge of Consorts and their children returned, as did the last bua I'd watched executed publicly by the Sisterhood. This did not count those taken to Auranka's Pit or forced onto the altar by the Priestesses.

I was having dreams of a bua with gold eyes in the Desert, pleading rescue from the same fate, whom I was fairly sure had been the Valsharess's son. Cris-ri-phon had been too late returning because he was afraid of angering his Queen.

I felt sick. *Oh, Goddess.*

I croaked, "Not all of us are like that."

Such a lie when it was easier to comply to survive. Yet when I'd been new to the Sisterhood, how I'd dreaded when it was my turn to prove myself in an execution.

Then came the Queen's purge. I'd felt so numb afterward. I didn't know *what* I'd proven. I hadn't felt anything at all until Shyntre admitted his desire, reluctantly, despite what I'd done. How he'd yelled at me. But then my wizard had returned my touch like I was someone of worth, and I'd wanted the reassurance.

My Elder D'Shea couldn't reach me in her bath, but if her son thought I could be touched and feel pleasure...

Him. The most stubborn wizard in the tower.

Then again, it could have been because I was pregnant. Mourn said "brothers" will look after each other's offspring if it is known to them. Was that all it had been to my wizard? Why he'd made the pellets for Rausery to give to me? To preserve Auslan's child, what really mattered to him, and I was just willingly carrying it?

He fucked so fiercely hearing me say it. We coupled twice more after...

In the awkward silence, Mourn could have pressed his point, could have forced me to defend how things were in Sivaraus, in the Sisterhood, as I had attempted with Elana in her own kitchen.

"It's just the way things are," she'd said.

And I'd agreed.

"I wouldn't like living there at all," said little Layne. *"I don't want a woman to take care of me."*

The Human boy had meant to protect and decide for him; I'd understood him correctly. This was how Cris-ri-phon took care of Elana, and had wanted to take care of me. Except she wanted it; I didn't.

I'm not like a Witch Hunter, though... I'm not that...joyous in causing pain.

My eldest leader was; the Prime relished it for many centuries beyond the lifespan of any man at Manalar. She who'd established the Sisterhood's reputation to the rest of the city, who wielded a power I had looked forward to gaining if only because it protected me from the Priestesses.

Fadele, who mistrusts anything psionic and wanted Reishel and me killed for listening to an Ornilleth in our heads.

The merc did not press me but still sounded curious. "If your chosen sire is a noble servant, I assume his brother is a noble mage?"

"Yes."

And that mattered to me, did it not?

"No blood-bond, however," I added, slouching, looking around for more pork to eat. "But they shared their youth."

"Hm. Unusual." Mourn reached to the far side of the fire and picked up a warm piece of meat on a stick, handing it out to me. "Especially for nobles."

Nodding, I accepted and chewed on it, feeling resentment alongside the deflation and... shame? Mourn had a clear prejudice against females trying to control him, but why did I blame myself? Was this big male trying to manipulate me, to suggest there was no pride in where I'd come from or who I was? Or was I just afraid he was right?

It's not that simple. I wanted my sisters. I chose them, they chose me...

I wanted Jaunda to be alive down below when I got back; I wanted her to succeed in whatever her mission was. Gaelan might have been out there, sick, or hungry, but I'd failed her as I'd failed Reishel. I had been sick too long and it was too late.

What about Jael? She was the last one in my power to help.

I swallowed my pork. "Gavin?"

"Hm?"

"What are your intentions for Manalar?"

Both males peered curiously at me. They each had such strange eyes. To think I was sitting here like this, with the two of them. I would have never imagined it when Rausery turned us loose to brave the Surface.

Gavin tugged from his own belt pouch the shard of black glass he'd created by Human sacrifice. I recalled my current company; each of us had killed for vengeance, reward, and survival, and we would again. Maybe that was why Mourn hadn't pushed the comparisons farther. He was a paid assassin, and I did not know if he refused *any* job if the reward was right.

"Sarilis intended to aid Kurn and Castis," the Deathwalker began, "and by extension aid the Ma'ab, by providing something which would disrupt the control the Bishops have over the sacred pool inside the temple, a great source of magical strength and a key part of the city defense. He claims they are 'hoarding' it, and he can't use it."

I recalled, while Mourn just listened.

"The vials you threw to cleanse the warp rot would have accomplished this goal as well," Gavin continued, "but the cost to every mage nearby would have been excessive."

"What cost?"

Chilly eyes focused on me. "Burning out the affinity they possess, closing off their talents, leaving fewer mages at large and guaranteeing a rise in violence and death rooted in insanity among Humans around Mount Sonai for decades to come."

Could that have included him? Could it have disrupted his dreams to his Greylord if he had followed through? Maybe he hadn't known that until he'd died.

"Hm," I said. "As a Deathwalker, are not deaths the same regardless of cause?"

"Absolutely not," my scholar retorted, peering directly at me as if surprised at my ignorance.

I could have brooked insult at this tone but felt a familiar twinge of interest, knowing I'd hooked his passion with that offense. I settled down to listen, hoping Mourn knew enough to be quiet.

"As circumstances of gestation, birth, and early life aid in determining the overall health and nature of the young living," Gavin explained, "so do the circumstances of death and transition form the nature and available pathways of the young dead. There are as many outcomes for Vis becoming what they are beyond the veil as there are for the living souls coming to us through birth. Perhaps *more*, as the circles can be far-flung, like living many existences at once or in sequence."

Death is complex.

Mourn was as silent as I was.

"The old goat in the Ley Tower does not understand this," Gavin stated with a sneer, studying the glossy flint in his mist-white palm. "For his ambition to harness greater power from the Ley Lines, this one action would do worse to the living *and* the dead than the siege itself. I doubt he would ever recognize it, death mage or not."

"Then what is in your hand?" I asked, fascinated. "Why did you create it?"

Gavin glanced up from his flint. His stare confirmed he knew but didn't want to talk about how I'd witnessed the flint coming to be despite not having been there. "This is the Witch Hunter's soul made manifest. His transition contained and whole, unable to travel yet."

"Yet?"

"Soon, he will, but not until I release him."

Mourn grunted. "Under what circumstances?"

Gavin looked at the Dragonchild, contemplated what I knew, then chose to back up in his explanation. "This flint contains the quality of the follower created by the Bishops of Manalar, familiar and recognized. It is an imbued soul trap attuned to the sacred pool inside the temple, which they call *Pisc'sagrad.*

"Throwing the shard in will disrupt the Ley in a similar way as Sarilis's vials, but the backlash will follow the threads to those bonded to the pool: the Bishops and their acolytes. Other mages who have no hand in drawing their magic from that source are likely to survive sane and with their affinities intact."

Mourn's tail moved, perhaps without conscious intent. "I did not know such a thing could be made."

At last, Gavin looked away. "Only because I know these followers well. And only this once."

"Why not again?"

The Deathwalker offered a dour look. "The cost and wisdom of doing so."

Mourn nodded, and I glimpsed his admiration. "You need someone to throw this shard into the pool?"

"*I* must throw it in," Gavin clarified, his tone unbending.

The half-blood reconsidered and spoke again slowly, like he had something to debate. "If you do this early in the siege, then the Ascended will claim Manalar. Sarilis's method would harm the Ma'ab invaders as well, for he sides with none. You target the Bishops, a scalpel used to cut the string on a drawn bow, which will collapse Manalar's power in a catastrophe and leave the city undefended."

My scholar's expression reminded me of the few times he had spoken of his father. He was unmoved. "As it shall be. As my Lady guides me."

"Your Lady *wants* to give the City of the Sun to Ennikar?"

"I claim no knowledge of her 'wants,' if she truly has any."

"Blind faith does not become you, Deathwalker, any more than it does the *Dyos Guerrimos*."

Gavin waited several beats, watching the other with slightly narrowed eyes, and I could not tell what he was thinking. Had that stung as much as Mourn's remarks on my Sisterhood? If so, the Dragon's son was good at that. Where did *he* stand in the balance to judge us so, as one who shoots dissolving arrows and assassinates from the dark?

The pale mage rasped with resentment. "My father was blind to his actions against the living while I could not close my eyes to the dead even in sleep. My mother's blood allowed me to see enough to know my task at Manalar does not stop at favoring the Ma'ab, which is happenstance, not motive. It goes beyond battlefield strategy, To'vah. What happens in mortal wars is not up to *her* but those engaging in it. This is where I beg to differ: I am not as blind but certainly as driven."

Mourn considered this and granted the speech another slow, accepting nod. As with me, he did not press.

Gavin turned to me to change the topic. "I have a question, Sirana."

Sigh. "Yes?"

"You said your younger 'sisters' could not tell you carried, though your leader could. Plural. How many sisters do you seek, if I may know?"

Mourn looked at me.

Uh-oh.

I did not answer at once, so my scholar pushed his reasoning.

"You urged strongly in favor of seeking one sister near the warp rot, but you were prepared to go to Manalar as far back as when we left the tower. Or so it seemed to me. Brom assumed your queen was an oracle interested in this battle, and this was why you were present in our party. Is that true?"

I swallowed several times, trying not to lose my pig. Another glance at Mourn worried me that he had overheard my stupidly telling Tamuril about Jael's assassination mission outside the Ley Tower.

"I wanted to find both my sisters," I confessed to Gavin. "There are two. The other will be near Manalar if she is not already there."

"Her mission?" Mourn asked.

I offered the half-blood the most amused and exaggerated sneer I could muster. "I do not *know*, mercenary. I can lie well enough to prompt a reaction."

He narrowed his eyes. I saw no confusion.

"What do you mean?" Gavin asked. "Lie to whom?"

"The Druid mentioned earlier," Mourn said. "A pale-skinned Elf who lives near the Ley Tower and bears witness."

"Ah. The one hurt by the 'Baenar.'"

"Correct."

"I admit I never saw sign of her in the five years I lived there."

"That is as it should be."

While they spoke, my feet felt cold inside dry, clean boots. *What have I done? Has the Dragonblood told anyone about Jael? Was that why he was gone from Troshin Bend that night? Or has Tamuril sent a message to her sister in Augran?*

"The truth is between her and our queen," I finished, my stomach too weak to continue. "I do not know what she is to do at Manalar."

Mourn watched the dark river flowing South. "If she is captured, Sirana, it will be a painful death."

I gritted my teeth, ground them. It was audible. "And what am I to do with *that* knowledge? As if I could not imagine what may happen to her, meeting Jacob face-to-face? I did not *send* her there."

"But you would join her."

"Not to be burned as witches."

"Indeed not, but to help complete her mission even if you do not know the purpose. As you did the sister sent to cleanse the warp rot."

No doubt my tears were obvious in the firelight. Jael had wanted to meet up later. She'd insisted, wanting to be kissed as if to seal it; our last time as we ate each other's slits against that tree, taking turns with our noses buried in fragrant fur and folds.

You mean to come back, Sirana.

Yes.

Me, too. Meet you here? We could go home together.

While Gaelan had left to find warp rot while I'd distracted myself from her pain, and from my fear.

I was grateful when Mourn lifted his heavy focus off me and shifted to Gavin. "Meanwhile, you must get inside the temple sanctum, somehow. Unless you are a master of illusion, Deathwalker, they would torture and burn you at first sight as they would any Baenar."

Gavin stared at him for a few seconds. "I am no master of illusion. I know *what* I am to do. Not how."

The humility in his tone was unfamiliar. I wondered where he'd learned it. Would his Archimandrite father have ever expressed such self-doubt to an outsider in service of his faith?

"Hm." Mourn did nothing with his large hands while he thought; only the tip of his tail moved. "Where were you planning to go if you survived the warp rot? Straight to Manalar with no plan or supplies?"

Gavin and I glanced at each other. I shrugged.

"Not discussed. Very well. I work out of Augran, and I could lead you there. I must close my contract on the Ma'ab fugitives regardless. There are many in the city with investments in the conflict rising, with resources which may support the Deathwalker's task."

"We would have the same difficulty with our appearance as the city farther South," Gavin noted, probably for my benefit.

Mourn smirked, opening his rough broad hands, showing off his talons. "I have connections who may help if we might come to an agreement, though it need not be tonight."

Go to Augran, first.

Gavin nodded, interested but not visibly eager, while I wanted to ask about a pale-skinned Elf in the city where he worked.

"Tamuril has a sister in Augran," I stated with confidence. "A Naulor Elf. Have you met her?"

My death mage paid rapt attention; it was clear he wondered how I knew these things, while I wondered the same about him. Meanwhile, Mourn peered at me for many long moments as he contemplated how to answer. I waited, feeling somewhat pleased.

Finally, he showed fang in subtle threat. "I have. She is worth my protection, Baenar, and it is better you do not meet her."

That door firmly slammed shut.

I exhaled in frustration. "I was to ask how she lives among Humans every day?"

"Illusion. They do not recognize what they see."

"What does she do with her time? For how many years had she lasted?"

"That is not your business, and your Grand-mothers at present prefer to forget the Naulor exist."

"Most daughters never knew!" I retorted.

"I am not here to fill that gap for you, Sirana, and Tamuril's sister would not be eager. Ask yourself if you imagine there is good reason."

"Asking that helps *nothing*," I said through gritted teeth. "You are only warning me not to look inside the box! Like the Sorcerer!"

"Enough," he snarled back, tail punctuating with a quick lash at the rocks.

The campfire crackled while my mood stewed; Gavin added more branches, stirring the embers as sparks floated up upon the heat. It was telling that Mourn would state it so clear he would protect this mysterious Naulor; there was a history. My being blocked in this manner, however, pinched my resentment to be as sore as at Troshin Bend.

The Davrin had forgotten the Naulor and their victorious Queen since the last war in the Red Desert, and unless the Druid's sister was older than my Valsharess, she may know even less than Cris-ri-phon. I could question how much Mourn knew as a runaway of not yet five centuries as well.

I smirked at the thought, but this brought me to the defeated Dark Queen, Innathi, who was trapped in the cursed dagger. *If that's her, if she is real, then she would have answers that Mourn and his Naulor ally don't.*

I lifted my eyes from the fire. "Gavin, may I see the relic?"

Both males stilled, pulled from their own thoughts to peer at me in the dancing light and shadows.

Irritably, I waved my hand at Gavin. "Just unwrap it. Show me you have it. I must see."

"Do you mean to draw it?" he asked.

"No." I read their faces. "You clearly don't think I'm strong enough yet."

"What purpose would it serve?" Mourn asked.

"I cannot say."

That was truth. I still felt a twinge.

"Just show it to me," I insisted. "I'll not touch it. Then you can rewrap it."

I watched for it but Mourn made no signal to Gavin I could detect. Seemingly by his choice, my scholar reached down behind him for his full pack. Loosening the top, he removed the same grey-tan leather wrap from when they sheathed it for me. The knots looked the same, many days old, while Gavin tried to tug them loose in his lap.

Mourn's tail had stopped. All of him had.

It began with this blade.

Careful and deliberate as any of his surgeries, Gavin unwrapped the bundle to reveal the weapon in plain view. The red runes of its hilt glowed briefly at me, and the glossy edge of the sheath reflected the firelight, setting my heart to racing. No sniggering voice entered my head but in staring at it, I relived the chaos of the slime-dripping forest and festered crystal jutting from the earth.

Gaelan speaking to me.

Soul Drinker screaming at me not to disappear again.

When Gavin had pulled me out.

From somewhere.

At some point, I *must* speak with Innathi again, to determine if that was truth or a demon's trick. To learn the Davrin's Desert history. To do that, I must draw it again, knowing what I knew now, and get past the gatekeeper. The will of the dagger was powerful, strong enough to wear me down to a nub with constant conflict demanding my compliance. Punishing me severely for disobeying.

Had Soul Drinker been lulling me at first, when I'd been able to sheath it of my will in front of Osgrid, because it wanted to escape with me? Or had Shyntre's pendant, which Mourn now owned, offered me some protection as it had against Priestesses of Braqth?

I thought it was a good sign to feel a trickle of fear in recalling that moment I attempted betrayal midbattle, when Mourn had been my only protection against a hurtling horde of cannibals. The compulsion placed by my Valsharess had been the final barrier stopping the dagger from using my body to stab the Dragonblood in the back.

The mercenary never knew though Gavin might have glimpsed it.

"Put it away," I muttered. "Please."

Wordless, Gavin rolled it up and tied good knots, replacing it in the pack, which then left my sight. I exhaled, and Mourn's tail moved again in my periphery.

"Have you finished your queen's mission, Sirana?"

Mourn's question took me unaware, felt like a rock plummeting down my spine, from neck to tailbone, fraying nerves as it went. Shock prevented a peep as my eyes widened.

"Is that why you're following your sisters to finish theirs?"

Stop.

I began packing my dry and mended things. Mourn tilted his head but kept speaking. "As I've watched, your purpose seems muddled and drifting."

I can't speak.

Fingers quivered, spiders nervously hopped about my shoulders, my throat couldn't open to breathe. Everything ached.

"What is your goal, Red Sister?"

★...*if you find any, bring them to Us.* ★

"Perhaps I might help you achieve it."

A soft wail escaped my lips as I grabbed my pack.

"Sirana?" Gavin asked. "Where are you going?"

I had no answer as I fled from the riverbank. Neither male called out or pursued me while I took long leaps from stone to stone, heedless of twisting my ankle among the black cracks. I ran past the dead mare standing in the dark and kept going.

The sound I'd made echoed in my ears, too much like Gaelan when she had run from me. So did the Valsharess's command, for the hundredth time.

Listen to rumors of half-bloods. If you find any, bring them to Us.

If my compulsion had urged me any other direction but to the crouching hybrid behind me, I'd have left them as Gaelan had left me. I'd have run away until dawn. Until my feet blistered and bled.

Instead, I stopped two hills later, collapsing outside the sealed den of the Dragonblood. Huffing for breath, I attempted one enormous and futile effort, shoving the boulder to see if it would move. When it didn't, his ward convinced me I wanted only to sit, and I landed with my back against it, shaking.

Even thinking to move a few ticks later, I couldn't lift my pack. I wasn't sure I could stand without using it as a crutch. My muscles were mush.

Fucking cock piles.

In dimness and solitude, my thoughts sought an anchor following my panicked bolt, to slow my heart, to somehow coax my tired body to be comfortable. It was harder to achieve than I hoped.

Muddled and drifting, he said.

Not so. The path was not direct, but it was clear. I only couldn't speak my true goals to them, and I didn't know enough to do more than I did.

If I had been traveling this far over many weeks, following the century-old scent of a Sathoet among the Ma'ab, then those signs had been obliterated by the firm flesh and beating heart of a former slave who'd reached the Surface several centuries before the Priestess and her Son had been captured near the Ley Tower.

Bring him to Us!

I shook my head, though knew, in the end, I'd be unable to deny Her.

Gavin had said he knew *what* he must do next but not *how*. I was in the same state. I hadn't the first vision how I might coax Mourn underground, to bring him to my Valsharess. I certainly had no tools to force him such a great distance, except one.

Mourn had told me on our way to the river that he could be persuaded to help kill Sarilis and let Gavin take over the Ley Tower. That was a two-for-one to satisfy the geas: kill the old man, lure the half-blood back West, closer to the entrance to the Deepearth.

And then what? Fuck me. I shook my head. *You're looking too far, Sister. Focus in front of you. On Manalar.*

War was coming, and Jael was directly in its path.

She won't survive alone.

Pure night sounds surrounded me, continuing unabated while I chased my fast-breeding problems, overlapping yet pulling me in opposite directions. I reached for my spiders, cradled them in my hands, and envied their simplicity. The To'vah-krav's words returned, from when he'd denied me a bargain to search for Gaelan.

There is a conflict within you which concerns me.

I huffed a dry, self-deprecating laugh.

Little do you know, half-blood!

But he might figure it out. The geas was too strong, too apparent. How could he not ask further questions after this and trigger yet more pain? How would I react next time, with greater insanity than I had thus far? Would I hurt myself or my baby without self-control?

*What can I do to save myself when I can't **speak** for myself?*

Perhaps I could ask Mourn for something first. I could set a clear goal, for the mercenary preferred those. He had offered to help us meet connections in Augran, those he knew who had "investments" in the conflict.

Who might they be?

Others not joined in the two sides, like Brom and Mourn, who did not simply want Manalar to lose. The innkeeper had quite a snarl on that topic. I closed my eyes, drawing the memory of his passionate reply.

*"I **want** the Temple heart freed of the Bishops. The same as Sarilis. The same as the Ascended. The same as the Guild, and others aware of the change in the Ley Lines since they took over Mount Sonai."*

The Guild. *Yes.* I would lay a stiff wager in favor of this Guild hiring Mourn for his contracts. Would he know others who could help me locate Jael? Maybe they had spies and informants, like in Sivaraus. Maybe someone would know what happened to her.

Unlike Gaelan, who vanished in the wild unseen.

I must try to explain, although hiking to the river might be a challenge my body would reject this instant. Should I stay here? Mourn could track me without trouble, but would either of them care to come looking before I needed food?

All that good meat left at the river. To be dried tomorrow under the Sun.

Damnit.

Hooves sounded in the distance, tromping down the hill behind me, and I straightened against the boulder, listening. There were no other feet, so either Gavin rode the horse or he had simply sent her to me. Mourn wasn't with him.

I waited in silence as the horse came closer. No burring, wickers, or snorting nostrils; no breath at all. She stumbled once from the Deathwalker's weaker night sight, and champed her teeth out of old memory of muscle.

"Gavin?" I asked, my voice slurred from the ward's effect.

"Yes."

He reached the ridge, guided her through the foliage until he was in view, and stopped. His eyes vanished into void-like eye sockets at this distance, his pale face gaunt and skeletal. The robed man of death sat atop a too-still horse. Waiting for me. Had I been given time to drift off, I might have thought I was trapped in a dream.

He said, "Mourn sent a message if you would hear it."

I arched my brow in surprise. "Um. Alright."

"He apologizes for causing obvious distress. He says he will give you privacy if you wish to travel to Augran."

My brow furrowed. "Oh? He sent you to say that?"

"No, he made the request as I prepared to leave."

My lip curved cynically. "To bring me back?"

"To return the black dagger to you if you cannot go to Augran."

Cannot. Something pricked in my chest to imagine he somehow understood my struggle, perhaps better than most non-Davrin.

Then I grasped what else he might mean. "You wish to go to Augran with Mourn?"

"I do. An opportunity I must take."

The image of sitting alone with Soul Drinker while the Deathwalker left to go his own way was…terrifying. My tongue was heavy as I made it work.

"I must go with you both. I still seek my sister as well."

There. Pure truth, if not whole.

My scholar accepted this and did not demand more. "Do you wish to rest here? Have time alone?"

I smiled with chagrin. "It does not matter what I wish, my belly will overrule me soon. I did not take any food."

"As you please."

Heh.

I used the rock to stand despite the gentle ward urging me to stay. It was an odd choice for the protection of a den, I decided, and would ask the half-blood about it. Stamping feeling into my feet, I asked, "Are Mourn's words truthful? He will let me be?"

"I think they are." Gavin dismounted and motioned to her swayed back. "Here, better if you guide Nightmare with your eyes. I will walk."

I paused at Gavin's unusual lack of precision. "You mean the night mare?"

He sounded puzzled. "I thought you chose a name. It is suitable."

I blinked. "I did? When?"

"Before you arrived to wash. Mourn mentioned that you woke from a nightmare and called the horse this as well."

"Yes, *the* night mare. She will run without Sunlight flooding her path, as you explained to me in the barn."

Astonishment mixed with a trickle of discomfort filled me when Gavin peeled back his lips in a deathly grin, grotesquely amused. "I see. Well, I never named her as a living man, knowing she would die without traveling beyond. I am surprised you didn't ask."

I shrugged. "We do not name our mounts below, either. Similar reason."

"Ah. Well, then. Perhaps you should know that the Dragonchild is of the firm opinion that formal names are worthwhile for anything of value to you."

Odd. "Why so firm?"

"I asked the same. He said a name draws different essence to it when it is spoken or thought. This can alter the pathways within an aura or a mind." Gavin paused to consider. "An intriguing idea, possibly with some merit, for I have noticed...hm."

I tapped my foot. "Noticed what?"

"Clearer direction. When I am still."

I grimaced, failing to follow that. Osgrid had called him a "mystic," a flavor of mage who caught glimpses of chaos in his magic. This became apparent just being near him. My Elder D'Shea, by comparison, was anything *but* a mystic.

Gavin looked at me, noting my expression. "Ever since you expressed a strong preference for calling me Deathwalker at Brom's inn, Sirana, my insights and discoveries possess a precise nuance in this direction which surprises me. In hindsight, I am glad you took to the name, for I may have discarded the deathless one's haunted memory otherwise."

I blinked at him. "Oh."

Yes, I remembered that. Perhaps I'd taken a liking to it only because of the Sorcerer-General's dreams. I knew I'd *wanted* there to be some connection between those ancient dreams and this day which wasn't a threat to me.

At least this study appeals to the apprentice.

I scratched an itch, became aware of the familiar hollow space opening in my middle, demanding more roast pork, while my presently nameless spiders awaited my next move.

A name is worthwhile for anything of value to you. Hm. Strange habit, Dragonblood.

With a sigh, I searched for the knucklebone talisman on my belt. "You prefer Nightmare, then?"

Gavin contemplated his mount, who seemed in better shape than the night she had died. I hadn't yet asked how he accomplished this.

"A disturbing dream that does not shy from speeding through the dark. Heh." His bony chin dipped down. "Yes, I think I do."

Reluctantly, I smiled as I attached my pack and mounted up. "Me, too." I patted her withers knowing she couldn't feel it. "Come, Nightmare. To the bank."

And to the bargains which awaited us from the Dragonchild, who insisted I call him by his own tongue-tangling name or by a different sound entirely.

CHAPTER 10

MOURN HAD EXCUSED HIMSELF SHORTLY AFTER GAVIN AND I returned to watch over his catch and the campfire. He stayed long enough to confirm we both meant to accompany him to Augran.

"I will forage food to add to the boar."

I did not argue or try to delay him, though I did not relish being alone with my thoughts while Gavin kept himself occupied. I hadn't the energy to needle the Deathwalker to make conversation, nor did I want to abrade his mood when he'd made much effort on my behalf.

Instead, I selected some noiseless endurance exercises using the many rocks, rested, and worked. Gavin glanced at me on occasion but left me to my activity.

If I was to infiltrate a large Human city with the help of a resourceful and stealthy mercenary, then I must strengthen my reflexes and agility, and lengthen my endurance to the Sunlight again. Better done sooner rather than later, and if more food was on the way, in addition to whatever I found, then I could afford it after that galling, utter collapse following the warp rot.

How could Gaelan have been expected to accomplish that mission alone?

The answer was as clear as the burn in my arms while pushing up my body weight. *She wasn't.* She either needed to find help or die in the attempt. Or both. Jael's mission was of the same nature; the Valsharess had told me I was the only one expected to return. Jael wouldn't seek help, but nothing prevented me from bringing that help to her.

I had lost weight during my recovery. I could prod my gut with my fingers and feel the heat and hardness of my womb close to the surface despite it not distending outward yet. Given how often I thought about food and ate more in one sitting these days than I ever had, I wondered when my leathers or my armor might not fit so well. What would I do then? I had been trained how to mend my clothing, but I was not a seamster to alter whole designs to account for an imminent, new shape.

Maybe the city has something.

Though the problem remained of what I would trade for it. I had so little, I might have to become like a sneak of Low Gate and steal what I needed.

Except no stealing from the half-blood. As agreed.

Panting sooner than I wanted, my brow damp, I cooled down wandering the lush forest and gathering pre-dawn mushrooms, digging up grubs and roots, and harvesting some of the flavorful herbs I recognized from watching Gavin. I didn't know when we were leaving.

Perhaps he can make a stew. He is good with those.

"Hm, impressive," the Deathwalker said of my stash as the sky lightened in the East.

I smiled. "I will try to scoop out a fish or two. Perhaps I can double what the half-blood collects."

A grunt and a nod as the Deathwalker reached to hand me a stained, rough-woven sack. "If you discover any carrion, would you bring it to me in this?"

Carrion? I wrinkled my nose but took the bag. "Why? More study?"

"To feed Nightmare, so she is not taking fresh meat from you."

"What?"

His gaunt face barely changed. "I have been introducing a new diet, of sorts. She cannot heal but I've given her enough of my blood, she has a non-dependent aura which can rebuild and strengthen her form by consuming flesh." Gavin looked at where she stood farther from the fire. "She may soon pass for a living horse if one does not inspect her teeth."

I made a face. "Her teeth?"

"They are suitable for tearing flesh and crushing bone instead of chewing grass or grain."

Well, now I *wanted* to inspect her teeth. "So, she is a scavenger, now."

"As useful a role as a grazer or predator."

"That was not an insult, Gavin," I said, smiling at his defensive tone. "Most of us are scavengers underground, whether we recognize it or not. We do not have the green abundance to have grazers at all. I will help find carrion if she needs it."

The Deathwalker considered this and accepted. "Perhaps I can revive or rebuild enough of her senses where she may be able to smell the decay and feed herself, but that will take further time and study."

If the death scholar wanted to make it sound as though he had nothing but the time in which to study, he'd succeeded.

"Are you 'deathless' as well?" I asked curiously.

He made a face. "I have experienced death."

"You do not expect to age and die again."

"Not as one born would recognize. I may expect further transitions."

"But you eat. Do you sleep?"

Gavin nodded. I could not tell if he was pleased about that or not. "I remind you that the Deathless also eats and sleeps."

"But you aren't the same creatures."

"No. Our transitions are vastly different."

"Oh? What was his like? You seemed to have learned about him in the Greylands."

"He is known there, from many lives and transitions. That is the best I can describe it." The Deathwalker stirred and fed the fire to keep it alive.

I glanced at the river and back, not wanting to miss the window of active fish but pulled to this topic all the same. "Is he Cris-ri-phon?"

"Yes, but not only. Brom Troshin was as real, though you may have 'killed' him in the kitchen. Cris-ri-phon came first, it seems, although I learned that from your experience, not mine. As you say, you 'woke' this ancient one, somehow."

Reluctantly, I remembered Toushek in my last nightmare. Even if the Davrin trader was not what he appeared, he still had interest in the Davrin fate. And there remained a Dark Queen having half-Human children.

"So, it is the Davrin who made him. Interfering with a Human's mortality."

Gavin contemplated and shook his head. "Many factions have become involved with the Deathless, and he did not become that way against his will. His own search and desires opened the way, much as mine did for me."

Worried, I glanced South. "Do you think he will pursue us?"

Ice blue pupils settled on me. "I may not be of much worth to chase, though he would attempt to destroy me given the chance. You, however, and in possession of the relic…"

I knew that answer. *For certain, yes, he must come after me.*

"The Dragonchild's aura is significant," Gavin informed me. "Although we have not seen the Sorcerer-General's full effort, we only needed Mourn to alter the outcome with the warp rot. He may be a match or better."

I made a face. "You suggest I bargain for his protection?"

"He defends another Elf by his own word. His mother was of your race, and you are pregnant. By his actions alone, I estimate that this matters more than he says to you. He possesses enough magic and martial ability to challenge any Human enslavement attempt on you, certainly against Witch Hunters, and against stronger Ma'ab agents."

They get stronger. Of course, they do. Folding my arms, I sighed. *I need to herd him West, anyway.*

"He might accept the ruby as payment," Gavin continued. "He is still interested in it."

I made a face. And Mourn could use it. To give it to him now, so far from Sarilis's tower, there would be nothing to stop the half-blood from stabbing me in the back then, unlike me stabbing him.

I felt cold and small.

Nodding acknowledgment, I excused myself. "I am going fishing. I shall return later."

MOURN WAS GONE FOR MOST OF THE DAY, AND I BEGAN TO wonder, since he had spoken of drying the pig meat. Nothing prevented Gavin and me from doing this, so we began the process along with the few fish I'd caught and cleaned.

I hadn't found any carrion but gave Nightmare the fish bones and guts; she readily consumed them. Glancing Gavin's way—he was occupied—I checked her teeth. As he'd described, she had canines, and her many grinders had points capable of splintering bone into shards.

How did he do this? It wasn't a matter of having removed the old teeth and sticking in new ones. They looked like those she had died with, just…

Modified.

I gave her some of the aged pig meat, astonished that it seemed to be helping her scent. I sniffed closer. She didn't smell like a horse, but she didn't smell rotting, either. Not as before. I considered this scent.

Somewhat like the dogs in Troshin Bend. One that isn't excreting.

Through the morning, I had expected the lingering crows and other scavengers to come in and try to steal the meat as we dried it; we were out in the open and would see them coming. Yet there was an odd lack of animals to make the attempt. A few bare-headed raptors circled high for a while but did not descend. By the time the Sun had passed overhead, and I was wearing my sunblind, they had left.

"This is strange," I said, explaining my observation. "Are you doing this?"

Gavin shook his head. "I had not planned to but wondered if the mare and myself somehow put them off."

I shook my head, narrowing my eyes in thought. "Not that alone. They stay away like a predator is here. Or close by."

Gavin's pause was brief. "Ah. Mourn. Perhaps his presence lingers to our benefit."

I smirked. Maybe the "Dragonchild" had needed to piss several times last night but wouldn't pull down his pants in front of me again after he'd caught me inspecting his member. Maybe he'd gone into the treeline and purposefully made a boundary to warn other competitors away from his kill.

Although, it was amusing to consider Mourn being modest about that. I doubted he knew I'd been looking for signs of demonic taint, not appraising him for potential performance. I hadn't said anything, and this didn't seem a topic Gavin would bring up to re-assure, if he even noticed.

"Well," I began, "I had planned to stay to defend the meat, but if it may be this quiet all day…"

"Hm?"

Gavin wasn't following me.

"It seems strange Mourn has not returned when there was a plan. I will search around for him, beginning near his den."

"I have a means to summon him if we are approached," Gavin reminded me.

"Oh, yes. How is that done?"

The Deathwalker smirked. "A thunderstone. One you obtained from the Ma'ab."

I grimaced. "Wonderful. Well, you can use the same method to 'summon' me, then."

"As you will."

I took a skin of river water and a pouch of forest food with me, so I need not hurry back, and left the last direction I'd seen him go. As I expected, it was not so easy to track him, especially in daylight. I lost clear physical sign early on; the mercenary wouldn't leave behind a trail of fresh broken twigs, torn fronds, scuffed rock, or disturbed soil.

Soon, I turned toward the hillside den, keeping careful measure of my strength. The path was familiar, and the Sun was intense, so I moved as I did underground: using a mix of scent and sightless perception to lead my way. It was as though another side of the forest lingered at the edge of my periphery; I detected warmth from a living creature, some unusual musk, or a sound which left an echo for me to drift toward, floating on that natural current.

My eyes snapped into focus as something large moved over the next rise, where the hidden den would come into view. I crouched down, lightly touching the ground for balance on the slope, and held still. The sound offered the mental image of a bear scrubbing an itchy spot against rough bark. A growl of relief followed, but I decided it wasn't a bear.

My lips stretched without showing teeth. *Returned already, half-blood?*

I crept closer, quickly as I wanted to gain sight of him before he scented or heard me. It was a self-test for practice only; I would not try to get stupidly close. It would prove nothing, and I wanted to keep my head.

I chose my approach, reached the hillcrest, and peeked above a stone, managing to catch that brief glimpse. Like the bear I'd first taken him for, Mourn scratched his back against the tall stone outside his den, which was open. He focused on one side of his spines as if his left shoulder irritated him intensely. He had removed his harness to do so.

Or perhaps he hadn't yet put it on, I thought as I sniffed the warm body heat and musk drifting from the cave. *Did he just wake up?*

The next moment, the Dragon son inhaled through his mouth and moved his head. His tongue flicked out, his metallic gaze fixed right where I was crouched as I tried to get lower out of sight.

He rumbled, "*Salsis, velxun.*"

Well, damn.

I offered the requisite reply to avoid a fight. "*Gre'as anto.*"

His tail swerved while he lifted his hand to form the familiar motion of accepting peace, and I stood up. My approach casual as I looked about, I was impressed most of the signs of Gavin camping here while I recovered were gone.

"Needed a nap?" I said in Trade.

"Yes." Mourn smirked, shrugging into his weapons harness, cinching it tighter in front. "I have not slept since you entered the storm on the Midway."

My smile fell as he adjusted the fit around his torso. *Shit.* Between Gavin and this half-breed, was *I* the one who needed the most sleep, the weakest link? Quite a reversal from traveling with Humans and Dwarves. I didn't like it.

"Why are you here?" he asked.

"You mentioned drying the pig," I said, "and seem to follow through on tasks rather than be distracted on a whim."

He lifted a heavy brow. "You suggest either you were wrong or if I'd found trouble?"

"And I wanted to discover which, yes." I paused. "Since you did not suggest being tired when you said you were going foraging, I assume you didn't want me to know you might be vulnerable."

"It came on suddenly," he murmured, sounding resentful. "Though you assume correct. No Davrin I knew slept while knowingly vulnerable."

True enough.

His harness in place, his pants and bracers snug, Mourn ducked briefly into the cave and pulled out a large, heavy sack. He handed it out to me.

"Here," he said. "For our travels."

I took it but barely managed to keep it from plummeting to the ground. I looked inside though my nose told me what to expect. "Impressive. A sampling of the entire forest."

Mourn had crouched, his tail braced against the ground as he prepared to move the boulder into place.

"Are we not coming back here?" I asked.

"No," he grunted, straining to get the boulder moving before letting it settle and proceeding to cover up the signs. "You are well again, the weather will be fair for the next few days, and Nightmare can pass as living from a short distance. I must return to Augran, and you have agreed to go there, pending a formal bargain."

"Are we leaving now?" I asked, wondering if he would rather negotiate on the road.

"This evening." Mourn gauged the shadows cast by the trees rather than the placement of the Sun itself. "We have enough time to prepare and preserve the food if I use some added spells."

I certainly wanted to see that.

Slinging the foraged goods over my shoulder, I followed as he walked in the direction of the river. "Where are your long weapons? I see the pouches and short blades on the harness. What of the bow and quiver of black arrows? The sliding swords?"

Mourn paused on the hill and half-turned. Considering a moment, he opened his hands, palms up, drawing my attention to them. His soft growl sounded like *vaex-vur-vaess*. Then, from thin air, the oversized archer's weapons used to kill Witch Hunters and shoot Kurn appeared in his hands.

I blinked. My mouth opened but then he motioned and spoke again, in a few words, exchanging his bow for the sliders he'd used against the cannibals. He didn't threaten me with them, but a nearby tree lost a few twigs.

I studied the metal whorls that made up his bracers, avoiding his face in case he was mocking my ignorance again. The shapes were abstract and did not glow like Soul Drinker, but I recognized at least one as a wizard's symbol for a bow and arrow, and two which could imply the double blades. There were ten and two more beyond what he'd shown me.

"Elegant solution for the weight," I said. "And an impressive selection."

His tail offered advance warning that he was angry with my response.

Uh-oh.

I hurried to add in our Mothers' tongue, *"Did the Davrin make these for you?"*

His tail slowed to a stop, but I heard the quiet, bitter elaboration in his distant city's accent. *"They did. I cannot remove them, Baenar. Neither will anyone else."*

Cautiously, I lifted my eyes to his face, evading the reptilian pupils grown so thin but acknowledging the tension everywhere else. *"They will not?"*

Mourn showed me his fangs in an unpleasant manner. *"The few who might have done so without rupturing the bracers and severing my arms refused. Fortunately, the maker had the foresight to imbue them to grow with me in size."*

Implying they'd been bonded to him since youth.

My pulse throbbed quietly in my ears. *"Who refused? And why?"*

"My Priestess-Matron. My Grandmaster. My Sire." He paused. *"I know why the first two refused."*

Mourn opted not to complete his story, turning to head down the hill. I stood there a few moments holding his bag. Perhaps he intended to prove himself as broody as Shyntre, and with as much cause for his blame felt as heavy. I shook it off and got moving.

I didn't do this to him. I don't know what they did.

I called out, *"Does your Aunt still live in Vuthra'tern?"*

He slowed so I could catch up, turning his Elven ear toward me, but I couldn't see his eye. *"No, she is dead. Nor does my Grandmaster, though he died first."*

My brows went high. Did he kill them *both* for what they made him?

*It must be. Knowing what I do now, how could anyone think a magic-laden half-blood would **not** turn on them?*

Then, inside, I sighed. Wilsira had thought it was a good idea to tease and provoke Kerse for five hundred years, and to lie about the Consorts. Shyntre made it well-known how he felt, having taken enough abuse to turn against any female with power over him the moment he had an opportunity. My wizard simply wouldn't talk about whatever the Valsharess had done to him.

"Any particular reason they turned you into an intelligent weapon," I groused, adjusting the heavy sack, *"or was it because they could and didn't consider if they **should**?"*

Mourn's shoulders lowered and his tail weaved gently as he stepped down the hillside. He took a moment to answer. *"Fairly simple. The Elder Mind had become an imminent threat. The Priestesses were afraid, and the first Matron who could deal with it would become the First House. It was ambition."*

I shuddered. *"And did you 'deal' with it? For your Matron?"*

"Yes," he answered. *"Though, not alone. And my Matron did not enjoy her new rank for long after."*

I could well imagine, like Wilsira, she had made a crucial mistake in her success and hubris. *"How long ago was this?"*

"I already told you."

"Four hundred and forty turns?"

"Wait…" He looked at a bird that caught his attention. *"Apologies, that's incorrect. Four hundred and thirty-nine."*

I strained my eyes in a hard roll. *"Hilarious, half-blood."*

"I am not jesting, Baenar."

"But there is an Elder Mind threatening Sivaraus, do you know?"

Mourn shrugged. *"There is more than one Elder Mind in the Deep-earth. Now, may I ask you a specific question about **your** blood family?"*

Nice chafe.

"Sure. Ask it."

"Does anyone else at your House have blue eyes?"

I squinted, puffing my way up the second hill. *"No. I am alone in my shade, there for everyone to remark upon if they so desire."*

"Hm. Who is your sire?"

I waved my hand. *"Some registered spurter in the Eleventh House. I don't know, I never met him."*

"Registered? What does that mean? An elder?"

"What? No, he wasn't above two hundred when my Mother caught. It means he met and was acknowledged by the Palace Court in the House records."

He wasn't too interested in that. *"Under two hundred. Aren't there older males in Sivaraus who breed?"*

"In truth? No." I paused. *"Well, wait. One. The Headmaster of the Wizard's Tower. He must be a thousand by how many wrinkles he has, though his son passed two hundred. Besides him, you are the oldest bua I have ever met."*

"Hm, except I don't breed," Mourn said with a sneer.

I didn't know what to say to that, and he did not invite me to try.

Still, it opened many questions. Did he have no urge for sex like Gavin? Or was it that the pleasure had been twisted to serve another, as it had been for me, and he felt revulsion? The challenge to discover an unforced climax with a bua defined my first turns at Court, but I had many opportunities to try and could not avoid facing Jilrina's legacy regardless.

In contrast, this half-breed had escaped to the Surface where there were no Davrin to mate with; certainly, no Dragons walking around, either.

So, what is his view on sex? Does he ever think about it, or act on it?

I was somewhat surprised the geas hadn't hit by now. I was talking about Sivaraus in the hopes of learning about this other city of Dark Elves. Perhaps the trick was not talking about the one who ruled it.

The mercenary was quiet long enough for me to return the ball.

"Why is your question, of all things, about old males and blue eyes?"

He grunted, implying that he wouldn't answer.

We'd see about that.

"What was your House name, by the way?"

Slowing to a stop, he turned to me and answered this without a squabble. *"Dar'Prohn."*

My arms lost some of their strength, and I had to set down the bag, remembering an exiled Captain of V'Gedra. She'd been near death but found by Cris-ri-phon and his brother in the Desert. She lived with Humans to survive.

If any of that was real. *Fuck.*

Meanwhile, Mourn studied my face. *"Hm. You know this House?"*

"Um. No. But there was a House Ja'Prohn in the Desert, was there not?"

"Likely," he answered with a detectable caution.

I called his bluff. *"You do not know?"*

Mourn exhaled, looked to the side.

I retorted heatedly under my hood, *"So, you lied."*

"Correct," he rumbled unapologetically.

"Pfeh! You can't 'fill the gap' my mothers have kept from me even if you cared to."

"Not fully. I know of a war that caused a cataclysm which drove the Dark Elves underground to escape it. I know their Queendom had once been in the Red Desert, though the capital city is buried in sand somewhere, and the soul dagger you possess played a role in its downfall. Having met your Deathwalker, I know that somewhere this gave rise to the deathless one I'd taken for a long-lived sorcerer who appeared from time to time."

I waited. *"Is that all?"*

"For now." Mourn looked toward the North for a reason I couldn't fathom. *"I have not cared much for this part of my heritage when there were many aspects to explore."*

I exhaled. *"What of Tamuril's sis——"*

"If the Naulor in Augran is knowledgeable of that time," he said with force, *"her insight is not open to me, Baenar. I do know she is too young to have been living then, so she would be a scholar at best. Though, I'm sure you have seen,"* the Dragonchild sarcastically opened his arms to either side as if embracing the world. *"Not even the Naulor Elves are out in the open building cities and expanding on their past where Yungar and Tundar can see."*

I stared. *"What and what?!"*

Mourn palmed his brow. *"Humans and Dwarves. Yungar. Tundar."*

And Baenar.

"More Draconic," I grumbled, dragging the bag for a few steps after we got moving again.

"To'vah. Yes."

I harrumphed. *Do only the Naulor have a Draconic name they call themselves as well? Why is that?*

Finally, Mourn reached out for his harvest to carry it. I let him take it and asked, *"What of blue eyes and old males?"*

Mourn smirked that I was stubborn enough to circle to this yet again. *"If you know your lineage, Sirana, I need not cast any doubt of it. I was only curious."*

"Why?"

We'd crossed a line of brush, and I could hear the river now. Mourn's silence was that type that felt like he was choosing his words. I waited.

"Once," he said, *"at my Matron's command, I chased a blue-eyed Davrin bua out of Vuthra'tern. Seeing you, I wondered if he made it to Sivaraus for he fled that direction, although it is more likely he died in the wilderness, as he was injured."*

I disbelieved the possibility. *"When was this?"*

"It was four hundred and fifty turns ago exactly. If the bua had lived, he would be five hundred and seventy, seven turns older than me."

And approaching Elder D'Shea's age. Older than my own Matron.

I repeated stubbornly, *"There are no buas that age in Sivaraus."*

"So you've said."

I scowled, watching his large, scaly feet pressing the dirt and downed leaves. How this bootless Dragonchild *loved* to count, I thought, though made no such observation aloud. I wondered how often a fugitive exchange might happen with the two cities. Who knew about this already?

Elder Rausery, maybe? When she was training with Jael on the Fringe, she was talking about Davrin avoiding Valsharess laws.

I was also struck by the link between the Deep traders and my Matron-Mother, recalling when I had accompanied the Conceiver on an unplanned stop at my former House as a Red Sister.

That scroll Mother dangled in front of Wilsira to satisfy her enough to leave the plantation sooner rather than later. She wouldn't...?

Well, my Mother could fuck any bua at any time, but she couldn't keep any accidental issue from such a tryst. Regardless, this portrait didn't suit my Matron. She was too meek, not that adventurous.

"If a Vuthra'tern exile made it to Sivaraus," I said, not yet releasing the bone, *"he would be Houseless. Fringe, Low Gate, commoner, or trader. No Matron would take him for a Daughter because her heir would not be recognized by the Court. There is no chance the bua you chased out could be my sire, or not even a grandson of his. None would be registered."*

Mourn's tail weaved between trunks and bushes without touching them as we made our way. *"I believe you are right, if all the breeding buas are young and meticulously tagged in that way."*

I heard the swipe but didn't have a chance to respond.

"Besides, there are bloodlines with other eye colors beyond red. Surely you have seen evidence of them?"

"Yes, one Priestess has green eyes." As we finally left the shade, I hopped from boulder to boulder toward the water, and a grin struck me. *"Although, in truth,"* I added, *"I much prefer Tamuril's lush leaf color to Tarra's creepy jade."*

I waited for his response.

"Hm, you've been that close to the Priestesses?" he rumbled. *"My condolences."*

My grin melted as I frowned at his broad back. *You have no idea, merc.*

My grey-robed ally stood up from his seat as we got close and said to me, "Ah. You found him."

I smiled. "I did. He was sleeping at the den."

Mourn tossed me a look while Gavin's icy black eyes glanced at the bag gripped in his fist. "If so, I still see a fair haul."

The half-blood grunted. "Thank you for beginning the drying in my absence, Deathwalker. I can finish the rest by sunset, then we may leave North to the Great Lake."

I shared a glance of confusion with my scholar. "Isn't that the wrong direction?"

"Not in the long view. Catching a trade ship to Augran would be the fastest way to get there from here."

"A ship?" I echoed. That sounded concerning.

"Hm," Gavin said with mild curiosity. "I have never been on a ship."

Same. But I wasn't curious at all. "What about Nightmare?"

"Horses board passage frequently enough, some vessels have stalls below deck. I imagine the crew will be glad she is a calm one."

Maybe too calm. "And we would happen to find a horse ship at the right time?"

"Likely. Port Fortnight brings the main trade for this side of the Great Lake. Livestock is common."

"Wait, this side? *Which* side?"

The mercenary didn't blink. "Southwest."

I rubbed my temple, and Gavin tried to help. "I believe there are four major trade ports on the Great Lake. Augran is Southeast, Fortnight is Southwest—"

"And the two are roughly sixteen days apart," Mourn interjected with baffling humor, "traveling by horse in fair weather."

"What's so funny about that?" I asked.

"Fortnight."

"So?" I read their expressions and sighed. "I forgot that word."

"A time measure," Gavin said. "Half of one month, or two weeks."

I stared. "They named it Port 'Two Weeks'?"

"Humans have chosen stranger names," Mourn said. "It suits."

I groaned. Right. This To'vah-krav enjoyed his proper names as much as he loved to count.

"So," I pointed in two directions for review. "Augran, that way. Port Fortnight, this way. The other two?"

Mourn pointed Northeast. "Taiding."

I took note. "I have heard of Taiding. The Dwarven city."

He nodded then pointed Northwest. "Yong-Ch'hai."

Even Gavin was quiet.

"Did you clear your throat halfway through?" I asked. "Yong what?"

Mourn looked like he was trying not to laugh. "No, that is the lake city to the North and West. Yong-Ch'hai."

"Who lives there?"

"More Humans. They call the land Yung-An. They are the Yungian breed."

I shook my head. "Which breed have I met, then?"

"Paxian, of Paxia. And Ma'ab, you know."

Trying to memorize these new words, I was reminded of my lessons with Shyntre in the Wizard's Tower. "What is the difference between Yungian and Paxian?"

"Appearance," Mourn ticked off on his fingers, "culture, magical lineage. They can interbreed, however."

"Hm," Gavin said. "I have not heard much of Yungians around Manalar, except they are not welcome."

"I know."

"Why not?" I asked.

"Their skin is too dark," Mourn began then clarified, "Not as dark as us. Brown-earth skin."

"Like the Zauyrians of the Desert?"

It was Mourn's turn to blink. "Ah, well. Yes, but perhaps lighter. And that is an old name. No one on the South Sea will know it."

I tried not to stamp my foot. "What is the current one?"

"Sal-zayr."

"Close enough."

"Not for Humans over three millennia. Rulers and so-called empires have risen and fallen many times, the Ma'ab are just the newest. Manalar has gone through many identities, the Bishops are the present power."

I exhaled, feeling overwhelmed, and looked at the light glinting off the river's surface with crossed arms. My empty middle gave me a threatening cramp, so I dug into my travel mix and tossed in a mouthful, chewing, preparing my waterskin to take a swig and wash it down. Seeing this, Mourn got started on the other food preservation.

"So, how long to sail from Port Fortnight to Augran," I asked, "if it is not two weeks?"

"In fair weather, half that. Assuming a storm does not rise in the archipelago."

I hated storms. The Surface was an uncertain place because of the weather, but Jael was waiting.

I made a face and continued to eat, resolving to ask about the arky-something when we got closer. "We leave tonight but do not have a bargain."

"I know. This can be worked out on the way."

Hah. The mercenary was damned sure we'd come to an agreement. Although, if we didn't, I supposed he could leave us on the shore of the Great Lake and return to "close his contract" on Kurn and Castis.

Then I was reminded that Gavin was going for sure. He had a task both which he must do and was probably something that the Guild would want. Mourn must have something to gain by introducing them. I was the one with nothing to trade for what I wanted. Nothing I *wanted* to trade.

Work it out on the road. We'll see.

THE SUN WAS A DEEP GOLD WHILE MOURN SALTED AND DRIED our supplies, hot on our backs and the apparent base of the half-blood's spells. When the shadows became long and the sky had shifted toward pink, orange, and purple, I aided Gavin in sorting, wrapping, and packing enough food to keep us well-fed for ten or so days if we didn't gorge. Longer if we supplemented it with further hunting and gathering along the way. I said as much.

"A good idea," Mourn agreed. "Good food and water aren't plentiful on a ship. There will be rats for the horse, but I do not recommend you eat them, and you'll never catch fish directly off the side. The more you use your own stores below deck during that time, the less you'll draw attention from the crew."

I released a quiet sigh and didn't comment how I'd most certainly drawn the attention of the innkeeper with my eating.

"I presume you will provide disguises as well?"

Mourn nodded. "Necessary."

It certainly was, also like the innkeeper.

Dusk was soon upon us, and while Mourn and I erased signs of our camp by the river, Gavin waited with Nightmare on less rocky ground. Perhaps the other two were as drained as I was with the discussions into which we frequently fell, for we spoke no more the first half of the night. Instead, we focused on making distance with me guiding Nightmare, Gavin sitting behind me, and Mourn jogging beside us.

The horse would fall apart before she would stop on her own, I knew, and Gavin apparently had a lot to occupy his mind, as he began no inquiries. He would barely touch my sides for balance when the way leaned hard, but otherwise the scholar's body behind me might as well have been another pack for the attention he drew and the warmth he generated.

Meanwhile, the Dragonblood did not grow tired or winded for hours at a time. He also didn't complain. I ate and drank atop the mare but was also the one to speak up and request a stretch-release break. At least he no longer asked me if I needed help, and if he drained his bladder half as much as I needed to, he went somewhere I couldn't see.

Eventually, as I must have known it would, my mind wandered around to sex. I had recovered and relaxed enough to feel a tingling blood rush to my crotch against the saddle, although my memories and wishful imaginings were unfocused and shifted readily.

I drifted in the pure pleasure of mounting an exhausted, sweet-smelling Auslan at last, in listening to those soft moans of submission next to my ear as I lay upon him in my mind's eye. My hips shifted in the saddle. We shared something I'd never done before, him and me, but had I imagined that I'd seen his aura in truth? That one time? *They were such beautiful colors.*

As Nightmare stepped slowly through a deceptively level meadow, I closed my eyes, listening to the horse's hooves, but in my mind sat on a heavy table, spreading naked, eager thighs for my wizard during a study break in his sire's library. I was gasping with want even before Shyntre pushed in two fingers together. I writhed and ground my hips as he sucked mercilessly on my clit, refusing to let it go until I heard the pop inside. Magic jumped from those fingertips massaging my cunt from inside, and I shrieked, my body jolted. I saw stars like he'd described, thought I'd pissed all over his face. I hadn't, but he was no happier about the clean-up.

"Careful," Mourn said. "The slope is steep here, but we are close to a road again."

"Huh? Oh."

My crotch received a couple bounces as I navigated Nightmare, focused on the bone in my glove. It took a while to reach the bottom. I bit the inside of my cheek.

Finally, on a remote, dirt road formed by cartwheels, I felt Jaunda. She had me bent over after a wrestling match I'd lost in the Cloister. Again. My limbs locked, her scalding skin and dense weight on my back, the blunt tip of her imminent pole pressed a randy warning on my twitching pucker, which began to yield beneath her lusty growl and the nip on my ear.

Relax, novice. That's it. Let's loosen this tight Noble netherhole for a few Sisters after me this eve. We can all unload some stress.

Ohhh, Goddess, fuck me, Lead!

"Stream coming up ahead. Shallow, no bridge."

Damnit!

After the crossing, I resettled my mind in the Cloister.

Jael was grinning, looking proud of herself as she loomed above me, stark naked and on all fours. She had finally stayed focused long enough to make my slit sing against her mouth, and as a reward, Reishel finally stopped teasing the youngest's dripping folds with her own tongue and fingers while Gaelan kneeled behind her, stroking the thick, sensuous phallus.

Bright, burning eyes rolled up as we filled her cunt, and I stared at her lips, so swollen and messy from pleasuring me, as they opened in a moan. She gasped both before and after I leaned up to steal a kiss, pinching and pulling her nipples as she liked. Gaelan fucked her harder, watching us, and I didn't let up either the kissing or the tit-torture.

Sharing a mischievous look with Reishel, I watched her lick her fingers and attack the helpless novice from the front and the rear. One hand vigorously rubbed Jael's stubbled mound, the other screwed two wriggling fingers up her netherhole, twisting her wrist again and again. Jael struggled, protested, but never tried to get away. She was unusually, deliciously vocal when she peaked, sometimes yowling like an animal. Within the privacy of the Cloister, we enjoyed that about her.

I moaned.

"Are you well, Sirana?"

My eyes popped open. It was still dark. I was mostly upright, riding Nightmare along the cart path, surrounded by the overlapping song of night chirpers.

"Something you ate?" Gavin asked.

"Uh. No, I am fine. But I could use a stretch break."

"Very well."

I slowed the mare but looked around baffled. "Where is Mourn?"

Gavin dismounted first, his bootheel skimming his shovel. "Scented a hunting opportunity, I believe."

I landed on the grass feeling my face warm. *Scented.* I wondered then if the half-blood could smell my arousal on the saddle or knew what the moans meant better than Gavin. Maybe that was why he left. Was he concerned I might ask him to serve me like that? To "scratch an itch" for me?

Bah. I can do it myself.

The mercenary would probably ask for payment anyway.

Gavin did not question my moving deeper into the trees and out of his sight. My guardians were out and waiting patiently on my shoulders as I leaned against a tree, removed my gloves while leaving the talisman inside, and pulled up my belt higher on my waist. Gloves tucked to one side, I pushed down my leathers and reached above me to grip a comfortable branch with one hand, bracing my feet and legs flat and wide.

Now. Don't linger too long.

While my fingers coaxed ever more sensation from me, inside and out, I kept my thoughts fluid as well, exchanging out the Davrin-only scenarios which had kept me aroused in the saddle for hours, refusing to let them wander farther than that.

Keep it simple. Only pure bloods. Ohhh…

I tried to keep my breath quiet but needed to suck deep as I shuddered, stroking harder beneath the tree. My cunt drooled and made noise as well. Everything seemed so sensitive, the night breeze was adding its own titillating caresses while I enjoyed my private visions, pushed them harder.

As they pushed *me* harder.

I started by straddling my Consort, welcoming his fertile cock back inside without fear of what might happen. Then, like at the Priestess's orgy, someone pushed between my shoulder blades, easing me down until I lay belly-to-belly with him, and another Davrin prepared to mount my netherhole. I looked over my shoulder. Grinned. Shyntre couldn't wait for his turn, and I didn't want him to.

As I double-fucked them, another stepped up and grabbed my hair, resting a soft, smooth glans against my lips, nudging until I licked and sucked. I could take another. I lifted my most inviting gaze, and Jaunda pushed her magic pole into my mouth with a throaty moan.

Oh, Goddess! Fuck!

"Yes…"

A little more.

"Ah, tha's… good…"

So close.

Harder. Fuck me deeper.

They did.

The goodness started as one ripple, then others followed. *Yes!*

Ripples became waves rolling up from that single point.

Ah! Ah!

Sweeping, overwhelming.

Ahhh, yeahhh….!

The heated, sweaty pile in my mind's eye vanished as soon as I came down, not only clutching the branch but practically dangling from it. I wasn't sure if my lovers had come in my dream, but I certainly had!

With a long exhale of satisfaction, I got my legs under me, releasing the branch one finger at a time. Flexing my hand, I stretched my arm, rotating it at the shoulder, then sought a cloth on my belt to quickly wipe down my crotch. Gradually, I noticed there were fewer insects making noise around me, and I paused. Was that from my activity, or was I being watched?

I once watched Kurn stroke to release from the trees, didn't I?

He had looked around paranoid after finishing. *Just like this.*

Pursing my lips, I decided Mourn would say something or he wouldn't; he would show himself or he would stay hidden. Or maybe he wasn't there at all.

I cleaned up, sorted out my leathers and gear, and returned to Gavin and Nightmare on the road.

"That took longer," he commented.

I shrugged, mounting up first so he could get behind me. "I needed release so I can focus."

"Hm."

The mare shifted with his added weight, and I grinned. "Do you want me to be clearer?"

The death mage paused. "Clearer than acutely active bowels?"

A laugh escaped me, and I covered my mouth. "No. Not that."

"Then I do not want to know."

"Aw." I got the horse moving, feeling much better, alert, and relaxed. "Very well, apprentice."

Gavin grunted. "I do not think that suits anymore, do you?"

"Apologies, you are right." I considered. "Do you claim 'master', now?"

"No. If anything, I am still a seeker. 'Apprentice' is too… small."

I smiled with a chagrin he couldn't see. "Seeker. A learner. Scholar. Mystic, perhaps?"

"I do not need that many names."

I shrugged. "If you are to meet the Guild, you might try several if they do not know Deathwalker. I will watch for the one they respond well to."

"Oh, will you?"

"Unless you are comfortable enough to judge them yourself."

Gavin didn't reply at first. "Then what status have you and me, if they ask?"

"Allies," I replied easily. "By choice. This is how I have been thinking of you."

He murmured in a way that told me it was good enough for him.

Going by the moons, it was an hour later when Mourn joined us again. He stepped slow and cautious out of the shadows, giving us plenty of warning. He carried the remains of a ground bird, plucked, cooked, and mostly eaten. He offered me a large leg, which I accepted eagerly, and a few ragged bones to Nightmare.

"Feel better?" he asked me.

I replied after a smart nod, bird meat tucked in one cheek. "Do you?"

The Dragon's son looked at me and smirked, gold eyes shining in the dark in a hauntingly familiar way. He let me know he was aware of why we'd stopped.

"Good sign," was all he said.

CHAPTER 11

I COULD SMELL THE GREAT LAKE WELL BEFORE WE SAW IT BY dimming moonlight. It was cool and fresh, though the shore held a complex underlayer of decomposing plants and animals.

Despite the cart trails becoming wider and well-used, Mourn led us off-road before we could meet any natives. We circled around to the view of the water and its Human port, well inside pre-dawn darkness. I volunteered to get off Nightmare and lead her, choosing the closest path to the Dragonblood while imagining how the haphazard spread of shelters might look in the day.

"Welcome to Port Fortnight," Mourn murmured.

I traced the apparent boundaries. *It's a lot larger than Troshin Bend.*

Yet the Humans formed a mere dot on the shore compared to the lake which was *massive*. The rippling blackness shimmered with the shattered reflections of two setting moons, meeting the stars at the horizon and disappearing. I could not see any land on the other side, and the shorelines to my right and left stretched as far as I could see.

The half-blood added, "This is a small city. Not without its charm despite the dung heaps."

I blinked at his straight face and sniffed. "I just smell the water. It is giant."

"Offshore breeze at night," Mourn said with amusement. "A less smelly time to approach from this direction."

Uh-oh.

He was right, of course; there would be plenty of dung piles, heaps of them if they consolidated it anywhere specific. I could hear rising numbers of foreign livestock; not only the docile versions of the pheasants and wolves like at Troshin Bend—chickens and dogs, I reminded myself—but I discovered they had pigs as well, far more horses, plus something like the bulky, lowing *uroan* down below. I detected their manure evenly spread out over tiny plots of land which grew tidy rows of plants as well. It wasn't unfamiliar, like the mundane but necessary parts of home, although the many small, bobbing boats strung out into sparkling water kept me firmly present on the Surface.

Mourn pointed beyond those. "Our timing is good. Those are trade ships anchored at port. High chance one of them is leaving for Augran soon."

Gavin grunted, noting the shapes but unable to make out as much detail as I could. Three water vessels were farther offshore, and they seemed to be made of large trees, many of them. Their wood had been sectioned and formed in the way that the Davrin formed stone, ore, and fiberstalk, not only for the bloated body but several massive poles jutting up into the night sky.

Without the magical tools the Davrin used, it looked rough and without much attention to aesthetics. Functional and sturdy, not pieces of art to serve a picky eye. Still, I wondered how Tamuril would judge one of these things.

Wait, we're climbing onto one of these things to ride South.

I grimaced, wondering how much that slow rocking would be exaggerated the moment the vessel was beneath my boots.

Even assuming a storm doesn't rise in the 'archipelago.' Ugh.

I'd since learned what that was: a chain of numerous, small islands that cut the entire way across the Great Lake, North to South. These isles were an obstacle course when sailing on a fair-weather day, but deadly if caught in a powerful storm like that which had plunged down the Midway as we'd been crossing it. Mourn had also informed me that specific storm had first formed on the Great Lake, where we'd be traveling for a week.

Comforting.

While we had found useful things to discuss the last two days on the way here, Mourn and I still hadn't reached a bargain; he had not insisted, and I hadn't opened it with an offer. I remained baffled—and wary—that Mourn had not mentioned the Ma'ab ruby or Soul Drinker as additional payment to the saphgar I'd given him.

Meanwhile, from conversation and actions alone, I had concluded that Mourn and Gavin shared the opinion that Jacob's soul shard and its intended use was valuable enough on its own to warrant safe passage with the Dragonblood mercenary. As both a war tool and keen strategy, he didn't want to let the Deathwalker out of his sight, perhaps.

Gavin's mistress is clever for his claim that she does not care to influence the outcome of this siege.

Our trio had rested at staggered intervals, mostly when I needed sleep, but I hadn't dreamt again. Not of the Desert or the Abyssal prison, nor of my buas or the Valsharess, or… of anyone else. I was glad but anxious the next time I would.

"Have the dreams of your child come? Have you seen her face yet?"

Innathi's immovable certainty that I would see the face of my Daughter, *and* that it would be an irreducibly *good* thing, discomforted me.

What was the benefit of seeing the face of someone who might die before being born, despite what I could do? If I returned to my Valsharess with Auslan's spark burning, why should I delight to recognize exactly who was to be taken from me, likely still wet from the womb? Wouldn't it be less painful if I didn't know the face so well, as D'Shea knew Shyntre's?

There's also that other obvious thing.

What if I carried a son, not a Daughter? Did this matter if the mother was a Red Sister? The details, maybe, the child's fate would have the same end of serving Braqth over anything I wanted. I heard Rausery's terse reply in my head having stated that she'd birthed a Daughter once.

"Dead. Somewhere in the Sanctuary. Priestesses used her up."

Worse for me, it wasn't the Sanctuary who knew about and wanted the child, but my Queen who compelled me to return, now *with* Mourn at my side.

When this had struck me once again on the way here, I'd stifled a groan of fear and, for the twentieth time, wondered if Mourn should not have tried so hard to save us both. He did not understand the role I served in Sivaraus; he couldn't imagine the lack of choice I had, especially after what Cris-ri-phon had done to lessen them further in destroying my Elder's vial.

The fact that the Dragonblood *had* tried lent weight to Gavin's assurance that I could bargain with him, while also suggesting why he wasn't insistent in defining the terms. This still concerned me.

If Mourn was of Davrin-blood, male, and a loner, he would not dare try to claim responsibility for my giving live birth like the Sorcerer-General. Would he? I wanted to tell this large male, as I had the sorcerer, that my baby was *not* his responsibility. I wanted to tell myself that I expected nothing from him.

Yet, at no point thus far had I refused the half-blood's help when it was in fact needed. Not after what Soul Drinker had done to try to purge it without my knowledge or consent.

Somehow, I wanted to think I felt less threat and offense with Mourn than I had in the sorcerer's quarters, but I also did not understand why. Perhaps I simply *couldn't* refuse his help, for this helped the Valsharess's geas?

The compulsion I could not warn him about.

"Wait here," Mourn told us. "I will find my contacts and return by dawn with passage to Augran."

THE NIGHT WOULD BE ENDING SOON. GAVIN WAS WRITING BY the soft blue glow of a familiar knucklebone. I sighed.

"How far does the Great Lake extend?" I asked in a whisper, looking out but unable to differentiate much between the night Sky and the dark horizon of the water, for the moons had set and new clouds had appeared.

Gavin shrugged, his grimoire and ink bottle balanced on his lap, his drying sand in easy reach. He didn't enjoy me looking over his shoulder but did not try to block what I could see by sitting nearby. It wasn't like I could read it.

"I am uncertain," he said. "I've heard vague tales of sailors being gone for months on a 'tour' following the shore and visiting various ports, but this is my first time seeing it."

My eyes were wide. "Months?"

Gavin nodded. "The wind does not always favor the sails going in a circle, from what I understand. The location of the largest ports would, by logic, reflect the strongest wind streams in certain directions. At certain times of the year." He paused again. "Or at different phases of the moons, as well. I am not familiar with the details."

I tried not to appear horrified at this implied complexity of sailing the Great Lake, but I doubted I succeeded the longer I thought about it. There were similar obstructions and dangers belowground when the molten hotspots changed course or tunnels simply collapsed. One learned and adapted by necessity, I knew, and no one learned it all at once.

"At least the stars would be consistent to navigate by on clear nights," I suggested.

The pale man's black, stringy hair dipped down. "There is that."

I paused in thought, then asked, "Could we be in danger, accepting passage on this ship?"

"Always. I recommend making that bargain sooner rather than later. Mourn seems the type to keep his agreements."

Now someone decided to nudge me.

"What is your bargain with him?" I asked bluntly "How far does it go?"

"Only what you heard. He will guide me to an interested party within the Guild of Augran who will listen to my task and likely assist in a plan to help it succeed."

"What does he receive as payment?"

"The allowance to be present during the planning."

Not having heard that part, I squinted. "He has an interest in going to Manalar himself? Not dropping you off with his contact and leaving to find another contract?"

"That, or he needs more information from the Guild to decide this. He also waits on you, and you are determined to go to Manalar for a different reason yet have not spoken on it."

I fiddled with the fit of my gloves while I considered. "It would not be...wise to make a contract with him for mere treasure. That allows him an opening to take other contracts at the same time. I cannot aid you with the shard, find my Sister, and allow him close and in possession of the ruby used against me."

"Ah. I can see why you are teasing him with the possibility."

I scowled with searing resentment. "I am *not* teasing him. I have not once proposed that I might trade the ruby. It is not my doing if he still wants it. If he is that greedy for magic trinkets that he cannot think of anything else..."

I paused there since I did not have an "else" ready to suggest.

My scholar considered that and grunted, lightly sprinkling the fine sand to fix his letters onto his page. "You are correct. You have not made the offer."

If only Kurn could have accepted that the first time, or Brom the second.

My scowl remained. "If you admit that so quickly, why did you make the accusation?"

Gavin considered this and shrugged. "My father and the brotherhood were of the strong opinion that women held onto stolen valuables they knew they could not keep but would inevitably try to gain something in the process of giving them up. I …assumed this was your goal, as it is effective if she is also considered beautiful. My apologies."

Annoyance and a baffling sting roiled inside me, but I kept my lips closed, jaw tight. The death mage had assumed I *knew* I could not keep the ruby? Why, because Mourn wanted it?

That makes no sense!

It was searingly insulting, this implied imbalance on who kept powerful magic items on the Surface. *What makes him the assumed owner? That he is a large male? Pfeh!*

Gavin was studying my face. "I see I was quite wrong. My error, Sirana. I did not intend to insult you."

I waved my hand. "It is fine. I am not angry with you."

He nodded acceptance.

Although, I *wasn't* fine, given where my thoughts headed next, away from the death messenger to the dark city far below my feet. I recalled many buas at Court, many I had sought to lie with, who were assumed or accused to do this very thing as the manipulative teases they were. Often enough, they *did* steal to tease and negotiate, proving us right.

Or so I'd thought before I met Shyntre, who did not try to negotiate with the saphgar or those pellets, but simply made them and gave them up. Callitro had negotiated a little but without much guile; he simply wanted attention and offered to craft a ring to coax me to the Tower multiple times.

A gold ring which made a difference to me on the Surface, several times.

What choice were buas like them given but to hold on to something they *knew* they could not keep, delaying and negotiating with it, or to not fight and do without it? The harassment to give it up would not end once a female thought about what he might do with it. She would take it away; as I'd told little Layne, their Mothers would not allow them to own their own land or wealth.

And if the Davrin son was resistant, there were ways to "convince" him.

My personal view this far outside my home city was simple: I didn't want yet another large male to hurt or possibly break me with a magical focus attuned to me. *Kerse... Kurn... Brom... Both of them together...*

How had I escaped that many times?

I winced, already knowing the seed to my fortune had been Shyntre's gift; a counter-focus for the psionic shard left in my mind by Kain. D'Shea had known, had been using it to help me cultivate my will, to shield my thoughts against Davrin mages. It had worked well before everything went to the Pit. I hadn't been strong enough to face a demonblood backed by an Ornilleth prisoner.

We all have a breaking point.

Mourn possessed my blue gem, now. I'd given him something far more valuable in the long term for short-term survival, and I was *afraid* now. Did Mourn *agree* with Gavin, that I was deliberately teasing him with the ruby as payment? If he did, I was in ruthless danger once again. I'd watched Mourn fight against the warped cannibals; I could not go hand-to-hand with him in the same way Shyntre could not with Jaunda.

Although, Shyntre has spells to fight for real, if he can keep distance.

And if he could not? My wizard was defiant in his eventual domination which overwhelmed whether he had "teased" her or not.

He had screamed at me often enough that he hadn't. *"Just give me space! Let me breathe! ...You all look ridiculous wearing the Feldeu, anyway!"*

I sighed. I wondered if I could ever convince Shyntre that I'd thought about this, and he was right. After the Deathless and the

Ma'ab in the kitchen, I might know what he had been talking about, and… what? Apologize for the way I'd acted?

Too late for that. Now what?

Offer to trade the blue stone for the red one after all? Negotiate for something I "knew" I couldn't keep anyway. I wanted the blue stone back, but dare I explain why? *Could* I explain it?

When Mourn next approached us, I recognized him only by his soft rumble and his hand sign.

"It's him," I warned.

"Oh, good," Gavin replied, deadpan, getting to his feet.

I stared. The Dragon's son looked like a smaller brother of Kurn, with the raven black hair although his skin was not so deathly pale, and his face was without the permanent sneer. His clothes had changed to cover him from neck to wrists, down to his illusionary boots. He'd also taken on blue eyes.

Is he mocking me?

I caught my impulse long enough to ask, "How common are blue eyes in Humans?"

"Very," Mourn replied. "Enough that they do not remark on it."

"So, except for that, are you Ma'ab?"

The false Human shook his head. "Noiri."

Zauyrian, Ma'ab, Paxian, Yungian…argh.

I folded my arms. "Noiri. Very well. Who are they?"

"The Yungar who live in the North. They were there before the Ma'ab invasion and fought the first wars taken by surprise. They've interbred the most with the Ma'ab, largely through war violence and enslavement, but are numerous enough to exist apart from the Empire for now. Many Noiri sail the Great Lake, so no one would look twice at me in this form."

I eyed him again, not yet accustomed to Mourn being this slender. Kurn's smaller brother with blue eyes and rosier skin was a fair description, and it made sense with that story. He was not mocking me.

236

Gavin evaluated the form as well. "I do not see an aura, illusory or otherwise."

"I am suppressing it. If you will do the same with yours, both of you, my spell's aura will be the only hint you are not what you seem. It will take a trained mage to look for it, and we are unlikely to be close to one for long."

Gavin nodded, and I smirked. "No mages on boats? Ever?"

He looked at me. "On larger vessels. They would have a designated purpose to be there, and the smart ones do not work cheap. I have confirmed the trade ship we will be taking does not have a permanent cabin-mage."

Good for us, given we'd be trapped on rocking wood atop that massive, moving surface. I grimaced to imagine, looking at it now, while Gavin waited patiently for a modified appearance.

Mourn motioned a simpler sign I did not recognize. *"Jiilral ehaism…"*

As at Brom's Inn, Gavin's coloring changed, but his appearance did not shift dramatically in his height or form, though his facial features lost the corpse-like gauntness and filled out. The striking, black sclera changed to white, his ice-blue pupils warming to a brown that would also match his long hair. His skin became Paxian tan like Mathias's.

Gavin inspected his hands and forearms, noting the warm tone and clear fingernails. He looked to me in question.

"Show me your teeth," I suggested.

His lips clamped tight at first; I smiled in response, showing my teeth plainly. It took the death mage actual effort to stretch his lips enough for me to see. The awkwardness was as disconcerting as when Nightmare showed her new shredders.

I glanced away. "Your teeth are mundane. Eyes are brown and white. You should not frighten anyone."

Gavin nodded acceptance.

"Any preference?" Mourn asked me then.

"Not the youngest of all aboard," I answered firmly. "Not ugly, but not too pretty. *No* copper-red hair."

The mercenary smiled with amusement—he knew exactly what I meant—and agreed. "Male or female?"

I squinted in thought. "Do women sail?"

"They do. Not as many, and not every Human vessel welcomes them. Some groups of men consider them too weak, or distractions, or just 'bad luck' and ban them from working their ship, though they may accept female passengers with coin. But this one has three women as sailors, another five as traveling traders."

"Three of how many?"

"Twenty-eight."

"Only three?"

"It is worth noting they are not pretending to be men, as some do on other ships. The men will accommodate them aboard this ship. I selected this one so you may appear the same if you prefer to remain female."

I blinked at him, taking some time to sort that out in my head. Humans were complicated, and the half-blood had been walking unseen among them, studying them for a long time. I was fortunate he could distill and guide me in this way. I had already stumbled and broken into one town. Despite being so small, it had been as threatening as Sivaraus.

"Are you suggesting, as the innkeeper did, that I would not move like a man if I wore his face?"

Mourn's tail moved in that precursor to a carefully chosen answer which was becoming familiar. "Correct, but it is less a masculine way of moving and more Elven, but Yungar would not know how to interpret this except to wonder if you are pretending to be a man."

"Hm. Very well. A woman, not too pretty or too young. No copper hair. In fact, make it brown like Gavin's."

"Done."

He used the same words again in his spell, and in the span of a deep breath, I beheld rougher, pale hands which pulled a light brown braid forward. *Strange.* I wore a shirt and pants under my cloak; thank Goddess he did not change it to one of those "skirts" worn by the women in Troshin Bend. The appearance was not of leather but a rough-woven, grey-brown cloth. My weapons and pouches remained where I could feel them, but they were masked in the illusion to not appear at all except for one sheathed dagger.

Gavin approved. "Good. The same blue eyes, I would know you, but with rounded ears and this face, you should not draw the eye of those collecting beautiful women."

Those collecting…?

Mourn beckoned, turning toward the faintly lightening shore. "Dawn comes soon. We should be on board before sunrise."

THE DIRT ROADS LEADING INTO THE SMALL CITY GREW WIDER AND chunkier as a greater number of shelters surrounded us. I guessed this was from more animals landing their dung upon it plus regular churning of the mud by many feet whenever it rained. This close to the water, I imagined it must rain readily. With some grim amusement, I noted damage caused by a recent storm and imagined it was the same one which had driven us quickly into Brom's Inn.

I was less amused that the clouds covered the stars as the dawn arrived as a dark grey. *Please, no storms while I'm on the boat.*

Some early-working townspeople noted us walking by but quickly lost interest. We had enough stores on Nightmare not to have to barter, so Mourn simply led us to the subtly leaning docks and its array of smells. While the environment had similarity to the underground lakes large enough to ferry small boats, there was greater variety and complexity in what grew or lived there.

As with everything on the Surface.

I was sniffing the air, detecting both fresh and rotting at once, considering these Human-built wooden planks beneath my feet. They hovered over the water but would likely remain in place for only a few decades. Perhaps Humans were used to rebuilding things frequently or never noticed doing so with their short lives.

We stopped by a boat with a lantern lit; it was too small to carry the three of us and Gavin's horse. There was also a man wearing thick, dark clothing, preparing things.

"This is Parey," Mourn said in his Noiri disguise; his polite, smiling voice wasn't as low as normal. "He will take us out to the *Trickster of Isles*."

"Mornin'," the man said neutrally, better securing his warm, clinging hat before shifting a bulky bag to one side, rocking his boat. He was dressed in old layers of clothing and smelled of sweat, salt, and oil.

"Trickster...?" I began.

"The ship's name."

Of course, it has a name...

"*Trickster?*"

"Nearly ran tah rocks thrice, milady," said Parey in the boat. "She's a lucky one to be on passin' through in the archipelago."

"Good crew," Mourn added with a smile. "Light and swift design."

The sailor shrugged.

"How will we get the horse onto the vessel?" I asked, deciding not to share *her* name.

"We remove her pack and saddle." Our guide indicated a ramp leading down into the water farther along the pier. "She can swim out alongside the boat, and the crew can use ropes and a harness to lift her up. Common enough."

"Huh."

I exchanged a look with Gavin. A good thing he had spent all this time grooming her to look alive.

Nonetheless, Parey squinted at her behind us. "Calm one. Heard th' hooves behind me but fergot she was there."

"Well trained," Mourn assured him. "Are we ready?"

"Aye. Climb aboard, milady. We'll catch yer man at the end of the ramp with the horse."

Gavin turned his head away, probably to roll his eyes without being observed, before stepping to Nightmare and removing her present burdens. I accepted those holding the food before turning to climb down the ladder into the boat.

"Here, hand 'em to me," Parey said, holding out his hands.

"I am balanced," I insisted, my boots finding the sturdy rungs. "These are mine."

The sailor dropped his arms and stepped away. "As you like. Just saying… odd yer manservant made you work an' you said nothing."

I stood on the boat, feeling it weave side-to-side as we adjusted to my presence. Gavin did not protest this incorrect assumption, but his back was as tense as any time he was around other Humans.

"He is not my manservant," I said, carefully resting my food supply where it wouldn't get wet.

"Ah." A pause. "Husband, then?"

Gavin made a noise. I tried not to laugh.

"Why does it matter?" I asked, deflecting his prodding.

Parey looked at Mourn, who shrugged, offering no guidance. The bearded man licked his lips nervously. "Manalari women don't travel alone. Your brother?"

I sighed. "Yes. My brother."

The man's curiosity wasn't sated. "Is he mute? He ain't said a thing, you do all the talking."

"Your questions annoy me, *marine descito*," Gavin said, having loosened Nightmare's saddle. Mourn offered to take it; he accepted. "Mind your business."

Parey blinked, at least confirming we had the same accent and that the death mage had ears. "Er, 'pologies, sir."

Mourn joined me in the boat with the heaviest of the tackle, and Gavin led his horse by the reins toward the ramp while Parey unmoored his boat. The boatman settled down with one oar while the Dragonblood in disguise took the second without remark. They pushed off, and I quickly sat down, gripping the wooden bench.

At the end of the ramp, Gavin climbed in last, retaining hold of his horse's lead, and she willingly entered the chilly water and began swimming behind us. I watched Mourn while trying not to smirk. In this form he deliberately held his strength in check, to match the stroke of the Human man.

We'd be going in circles, otherwise.

Parey grunted as he pulled at the oars, "Horse jus' followin' 'long in dark water withou' even a snort."

"So?" Gavin asked, annoyed from the sound of it.

"Horses with water legs are rare. Don' sell 'er cheap."

The mage grunted. "I will not."

We made steady progress toward the ship, and other sailors were ready to lower down the canvas and pulley for Mourn to wrap beneath the horse's belly in the water.

"Come on up," someone above us called, throwing a rope ladder over the side. "In case the horse kicks, don' want tah be 'neath!"

Nightmare wouldn't kick unless Gavin told her to; we both knew that.

"Make her kick," I whispered near his ear as I stood up to balance the saddle packs over my shoulders.

A brief nod, and I began climbing first while the males held the boat steady, scaling the rope ladder with considerable ease. I probably should have slowed down when one of the sailors was taken aback seeing me peeking above the ship's railing.

"Ah! Oh, here, milady, let me help you."

He reached for the food packs.

"No!" I barked, and the scruffy man withdrew in a second surprise. "Let me be. I can do this."

Like Parey, the man backed up to make room, helping instead to get the horse on board as the sky had overtaken the paltry light of two hanging lanterns. A few grunts of effort, a word of warning when I saw Gavin gesture, and the horse simultaneously kicked and snorted in a believably frightened manner, but otherwise it was smooth and successful. Mourn was the last to join us aboard a moment later.

"Thank you, men." The mercenary passed a pouch of coin to one in a thick, dark blue coat.

"Welcome aboard the *Trickster of Isles*," he responded, accepting. "I'm Kelli Tremain, the Captain. You are the last passengers, so just waiting on one boat of supplies. We'll set sail soon as they reboard."

Human Mourn nodded. "We will wait in the hold with the mare."

"The lady, even?"

"We'd accept spare blankets if you have them."

"Sure thing. We'll call when the cook has the stew."

Gavin was hunched over again, disguising his usual height around these non-Ma'ab Humans, and seemed shorter than Mourn's Noiri form at first glance. Curious eyes were on me rather than him; they tended to look at him next if they looked at all. We said nothing and were guided to the ramp that would get the horse down below.

The ship assailed me with scents of close-working Humans, of dank wood combined with something like burned sap, of old fish, urine, and vomit. It was far more pungent than Brom's Inn, but no worse than the dungeon below the Palace in Sivaraus. Better than a greasy-bearded Dwarf with his trousers down, pressing me to the stone and breathing in my face.

Fuck.

I grimaced at the unbidden memory jog, wondering how long it might be before my nose became inured. As the large ship swayed and groaned upon the lake, as my legs constantly fought its tilt, I knew I would have preferred the fresher effort of traveling in the mountainous forests on solid ground.

I reminded myself that this was the fastest way to reach Augran, the fastest way South, with many potential eyes and ears who might have seen or heard of Jael. I had to secure a deal with the half-blood, of course. Somehow.

It's impossible to walk away.

We settled down in the hold to wait for the anchor being pulled up, listening to the men's thumping footsteps above us and to the ever-creaking wood. A low, constant shush of sound on the other side confirmed I must be below the level of the water. I could only hope that the workmanship of the Human builders was competent, and the vessel would hold up in rougher waters.

If not, I am sprinting topside at the first sign of a leak.

Mourn was watching; I must have seemed as tense imagining the deep waters outside as Gavin was around other males. He rumbled softly before speaking privately. "In the event of a storm, staying below the top deck would be safest for you."

I gave him a skeptical look, my eyes squinting.

"You can be easily thrown overboard by a wave of water or sharp tilt," he said. "The sailors know how to secure themselves."

"What if the wall leaks?" I asked, pointing at it. "Or breaks wide open?"

Mourn looked. "If it does, the situation is dire. Leaks, we can do something about. If a breach, I could not save the horse, but I would aid you and the Deathwalker."

"How?"

"It depends on what is happening, and speculation would not help right now. I have experience with sinking boats and storms on the Great Lake, but you would have to choose to follow my direction under pressure. I cannot make you do this, Red Sister, but know I am not trying to kill you or watch you drown, and I have agreed to help Gavin reach Augran."

I could appreciate his plain-speak. He was like Elder Rausery, leaving it open that I could follow those with greater experience or not, even to my detriment. Cris-ri-phon would have said he knew what was best and would protect me no matter what, as every pregnant Davrin needed it for some reason. Mourn didn't mention it either way.

"Will the sailors get too curious?" Gavin asked, looking behind him at the three empty stalls filled with cargo, the fourth containing Nightmare.

"I have requested privacy as part of the bargain with Captain Tremain, though there is another exit to the deck at the far end."

The death mage grunted. "Good to know."

"I saw your escape from the second floor of the inn," Mourn said, "so I know why you ask, but try not to overreact. I have used this ship for passage into Augran before. Crews change but the Captain is the same. He is discreet."

Gavin grunted. "And where will we be let off?"

"The *Trickster's* route will see us leave the Great Lake and sail inland by river, through the city, to Yong-wen. We will disembark there."

"Yong-wen?"

"Yes. The Yungian enclave."

Mourn looked at our faces and seemed to realize we didn't know anything about the city. "Apologies. Let me begin again. Augran is the largest Human settlement I am familiar with, larger than Manalar, Yong-ch'hai, and even Ennikar, for it has four quadrants, each a city unto itself, but they have grown enough to merge."

I was about to ask for details when Gavin interjected skeptically, "Are you 'familiar' with Ennikar?"

Mourn shook his head firmly. "No. I am familiar with Manalar and Yong-ch'hai. I have run the perimeter of Ennikar without getting caught. I have also visited Yung-An and their cities on the Sea of Fish, and Noiri Dargevold along the Dragon Coast."

Dragon Coast. He must enjoy that.

"*Are* there a lot of Dragons along the 'Dragon' Coast?" I asked.

Mourn smiled. "No. Just a lot of stone."

Hmph.

Abruptly, the shouting and thumping boots above us heightened, and I tensed as several loud noises I couldn't identify captured all my attention.

"We are setting sail," Mourn told me.

Just as the boat tilted and groaned, I grabbed on to a crate and asked for distraction. "What about Taiding? Have you been there?"

"I am familiar with the Dwarven city. With all the big cities on the Lake's shore."

"Have you been everywhere?" the Deathwalker asked.

The Dragonchild's Human smile seemed genuine rather than threatening, like he was pleased to answer. "No, but I have kept myself busy the last three centuries. I have yet to reach the cities of the Southwest, Break Water and Salton Deep, but Ahj-Zayr on the South Sea has been relevant to travel to recently."

I watched Gavin's face as he removed his grimoire and bluelight knucklebone, opening the book to turn a few pages like he was checking something. I had to take it on his superior knowledge of the Surface world that this covered immense distance and yet *still* didn't cover the land as anyone knew it.

As water shushed outside and the ship drifted and settled down, I tried to picture this Surface if I had a larger map made by Shyntre. One place was missing. The Sorcerer said it was to the Southeast.

"What of the Red Desert?"

Mourn's smile faded. "I have seen it briefly. There are no cities of appreciable size."

I squinted. "You like 'cities.'"

"I do. I am drawn to them."

"Why? You're curious?"

"There is that." Mourn shrugged. "I can spend time alone out in the wilderness as needed, but I always feel the urge to locate and explore a settlement. I have no cause to resist it."

Not with his illusion ability, no. I smirked. "Not a Druid, then."

"Absolutely not," he agreed. "It is difficult to drag a Druid into a place the size of Augran."

I bit my tongue rather than draw the obvious comparison between him and Tamuril's mysterious sister. "And Augran is essentially four cities in one, you said?"

"Yes." He extended his fingers one at a time. "Alran, Bor, Niss, and Yong-wen."

We both noticed Gavin making a quick cross shape in his book and taking notes. I leaned to watch him draw the square; Mourn waited until Gavin paused and looked up before continuing.

"Alran is the Northeast quadrant, most heavily used by the Dwarves and Noiri Humans. To be expected, as it rests on their side of the Great Lake, North and East."

Gavin's quill scratched across the page.

"Niss is the opposite side of the shore, Northwest, and heavily Paxian. Recent escapees, exiles, or the excommunicated from Manalar are showing up there. This part of Augran is changing quickly right now."

"Hmm," the scholar grunted without looking up.

"Bor is Southeast and tends to be a mix of older traditions of Paxian and Noiri and some Dwarven." Mourn paused. "At times, Kurgan also come off the Steppes from that direction."

Gavin's quill stopped, and I looked at Mourn.

"What?" he asked.

"*More* 'breeds' of Humans?" I added, my pitch going up without meaning it.

The half-blood chuckled at me, and I was glad the sailors were busy working and couldn't hear us talking down in the hold.

"Yes, another breed, although Kurgan is a loose name for many nomadic tribes. They don't build cities. Their horses and their dogs are more valuable to them than any gold coin."

"Interesting," Gavin said. "I have never heard of them."

Mourn looked at him. "Their stories don't have far reach off the Eastern Steppes. They do not talk to outsiders beyond brief trade meetings on neutral ground. Ironically, I've begun to see evidence that the Kurgan are surprisingly strong deterrents to the Ma'ab spreading down into the Steppes and the Green Sea to the East. This is why Taiding, Augran, and Manalar are the Ma'ab's preferred targets. I believe the tribes' sole focus the last two centuries is disrupting Ma'ab communications and raiding any new settlements, so they don't gain a foothold."

Gavin made a face. "I am surprised the Ascended allow that for so long."

"Perhaps it is not a long time to the Ascended," Mourn countered like he enjoyed the discussion. "The evidence suggests the Kurgan may also have death magic of a greater strength and consistency than the Noiri, and this may be why they were not overrun like them. Numerous, fast, with no center to attack, and able to match the Ma'ab with their methods on the battlefield."

"Hm. Intriguing."

More scritching.

I sighed, counting on my fingers. "Paxian, Ma'ab, Zauyrian—"

"Sal-zayr," Mourn corrected me.

"Mm-hm. Noiri, Yungian, and now Kurgan?"

"Yes. There may be another breed around Break Water."

I rubbed my face. "When did they get so numerous?"

And why were the Elves mostly unseen? Rithal shared his oldest tales as claiming the Elves, Dwarves, and Orcs came first, but the young, short-lived race grew so widespread and so fast.

The two males chose to take my question as rhetorical.

"So Augran is Alran, Niss, Bor, and Yong-wen," Gavin prompted, waving his stylus at the half-blood.

"Yes."

"Tell me about Yong-wen."

"This is the newest enclave, not yet three hundred years old while the rest of the city is over a thousand. Yungian settlers from Yung-An moved inland to the Southwest. This is why we must sail inland from the lake to get to them."

"How far?" I asked.

"Only takes a morning."

Gavin asked, "Any particular prompt why settlers from the North and West came all the way down here?"

Mourn had an expression that, in his Noiri Human form, I could not easily interpret. Perhaps I wouldn't with his half-Dragon face, either. "Hmm. Well…"

The death mage crossed his wrists to rest above his book and waited.

"The 'prompt' was me," said the exile from the Deepearth. "Nothing dramatic. No singular event or war. Just… encouraging trade."

My curiosity tingled all the way up my spine. Yung-An was notable in his history on the Surface. "Did you meet the Yungians first? When you escaped the underground?"

Mourn dipped his chin but did not elaborate.

"You seem involved in Human events. Maybe Dwarven ones, too?"

"I like cities," he repeated.

Indeed, he'd gotten us through Port Fortnight and discretely onto a ship with truly little trouble. Nothing like the previous group leading me into a tiny town of loggers.

Gavin shifted. "And why is disembarking at Yong-wen among Yungians better than getting off around other Paxian and Noiri to match our appearances?"

Mourn nodded to acknowledge the question. "Fewer eyes overall, others which will avert their gaze if they happen to glimpse a magical aura. Yungians collectively give mages and 'spirits' more privacy and deference than the other breeds of the city. It is part of their culture. Those who act alone to offend the spirits are shunned. With the right introduction, you and Sirana may be able to show your real form and be treated as extraordinary guests with whom to make a good impression."

I narrowed my eyes suspiciously. "What does 'yong-wen' mean in Trade?"

Mourn smirked at me. "City of the Dragon Spirit."

"I knew it," I accused. "You 'encouraged' its growth in more ways than trade!"

"You might be glad for that, Red Sister."

I narrowed my eyes. "Do you claim ownership of Yong-wen?"

He pointed a claw at me. "That, I do not. The Humans run themselves, better not to be involved in their daily doings."

"Just profit from it."

Mourn chuckled and opened his hand to wave it over Gavin's rough, new map. "In contrast, the older parts of the city have long, deeply woven bonds formed centuries before I arrived. They are based solely on the merchant class and their history. There has never been a 'king' of Augran; though many have tried, none have kept it. Men can build and destroy networks in one lifetime, and gain or lose fortunes on fortune's whim.

"It can be exceedingly difficult to wander around long before being noticed if something seems strange about you. Any of them might act on individual suspicion or report information for a larger and coordinated confrontation. In fact, this is encouraged and gathers a mob quickly. You saw this in Troshin Bend, yes?"

Nodding sullenly, I asked, "Is there a 'king' of Yong-wen?"

"Yes, but he is far away, on the other side of the Great Lake at Yong-ch'hai. The tradition of the king currying favor with 'spirits' remains, but the people here can live on networks and fortune like the rest of Augran. You will find this blended order easier to exist in safety than most places of the city."

This was a lot of information to take in. I was hungry but growing tired as well from consciously controlling the troublesome anxiety born from the constant shift of the boat. Gavin asked no further questions for now; I watched him put away his glowing knucklebone and writing supplies then settle down with one of those spare blankets.

Was he going to sleep?

"I should meditate on this," was all he said before closing his eyes.

Within moments, I was convinced he wasn't aware of us anymore.

★Eat and rest, if you wish,★ Mourn signed to me, getting down onto the floor and leaning against a rough woven sack stuffed with what sounded like hard pebbles. ★There is naught to do for now.★

I was surprised that I understood him; I took that extra tick to be sure. My hands replied, ★You know the silent tongue?★

He signed an affirmative.

★As with your speech there are differences, but the overall language was kept intact.★

★Yes.★

I pursed my mouth. ★Sivaraus came first.★

He didn't blink those blue eyes. ★Correct.★

★When did we split?★

Mourn paused and shook his head. ★No one in Vuthra'tern remembers. If none in Sivaraus know then only my sire does, now.★

I added wryly, ★But like refusing to remove those bracers, I wager he refused to tell you when it was, and that you do not know why.★

His expression shifted closer to stone. ★Correct.★

I weighed my next sign. ★Do you interact with him often? The Black Dragon?★

Blue eyes slid away to study one of many rope knots and straps keeping things in place. *Not often.*

But this Dragon's son *had* met his sire in the flesh, though his mother had died in birth, leaving him to the non-existent mercy of a Priestess of Braqth who'd broken from our Valsharess some unknown time ago.

At least five centuries, probably more unless Mourn was conceived in celebration of that severance. Then they promptly forgot what just occurred...? No, it must be longer than five.

This assumed Mourn was truthful about everything he'd told me from before his escape, which was little, all things considered. Basic truths of how he came into being and how he was here. He'd had a chance to mislead me about Tamuril's sister but did not deny her existence; he'd simply told me to mind my business.

Even offering small tidbits about his living on the Surface, Mourn had kept his word and had not asked about my mission after I'd run from the camp. He had not asked about a bargain between us, either. Gavin's value alone was good enough to make this journey.

What do I want?

Help in finding news about Jael at Manalar. Help locating her, for certain, but what of asking for aid to help finish her mission, so she could be free to come with me? That depended largely on what it was. If it was possible, or not too late.

For any of that to do any good to her—to us both—I needed not only a teacher about Humans but a defender against their fear and greed as well. Mourn had shown with clear extravagance that he could provide the service.

And what will I give him to receive it?

I still didn't know.

Mourn did not pick up our silent conversation when it stopped, and I dug into my stores to eat, slow and careful, as I grew accustomed to the movement of the ship. Gavin did not toss or turn in sleep as he used to; he was as unmoving as Nightmare when we didn't think about moving her.

After I'd finished and secured my food, I closed my eyes, my chin dropped down. My belly cooperated, and I breathed deeply to relax.

At some point, when I wasn't searching for it, I slipped into Reverie while sitting upright.

CHAPTER 12

THERE WAS TOO MUCH WATER TO WALK THE DRY SAND, TOO much cold rain to build a warm fire, too strong a whipping spray to prevent the wind from stabbing like needles. How ironic that we needed water every day, and yet I was trapped when there was too much of it and only wanted it to go away.

I was trapped on an island of sensations too strong to escape, my hair plastered to my skull. The chain of storms along the horizon held no end. Far out among spear-tipped waves, a giant, purple pincerworm breached the surface and dove down again, and I froze in place. There was nowhere to run on the island; I could only panic in circles.

If I hold still, maybe it won't see me.

To my left, a wave tumbled forward, throwing itself upon a small, red gem glittering like a beacon. The water pushed the necklace higher up onto the island before dragging it partway to the deep. I looked out at sea, saw no creature. Darting forward, I snatched up the half-buried necklace in a clump of saturated sand which fell from my fingers to land in heavy splats. My breasts ached as my nipples pulled tight and hard.

Sssirrranna…

Soul Drinker?

My heart drowned out all but the lowest of distant thunder. I wiped greyish mud off the glossy red surface, subtle vibrations caressing my fingers as the demon called to me.

*Where are you? I sense you close… Reach out to me. I have something to tell you about the Dragonchild. Something you **must** know.*

Rain streamed down my skin, through my hair, and I shivered with cold. Fear. I was not strong enough yet.

Come, come. Are you hiding? I am sorry the warp rot was so difficult, but you did well. You were tough to the end! Brave Red Sister!

In my periphery, I saw the pincerworm again; far out in the water but closer to where I stood. Behind me were no trees in which I could hide off the beach; this was not a forested isle. There were grasses covering the hills, long and waving in gold and green, and many rocks with dark, straggly shrubs reaching up stubbornly between them.

Nowhere to hide. Breathe slow. Don't move.

On the Surface, I shared color with shadow. With all these dulled noses and sight inured to the light, my silent stillness so often worked. With my limbs together, ruby clutched to my bare chest, I hoped to resemble the deep crease of a boulder with a streak of quartz.

Sirrannaaa! I know you hear me! If you fear for your unborn, your time is thin! The longer you stay near the Dragonchild, the harder it will be to hide from the To'vah.

Why would I want to do that?

As if hearing my question, Soul Drinker continued. *The mercenary may not intend it, but he would show them what you do not want them to see. I tried to protect you when he first appeared, but that infernal geas interfered.*

My heart refused to slow, and again the sea monster showed itself to my right, this time leaping impossibly high above the turbulent surface of the lake, continuing to rise up to the storm clouds. Massive wings opened up, the underside paler than the rest of the body, the tail long and curving like wind trails.

Not a pincerworm.

A Dragon.

Ssirrana! Listen! I can help you to stay unseen from their prying gaze.

I wanted to sprint the opposite way from that flying beast. I wanted it more than my thirstiest drink of water.

Don't move!!

My eyes fixed to the armor of scales which appeared hard as amethyst. Wings beat the air, long body flowing past me. It did not bank toward me. Soul Drinker could scream into the Void as it liked; I would stay in place until nightfall, if need be.

Then, as the Dragon circled the island from the sky far to my right, the rain eased, and a bank of grey mist rolled down the hills from behind me. I welcomed it, that rising haze obscuring me, flowing first around my legs like a cool, gentle breeze. The patter of innumerable droplets was suspended in silence, submerging me in fog. The ruby stopped quivering in my palm; Soul Drinker had quieted.

Should the amethyst beast dive now, at least I would not see it coming.

The mist swirled as I turned carefully in place, my ears straining for any breath or shift besides my own. I was naked, a dark silhouette within a light backdrop. When I stumbled upon another figure sitting cross-legged on the sand in front of me, I started in fright and bit off my gasp.

It was not just thin or emaciated, but a skeleton picked clean of flesh. The bones were visibly longer and thicker than a Davrin, the dark cranium like a tall, blunt club. The skull twisted on its exposed spine and leveled empty sockets at me as if it could still see.

Then it climbed to its feet, smooth, slow, and deliberate.

The urge to pee or weep rose strong, but I pushed past it. I'd first seen grey clouds from afar in Reverie, but now I was in them. I knew who my ally was, and he would always be tied to images of death. It was not the existence of which mortals feared; we saw it every day to eat. We feared the pain before our own death. *Alone.*

I understood this.

A skeleton was not in pain. It was far beyond it.

I reached out first, as I had refused the black dagger. ~*Gavin? Is it you?*~

The black skull tilted to one side; there were no lips or tongue to form words, so it replied in kind. *We journey faster than expected to where we await ourselves.*

There arose the tiniest trickle of doubt. It *sounded* like him, somewhat, but I could not make sense of the riddle. I wanted a plainer response. ~*Did you see the purple Dragon? Did you or your mistress send the clouds to help us hide?*~

The articulated bones stood without reaction or response at first. In the quiet, I noted the odd, sharp points or edges in the form, some glossy facets, like it was not pure bone but laced with that odd flint. Like Jacob's soul shard.

Its next thought came as if our minds shared space. *You are simply here, Sirana.*

My heartbeat was muffled inside this mist. ~*You know me. And you are Gavin? Tell me. I cannot see your face.*~

No, I suppose you cannot yet.

We heard distant snarls then, somewhere beyond the mist. It put to my mind two wary predators facing off, but my ears could not pinpoint their location. Worrying. More so when I remembered that the skeleton had not answered my question.

~*What do you see in my unborn?*~ I asked.

The skeleton lowered its eye sockets at my middle in contemplation, and I smiled. It *was* him, although what he thought next added little comfort.

Learning.

My smile became a grimace, the black bones continued to speak with teeth flush and jaw immobile.

You entered the grey unseen, though someone tried to follow you. The harm is unknown but unavoidable if they succeed.

~And if I didn't know how I got here?~ I responded. ~What should I do now?~

Somehow, the sightless skull communicated baffled surprise. *If you must ask what you already know, then choose your guardian and make it known. Soon.*

I frowned. ~One other than you?~

I am not your guardian. And we are in a turbulent place for you to remain uncertain.

~I do not know enough truth to **be** certain!~ I blurted. ~Everything changes, every time I wake up, and I do not know where I stand. It seems I only grasp my lack in all I do not know, from sand to water to horses and boats. I dream of lies and truths both kept from me, and it is from **these** I must choose!~

Gavin's skeleton paused again. *I remember. Yes.* The skull twisted to one side. *Often that was when I picked up the older tools. The first ones I found for better or worse, to mark the ground where I could rest.*

I huffed sardonically, listening to the waves beyond my sight as the sand seemed to tilt like a ship. ~I am not on the ground to mark it.~

Indeed, not.

Gavin's attention turned to one side. As I followed his empty gaze, I spotted a shrouded woman in the mist, gauzy veils obscuring her face. Tattered, undyed cloth wrapped simply about her small body, practical as a monk. I knew her. She was there the last time I'd invaded Gavin's memory, when I'd been found out. Her voice whispered distantly, *When shall we become?*

Shit. Had I done it again? Now I wanted to leave. This standing in the mist was getting me nowhere.

~How do I escape this isle without harm to Gavin, me, or my baby?~ I asked her.

Wordlessly, the woman pointed in a direction, and an instant later, the massive flyer's snarl aligned with her arm.

Uh-oh. I checked that my hand clutched the ruby. *~And if they see me?~*

She held her pale hand out toward the black skeleton man, who thought nothing I could hear. They waited.

Sigh.

I turned in the mist and hurried toward my guiding sound, quickly discovering the faster I sprinted, the sharper my ears became amid the growls and rumbles filling the grey. Within the blurry haze, I could judge the shape and height of the isle's treeless hills without my eyes, as I could underground or like in the canyon after Kurn's thunderstone struck.

I did not slow, for my swift and light touch with my feet meant a quicker recovery if I skidded or tripped. For as long as I made less noise than the beasts above me, they covered my escape.

Escape from whom or where—*or when*—I had only a fragment of a clue.

I OPENED MY EYES LYING NEXT TO A DISCONCERTINGLY COOL, Human body who did not seem to be breathing. His eyes were closed, his long, pointed nose aimed toward the creaking ceiling. My arm was outstretched and trapped beneath his tan-brown neck, gripping tough leather and bulk of something next to his far shoulder where I could not see at first.

As was often the case, I did not have to look to figure it out. I could feel my spiders crawling over my wrist, nestling, tickling me on purpose. They were trying to get my attention.

Ssirranna… Can you hear me?

Fuck.

Gavin lay heavy and comatose, breathing only once every several minutes as I watched and waited like a frightened rabbit. I slowly lost feeling in my arm, which removed the stubbornness of my grip, and I tugged like a tree-gnawer attempting to extricate its limb from a trap.

Sssooo clossse…

I rolled away from Gavin, my brow damp with sweat, as I waited for my arm to cease tingling before testing the flex of my fingers again.

"Damn you," I whispered.

My guardians had hopped off when I pulled free, crossing over Gavin's chest to join me. I was able to see the bundle containing the red rune blade partly extracted from Gavin's pack, one of the knots loosened by plucking fingers. Presumably, mine as I slept.

I considered reaching for those leather thongs—to retie the knot, to prove I'd won the test of wills again, and I could return it how it had been. I could prove I didn't need Gavin or Mourn to do it for me like some weak woman or child, couldn't I? I scoffed at myself, reaching immediately for my food. Just hubris goading me, for I hadn't stopped looking for a way to approach the bundle safely.

There is no safe way. Soul Drinker would only laugh.

I ate a lot; it took a while to quiet my rudely woken stomach. As I sipped the good water which recalled for me the peaceful river where we'd stayed, I told my fretting spiders, ~I am fine. Nothing bad happened.~

This time.

After I'd used the relief bucket as well, an odd rumble sounded above me on the deck. I thought instantly of my dream. The shrouded woman pointing a way to escape without harm to Gavin, me, or my unborn. As I'd woken reaching for Soul Drinker as it spoke to me, could there be something to this waking sound, something real infiltrating my dreams as the rune dagger had or as I had done to Gavin?

I peered around the hold, at the reclined man and his steed wobbling on her hooves, at the cargo shifting within its ropes. What time of night was it? It was not day; the hold did not have a hint of diffused sunlight leaking through the closed cargo door which doubled as the deck.

Where is Mourn, anyway?

The rumble above came again, and I secured my food after grabbing a snack pouch, rolling with the ship to gain my feet, and moved quickly to resist drifting to one side. I took to the ladder as the in-motion alternative to the loading ramp, which was inaccessible after having been winched up against the underside of the deck.

Two small platforms up, I listened outside the trap door before peeking out, spotting the last, retreating daylight behind the ship. How odd it must seem that the *Trickster's* passengers went willingly down into the cargo hold and stayed put for the entire day. I should *not* have slept so long, from dawn to dusk. That was longer than any healthy Human, longer than when I'd been at my most ill following the warp rot cleansing.

What happened?

Should I be worried? Had Gavin been "meditating" all this time or had he risen while I slept then returned later? Was something wrong with him? Should I go check?

And do what? Check his pulse? Press on his heart to make it beat? It's not like I have another silver dagger to remove.

I sighed, watching the evening activity. I was sure Mourn wasn't down here, and neither Gavin nor Nightmare made any noise, yet plenty of smelly men worked on deck by lantern light, shouting to each other and plodding heavily atop the damp boards.

I smelled hot food being prepared somewhere nearby, motivating the crew to finish up. I waited until most shuffled off to the mess for their meal. I did not glimpse Mourn's Noiri face among them.

Has he changed his face again?

As the first stars shone through gradually dissipating clouds in a moonless sky, I left the hold with hood up, guardians again beneath my hair, trying not to look too far out at the vastness after glimpsing no land. The air was certainly fresher than below, and the ship seemed to cut through the water at great speed. I avoided the railing where the shush of the water below was loudest.

There was a plethora of deeper shadows to aim for which helped me focus and evade a random sailor. Hugging them and the center of the vessel, I stepped as light as I could on a constantly moving vessel, swallowing down a lurch in my stomach.

The front of the ship was empty of men for now; no one stood at the railing, though my straining ears again detected that low, dream-like rumble toward the rear, up on that higher deck. I reversed course and followed the sound, approaching the stairs with caution as I believed a low male voice responded. I questioned my certainty that it had been an answer to a question; I questioned if these were real words, at all.

Eventually, I peeked onto the upper deck. *There he is.*

The black-haired Noiri was frowning at the center point of the deck, his shoulders squared, hands fisted loosely. I rather wished I could see whether his tail would be dancing or not. Then he turned his head my way and breathed out like he'd been holding it and made a gesture of greeting that a Davrin would understand.

I climbed the rest of the stairs, looked around, and found us alone.

"Sleep well?" he asked, approaching the railing, resting his weight on his elbows and looking out at the water.

I arched one brow, sweeping the deck again with my senses. "With whom were you speaking?"

Mourn tilted his head. "No one. I've eaten. Just relaxing."

"Oh, really?" I approached on his right side, neither touching the railing nor glancing down at the rippling lake. *Ugh.* "It seemed the right time to leave Gavin and me unconscious? There was nothing unfortunate that could happen?"

"Your spiders were guarding you," he pointed out. "You were safe."

"Ah. I fell asleep with them secured. *You* let them out?"

"I did."

I narrowed my eyes. "I heard something, first down below and then above. A rumble. Too low to say what it was, but I thought it came from you, or one around here. You acted like someone was here."

Mourn's surprise seemed real. "Hm. Could have been the ship groaning."

"Do not insult me, mercenary."

"Or it was the song of a deep swimmer below our feet."

"Unpleasant to imagine."

"But true. They exist."

"Under my feet is *not* its origin, and you are deflecting." I crossed my arms. "Can you offer anything other than I was 'imagining' it, *bua?*"

Mourn shrugged, his Human mouth in a straight line. "The Great Lake has many mysteries. Sailing near the Archipelago can bring strange dreams to mages sensitive to the Ley Lines. I do not doubt the Deathwalker will see things. And now you, apparently."

I frowned. Should I tell him about the dream I'd had? *Or is that privacy for Gavin like in the shed?* "I say again, I am not a mage."

The half-breed checked around us then hand signed, ★You are a Baenar who uses magic gems. That may be enough.★

I exhaled but ignored the oblique reference to the Ma'ab ruby. ★Has it begun, the place of strange dreams?★

Mourn decided to speak this part in Trade. "It seems so. We are making faster time than the Captain expected. The next three days could see different dangers arise: a sudden storm, reverse currents or whirlpools, hidden reefs just below the surface at low tide. This was the quiet day, though the two on the far side of the island chain should be better as well. I am glad you were able to rest."

I smirked, gingerly resting on my elbows as well, mimicking how the hybrid was moving with the ship. Better. I wasn't fighting it every moment.

"Seems all I am doing around you is resting. How could I sleep all day this first time on a ship? You did not do anything to encourage it, did you?"

★Not beyond feeding some rats to the horse to keep her smell down,★ he replied in sign with a straight face. ★It seems clear to me why. If you rested only a quarter of each night since you surfaced, were never safe among the men you travelled with, suffered at their hands when in dire need of escape—★

I lifted one hand. ★You may cease bringing that up. It is not an excuse for continued weakness.★

Mourn seemed to weigh debating that but chose the practical part first. ★Even without the daily threat, fighter-matas *will* need longer rest than a fighter on her own, sooner or later. The lack of it compounds on itself until she falls into Reverie for a week.★

The hybrid stopped signing while I chewed on my cheek in thought. ★You have experience with fighter-matas?★

His massive shoulders lifted. ★A little.★

★A squadmate? You mentioned those.★

He nodded but, unlike when Gavin had asked about cities, Mourn was not eager to explain. Instead, he finally asked the inevitable.

"I have most of what I need to close my contracts with the Ma'ab in Augran. I am only missing the *Ridhian*."

My hand grappled for the ruby in my pouch. *There it is.*

"You know its name?"

He levelled a dry look at me. "I am surprised you do."

Another test, damn him.

"Soul Drinker told me."

"Ah. Your resistance to giving it up makes sense."

"What, because I'm listening to the dagger?" I retorted. "No, it made sense *before* that. I told you, the Ma'ab and the Deathless used it against me three or four times!"

"That many?"

I couldn't tell if Mourn intended to play ignorant to keep me talking, but it worked as I snarled in frustration. "You watched us the first time in the canyon!"

"Yes. Your resistance while trapped in the webbing was impressive."

"But not without its limits."

"I believe you. What of the other attempts?"

"Inside the inn where you didn't see. First the sorcerer in his quarters, then him *and* the Ma'ab trying harder in a pile!"

His mouth tightened; he lowered his gaze briefly. "I *am* sorry this happened, Sirana. I underestimated both the innkeeper's threat to you and the strength of your alliance with the Deathwalker. I expected you to leave quickly. As I hear more what occurred and why you stayed, I am amazed it did not go worse."

"But it could have gone *better*," I said, tinged with bitterness. "Any pregnant Davrin would have 'finished' it, remember?"

He did not blink at being reminded. "I regret that I questioned your actions. I did not know of the rape when I said that. There is no 'better' way to act after surviving that violence on body and mind. As you remind me, I wasn't there. I *would* have interfered had I been but, given my own path to survival, I might have also provoked something for which none were prepared, if this Deathless is what you say."

Another oblique reference to his Matron-Aunt? Or something else? I shook my head and shrugged, trying to calm down. Despite my insistence that the attack in the kitchen was not an excuse for my recent lethargy, I was certainly talking about it a lot.

And he's listening. Drawing back on his assumptions without reluctance or hubris. *He has nothing to prove.*

"I have no idea *what* the Deathless is," I said, ready to move on. "I only met Cris-ri-phon in disguise, and he had been 'asleep' for a long time."

Mourn checked around us again for lurkers. I did the same. Then he asked, "Did the sorcerer tell you how he came to his immortality?"

"No. I am not certain *he* knows, but the relic is a strong motive to search for and keep, for he'd gifted it to his queen once, earned on a quest to be worthy. Brom Troshin recruited the Ma'ab to help him find it again in this last century."

And he might have recently spoken with that queen, if she's real…

"How did you learn this?"

"From him, from his Ma'ab daughter, the relic itself." I paused, but didn't add, *From his dreams.*

"Do you have any hint at all how it started?"

My mouth split into an ironic smile. "With a 'wedding,' I heard, followed by half-blood children born to a Davrin queen. Many were hostile to this but hid their faces from view. Eventually, the queen and her children were assassinated. Cris-ri-phon lived, somehow."

Though, what had this to do with my dream of him and Toushek meeting that skeleton in the isolated prison? I didn't know which happened first.

Mourn let the silence stretch but returned to where we started soon enough. "Sirana, what do you want for the ruby pendant?"

I don't know.

"Start with where it came from," I said. "Given how much trouble it's caused me."

He sighed. "Kurn Divigna stole the *Ridhian* after raping and killing a Ma'ab sorceress. The noble family wants it returned. That is part of my contract, in addition to Kurn's torment and his execution, along with Castis who aided in the theft and tried to hide the evidence. I must keep my bargains, so I would like to bargain with you. What do you want for it?"

My first impulse was that I wanted nothing for it if only Ma'ab wanted it. I hissed, "You can well imagine what the 'family' will do with it. Have they any more restraint than the one who stole it?"

The half-blood shrugged. "No. But that is not required to take a contract." He saw my stubborn look. "We will know where it is. It can always be stolen again, if someone were to hire for that task."

Offense burned in my gut, and I clutched the ruby harder. "What a ridiculous use of time, Dragonblood, to lose sight of an item hard-won so you can close a contract, and then go to steal it again!"

Mourn's Human face smiled with genuine amusement. "Sometimes it is necessary. I grant that a *mata* intercepting someone at a siege does not have decades stretching before her to plan her aspirations, although you might find it less ridiculous if you were in my place."

"I am not greedy like you, To'vah-krav. I do not care about building wealth with bargains and contracts. Such narrow pursuit of objects only brings trouble, from what I've seen."

The mercenary chose not to debate that, but he did use it. "Then surely there is something of less tangible worth to you, that I may trade with you instead of tricking or stealing from you."

"You said no stealing."

His gaze levelled, and I thought I saw a glimpse of metallic gold in his blue eyes. "I would rather not. But, fair warning, Sirana, that is up to a point, and only regarding the *Ridhian*. I would steal this ruby from you to complete my contract if you refuse to bargain."

I gritted my teeth behind my lips. As Gavin predicted, Mourn had been humoring me, willing to let me ask for something I wanted before giving up something I couldn't keep. *He's made it clear as crystal.*

This wasn't any different from what Wilsira would say to a lesser Noble, was it? My mouth tight, I asked, "Any similar plans for the Desert dagger?"

"Not at this time," he answered readily. "Though it's possible, giving this type of object enough time and exposure, someone else could make a bargain before you."

Goddess-damned, insufferable rough-skinned…

"Why ask to bargain now?" I demanded.

"You have shown me you are not only a vivid dreamer on calm days," he answered seriously, "but sensitive to the Ley of the Archipelago. I have run out of time waiting on you to bring it up first."

"What?" I laughed. "What do vivid dreams have to do with a magic ruby?"

Mourn just studied me for a moment; perhaps he could tell I knew more than I said. Then he said, "You are attuned to it, and it was the dark relic that told you its name. The dagger will likely attempt to use any Ley flux among the isles to snare you and coax you to draw it again. Had I known this, I'd have not left you alone down below. I apologize, I will not do that again."

I tossed my chin. "You are trying to frighten me into trading it."

"We *both* know demons," he growled. "Tell me you do *not* see it willing and eager to try this. And you have no defense."

"And if I just give it to you," I replied, "I *still* have no defense!"

"Is that it? You think to use it in defense of the relic?"

"Can it be done? Will you teach me?"

He grimaced as I clasped at anything. "I am not sure. Nor would we have time. The isle maze is ahead, and I must close my contract at Augran. I would rather bargain for your defense a different way."

I ground my teeth, fingers clutching the railing through my gloves, caught in indecision as I closed my eyes against the constant motion beneath us.

Where is the truth? Where are the lies?

Mourn looked behind me, and I expected some sailor to be butting in where he wasn't wanted.

"Deathwalker." He nodded in greeting. "Is something wrong?"

I turned quickly, spying the hooded monk coming toward us…

Holding Kurn's sword.

It was sheathed, and the death mage held it single-handed just beneath the cross guard. I couldn't see his eyes as he looked down at his feet climbing the stairs.

He spoke as he approached us. "Not for me. I wondered, mercenary, if you would bargain for this sword?"

What?

I glanced at Mourn. Whether he meant to show it or not, he was quite interested.

I hissed at my scholar, "What are you doing?"

"No harm to you," Gavin said, lifting the Ma'ab's sword where it could be better seen. He also carried the satchel which would contain his grimoire and Soul Drinker.

"May I inspect it?" Mourn asked, holding out his hand. "I will not keep it unless we are agreed to trade."

"For what?" I demanded between them.

"I don't know, Baenar, he hasn't said."

Gavin offered the sword two-handed to the Dragon's son, who took it and pulled the blade free, handling the weapon with ease. I spotted his Human tongue flicking out to taste the air around it.

The death mage spoke plainly. "I would like to trade it for the sapphire in your possession."

What?! That's mine!

I refrained from blurting my fury but stood bristling with my mouth open, one hand anchoring me to the railing with a vengeance.

Mourn glanced from the sword to me then to Gavin, tested the heft again, nodding with appreciation. "Any aspect of the bargain not yet spoken, Deathwalker?"

"No. One for the other, and the deal is finished. Nothing unspoken."

The Dragon son grunted. "I should clarify it is not true sapphire but a denser, non-crystallized stone which appears like it. It could fool most Humans, but a Dwarven trader would be able to tell the difference rather quickly. The two stones are not valued the same."

"Hm, interesting. Thank you for clarifying."

I outright scowled listening to the two of them barter over my stone. It took effort *not* to insert myself in the dealing, because I didn't know what Gavin intended yet. I bit my cheek and waited.

Mourn seemed to notice, sly eyes flicking to me again before one final inspection of Kurn's blade. He withdrew my pendant from a different pouch than where I thought it had been. "Done."

He made the motion to toss it, offering Gavin the moment to prepare before gently lobbing the stone past me to the Deathwalker, who caught it.

"Thank you." Gavin turned it over, using all ten long fingers to trace its shape in the dark shadow of the rear deck. "Ah. A crescent moon. Skilled work."

Now he's taunting me.

I waited for the death mage to ask me next to trade him the ruby for the saphgar, which he would then give to Mourn and be done with our argument. I discarded several things I would say in reply, distracted when the ship started to lean again.

If I wouldn't trade the ruby to Mourn for the blue stone, what makes you think I'll do the same with you only to see my wishes circumvented? I'm not that stupid.

Gavin placed the blue pendant in his pocket, nodding in satisfaction.

I blinked, palming my face. *Arrrgh…*

"Are there legends of an amethyst Dragon in the Archipelago?" Gavin asked, looking out at the water with less apparent trepidation than I felt.

Mourn had attached the sword to a belt I knew he didn't wear with his harness, but it was his turn to blink in surprise. "Um. Yes, quite a few."

"Perhaps that explains my dream."

"For certain," I offered. "Mourn told me your dreams may be stranger the next three days, as mystics like you are sensitive to its flux."

Gavin pondered. "Indeed? Good to know."

"Mystics?" Mourn asked me.

"Yes," I said, glad to feel a solid grip somewhere. "The mages who see glimpses of chaos, yes? Not every mage does."

I'd made an impression on him.

"Where did you learn that word for such an affinity, Sirana?"

He sounded curious.

"Osgrid," I said. "A Dwarven eve witch outside Troshin Bend. She was mystic and said Gavin was, too, from looking at his book. If she took my advice, she has left her cottage in the woods rather than stay to take the blame for what happened."

The mercenary nodded in agreement. "I hope so."

"I do not know where she would have gone," I continued, "but Rithal mentioned meeting her in Augran when he fled?"

"Yes, I recall."

"And you weren't surprised when I mentioned her in connection with *genethsa*. I wanted to ask if you have spoken with her as well in your travels?"

Mourn considered that. "She would recognize one of my faces, yes."

"Cris-ri-phon accused her of reporting his doings to the 'Guild' of Augran. Is that true?"

"Probably," Mourn granted. "We were both outcasts with links to the Guild, so we traded information on occasion. She knew I wasn't Human but did not insist on seeing my true form."

Once I'd paused in my questions, momentarily satisfied, the mercenary asked an odd one of his own. "Are there mystics in Siva-raus?"

I blinked. "What?"

Mourn pointed at Gavin. "Someone who feels like him. The Deathwalker's stranger manner or aura does not unsettle you, as he does many."

I froze, body and mind; I could not think. I did not understand why.

"There are no death mages below," I evaded.

"Nor should there be among Baenar. But there may be mystics, though I understood them to be mages who could sense simultaneous possibilities or influences. It would look like chaos or hallucinations to anyone mundane."

Hallucinations, or Visions.

I rubbed my temple rather than cover my womb, which had been my first impulse. "I am not well enough for this conversation."

"Hm. I will take it as likely but let you be."

For now.

I was too aware of the movement of the water and becoming hungry at the same time. There would be no peace between the two.

Damnit. Not again.

"I am going below," I said. "I must eat. And *not* look at ceaseless motion for a time."

Mourn nodded, and Gavin said nothing as I left. I loathed what I might miss leaving them to talk alone, but my irritability and illness were rising quickly. I reached for one of Shyntre's pellets.

I still didn't know if they were neutral or worse than they had been before the warp rot, but I just wanted to be *well*. I recalled how the Druid had not spoken of magic at all when she described using the mushroom as a base. Neither had Osgrid. They were each mages of a sort, and capable with mundane medicine, but neither were magical healers.

It was different when the medicine brewer was a mage like Gaelan. Often, there was a gesture or a word that had to go along with it to gain the full potency. There had never been anything like that for these pellets. Even Elder Rausery had complimented my wizard on his skill making 'fresh' pellets for her exploration up top.

"This is more potent than the mushroom alone," Tamuril said. "If only you knew how they are made, Sirana, you could save many lives up here from too-early deaths."

I placed one under my tongue to dissolve on this reasoning. I must know soon or else I would not keep carrying them around. If I became ill, I would alert the males. I was willing to bet Mourn kept a healing potion or two.

When I returned to the hold, I was further irritated to find my packs of food had been stolen. *Damnit, Gavin!*

My cursing did not last as I located them stored in the stall behind Nightmare, who showed me her teeth briefly, as if she would bite whoever entered. I retrieved my knucklebone talisman, and her rejuvenated lips covered those sharp teeth again. Stepping past her, I found everything as I'd left it.

Very well, good move.

While eating slowly, my nausea retreated. I wasn't sure if it was Shyntre's pellets or the food or that the tilting horizon was hidden from view, but I was glad regardless. It wasn't becoming worse.

Sooner than I expected, Gavin joined me again in the hold. Mourn had not followed him. He sat down near enough that we could talk privately. I arched my brow, waiting.

He let me have it.

"This was the second time you fled into my dreams while we are both unconscious. I recall enough of the visions and your frustrations, as well as the concerning details around me after I awoke, that I understand why. But... this cannot continue. You must gain control of this."

It felt like a stone had landed in my middle.

"I *had* better control, once," I muttered, breaking off a piece of pressed nuts and berries and placing it on my tongue.

Gavin considered. "You said you were injured, and the talent had vanished for a time."

I nodded, chewing.

"This talent is becoming stronger as you have healed from whatever happened," he said. "You have agitated Human men without intent, and they have posed a greater threat to you than they might have been without your sharing their dreams."

I was about to snarl at him for that but refrained. I could not deny it.

"I do not want to share dreams with you unbidden," he added plainly. "Mourn has been wise and has left your vicinity when you begin dreaming. He senses something but has practiced defenses which give him warning. He has agreed to teach me a few of these methods, if possible."

I ground my teeth. *Great. Both males allying against me for something none of us understand.*

"Meanwhile," Gavin continued, reaching into his pocket, and withdrawing Shyntre's pendant, "I think you need to pick up an old tool again. Rediscover how to use it."

I stared at the stone, blinked at him a few times. "What, you are *giving* it to me?"

"You need it, even if you will not ask me for it."

I looked away. "I expected you would want to trade something else for it."

Gavin considered that. "I suppose I do."

Here it comes.

I sighed, "What do you want?"

"For my returning this illusory sapphire to you, I request that you return to the Ley Tower with me to confront Sarilis, as we first bargained."

That was a long time away.

Gavin held out the pendant, but I hadn't taken it yet as I stared at him. He tilted his head. "Have you changed your mind on that?"

I was sure my lower lip quivered beyond my control, as the surge of aging, tattered dreams and their heavy chains in the geas came to the foreground.

Argh!

My spiders skittered beneath my hood as I pulled off my glove, reaching with my bare hand for not only the blue pendant but the Deathwalker's pale skin. I gripped them both, tugging his hand, and insisted he look at my eyes. He did so reluctantly.

~My Queen says I must destroy the tainted death mage at the Ley Tower before I can return home. That target is not you.~

Gavin's eyebrows lifted in surprise, and he leaned away.

Did you hear me? Please, let it be so.

I could not tell. The Deathwalker said nothing before he turned my grip so that the blue stone rested in my palm then withdrew his hand, breaking contact as soon as he could.

"The gem is yours," he said. "The deal is finished, Sirana. There is nothing unspoken on my end."

My throat closed, ached, but I nodded. There remained plenty unspoken on my end, whether I liked it or not. I smoothed my "old tool" between my thumbs, inspecting it for damage but found none. It felt good. Now maybe I could begin rebuilding that defense against Soul Drinker.

And somehow come to agreeable terms with Mourn.

"Thank you," I whispered.

CHAPTER 13

BY MIDMORNING THE NEXT DAY, I CONFIRMED SHYNTRE'S PELLETS were unspoiled and potent. Three times they soothed my churning stomach from the unseen waves and allowed me to keep my meals while I remained down in the hold. I told Mourn and Gavin this when they watched me put the third one in my mouth.

"Interesting," the Dragonchild said, bringing us our share of the morning meal, which wasn't bad and helped stretch my snack supply. "I do not recall smelling anything much like it on the Surface. Would you be willing to trade one to an apothecary I know in Augran?"

"Why?"

"She would study it. Possibly recreate it."

I squinted. "Would you care either way if I did?"

His mouth stretched; I wasn't sure if it was a smile. "Yes. A healthier childhood is better than an ill one, and stronger, skilled adults means shared labor and difficult targets for would-be tyrants to suppress a populace the size of Augran. This leads to quality wealth for me through less brutal means. I can help you barter fair payment."

Gavin spoke before I could. "Do you often plan in Human lifetimes?"

Mourn's eyes lifted to the ceiling. "One of several measures, yes. It has been useful."

The former monk added, "And you unashamedly plan to collect gold from a healthier and wealthier city over centuries?"

Fully metallic eyes appeared, shining in the half-blood's Human face; reptilian pupils expanded to show his interest. "Yes. Rare metals, precious stones, or well-made crafts of many shapes and purpose."

"Goddess," I made an exaggerated display of looking around, "where do you put it all?"

The mercenary glanced at me, seemed able to tell I was jesting, and chuckled. "I *am* my Sire's son, Baenar."

The gold color faded from his eyes as he stood up and did not stay to let us ask more about that.

The next evening arrived after having passed around and between island obstacles, no storms or strange whirlpools accosting us. Constant bootsteps sounded above my head, the men shouting at each other all day in what sounded like instructions, but Braqth bind me if I could translate it.

"Do they speak in Trade?" I asked.

Gavin did not glance up from his book. "As relevant for sailors, yes."

I squinted. "Then what is a jib? And why must they trim their heels?"

The death mage shrugged, continuing his writing. "I have never sailed before. I follow them no better than you. Perhaps ask Mourn."

I might have, but he remained up top, or "above board," most of the day. I was not sure how he entertained himself; I never heard his voice. I also neither felt the pull of Reverie nor could bring myself to leave the hold in broad daylight without need. It made for an exceptionally long day.

Eventually night fell, and I crept out again when there were fewer passengers and workers tromping about. The moonlit waters were no longer unbroken vastness; plant-covered islands dotted all around us as black shapes, their presence altering the unseen currents below and the drift of the waves up top. I could not pretend I was as sensitive to these subtleties as the working people who lived on the boat and had traveled here before, but I was no less alert for the path looking so broken and unpredictable.

By now I'd sorted out a few voices of women on the ship over those of the men by timbre alone, but I had not yet counted the five traders and three sailors Mourn claimed were here. At last, as I made my way in shadow, I noted two of the female sailors doing things with the ropes and sails, cleaning up tools and putting things in their place. This was no different from what the numerous men were always doing.

The women were "tolerated," as Mourn said, and I could tell they were stronger in body than the kitchen mother, Elana, and could match some tasks with smaller men their own size. Like me and Mourn, though, there remained tasks consistently given to the bigger bulls who were less likely to fail or injure themselves in the attempt.

I had gone to the front of the ship, looking into the eve without lanterns interfering in my periphery. My stomach was full, any motion sickness quelled with warm thoughts of my wizard and his little dirt balls. I wanted to study the stars and smell the clean air, try to guess our route and select which isles we'd be "tricking," by which the ship might glide past remarkably close. It was windier than yesterday, my hood would not stay up no matter what, so I kept my spiders safe in their pouch.

I had not a sixth of an hour at the ship's front before someone approached from behind. When I turned, she was peeking around crates of cargo. Another moment, she realized she was detected, ducked back—which made me smirk—then decided to step out plainly, confirming she was one of the sailors.

The woman had tousled, dark blonde hair, cut short but long enough to tangle and fall in her eyes. Her skin was ruddy brown and speckled with dark brown dots across her nose and cheeks and down her arms. Her drab clothes were loose for ship work, both the sleeves and pant legs rolled up to reveal forearms and calves to the air. She wasn't clean; I could smell her every time the blustering wind changed.

Paxian, I decided.

The Human shrugged her shoulders with exaggeration, showed her empty hands, and strutted forward to approach me without invitation.

What does she want? I glanced up and around in case Mourn was nearby; if he watched, he did so hidden again.

"So," she said with an odd, hoarse voice, "where's yer head veil?"

I stared. *Head veil?*

She scowled when I didn't answer. "I said, where's yer veil, Manalari cooze? No showin' yer hair, I know, an' yer a bit far from yer brother tonight."

Ah-ha.

"What is your authority to ask, sailor?" I replied, emphasizing the Davrin lilt that Mourn would consider Noble.

As expected, she second-guessed herself. It was a Manalari accent she had never heard before; I imagined she wondered what my connections were. I smiled, and her eyes narrowed. The half breed was right; blue was a common eye color up here.

"Sound rich. Bishop's spy?" she guessed. "Or one o' their sluts? Running back to tell 'em how they're fucked? North is comin' fer them but will leave Augran alone."

I hoped her intent was to insult and show contempt for Manalar, and *not* to glean information for the coming siege. If so, she was poor at it. What Mourn had said returned, that it may be safer disembarking in Yong-wen than let Paxians drift and whisper at our backs, speculating, suspicious. Hostile.

I asked, "What is your name?"

She stretched her lips, showing teeth like a dog. "What's yers?"

Hm. "Elana."

Her turn to wrinkle her nose. "*Hmph.* Spoiled rich girl name. Never worked a day in your life."

It was easy to keep my smile. Humans could be rushed and all wrong about their assumptions, but it didn't slow their words. *Worse than Davrin.*

The wind muffled many noises and maintained the risk of blowing my small guardians over the side of the railing. They were alert inside their pouch, chiming, waiting on me, but I wasn't convinced we needed to take the risk with this lone Human. *If more show up to support her.*

"And your name, sailor?" I prompted.

"Pete," she replied with clear defiance.

At first, I was reminded of the Pyte slaves down below but pushed that aside. She was waiting, hairless jaw jutting forward, fists clenched, ready to fight for some reason. It sank in that now *I* was missing something.

"What do you want?" I asked.

She spat on the deck. "You off this ship soon as possible. Don't like your cult here."

I rolled my eyes. Some of the sailors had been watching for me, apparently, though had avoided going down into the hold per the Captain's orders. And why? To issue a challenge to a proxy for the City of the Sun, while we still had four or five days left of me being on this ship. If all went well.

Meet this challenge now, or they will sneak down to disturb Gavin and me at some point.

"Do you want to fight, Pete?" I asked. "To test this night who is better?"

The blonde guffawed, slapping her thigh. "Not smart, God's dog. I'll kick your cunt drier than it is."

I grinned, swiftly closing the space between us, my hands empty. The smelly woman's eyes widened, and she brought up her fists.

She wasn't inexperienced in a brawl; she didn't fumble her first strike. In fact, she landed it, clipping my shoulder.

Lucky. But you didn't have Jaunda as an opponent in the Cloister.

I moved without thinking. *Block, deflect, strike, follow through.* One last move, I swept her footing out from under her, then toppled after her thanks to the tilt of the ship. My knee landed on her gut.

"Oof!" she grunted, eyes bulging, unable to inhale or speak as I regained my feet.

Then Mourn was there, holding his large, Human hand between me and Pete. "No more, Elana," he said. "You won."

I raised my voice above the wind. "If she picks another fight with me while I am on board, she shall regret it again."

"I do not doubt." He glanced behind him, motioning to a couple men, sailors huddled on the other side of the cabins. He said to them, "Can you take your shipmate somewhere else, please?"

Two came forward, one kneeling to pull the woman's arm across his shoulders. "Right, right. C'mon, Pete. On yer feet."

"Sorry 'bout that, m... milady," the second said to me, looking as apologetic as some buas down below. "I tried tah talk her down. She had a hard life at Manalar. Was lucky tah escape. She don't like reminders."

I quirked one eyebrow at him but said nothing as they helped the groaning woman stumble away. I glimpsed her jaw swelling. *Good.*

When they were gone, I flexed my hand and checked for a split knuckle or sprain. It had been a while since I'd thrown a straight and simple punch but had reacted properly. I was fine.

The mercenary sighed, arms crossed, and I lifted my chin and narrowed my eyes at him, daring him to criticize. "Challenges for simple tests of strength are best dealt with early and firm. And you know it."

Mourn did not counter that. "They will also remember us."

"Only by the face you gave me, and by the words Gavin taught me. I was not about to spend five days in potential storms evading a sneering woman's misplaced aggression and blame. Better she faces consequences for it like any barking dog that gets kicked."

"Hm. Well. There are other ways—"

"Oh?"

"—but they require time and patience. Perhaps next time."

"Ah. So confident there will be one?"

He was for certain suppressing a smile. "Now that I've watched you engage another aggressive female, inevitable. I ask you be wary of interpreting a woman who evades a physical confrontation with you as either weak or deserving."

Now it was my turn to suppress a smirk. "I know better than to assume either, *bua*. Believe me."

Mourn may have been suspicious or curious about that remark, but not enough to hold his attention as he looked out to the Archipelago. The wind once keeping my spiders tucked away had dropped off suddenly, and I realized all sources of night-light beyond the glow of a lantern were gone. The moons and stars were covered by clouds. The isles were fuzzy, amorphous blotches amid the black, trembling water.

"Mm," he said.

"What?"

"I am climbing to the crow's nest."

I blinked. "The *what?*"

"I'll return soon. Try not to gleefully accept another fight while I'm gone."

"Very amusing."

I watched as the mercenary moved quickly to the main mast, passing for a capable man instead of the decidedly inhuman half-blood I'd watched hunting pigs on a riverbank. Mourn began scaling the rungs which led him up to disappear among the sails and rigging. It was only as I kept my eyes upon the sky and tracked his progress that I spotted the obvious lookout basket built at the top. It was easily the highest vantage point on the entire ship and large enough to hold two men snugly.

Crow's nest. Heh.

The subtle fragrance of the surrounding isles came to me then with the wind calmer and the sails deflating. I knew I would find quite different flowers and trees in the middle of the water than I would in the mountains. The animals would vary based on what was available, or how easy it was to get from one isle to another.

I tapped my chin, imagining a moment where I might walk one of those isles to see something my Elder had not. Unlikely we would be stopping for a pleasure stroll, or that a craft this big could sidle up to a rocky coast to let me off for a while. If I wanted to see something Rausery hadn't, I'd have to see it from the crow's nest.

Which would *not* happen in the day.

"Hm," I smiled. *Why not try?*

Loping over to the mast, I began climbing the rungs, keeping my eyes on my hands. *Like on the cliffs underground, don't look down.*

"Hey, *hey!* Lady, no! Get down 'ere, no passengers on the rigging!"

What the piss was Mourn, then?

I climbed faster as two men ran toward the mast, measuring my breath, challenged by the numerous ropes crossing every which way yet comforted by the billowing spreads of massive cloth blocking my view of the horizon for now.

One sailor was climbing behind me while the other cupped his mouth with both hands. "Roewn! *Roewn!* Dodgasted fremin, can you get yer charge off the mast before she breaks her head?!"

Laughter burbled out of me to hear that, and it felt *good*. I climbed faster, ducking a look under my arm to confirm my pursuer wasn't closing distance.

"Roewn!" I called. "It's Elana! I want to see the crow's nest."

The half-blood poked his head over the side and audibly groaned, rubbing his temple. He didn't try to shout an order at me to climb back down.

"I will bring her down, Jahn," called Mourn. "Let her be."

"Captain takin' no responsibility fer this!" bellowed the one beneath me. "An' I'm not takin' lashes fer a chudderfwet! Where's her brother, anyway?!"

"I will take all responsibility for bringing the woman down safely, Chep."

"You better, Guildsman!"

"I will. Down to the deck before her boot kicks your face."

"Yeah." He spat. "I heard she's an ornery mare."

How Surface men loved to talk as if I didn't have ears. I made a face, wishing I had my sneeze powder to drop on Chep's face, instead. I refrained from taking a lethal alternative or even cursing because the man was already climbing down. Soon after, I knocked on the underside of the trap door I spotted easily in the crow's nest.

"Let me in, Guildsman."

"You must be bored tonight, lady."

The trap door opened, and his hand appeared for me to grab. The moment I did, my boots left the rungs, causing a stark moment of panic as my body was lifted up and through by one arm.

"*Yai!*" I cried, stumbling atop a spare coil of rope weighing down a few rough blankets.

The trap door thumped closed behind me, and I rolled over only to be shoulder-to-shoulder with the mercenary. I hadn't looked down on my way here and had been fine but, suddenly, this basket so high in the massive, open sky was even tinier than it had appeared from the deck.

I've made a mistake.

And I still had to get back down.

Mourn was trying not to laugh. "Good evening, Sirana."

I stayed seated on my rear, for I couldn't see over the edge this way. "Why did you climb up here?"

"I was about to ask you the same thing."

"To ask you this question."

He sighed. "You will not like the answer."

I said nothing and waited expectantly.

"The wind dropping like it did could suggest a storm nearby," he explained. "The Humans can't see far at night. I can."

Uh-oh.

I wetted my mouth before speaking. "Is 'Roewn' a regular who could also aid the crew if needed?"

"He is. He might know a few spells for seeing in the dark."

"He's a Guild mage."

"Close enough."

More activity sounded far below us than there had been a short bit ago. Sails and ropes started shifting around.

"What are they doing?" I asked, gathering the nerve to peek over the edge.

"What they always do."

"Do you see a storm coming?"

"Do you want to look?"

I couldn't read his tone. Breathing in slow and out again, I grabbed the damp wood tightly in both hands and leaned close and up to gaze out from the crow's nest. I stared for some time, as far as I could see, tracing the curve of the world as it tilted in a way I had never imagined in my life.

Ohhh, yep. Mistake.

"I see cloud cover and black isles in one direction," I spoke with care, as a starting point.

"North," Mourn agreed, then pointed to a specific glob of darkness to the North and West, behind us. "And there is our storm catching up. Hard to tell if it is short or long endurance, but the wind will start again soon."

My eyes followed his arm out that way. I could easily see the shape of the clouds, and yes, *those* would warn me to take cover.

"I must get down below," I said.

"I am glad we agree. Do you need help?"

I paused, realizing he hadn't asked that since the first time I'd gone to the river to wash away the warp rot and Troshin Bend. "I do not think so. Climb back down the rungs, right?"

"Unless you'd like to rappel by rope."

I smirked, trying to imagine how doing that from here would be different from doing it against a rockface in the Deepearth.

Easy. The wind.

On cue, it picked up, and my cloak flapped against my shoulder. As I turned my head toward the sails refilling with air, strands of my hair escaped from my braid and went into my face.

Oh, Goddess.

"I will climb down first," Mourn suggested. "If you slip, I can catch you. I must report what I can see to Captain Tremain, anyway."

The Dragon's son had proven he was strong enough to catch me by one limb if needed. "Sounds good."

Mourn opened the trap door, and I squeezed the wall to let him go first before turning away and shimmying into the square hole, seeking the first rung with my boot. He grabbed my heel and put my foot in place.

"Try not to kick my face, please."

I smiled though he couldn't see it. "Not intentional."

The ship tilted, slow and inevitable to one side, and I froze to feel the heavy lean of my body, clinging to the spindly tree trunk missing its limbs. My heart slammed the inside of my ribs, my eyes staring at a white spray splashing up over the side of the ship.

"Easy," Mourn's voice drifted up. "Keep moving. This will not get calmer for a while, Sirana. You cannot remain up here for the duration of a squall."

Right. Keep moving.

I closed my eyes, feeling the wet wind coating my cheeks, and made myself move. Down. Another rung, and another. It was easier if I couldn't see. If it was like the chasms of the Deepearth where one knew there was a floor, somewhere, but one had to descend into utter blackness to find it.

"Almost there. Good."

"Roewn! What in' blazin' skies ya doin' up there cuddlin' with yer silver?!"

Mourn squeezed my waist pulling me off the mast and dropping me lightly onto me feet. He didn't answer the question. "Where is the Captain?"

"His cabin."

After a nod, he asked me, "Will you go down below and stay?"

The storm coming wasn't as obvious down here. Not yet. Still, I nodded. "I shall prepare with my brother to ride it out. I assume you are staying up here?"

"Aye," he answered oddly. "I can do more up here to make sure we make it to shore."

A glorious thought. With quite a few sailors glaring at me and making crude motions I may or may not have read correctly, I left to warn Gavin about the rough waters about to hit.

NIGHTMARE WAS LAYING DOWN IN HER STALL SIMILARLY TO HOW I'd first seen her the night she died. Given that she would fall down at some point regardless, I didn't question it.

By the soft glow of his knucklebone, Gavin was checking and securing the crates and bundles which could topple or slide if the ship tossed about too much, and I joined him. The sailors were busy, the noise and activity growing by the moment, and we were the ones who could get crushed by a hurled object down here. It felt good to focus on something we could do to prepare.

"Did you hear us talking, or something?" I asked him.

"I feel imminent warning of disruption coming from the North regardless. That you tell me heavy rain and wind accompany it does not surprise me."

"What?" I jerked hard on a tightening knot. "Is it a magical attack? Maybe the Ascended?"

"I cannot say. This is large and beyond my experience."

Abruptly, I imagined Gavin falling comatose again to something I couldn't see, or both of us collapsing and sharing a dream, again. Could I stay awake and not go a third time where I was unwelcome? I wore Shyntre's pendant beneath my leather armor as before, and the *Ridhian* was tightly wrapped and stored in a rear pouch. The red-rune dagger was secured away from me, yet I didn't feel ready for another mystical test. I couldn't remember what Elder D'Shea had taught me, where to begin.

Was it passive resistance? Cris-ri-phon hadn't been able to break in, not at first; he'd made similar remarks as my Elder D'Shea and Priestess Wilsira when they tried. Yet, the saphgar alone hadn't been enough to prevent both the Conceiver and Soul Drinker from breaking in eventually, given the time.

A loud, metallic grind sounded at the rear of the ship, followed by a splash. We paused. It was repeated at the fore as well.

"The anchors," he said.

"We're stopping?" I asked.

"Many islands surround us," he pondered. "Perhaps this will aid in not crashing into one of them?"

That made sense. The mental image of stopping in place to willingly be battered seemed ludicrous at first, but as Gavin had said on the Midway, we couldn't outrun a storm.

I watched as Gavin double-wrapped his grimoire and writing tools in oiled leather, inspected and secured his surgical kit, then settled down to tie himself to a post which wouldn't move without catastrophic force.

"Wait," I said. "If you must get free quickly, I know a better knot. Secure, but one hard jerk in the right place, it comes loose."

The death mage paused, considered my offer, and nodded, holding out the rope for me to show him. I grinned and made myself useful, creating comfortable harnesses for both of us. Gavin tested how to escape, grunted in satisfaction, and I rebound him, trying not to chuckle. Red Sister games came in handy on a boat.

The patter of rain arose quietly as we waited without speaking; after a while, Gavin secured his source of light and sat in the dark, his thoughts and focus were elsewhere. While I wanted to ask him what he saw or felt, I had my own concerns. Tugging out my blue pendant, I cradled it between my hands, then thought to release my spiders and guided them up to the ceiling while it was dry. They found a few protective gaps to huddle inside and wait.

That seemed easier than before.

The wind got louder outside, muffling the sailors, and rocking the body of the boat. My heartrate picked up in anticipation as the rain pounded down, and I no longer heard the flapping of as many sails. I remained alert, listening to everything, seeking out Mourn among the Humans while never being sure it was him or not.

It may have been pitch black in the hold, but my Dark Sight made out Gavin's form. I realized he no longer occupied himself with his own thoughts in quiet, as he so often did. He sat slumped in his harness with his eyes open.

I watched with a spike of concern as Mourn's illusion faded, and the long, black hair and corpse-pale skin of the Ma'ab-blooded death mage returned. His eyes had shifted to pure black, as they did whenever he used his magic, but his lips were still, and his hands rested in his lap. He did not appear in distress, but he was alone in whatever he faced. I worried about someone coming down into the hold to check on us and seeing *this*.

I pulled off my gloves and checked what I could of my illusion. *Gone. Fuck.*

Either the magic had reached its limit and needed to be cast again, or this was a direct result of the "disruption" coming our way.

For the next few hours, the ship rocked and lunged up and down violently enough that the vanished spell didn't matter, and not even Shyntre's pellets could suppress the sickness of my stomach being pitched like a playing ball. I dared not eat, either. Clutching the crate beside me, I resigned to remain in this cursed state of ravenous nausea as strange noises, calls, and wailing sounded outside, above, and underneath the water. For good or ill, Reverie was impossible, and I wagered none of the sailors would be sleeping tonight, either.

At least there wasn't a whisper of a taunt from Soul Drinker.

Don't do anything ill-thought. Let the others handle themselves. Let it pass...

Despite this mental chant, there came a point mid-storm when the lurching was particularly violent. My saphgar began to glow a deep blue at my chest, and Gavin's body moved, his long arm lifting up. It was deliberate. He reached out in my direction, a black-nailed, large-knuckled hand grasping for something. A bit of black blood seeped from the corner of his mouth.

Uh-oh.

What should I do? He had told me many times, in many ways, he did not like to be touched. He doesn't want to share dreams, either. He'd been dealing with this his entire mortal life, I reminded myself; he often looked possessed or had seizures, experiencing troubled nightmares.

This is nothing new for him.

My mind was clear. Anchored. My tangible reality wasn't sliding into dissolving sand at the moment. Could I "wake" him, as I once had Reishel? Could I shield him, listen to him as I had D'Shea when she confessed about Shyntre, when Gaelan told me of being in the shed as I lay dying, of Natia, and each despite their compulsions?

I'm not that strong anymore. Not after Kerse. I don't want to see whatever it is that's threatening him.

Gavin's eyes remained opened, staring into the Void. He made no sound, but I realized he'd bitten his tongue; that's why the blood was dripping. He tried twice more to reach out to whatever he saw.

Or to me?

No, he's not aware of where I am.

Yet, he didn't stop. Three times, his arm never wavered in its direction, focused on me. My newly returned pendant continued to glow, casting shadows upon his pale face. If I reached out, too, I could take his hand.

And?

Well, if I always avoided it, never learned control, madness was sure to follow, Gavin said. I doubted he would argue that, as mastery of his heritage practically consumed him. And if he did, I was sure of my stance.

Must relearn control.

At least Gavin didn't use the blame to violate me in revenge.

With a quiet sigh, I removed my gloves, anxious and nauseated. I took hold of the warm blue stone with one hand and snatched hold of Gavin's hand the next time he reached across to me.

Gripping it tight, I kept only one thought. *~I am staying out but… come back, mystic. Return to us. I'm here.~*

The Deathwalker blinked. Gradually, his ice blue pupils returned, and his tongue pushed the dark fluid which had collected beneath it out, until it spilled down his chin. I grimaced but held on until I was sure he knew that we were holding hands.

He tugged free, always his first impulse, but then black clouds passed across the icy blue color and he immediately reached out to touch the back of my hand. The color anchored again. He tried again to withdraw but instantly pressed the pale pads of his fingers to my dark hand. I held still, kept my arm out, waiting awkwardly.

"Fascinating," he said.

"You are back?" I asked.

"Yes. Yes..." He was looking around, tracing the ceiling. "I believe I am."

The rocking of the ship, the rising and sudden drops kept me from asking anything for another half-hour; it took all my focus to keep my hand out where Gavin could reach it. He mostly held on to my middle finger, pressing it between three long fingers as if checking my pulse, and dealing with whatever pricked at his peripheral senses. My pendant continued to glow as it had in the presence of focused magic, and Gavin's pupils kept flickering, threatening to vanish yet never going dark while he held on to me.

Eventually, shortly before the ship would begin to calm at last, the death mage released me and leaned back, dropping his arm. Mine collapsed in burning exhaustion; I groaned, massaging to soothe.

"Is it over?" I hoped.

Gavin nodded, saying nothing.

We had done well securing what might come loose, and the hold appeared to suffer no significant damage; Nightmare and the cargo remained mostly in place. Now things were calmer, and I could detect the heavy dripping of water coming from above, presumably whatever had splashed onto the deck. The dank smell had increased.

Tugging hard to release the rope harness which had probably saved me many bruises, I got up and stretched, calling my spiders to me. Gavin quirked a brow.

"I will check for leaks," I said, "and stay down here. I know our illusions are gone."

He still did not speak. I wanted to know what happened, what he experienced, anything, but knew better than to push the stubborn scholar.

Hopefully once he has time to think it over.

Tracing the perimeter of the hold, which was not the entire length of the ship, I did not find anything too concerning, though not all was perfectly dry. My ears detected several unseen rats, and they were *not* heading upward although were nervous enough to be startled when my stomach growled.

I smirked, commanding Nightmare onto her feet on my way to Gavin and my thankfully dry food. I pulled up my hood and ate slow as I could manage, listening for anyone coming down and hoping Mourn would be first. That would avoid some unnecessary concerns all around.

Apparently, he agreed. He was coming down, telling someone, "I will check on them."

I greeted him with a wave and a wide smile.

He paused, looking at my face then Gavin's. "Hm. Allow me."

We waited while our disguises were replaced, and Gavin checked his hands and arms, nodding in thanks as his black finger-nails faded to a living shade.

"I didn't ask before," I said. "How long does this spell last? Did you reset it at any point, and I did not notice?"

Mourn smiled. "No. It can last several days unless we encounter a surge from a strong mage or like the one in that storm."

I squinted. "How long is 'several'?"

He thought about it. "I can confirm three days, at least."

"Not four hours."

He watched me, and I was impressed when he followed my train of thought. "No. Brom wanted to be certain you couldn't get far on a disguise. We both knew that."

"But you aren't worried."

He smiled without showing his teeth. "You're on a ship."

"Yes, I noticed." I frowned. "What in the Void was that? Could it have been a Ma'ab attack?"

Mourn shook his head with certainty. "No. The Archipelago has magical squalls as well as storms. The isles have some unique plants and animals as a result."

"It just…burbles up from nothing?" Gavin asked skeptically.

"It almost always comes from the North," the Dragonchild explained. "Many travelers have linked it to a land bridge with an impassable forest, called Blackbark. They don't know what's inside. No one seems to return from that place."

I waited two heartbeats, and Gavin was reaching for his grimoire again.

"And you've never been there?" I asked.

Mourn smiled and waited for the scholar before speaking again. "No, I've not yet. Worth noting that many an ambitious mage has attempted to harness these isle-jumping surges for their own ends but usually end up dead or gone mad."

Gavin grunted, shaking his head as he began to write. "Indeed, I can see how that might occur. How far is this Blackbark 'land bridge' from Port Fortnight?"

"Ohh, let's see." Mourn exhaled in thought. "At least as far as from the Ley Tower to Troshin Bend, but all water and broken isles."

The Deathwalker nodded, turning to a fresh page. He was far past the halfway mark; I wondered what happened when he filled up his book.

"There must be another body of water on the other side of the bridge."

"Correct. The Sea of Fish. Largely traveled East and West by the Yungian and the Noiri, between Yung-An and the Dragon Coast."

I was far too entertained watching Gavin feverishly scritch his notes.

Eventually, Mourn asked, "How did you two fare the storm?"

The Deathwalker looked at me, thinking to wipe his chin to see the dried, black blood. He pulled out a rag to scrub it off before we had to ask. He might have remembered biting his tongue.

"I would say I fared poorly," he answered, "but Sirana provided a raft for me to cling to until it passed."

"What?" The Dragonchild pinned me with his gaze. "How did you do that?"

"Uh." I lifted the leather thong of Shyntre's pendant, letting it swing until he recognized it. "This helps me focus."

Mourn was skeptical, briefly glancing at Gavin. "But you aren't a mage, you say."

I shrugged. "It's… mental training in defense of some magic. Like breaking wards, it blunts the spell trying to bend the will."

His Human brows lifted high. "And you gave it to me?"

My eyes slid to one side. "My only option at the time. You couldn't have the ruby or the dagger for a threat you would have helped with regardless. And I did not realize how much the *saphgar* had been protecting me from Soul Drinker."

He caught that. "You've reevaluated giving me the ruby?"

I put up both hands. "I need time to think. But yes, I want to bargain with the ruby for something else. I will make you an offer by the time we reach Augran."

The half-blood showed me that he was pleased. "Very well. Let me know." He turned his head toward the ladder up and sniffed, flicking out his tongue. "The cook is preparing a midnight meal for everyone before they try to get some sleep. Would you—"

"Yes, please," I answered.

"I'll be back, then. And if you want to spend any time above board before dawn, I guarantee most of the sailors will be sleeping and won't bother you."

That sounded good. Even Gavin looked interested.

The rest of the night would be a collective sigh of relief for everyone.

CHAPTER 14

WE MADE IT THROUGH THE ARCHIPELAGO IN FAIRER WEATHER, overcast gradually giving way to clear skies. There were a couple moments of shouting, heavy steering, and scurries through the rigging, but we managed not to hit anything destructive.

By the sixth day sailing, I'd run out of the fresh water I'd brought despite my self-rationing and my being the only one drinking it. I had only the diluted wine that came with the cheese, salt fish, and hard biscuits, which were the main meals aside from midday with either a hearty stew or mush of beans and grains with oil. I was given an equal amount as the sailors, which was probably Mourn's doing as he negotiated all the food runs.

"May I trade my wine and water for *just* water?" I asked after making a face. "I don't want the wine."

Mourn shook his head. "It'll draw from others on the crew and mixing it is how they make the water safe. You will be fine for another day drinking it."

"It smells like *tycka* and tastes like *vholk*."

The half-blood blinked. "It does?"

Mourn held out his hand for my wooden cup, which I gave him. He sniffed, sipped, and smacked his tongue against the roof of his mouth. "Hm. Well, no dangerous amount of it, Sirana. It may be your... well..."

I glared. "My 'condition'?"

The half-blood neither glared nor blinked, handing me the cup. "Yes. Some things taste differently while with child. I heard squad-mates say it enough."

"Same with Human women," Gavin remarked, who was nei-ther eating nor drinking. "Or so I've heard."

Yet I'd not been allies with enough caits in my life, let alone pregnant ones, to have heard the same at home or at Court. These two male outcasts knew more than I did what I might experience. I scowled in pointless accusation at my wine.

"If I may ask," began the Deathwalker, "what are *tycka* and *vholk*?"

"Sulphur and iron," Mourn translated.

The death mage made a note.

I sighed. "And once we reach Yong-wen tomorrow, I can get good water easily?"

The mercenary paused. "No. Good water is at a premium. Weak ale is usually what the pregnant women drink, as it has at least been boiled."

Yuck.

Now I needed coin to drink water in Augran? I was about to make a snide remark about predatory trade before I recalled the guarded well on House Thalluen property, its relative value, and the significant way my Matron negotiated her agreements with her neighboring Houses. I'd been spoiled by the free-flowing snowmelt and open waterfalls and rivers on the Surface.

I soaked my biscuit in the wine, holding it farther away so as not to catch whiffs of the stomach-lurching scents. *Maybe if I'm fast I won't taste it.*

Mourn chuckled at my expression. "What did you just think about?"

"Nothin'," I said, chomping the soggy biscuit.

"You were about to say something."

I shook my head with pudgy cheeks. "*Numph.*"

"Hmm." He glanced into his empty cup. "I will see if I can obtain water for one day and boil it for you."

I waved my hand, ★Not needed.★

The wine wasn't any better with the biscuit. *I'm going to be sick.*

"A sailor or two would probably enjoy their wine at full strength for once," Mourn reflected. "And we are only a day out. I will return."

Sighing, I sat alone with Gavin, aware yet again that our guide waited patiently for an offer. Mourn hadn't brought it up again since the night of the storm. Now we were only a day out.

"Hey, Gavin."

"Hm?"

"Do you think Mourn plans to go to Manalar for the siege? Has he said?"

The Deathwalker took his time to recollect before shaking his head. "He has given no slip or suggestion."

"But your bargain includes letting him stand in the room with his Guild contacts while you plead your case with the soul shard?"

"Indeed, it indicates he wants the knowledge. I cannot say what he would use it for."

"Would you ask him to help you reach the inner sanctum of the temple? He said he was familiar with Manalar."

Gavin shrugged. "I am not sure how I would pay him. It was to be his 'interested parties' who had the resources to fund the venture."

Good point. How much was the ruby worth to the mercenary, if he would steal it regardless to close his contract? Surely not all I could think of that Gavin and I wanted or needed.

Help entering the temple.

Help finding Jael.

Help finding enough food and water.

Help standing against would-be slavers and Witch Hunters.

Help in case the Deathless appeared again…

That didn't include my geas to somehow convince him to accompany me to the Ley Tower and help kill Sarilis. *So that I can go home.*

One little ruby in exchange for all of that.

Ha.

I counted how many of Shyntre's pellets remained, for I'd been taking quite a few for motion sickness. I frowned into the pouch. *Five.*

How to bargain with a Dragonblood taking jobs strictly to earn wealth without being "brutal," when I had little wealth myself? In fact, where did he learn *that* lesson, not to simply take what he wanted? Not from the Davrin of Vuthra'tern.

I scratched my chin but instantly recalled Mourn's protective reaction when I'd asked about Tamuril's Naulor sister in Augran. Perhaps if Tamuril had had enough time, if she had been able to escort me to Manalar, she would have wanted to teach me something similar.

Hm.

Nothing brilliant came to me by the time Mourn returned with steaming water in a kettle. He tested the heat with his fingers.

"Hand me a water skin," he said. "It will cool."

I handed an empty one to him but instead of thanking him, I closed my eyes and held my head. He poured, finished, and Gavin offered to take it instead.

"What's wrong?"

"Meal's not sitting well," I muttered, getting up to pace, rubbing my temple with one hand and holding my middle in the other, trying to breathe steady in the dank, stale air.

"Alright. Let us go up to the deck. The sun is down, and you need fresh air."

My mind was split on that suggestion. A few clean breaths might help my roiling stomach, but the waves and tilting horizon might not.

"Come," he suggested again, waving his hand and heading toward the ladder.

Getting the slight sense that he wanted to talk as well, I followed him up the ladder and out of the hold. I could hear the snores, grunts, and passing gas of sailors sleeping below deck as we moved through without pause, but neither I nor the mercenary made any noise.

The blast of cool, moist air as I exited was a greater shock than I might have expected, though it felt good, cooling my hot cheeks. The stars peeked out in bright patches between a few overhead clouds, with the larger moon setting to our right. I could hear the spray and the foaming burbles around the boat, saw the expected, black mass with glittering crests before me.

Unfortunately, the ship only had to roll again for me to groan.

Come to the side, Mourn signed, not taking my arm but lightly touching it. *It will help.*

I doubted it. The better part was that I had something to lean on, resting my back and working less to keep my balance. I joined him, breathed out, and squeezed my eyes shut against another wave of nausea that sent a high pitch into my ears. Mourn said nothing.

When I wasn't expecting it, he swept something beneath my nose, and I caught a whiff of something so strong it made my breath hitch and my throat gag. My stomach absolutely rebelled then. I heaved once, then again, and ended up hurling my entire dinner over the side of the ship in a few hard purges. Mourn held one shoulder and made sure I didn't go over the side.

"Now you will feel better," he murmured, low enough that it would disappear on the wind.

"Augh," I spat into the water and swallowed several times before croaking, "Fuck you, merc. What *is* that? Old piss?"

"Close. Smelling salts."

Whatever that was. I scowled at him until he withdrew and offered a flask.

"Extra water to rinse," he said. "If the wine will not sit, you might try the ale at port."

Wordlessly, I accepted the flask and rinsed my mouth, swallowing instead of spitting. I took another swig then passed it to him. He took it.

"Feel better?"

"…yes."

"Good sign."

I huffed a breath; my stomach was sore, but I relished the relative calm from moments ago. The half-breed waited with me, and I watched the Great Lake without things getting worse. I was finally becoming accustomed to it, and before I could grow unsettled again, I pulled out the *Ridhian*, wrapping the necklace around my gloved hand, gripping the stone in my palm so it wouldn't drop into the water. Mourn watched with interest.

"So, how long would this ruby retain you as a dedicated guide for Gavin and me?" I asked.

The hybrid blinked slowly. '*What?*' might as well have been written on his forehead. He began cautiously. "I have never parceled out measured time for each gem or coin. I do not know."

Try again.

"I lost one sister," I said, my voice tightening as sudden grief returned yet again. "I *am* heading to Manalar to retrieve the other. And, as nothing will stop Gavin where his mistress shows his path, we go to the same place. He told me you would be present in negotiations with the Guild, and I will be there, too, on my ally's side. I *shall* be going with him."

Mourn stared at me. I couldn't read him.

"You have... *ahm*... you have done much to show us how much we do not know without taking advantage of it, as others have." I looked away as my heart picked up. "My offer for trading away the *Ridhian* so you may close your current contract is that your next contract is with me, as my bodyguard for Manalar. Help me find enough safe food and water, as you have been doing, and protect me from capture. If I am captured, pursue me and try to free me."

He was silent.

Cautiously, I lifted my eyes. He didn't look eager.

"That is quite a lot," he said. "Such a bargain could last an entire siege as stated."

"If that is too much for one ruby, what additional price would persuade you?" I paused. "Other than the relic, any wealth I can loot, you may have."

Mourn stretched his Human lips, but he spoke in Davrin. *"That is not wise to leave open-ended, Baenar. The looting alone will draw unexpected trouble and you may begin to kill under pressure to entice me. You also do not know what we might find that, like the black dagger, either you do not wish to or cannot give away. Altering a bargain once agreed may work in Sivaraus, but this does not work with any of To'vah blood. I would rather not show you why that is and ask you to take this on its face."*

I exhaled in exasperation, covering up my consternation in how he spoke. What *had* the Davrin fucked to get a hybrid like this? I'd expected to land in this spot soon after making an offer to a male five centuries old, but I hadn't found an angle that favored me without lying.

"The only thing I want for a ruby that you would take regardless," I reminded him, *"is your continued tutoring and protection while I learn about the Surface."*

"What of your Red Sister?"

I shrugged, pursing my lips in worry. *"A moot point if I cannot find her. Is this a starting point for us to bargain, yes or no, one of To'vah blood?"*

"It is a starting point, but I have concerns."

"Like that?"

"The Deathless following you. Your unusually vivid dreams linked with your aura when you are aroused. The relic that the death mage keeps for you which wants to own you. Whatever you have not said about your mission and why that false sapphire is more valuable to you than it would be to any I have ever known."

Alright, those were a lot of concerns, and most of them I either had no control over or I could not explain it.

I'm so stuck.

"You mentioned trading one of my pellets to a potion maker," I said. "Would doing so at no charge to her add enough long-term benefit to your wealth?"

"Closer," he replied.

"But still not enough."

"It shows me you are serious. And most of my concerns could be addressed by another contact of mine in Yong-wen, if you would meet her as well."

"You have a lot of female contacts."

A low chuckle. "They are easily overlooked, and I know how to find the best among them thanks to my upbringing."

"A question, then, if I may?"

"Yes?"

"Are any also companions? Or information brokers, like many of our buas? Do they share you?"

He blinked. Based on how he leaned away on the railing, I could imagine how his tail might have coiled if he still had it.

He rumbled at me, his eyes glinting gold again. "I have never... **never** bargained for information using sex. Neither offering nor accepting. I also do not offer my skills in exchange for a mounting. I am not that easy or hard up."

So indignant.

"*Good to know,*" I said awkwardly. "*Um, I apologize for the insult, Mourn. I was not thinking I could hire you on such terms. It is relevant to know if your contacts are lovers, and a wise question to ask oneself in Sivaraus. It is a frequent pitfall at Court not to know in advance or try to find out. Do you not see that?*"

He took a deep breath, slowly let it out. "*Yes. I can see that. And to answer you, no. None of the female contacts I would bring you to are my current playmates.*"

"*Do you **have** a current playmate?*"

"*No.*"

"*Are any of these contacts a past playmate?*"

He hesitated, exhaled irritably. "*One is.*"

"Uh-oh," I said in Trade. "Not Osgrid, is she?"

At least he smiled a little at that. "No. Not Osgrid. I do not know where she is, anyway."

So, the hybrid knew *how* to fuck, but Goddess damn me if I could determine his experience relative to his age. Did it matter? Not for what aid I needed from him. It was only that niggling detail Gavin had told me after I'd invaded his dreams again.

"*Mourn has been wise and has left your vicinity when you begin dreaming. He senses something but has practiced defenses which give him warning.*"

He sensed something. *Hm.*

The half-blood had also left when I'd been unbearably randy riding to Port Fortnight; whether by scent or spying, he knew what I'd been doing. He'd fled, warned away by his keen senses, and approached only after I'd finished. That was a concern of my own: my potential bodyguard running away any time I needed to rub some tension out. No surprise, truly, after enduring a Priestess-Matron for an Aunt.

"*So,*" I began, "*the ruby, one pellet, and meeting a specific contact in Yong-wen to address some concerns. Before you decide whether to guard me in seeking my sister in Manalar. Is that where we stand?*"

Mourn nodded. *"Yes."*

"Do you accept that I would give them in reverse order? If your concerns cannot be addressed, I want something else for the ruby and I would keep the pellet."

His golden eyes shone for a tick. *"Fair, so long as you **do** bargain for the ruby if this falls through."*

"Agreed, yes." I paused, heard a Human rustling around in a cabin behind us, and switched to Trade. "Anything else, or anything unspoken?"

He shook his head. "Not on my end."

Indeed, that seemed always the case.

"I am hungry," I said, waving my hand at the water. "And I lost my dinner."

"Yes, I noticed." He smiled. "The boiled water should be cool enough to drink, and are there enough stores from our time on shore?"

"Only one meal."

"Go ahead and eat that. I agree to help obtain enough food for you at least until we determine what happens next between us."

I breathed out, nodded in thanks, and took my leave to go below again. For one unable to talk plainly about what mattered most, I'd expected to be in a worse position at this point. At least there was still hope for Jael. I must only meet this new contact to convince the mercenary to travel with us a while longer.

Past an army and their siege, right into the power center of a sacred temple. Simple.

THE SHORT REMAINDER OF THE JOURNEY SAW ME WAITING anxiously with my ally for the next Surface-dwellers with whom we would negotiate. Had Gavin and I thought to head to Augran to obtain help before traveling to Manalar, we could not have slipped ourselves *and* his undead mare through any perimeter with such ease.

The *Trickster of Isles* approached the dense port on a sunny, late afternoon, so I was below deck anyway, although I was well aware of the changing speed of the ship as well as the proximity of others soon enough. The scent of the water became fouler, as did the noise.

Next, Human officials of some kind boarded the boat. Mourn was up there with Captain Tremain. Tensely, I waited as unfamiliar steps and voices sounded above us, though they withdrew after a cursory glance down in the hold where Gavin and I hid in the shadows and, behind us, Nightmare did not shift one hoof. This experience repeated after setting sail down a crowded river, and not even "Pete" spoke up to give us away. If I had needed further proof of the mercenary's connections in this city, I supposed I had it.

The third time we docked, our guide returned to join and stay this time. Mourn looked ready to leave. "We're in Yong-wen. It is dusk outside but put your hood up anyway."

We did, Gavin leading his horse by her lead up the ramp which was finally dropped again. We passed the ship's crew coming down to grab the supplies which were double- or triple-knotted in some cases. Pete glared at me on the way by.

I made it a point to observe as Mourn interacted with the ship's leader and upper crew on his way out. I saw their hands move. It seemed familiar, as if I should recognize it, but there were new or invented signs that broke the intent for me. I spotted what I believed was an exchange of gratitude, and few men gave us a second glance as we left their ship and entered the enclave of Yong-wen.

There was a great mix of doings close to the water, many goods and property being moved, many bodies trying to stay out of the way. I saw dark wood panels and a pale plaster lining the river, large buildings stacked two or three floors tall, which would aid in conducting business. It was drab, however, utilitarian, with every spare finger-width taken up with something useful, a building, door, pathway, crate or barrel.

I leaned to Mourn. "A riverside place to store?"

He signed an affirmative. *"Puang-shao."*

I shook my head like I needed the water out. "What?"

He slowed down. "This dock storage is called 'poo-ang shuh-oww'."

He'd done something oddly familiar with his tone at the end. I stared. "That *cannot* be any dialect of Trade."

"It is not. It is Yungian."

"You are fluent in the language?"

"Very. It was the first Human language I took time to learn."

"Puang-shao," Gavin repeated slowly though not exact. "A close Trade translation?"

"Simple enough," Mourn replied. "Outdoor Fish Road."

Neither Gavin nor I had a reply, at first.

"Fish *Road*?" I repeated.

"Literally a river," Gavin pondered. "I can see it. Interesting."

"The Yungian language is older than some areas where Humans established their roots. It shows in some of the primitive ideas in their words, though do not mistake it for lack of nuance. It is an anchored and complex language."

I wondered what "anchored" meant to the Dragonblood if we weren't talking ships but was soon distracted by the crash of scents walking down the piers and boardwalks.

These Humans permeated *everything* here. Not only their bodies and clothes, but their foreign spices and crafts loaded up the crates, moved by horse and cart among rows and rows of temporary storage. The din was the worst of it as the noise battered my ears while any understanding of the talk slid away. No one was speaking Trade but this unfamiliar "old" language with which the mercenary was comfortable. I felt too far from home.

Amid the heavy labor, negotiations, inspections, and eavesdropping in close quarters, most were too focused on maintaining their space and task to scrutinize three new arrivals with an old, tired mare.

It wasn't until we slipped past this warehouse on the river that I discovered Yong-wen near-bursting with colors. It was a pity that the Sun had set. On a clear day, this Human settlement would be aesthetically gifted at a level closer to Sivaraus, the first of its kind I had seen on the Surface. If Mourn had much to do with seeing this place grow, then Yong-wen must offer him selection aplenty for those "quality crafts" he'd boasted to collect.

Following the taller male and walking next to Gavin, I risked making prolonged eye contact with many people walking, running, and pulling carts along the cobbled street going the other way. I also peered high up, as often as I could without tripping over a cobble or a dung pile.

All the roofs were slanted, their lines curved in similar ways, curled at the corners. This gave the town a singular style that seemed less chaotic than the docks. They were layered with earth-red tiles to shed rain, their eaves decorated with metal flowers or vines. Columns of dressed wood or stone served as relief against endless wooden panels. Doors were not only stained dark red but carved with relaxing patterns or painted with murals of waterfalls, gardens, and Humans dressed in finer robes and fabrics than those working industriously around me.

I also noticed the Dragon motifs all over: the door murals, the carvings on columns, panels, and eaves, as well as occasional metal-work tips on the curved rooftops. This did not count the clusters of decorated pots growing and cradling fragrant flowers and herbs suspended from the upper floors, from windows and balconies with chains or rope. In addition, the street was dotted with red and yellow parchment-like balls glowing from the inside, acting as lanterns to illuminate the main path.

I could not help but be struck by the difference in appearance between the paler Humans at Brom's Inn and aboard our ship, and those of this "enclave" that Mourn said began only three centuries ago.

Yungian eyes were familiar to me in their shape, though smaller in the face and possessing a different balance with those round ears. Their eyes tilted upwards and were feline-shaped over the rounder, wide-set eyes of the Paxians. Yungian skin was deeper in color than most I'd seen, somewhat like Cris-ri-phon's Desert brown skin, and they favored black, straight hair like Mourn's, or occasionally a deep brown, as a people. I spotted no blondes or redheads like those at the Inn or on the boat, nor anything remotely approaching the cloud-white, near translucent skin like of the Ma'ab.

I beheld many examples of the men and women, along with some children. The women were slender, smaller in stature next to the men, who were not stout giants by comparison like the Ma'ab. It was remarkably close to Sivaraus, if one swapped the caits and the buas, more so than the Paxians had been.

Suddenly, I didn't feel *quite* as far from home. Perhaps Mourn had felt the same in discovering Yung-An?

Our guide looked over his shoulder in his altered, Human face and gestured for us to slide off to the side of the flowing bodies. We had no reason to balk, and soon we stood within a narrow, straight pathway between two multi-story buildings, deep in shadow. Gavin's mare blocked us from plain view from the street. The death mage and I looked at each other as if to gauge which of us would ask what we were doing this time.

A moment later, that question was answered when the half-breed grimaced, and I watched his ears lengthen and his skin darken beneath his hood, his harness reappearing on a shirtless chest. His fangs and metallic, Dragon's eyes returned with the shifting of his brow and jaw.

Next, Mourn's tail appeared to grow down from behind him, slithering out from beneath his cloak and coiling briefly around his own ankle in a testing flex before relaxing. His claws emerged again from his fingertips, as did those on his feet, including the heel-spurs.

Briefly, I sniffed a concentrated scent and heat from him which reminded me of a stressed or injured animal.

Wait. Is his appearance not an illusion like ours?

"Did you just—?"

I stopped to hear footsteps and Mourn turned around as I made out their shape. Three of them. Male, Yungian, dressed better than the dock workers in decorated, long-sleeved shirts which looked smooth to the touch. Their faces were firmly set, near frowning, with carefully trimmed facial hair around the mouth and chin. Unfamiliar herbs and spices hovered around them in a cloud. A young, thin boy who began to enter the alley stopped quickly when he saw the men's backs and immediately turned around to leave.

Mourn pulled down his hood and offered a magical light by a pebble in his palm. His beast-Elf face and even his horns were quite clear, yet the Yungians did not jump back as I'd expected.

"Jiu-wen sha'ming," he said to Mourn, offering a formal bow at the waist, his spine kept perfectly straight.

The half-breed put his clawed hands out, showing them empty, and replied in a low thrum, *"Jiu-yan'shi."*

I would have said that the men looked pleased, although expression was as subtle as some Davrin at Court. There were a few formal exchanges, and from reading their bodies and hands, I guessed that they simply wanted to know what our purpose was here.

Mourn motioned to our hoods. "Let them see your faces. I will remove the illusion."

Gavin tensed. "Here?"

"Who are they?" I asked.

"Murei Shuang, an elder father, and his two sons, Baenfing and Wei."

Gavin and I received a triple bow at the introduction. Mourn continued. "The role of the Shuang family is to be the gatekeepers of the enclave. If one means no ill, a visitor or trader knows to check in with them first. Murei was kind enough to meet us halfway and outside in private."

The spike of fear in my gut was sharper than I wished it. Gavin showed similar hesitation.

Mourn had his hand raised. "May I? I told you the truth about Yong-wen and the rest of the city. It is better they see why I brought you in here."

City of the Dragon Spirit, indeed.

Exhaling, I lowered my hood. "Go on."

Gavin had to follow my example before Mourn would unravel his spell, which he did without enthusiasm. I could tell the moment our Paxian faces vanished by the looks on theirs. They weren't prepared despite not blinking an eye at meeting the tall Elf-Dragon in an alley.

"Bakgwei!" exclaimed the younger man on the left, his voice hushed. He looked away, strange hand gestures in motion.

"Le nirjwai, yun gel-siyu!" the elder Murei said with clear irritation at his son, who quickly bowed his head as if in apology.

Mourn smiled a tiny bit; it was not obvious, but he enjoyed the exchange. Gavin stayed in place through this reaction to his dry, pale skin and his night eyes, watching them without a blink. I glimpsed his long fingers twitch like he was prepared to act. Likewise, it would only take me an instant to summon my spiders in a leap.

After chastising his son with another grunt of a word, Murei avoided eye contact with Gavin, focusing totally on me. The elder seemed fascinated, going so far as to move a step closer and note some comparison between Mourn and me. He asked the half-blood a question directly, to which Mourn responded with hand motions and a verbal answer. They went on, back and forth, and Gavin and I sensed a mutual acceptance and relaxed.

The mercenary certainly was fluent in Yungian. *And not just the words.*

With more bows, Murei bid us welcome to their city, or so we were told, and granted a farewell before leaving with his sons. Their calm gait expressed the dignity of those accustomed to privilege and influence on those around them.

"There," said our guide, putting away the light. "Word will spread regardless but coming from Shuang will help it stay in the enclave, and you will not be harassed by mistake."

I smirked. "By mistake?"

"Thinking you are mere Manalari mortals and not spirits in flesh."

"Spirits," Gavin repeated with a flavor of skepticism that could only come from a death mage. "Is that the meaning of 'bakgwei'?"

Mourn turned his head to show his teeth. "Broadly, no. Specifically, *bakgwei* is a 'white ghost' and recently made a curse for the Ma'ab. But the ancient legends also tell of pale spirits crossing over from the land of the dead, often linked to the imminent or recent death of family."

"What startling precision," I commented with a smile.

Gavin grunted, lifting his chin to look around as we exited the shortcut between buildings. "And what did the elder deem a Davrin?"

"*Nirjwai*," Mourn answered. "The closest word they have to an Elf of any color." The Dragon son paused oddly. "Interestingly, Sirana, your white hair suggests wisdom to the elder Shuang. He thinks you are an extremely old immortal. If that spreads as well, you will be shown more respect than any woman in Yong-wen."

I bit my lips neither to laugh nor snarl. "But not respect above you."

"Dragon spirits are strong guardians and bringers of good fortune regardless of perceived age," he said in a reasonable tone. "The residents here are often glad to hear I am in town. But I wager most will not speak to the grey mage at all for fear of bad luck or death coming to their homes."

"As if ignoring death stops one from meeting it," Gavin said.

The dry quip made me chuckle.

"Some here would agree, Deathwalker," Mourn said. "You might meet some. Come. Let us continue."

We raised our hoods but Mourn did not replace our disguises. With greater trepidation than either of us wanted to admit, Gavin and I followed Mourn out into the street. I was aware of Yungians looking our way before quickly minding their business. It was as if the reemergence of three, unharmed males in an alley had given permission for the commoners to reveal that they were aware of us, whether or not they had been from the start.

As we moved deeper into the enclave, I tried to read the body language of those doing business in early evening by lanterns on the street. Several shared whispers and glances, some indelicate pointing. Some obviously thought of doing something bold; they were trying to gather the courage to act.

I paid attention to Mourn's body language, his hands for signs, and his frequent scenting of the spicy, floral air. He was alert but calm. Gavin wasn't enjoying the attention but merely looked down and frowned deeper.

Finally, one older female approached. Her head was uncovered, and she had streaks of white and iron grey in her long hair, which had been plaited and coiled into an accomplished bun. Her yellow and pink clothing was not ragged, though it was not as new and nice as what the Shuang men had been wearing, and it possessed the same silken texture and stylized, floral decoration.

Her eyes, elegantly slanted upward and without the deep eyelid creases of the Paxian and Noiri Humans, were direct and deep black, her mouth set firmly but with an emotion I wasn't sure about. I could see her wrinkles, the lines at her nostrils and the corners of her mouth, the loose skin at her jaw and neck. Her hands were more like Gavin's, gaunt with raised blue veins and prominent knuckles, though her fingers were quite short. She was close to my height.

If this was an elder female Human, then I could see where the assumption of "wisdom" might come from with the color of my hair. I could see her experience; she was a matron of some kind.

The Yungian elder approached Mourn, her voice soft and respectful, both her hands out, palms up, as she lowered her head in a bow. We slowed and stopped when Mourn did, and the woman was encouraged enough to remove a simple silver necklace with three opaque, blue stones, which had been beneath her silken shift.

She reached out and let it gently slide along the bracer of Mourn's forearm, muttering something that sounded like a chant to me, except I felt no magic pulse. Nothing had happened, it was a simple, mundane gesture.

Nonetheless, Mourn pulled a sleight-of-hand that I almost missed: one hand had removed a tiny vial, and he slipped it into her palm as he accepted her gift of the necklace with obvious ceremony. He said no words. The woman was not stupid; she palmed the vial, hiding it, bowed several times as she backed away from him, speaking the tone of gratitude, and left quickly.

Several others emboldened by the show started forward, but only to one side; they gave Gavin and his mare a wide berth.

"Keep walking," Mourn said lowly to us. "Do not attack them in any way, do not hurt them. If they offer you a gift with both hands, simply accept it no matter if you want it. It is a crippling insult and a shame to their family if you do not."

Rigid. I refrained from making a face. "How many might try?"

"Only the bravest willing to touch a spirit."

Soon, I saw exactly what he meant when a poorly dressed, younger female approached me and touched my cloak lightly with her fingertips as I passed. Had the mercenary not warned me, I would have thrown her to the ground long before she made contact.

"What are they doing?" I asked.

"They hope for some Dragon luck. Just keep up with me. They won't steal from you."

"Won't they?" Gavin muttered cynically, gritting his black teeth, which kept everyone away from him.

I hated this strange behavior as well, feeling surrounded except for Gavin's side; hearing many words I did not understand; smelling unwashed bodies and clothing and bad breath as they made their pleas and prayers. I didn't like them touching me, be it my glove or my bracer or my cloak covering my shoulder, but none reached for my face or my middle or impeded my gait if I did not stop. They reached for Mourn as well, but he was so much taller that he could still see in front of us. My view was blocked by the peasants.

My heart began to pound as I wondered if this would be continual the entire time we were in this enclave.

"Xi-ung gao, nirjwai," said an older female dressed in blue and black, probably of middling wealth. She offered me something wrapped in blue cloth, presenting it with both hands and bowing her head to look at the ground.

What I smelled inside made my mouth water.

What had Mourn said? Accept any gifts?

I took the wrapped—and warm—foodstuff with a slight nod, and the woman reached up to touch the edge of my hood, as close to my white hair as she could get, smiling to show one missing tooth before backing away, bowing like Mourn's first woman.

A few women approached and offered me fruits and wrapped edibles; one gave me a large, purple flower. Mourn received pieces of jewelry in addition to a cloth-wrapped meal or two. Our hands were getting full; a bad thing if we needed to use our tools.

Eventually, at last, we escaped out of the cluster of Humans onto a street less populous, only a few curious children following us any farther. Gavin passed me an empty sack from Nightmare's satchel for the food, and I tucked most of the pieces in, except for the first one given to me. My appetite had returned like a storm. I had to eat that delicious-smelling package this instant.

Mourn had pocketed his new jewelry. He smiled, adding his meals to my bag as I unwrapped the woman's gift, sniffed it again in a cursory attempt to detect any toxin my body might reject. I took a bite.

"Like it?" Mourn asked.

It was a small hand pie, wrapped in an incredibly thin, stretchy crust. The mixture of minced meat and vegetables inside was seasoned in an astonishing balance of sweet and savory. There was a lingering bit of heat in my mouth after the second bite.

Oh, fuuuck.

"Yes," I answered after I swallowed again. "It is *very* good. Complex."

"Filling, too," he reassured me on the third bite.

I smiled and continued eating as we eventually left even the curious children behind. Mourn did not lead us in a straight path toward wherever we were going but shed stragglers and gave me time to eat my fill from the bag. I viewed a lot of the streets on the way, mapping them in my head how I did underground tunnels and caverns, except Yong-wen possessed many unique landmarks. It was too easy.

Signs of growing wealth became concentrated as loiterers on the street lessened. There was an air of importance among those riding in their carts, pulled either by a beast of burden or a single other Human, depending on how much cargo was being transported. Flowerpots and boxes became common, freshening the air amid close living quarters.

Finally, we reached a well-crafted building of dark wood, approaching from the rear. Peering up the alley and along the roofs, I guessed it sat at a prominent corner with closed shops and the evening taverns opened farther down the way. At the back, there was a small stable with tending buas, and I could see some of the other animals deliberately bred to look prettier than Nightmare.

Mourn instructed Gavin to take what he wished off the mare, for she would be staying here among the others.

"Is that a good idea?" the death mage asked.

"Will she eat the other steeds?" Mourn asked in all seriousness. At our twin expressions of surprise, he added, "The tenders do not understand what we are saying."

How nice to be sure.

Gavin shrugged and answered the question. "Only if they are already dead. She won't eat any feed, however, and if they check her teeth…"

"Then let me warn them." Mourn grinned, turning to the buas. He spoke in their native tongue, using his hands where necessary, indicating Gavin's mount in a similar way he had introduced us to the family Shuang.

The two young males' dark eyes widened, and they bowed their heads in understanding. One asked a question, Mourn answered him, and an agreement was reached.

The half-breed took it upon himself to remove the saddlebags and drape them over one shoulder, somewhat to Gavin's annoyance. As my scholar removed the saddle, the mare was unnaturally still; it was not necessary for anyone to hold the reins. The boys looked convinced, staring with awe, and whispering to each other like they were planning their night.

"What did you tell them, exactly." I crossed my arms.

"That she is a mare of the spirit world and only eats meat," Mourn said.

"Hm. That is refreshingly accurate."

"Also, that they should keep her away from the others," he continued, "and need not exercise her or tend her as they would a mortal horse. They only need to feed her a few rats and come tell us if someone lingers or hassles her. They have agreed."

"On your reputation alone?" Gavin asked.

Mourn smiled. "More on your appearance, *bakgwei*, but they are glad to receive instruction from the Dragon Spirit, for I have been here before."

How often Mourn chose to simply be truthful, and yet this seemed to fit well into how the Yungians saw their world that they did not question it. The Witch Hunters would have been in screaming murder fits by now.

"And where is here?"

"A Guild house in Yong-wen."

Gavin grunted, seeming satisfied. "I doubt anyone without magic would be able to take her if they tried. She simply will not move. They must be strong enough to carry or drag dead weight."

I smirked at the pun and spied one of the young handlers trying to peer into my hood. I looked directly at him, and he moved behind a post, averting his eyes. I could hear his heart pounding from where I stood.

Mourn noticed as well, flicking his tongue once in the boy's direction. "No need to delight in scaring them."

I blinked. "He was staring. I only *looked* at him. He did it to himself."

"He hasn't fallen to his knees," Gavin muttered in my defense, "weeping and babbling incoherently."

"Yes, it was a thrill for him," I agreed. "You said I could show my face here. I was just standing here."

Mourn grunted, leaving it at that.

We waited for Gavin to direct his mare to follow the boys as they put her in the empty stall farthest from the door. The other horses grew nervous, and we left as the boys began shifting steeds to different boxes away from the otherworldly mare. It was useful they were so cooperative with the "Dragon spirit," but I pondered how much influence Mourn really had among these people, what he used it for, and what he had to do to maintain it.

We entered the building into a large, quiet kitchen which had space for ten servants to be working at once. Richly decorated pots hung on racks suspended from hooks in the ceiling. Bags of white grains and baskets of root vegetables abounded with drying herbs and a rack of spice bottles. Two wide cooking hearths, one on each side of the room, were clean, orderly, and well-tended.

There were two Yungian women present, which might have been why Gavin covered up as much as he could, including hiding his hands tucked in his sleeves. He hunched down, again hiding the fact that he was not much shorter than Kurn. I understood not wanting to be stared at further but did not think he needed to hunch. Mourn drew greater attention with his height and the fact that he left his hood down.

Across the room were stone steps leading up from the kitchen into a polished, wooden hallway; I assumed we would go there. Before we could leave the mat at the doorway, however, Mourn plucked up a stout bristled brush next to a bucket of fresh water, dunked it, and began to scrub his bare, taloned feet. Gavin and I stared at him as he knocked off dirt between his toes.

"Remove your boots," he told us quietly. "You may carry them with you, but there will be a mat on which to place them in your room. Use that."

Our room?

I glanced at the women's feet, noted they wore stockings and open, tough-bottomed sandals on their feet. Neither wore boots meant for outdoors as the stable buas had worn. By comparison, how muddy and travel-worn *my* boots were, even if I did clean them regularly.

So, Yungians were a people concerned with indoor cleanliness. Not a bad thing under an open sky with so much rain mixing with soil, not to mention the manure in the streets and stables which could be tracked in. Not having to constantly clean the floors or worry about filth getting into the food and beds *would* give the servants time to focus on other things.

I complied, using the bristle brush after Mourn to scrub the bottoms of my boots, making sure to land the clumps of filth on the mat to be shaken out. Gavin was much slower to follow.

"Not a custom at the monastery?" I asked with a smile.

The mage grunted, "No. The cleaning of mud and dung off the floors was one of my endless tasks."

I chuckled. "Yungians must think Manalari monks like sheep in a field."

Gavin had not seemed to consider that before. He removed his boots and dingy socks as well, letting his pale feet and long toes with their black tips be seen by the servants as he cleaned his boots after me. They averted their eyes and found ways to rearrange their herbs.

We passed through the kitchen to the far door, the stone beneath our feet smooth and clean swept, climbing three steps to what I assumed was the main living area, maybe a dining space. In another dark paneled, decorated alcove, Mourn greeted an older Yungian woman with a bow and a word. She smiled widely at him, well-dressed in a royal blue silk robe and possessing an air of authority as she returned his greeting.

I peeked out of the alcove and through a curtain of beads woven on threads hanging down, spying a large dining space. Three long tables and chairs, beautifully carved, exquisite trimmings draping, craft displays, and murals on the walls. The color gold and long, serpentine reptiles were common accents.

Hm.

I thought it odd that Mourn did not introduce us to this woman by name as she briskly directed two younger females to lead us to a smaller hallway to the left, away from what I noted was the street-facing front of the building. I tried to catch her eye, but she would not look directly at either Gavin or me. She excused us and herself before I could speak.

I sighed inwardly. I didn't understand most of these customs. I'd picked up behaviors from the Ma'ab and the Witch Hunters faster, which certainly spoke something of me.

There are better ways, the half-blood had said, *but they take time and patience.*

We followed two caits dressed not quite as well as their elder upstairs to the second floor. The wood creaked beneath the larger males' footsteps, though I stepped lighter than the two females who wore slippers and made less noise. We were each introduced to our own room barely large enough for a decent bed, table, washstand, and tiny closet. The mat for our shoes was right by the door. There was a window in each, covered in what looked to be the same parchment that made the streetlamps, letting in light but affording visual privacy, if not soundproofing.

"They will bring hot water and soap," Mourn said. "We should freshen up before we meet my contact here."

"Your contact will be offended?" Gavin grumbled.

The mercenary looked at him. "We should bathe."

The death mage sighed as we stood out in the hall; the girls had gone to get the water and supplies. "You say they won't speak to outsiders, only each other?"

Mourn nodded. "Yong-wen is a place not easy to learn what happens inside if you don't belong. The rest of Augran is quite different; starting rumors or panic is much easier among the merchants and workers, which can draw the attention of the guard or officials. In most places, I am likely to be taken for a demon—"

"Ah, there we are," I interjected.

He arched a brow at me. "—but I have safe places all around Augran. Stay with me to avoid stumbling into the dangerous areas for non-Humans, and you will be fine."

Gavin and I didn't really have much choice about that.

We each took our separate rooms—Gavin and I next to each other and Mourn right across the hall—and took our time to freshen up and spend some time alone with our thoughts.

CHAPTER 15

THE MOMENT THE SERVING GIRL ARRIVED WITH THE HEATED portion intended for washing, I asked her for drinking water.

"Drink," I said in Trade, pantomiming the act and pointing to her steaming bucket. It was difficult to get her to look at me, but she watched my hands, at least. She was rather pretty with those dark eyes, her smooth skin, her round ears covered by her glossy black hair curved into a practical but elegant up-do.

"Ai! Ci'qin!" she cried, nodding with anxious exuberance, setting down the bucket, and fleeing downstairs.

I stared at the hot water and the open door, deciding I wouldn't strip down until I had something to drink and some security. The girl returned more quietly than she left, quick-stepping and balancing a full metal pitcher of water and matching cup in both hands. She set it down without spilling any, bowed in a formal fashion fast becoming familiar, and stepped backward toward the door.

"Name?" I asked.

She froze.

I tried not to grin and pointed to her. "You. Name?"

She shook her head and looked about to faint.

Pfft, I haven't seen a youth this jumpy since finding Grelio under the table.

Then again, looking at it from that perspective, I tried harder, first putting both my hands where she could see them. My fingertips touched my chest.

"Sirana," I said.

She gasped in fright, covered her ears, then *did* collapse, no doubt bumping her head on the floor. I grimaced.

Fuck.

I needed to leave this stuff to Mourn. Not one girl or boy had passed out around him, yet. I poured and guzzled two cups of water before approaching the Yungian servant, kneeling down to check her pulse and her head for any cuts. *Seems fine.*

"Mai? Ching shyuoh, Mai?"

Uh-oh.

The door wasn't shut all the way, and the matronly elder who'd greeted us earlier poked her head in the same moment I stood up and took a step back, showing my hands as Mourn had. Her look of concern was no surprise to me.

"Um...misunderstanding," I tried.

The matron peered down at the girl then up at me, considering something as I tried to seem nonthreatening. Slowly, she entered the room, left the door open a crack, and kneeled to check the girl herself with a low hum in her throat. Mourn *must* have heard the thump; I waited for him to come in and tell me I'd mortally insulted someone.

He didn't appear, and the matron sounded satisfied. "Is okay."

I blinked.

"You touch her, *nirjwai?*"

She speaks Trade? Excellent.

"No," I answered. "I asked her name, told her mine. She fainted."

The matron's thin eyebrows lifted high, several creases appearing on her forehead. "Ohhhh, *gyina shu.*"

She chuckled, removed her shawl to roll up as a makeshift pillow to put beneath the girl's head, rearranging her limbs so she would not wake cramped. Using the wall, the elder woman pushed herself to her feet with a breath out.

"Pardon for disturb, spirit guest," she said. "Any I obtain for you while we await Mai to wake? I too old to carry and not ask guest."

Mai, huh?

I waved my hand above my water and my bag of village gifts. "I have plenty, thank you."

The elder woman stood against the wall near the girl upon the floor, watching as I dug in to enjoy what there was while it was fresh. Like the rest of the Humans on the Surface, she seemed fascinated by how much food I could pack away in one sitting.

Then she lifted both hands to press to her chest as I'd done. "You can call me Ai-ling, spirit."

"Sirana, not 'spirit'," I said, peeling a piece of stubborn fruit. "Greetings, Ai-ling."

Her eyebrows lifted high again, but she did not faint from hearing my name. "Hm. You are warrior. Been gone long time?"

That was rather insightful for a Human. I glanced at her. "I have no enjoyment being formal."

She shook her head. "Few in Yong-wen wish to hear true spirit name. It will follow them, for well or ill."

I sighed. "Do you have a suggestion, Ai-ling?"

The older woman considered. "In Yungian?"

No, in Manalari. I took a drink of water, which wasn't snowmelt but it was clean. "Yes. A name not to frighten excessively. As long as it does not demean or insult me in return."

Ai-ling smiled without showing her teeth. "*Hm.* Your eyes like clear sky, warrior. Like this? *Lantiu-janshi.*"

I considered. "Lonteeyu janshi?"

The woman nodded. "Meaning warrior from clear blue sky."

Fun. Especially as I was from the opposite.

"It is kind of long. Which part means 'warrior'?"

"*Janshi.*"

Ah. I like that.

"Very good. Thank you, Ai-ling."

She bowed and kneeled to check on the girl as well. Mai finally stirred, and Ai-ling tugged her wrist, sing-songing something in Yungian. The girl scrambled to her feet with a bow to the bed that almost sent her head over feet again. The matron sighed with patience, took the girl's arm to steady her, and steered her toward the door, giving her further instructions on her way down the hall.

Then Ai-ling closed the door and remained inside my room.

I arched my brow. "Something else?"

"Yes. The Dragon Spirit asked me to speak with you, if you are not too tired, *Lantiu-janshi*?"

Her Trade had grown noticeably better as she looked at my face, bold and expectant, different from every woman in Yong-wen so far.

Ah.

This was Mourn's contact he wanted to address his concerns? She seemed to catch me at a disadvantage. I must leave for Manalar with Gavin, but the geas *could* stop me despite my promises to him and to Jael. This was the first step toward getting the half-blood to voluntarily come as well. Clever of him to choose an older woman from a completely foreign set of customs.

Yet I must try to impress her, somehow.

I glanced at the bucket losing its steam, motioning to it. "He suggested I bathe before meeting you. I have not done so, and it seems a waste to not use the water Mai brought, heated especially for me."

Ai-ling contemplated that. "You do not offend as you are, *Janshi*. Apologies for rushing this."

That answer leaned toward keeping my clothes on but wasn't direct enough for my liking. If she was indeed "rushing" this, my desire to bathe using luxurious hot water remained.

"Would bathing as we talk offend?"

Her answer took some deliberate thought. "No, warrior."

I began stripping as I would in the Cloister, until I wore only Shyntre's pendant, with my clothing and gear ordered on the bed for inspection. The elder woman did not stare at my body, not in lust or distaste, and kept her face placid, watching what my hands were doing.

I gently removed my spiders from their pouch, placing them atop the table to make their way onto the walls. Ai-Ling's dark brown eyes widened, and her face paled.

"They are magic-touched and obey me," I told her. "Their purpose is to guard me. I do not use them to attack first."

The woman said absolutely nothing to this, and I shrugged and continued my task.

Two clean and dry cloths had come with the hot water, as did a small jar of soap too fragrant for my preference, but I would use it anyway. The scentless bar I had brought with me from the underground was long gone. I scrubbed and rinsed in small sections, keeping things in order from top to bottom helping me think since the Yungian had gone quiet. Mourn's concerns resounded in my head.

"The Deathless following you. Your unusually vivid dreams linked with your aura when you are aroused. The relic that the death mage keeps for you which wants to own you. Whatever you have not said about your mission and why that false sapphire is more valuable to you than it would be to any I have ever known."

Where to start?

"You are of some status in the Guild?" I asked.

"I am. An archivist and scholar."

"Hm. Will you be among those to listen to what the death mage in the next room has to say?"

Ai-Ling paused but said slowly, "I will. I am curious of this."

I nodded, satisfied, soaping up my pits after cleansing my face and neck. "What of a Dwarf named Osgrid? She lived outside Troshin Bend."

The Yungian again seemed surprised. She considered lying to me but sighed. "I have heard of her, and of the sorcerer in the same town. Osgrid is a wise friend."

Claiming friendship of the Dwarf, and her Trade was fluent. I listened to Mourn's contact rethinking her presentation, how deep a deception was necessary. Apparently, the matron of an empty, Yungian inn wasn't her top choice.

"By what name do you know that sorcerer?" I asked, rinsing my torso and leaving a subtle scent of blossoms.

She answered readily. "Brom Troshin."

"Any others?"

Ai-Ling considered while I kept dunking and squeezing the cloth before wiping briskly over my abdomen and hips.

"None that matter," she answered. "By what names do you know him?"

I breathed out, feeling nauseated to recollect. I waited for it to pass then refocused on her face. "Cris-ri-phon, a former Zauyrian leader from the Red Desert. My death mage ally knows him as the Deathless. From the Greylands. It seems he has existed for a few thousand years in some form."

This concerned her immensely, but I could not determine if they had been known to her before now until she spoke.

"Can you explain how you came to know of these...?"

"Personas?" I asked. "Or souls?"

Ai-Ling's face was a paler shade than before. "Yes."

Maybe.

"I can try," I said, gingerly soaping up my crotch and between my buttocks, "but only with Gavin present. He is a scholar as well."

She offered me a nod and let that rest, though she proved she had spoken with Mourn somehow with what she asked next. "Gavin safeguards a …relic which you stole from the sorcerer, now attuned to you. What are your intentions for this cursed blade?"

She did not sound Yungian anymore. Her Trade was better than mine, but a familiar lilt caused a rush in my chest.

"You know its name?" I asked bluntly, reaching awkwardly to rub my lower back and spine. "Anything about its past?"

"Not its real name. I have heard legends of the Soul Dagger of the Dark Queen. It was a gift given upon her union with a Human man. It vanished in a war but has resurfaced."

I stopped washing with only my legs and feet to go, narrowing my eyes at her. "Will you show me with whom I speak, Guilder? This is my face, and my name is Sirana. Using it will not make one such as you faint." I smirked. "What is *your* face and name, that the 'Dragon Spirit' trusts you to deal with me?"

The elder female bowed her head in a somewhat different way than Yungian. "Fair to parley in the open, Davrin. You are as forward as my sister described."

Although I'd begun to suspect, even hope, I was nevertheless struck by the foreign beauty revealed to me as the short, Yungian elder vanished, and a tall, pale-skinned Elf stood in her place against the wall.

Shit. She's almost as tall as Gavin.

She was also slender and long-limbed the way Tamuril was. Her large eyes were dark, silvery grey, her gaze calm, experienced, peaceful; she seemed old as an experienced Matron although I spotted no fine age lines at all around her eyes.

Her skin was as white and her hair as dark as the Ma'ab, while her cheeks and ears were touched by the same pink blush as the blonde Druid. Not a touch of age-white showed in the easy wave of tresses. Her tapered, upswept ears were longer and narrow, where mine flared wider off the lobe.

She wore a cream-colored, long-sleeved shirt beneath a functional dress armor of black leather with blue and silver trim. Her pants were a deep blue that matched her cloak. She possessed a decorated blade at her belt but no weapon which looked hard used. Her feet were clad in pale, sheer stockings; her boots were elsewhere in this inn.

"The Humans can't hear us," she said, touching her chest. "My name is Krithannia. I am a Naulor. The only one in Augran. A pleasure to meet the assassin who would kill my sister with three venomous bites."

The delivery was dry as sun-bleached bone.

I kept scrubbing, selecting my left leg, and bracing my arm against the table. "That went poorly. I say true, I did not want to fight. I needed water from her well, but her falcon flushed me out before we could negotiate, her constricting vines trapped me, their thorns punctured me, and my guardians did as they were enchanted to do: stop the mage using the magic. I... used a... venom-cooler to save her. I do not have many to spare, but I did not want your sister's death, Naulor."

Her fine, dark eyebrow was raised, but she listened. I gradually worked on my right leg as I watched some anger pass over her face as she looked away from me. Pass over and leave. In her contemplation, she was easily the most regal face and carriage I'd seen on the Surface.

She must be a Noble, or whatever the Naulor equivalent is. Maybe higher.

"I understand first meetings going badly," she murmured. "What happens after often shows the truth, not the fight itself. You tended her and yourself afterward for three days, allowed you both a healing and second chance despite the insult and threat to your unborn."

So, they had spoken. Mourn hadn't been following me before she and I reached the Ley Tower, it could not have been him.

"Where is Tamuril right now?" I asked. "She made the offer to take me to Manalar to look for *my* sister."

Krithannia looked at me. "And you could not accept her brave offer. I hope you can imagine how much courage that took her to extend it."

I focused on the cloth rubbing between my toes. "I was not part of the squad who found the trespassers belowground."

"Fortunately for you, she says the same."

When next I looked up, I saw the shimmer of tears in the Naulor's eyes.

"I take ultimate responsibility, Sirana, as much as I find what was done abhorrent. I arranged for the travel and sent her where Morixxyleth told me he'd escaped the Deepearth, knowing from his stories that what she sought grew there." Krithannia swallowed. "I never wanted her to get hurt, but she was desperate to help a sick boy in a remote village. I did not think the men I sent with her would let her go so deep."

"They didn't," I said. "My sisters were on the Surface then, a different mission. It was... bad timing they crossed paths in the same tunnels so near to the outside."

"You heard about it, then."

"The squad leader is my superior."

The Naulor's tears withdrew some and her expression hardened. "Why did your superior not kill or enslave Tamuril if she felt the drive to violate and humiliate her? Why force the helplessness and pain, finish with her, and throw her out like crumpled waste?"

I wasn't sure I could explain that, despite that Jaunda had described it to me in bed while stretching *my* netherhole in demonstration. The memory conflated with the peek I had of Tamuril's pink skin and caused my labia to tingle.

Stop it, slit, pay attention.

"My sergeant disobeyed the clerics' desires," I said. "The next step after breaking the Druid's will through pain would have been to bring her bound to the clerics of Braqth."

Somehow, Krithannia's face shifted whiter, and her silvery eyes looked haunted. I could not take insult, only shrug with my cloth in one hand. "My sergeant changed her mind, that is all I know. She threw the Druid out beneath the Sun, knowing she needed it, and warned her not to trespass again." I paused. "She was punished for this choice."

"That makes it no better," Krithannia said.

"But it is more than you knew before today. I am being truthful and generous."

The Naulor smiled patiently. "Only because you want Morixxyleth, Davrin. That is plain as the day to me. Whether he makes a bargain with you is his decision for I am not his keeper. But I shall *not* allow him to be misled by you if I see it. All your motives must be placed in the light where he can see them. He suffered greatly under the Davrin and was a feral fugitive when I met him."

Krithannia at last straightened up to her full height away from the wall and finished her speech. "There is something else to your presence and that of the death mage you found than his past, however. Such that neither of us would disregard your goals or its importance to Manalar, but there are shadows around your people where he may miss a warning. That is why he brought you to me."

I disliked her intelligent and cutting insight but admired her boldness to negotiate on a bua's behalf, and the clear boundaries laid down. Finally, a powerful Matron on the Surface I recognized, and probably the "one" female contact Mourn admitted was not a current lover, but a former one.

She can say his name correctly, after all.

Motives all in the light, she said. Alright, let us start there.

As much as I can.

"The Deathless knew Gavin and I were headed to Manalar," I began. "He tried to force me to stay with him, tried to enslave me with the Ma'ab helping. Mori... Mourn executed Kurn and Castis as part of his current contract and offered me protection should the Deathless recover enough from his injury to follow me and Soul Drinker before we made it here.

"I want to take his offer of protection further. I am not stupid to believe I can evade the Deathless each and every time, and if the sorcerer did not follow me immediately out of Troshin Bend, then he may try to cut me off where I go next."

Krithannia arched a thin, dark eyebrow. "What injury, if I may ask?"

"I stabbed him with the relic. Though I... do not remember doing it. I was, ah, trapped between them, and it was the first time I drew it..."

I waited for a moment of dizziness to pass, realized my skin was mostly dry, and I was chilled. I moved to dress despite my clothes smelling of the week sailing on a ship.

The Naulor noticed, her delicate nose sniffing, and offered, "Shall I clean them for you?"

So, that was where Mourn learned that trick. I nodded, watched her cast with word and gesture, and my clothing and gear refreshed before my eyes, all odors dissipating. I began again to dress.

"You were trapped, you said?" Krithannia encouraged.

I ground my teeth then smirked. "If you are angry at my sister for mounting Tamuril to try to break her, you may be satisfied to hear I suffered the same. The innkeeper and Kurn violated me at once."

A beat.

"I am *not*, Sirana," she replied with force. "I am sorry to hear it happened at all. I am also glad that you survived them and escaped, as much as I am glad for Tamuril. I have seen the bodies of too many victims who do not."

For a while, I couldn't say anything. I finished putting myself together, feeling the added protection around me, physical and in-tangible.

"I must go to Manalar with Gavin," I said with care. "Plainly spoken, Naulor, I want Mourn's protection should Cris-ri-phon appear again. I saw him fight the mass of insanity amid the warp rot. The Dragon's son is the reason I saw the next day, giving me the second chance against the relic overtaking my will. *And* he is the reason my child still rests in my belly when I was starving but tricked not to know it. He is supremely capable, and his skills are much in need. He wants the *Ridhian*, and I will negotiate that and more if he will be my bodyguard when we go South."

"Why must you go to Manalar?"

"That can wait until Gavin is present."

Krithannia dipped her chin. "And the Soul Blade? Why would you intend to keep it when it is so dangerous?"

"It is not for greed or desire to keep it," I answered fiercely. "I stole it in desperation, but I am afraid of the demon's manipulation, of its voice in my head. Yet who else may keep its interest when it wishes to learn what happened to the Davrin after the Desert war? I *know* how consuming the Abyss is. I have stared into that Void for all my life."

Her lovely, contemplative frowned slightly. "But you are young."

"Indeed, I am only a century old, yet in ways Tamuril seems *younger* than me," I said with every intent to keep the tremor out of my voice, "and I cannot tell *your* age, Krithannia, when you can't be less than seven centuries."

She did not deny this. Her calm silence pulled me to continue.

"If you know how the Dragon's son suffered under the servants of Braqth, you might imagine how I have struggled to live as one of many trying to avoid being slapped on the altar. You may know I *have* been broken, but I must stand up again or simply die. My elders lead by example, they have seen and survived worse than you have lived. They become hard as the stone cavern around them, though you can only ask *why* my sergeant did what she did, while most of our *buas* die young with even less choice, abused to catch children from them before being sacrificed to a hungry goddess."

The pale Elf was like a statue as I quivered. My vision blurred at the edges as I spoke again.

"I-I am astonished at the relative peace and plenty of the Surface, at the widespread travel and the trade with others. There is struggle and greed, always, but I seek not to spread Braqth's ways up here. Let her stay hidden below in the dark! The spider clerics deserve to fight over the Soul Blade after I toss it into the web among them, should I succeed in carrying it to my city as it wishes."

My voice slowed then stopped on that inevitability as I tried to read the Naulor's mood. Her face had softened in response to the words tumbling free out of my mouth; she watched me and did not look away. She'd listened.

I tried to catch my breath, my heart thumping in my ears, eyes blinking to keep that telling shimmer at bay. I had no further words that wouldn't burn my throat. After many long moments, when the Naulor had returned from her inner reflections and leveled her elder's gaze to me, she bowed her head and made a graceful, if unfamiliar, gesture with her pale hand.

"I shall count myself fortunate you are the first pureblood Davrin I have met," she said solemnly. "You are driven by more than you say, yet all you say is true. You and your death scholar recognize that you need help, and I may say with similar truth that the Guild *can* help you. I wish to hear from both of you together. Come, call your guardians and let us move to comfortable quarters with our allies."

I listened, numbed to consider it being that easy, but gathered my spiders and belongings. As I followed her, I turned over what she had said.

The Guild can help you.

This was good for Gavin's goal but uncertain for a major part of mine, if Krithannia meant she would recommend Mourn *not* bargain with me to become my bodyguard. Perhaps she hadn't decided yet.

What would happen if Mourn didn't come with us to Manalar? Would I leave Gavin and Jael to merciless Witch Hunters to follow him wherever he went next? What if he simply vanished like the Priestess and her Sathoet Son, but did so to avoid me? What would I be compelled to do next?

Those possibilities scared me more than dealing with Soul Drinker again.

To her credit, the Naulor knocked on Gavin's door wearing her Elven form and did not quibble about her introduction when he asked for identification through a tightly closed door.

"I am the Guild Mistress of Augran. Sirana is out here with me. I am here to learn about the soul shard you carry and the message you must pass to the Bishops hoarding a sacred site. Would you come with us to speak in a larger room?"

Mourn leaned against the door jamb to his own room, arms folded, watching us. Based on his tail twitching mixed with a lash or two, either he hadn't listened to a word we'd exchanged, or he heard every single one. I wagered on the latter.

As usual, Gavin took a while to gather his things before opening the door, though he had not yet verbalized his agreement. Perhaps he'd forgotten. Krithannia did not seem to mind. Finally, the scholar opened his door and stepped partway through the frame then stopped.

The Human death mage stared at the Naulor at eye level. Whatever irritable, rude thing he was about to say was on her, as she could have warned him. I didn't because I wanted to see his face.

I wasn't expecting his eyes to shift void-black immediately.

"Uhh, wait," I spoke up. "She's important to your mission, Gavin. Not a threat."

"I know," he said, his head tilting first this way then the other, staring at the pale-skinned Elf through glossy, black eyes. "But I have never seen anything like this."

Krithannia smiled in welcome. "What is it you see, Deathwalker?"

"Perhaps I'd best not say until I understand more. But… you are the primary essence?"

"Hm." Her smile seemed almost flirting, her eyes a lighter grey now. She apparently did not find him repulsive to look at for so long. "If you wished to intrigue, messenger, you succeeded. And yes, I always have been the 'primary.' You may call me Krithannia. What do you prefer?"

The former monk shook his head. "Nothing in particular. Gavin. Deathwalker. Death mage."

"He dislikes 'apprentice,'" I volunteered.

Gavin darted me a look that made me smile, while Krithannia seemed close to laughter.

"Please, come. If there is anything you need to make our talk open and undistracted, do let me know."

Taking two corners made the building larger than I had thought at first, then the four of us entered a much larger office with food, drink, and enough places to sit. Krithannia made it obvious she was casting a privacy spell to lock down listening and scrying.

"No troubles could arise from speaking as we did in the hallway?" I asked.

"I selected my cooks and housekeepers this night," she said. "This is to keep our own auras from unsettling those nearby."

Not to keep anyone out but to keep us in. *Uh-oh.*

"You selected Mai?" I asked. "She seems new to the spirit world. Easily flustered."

Mourn emitted a brief rumble in his throat and raised one brow at me. I was tempted to blow him a sarcastic kiss but instead raised both eyebrows in challenge. Krithannia noted the exchange and chuckled.

"Yes, she *is* new and easily flustered," said the Mistress. "I wanted to see how you treated her, Sirana. Simple enough."

I lifted my chin. "I did not hurt her. She fainted."

"I know, *Lantiu-janshi*. She told me."

Mourn responded to the joke of the name; his fang poked out as his lips stretched.

The Guild Mistress looked between us and waved to the food on the table. "Now, would anyone like water, wine? A snack?"

I'd just eaten and had drunk enough that I would need a bucket break sooner or later, but I glanced between Mourn and Gavin inquiringly.

Inhaling at an oddly slow rate, the Deathwalker stepped forward and did his one bite of food, one sip of water ritual with no visible enjoyment. Nonetheless, Krithannia watched with interest. Mourn helped himself to quite a lot more and sat down, slowly, in a stout chair. I followed suit, figuring I could have it nearby when I grew hungry, for there surely wasn't anything wrong with it.

In time, we were each seated on one side of a square table, our respective packs and equipment resting on the floor, staring at each other.

Krithannia led again with impeccable politeness. "May I see this soul shard you created, Gavin? That which must be thrown into the sacred pool."

The death mage sat for a moment before reaching into his belt pouch for a lump he kept wrapped in a drab cloth. He set it down carefully and unwrapped it slowly with one hand, revealing the glossy piece of flint, sharp at two ends, with a center that churned so gradually one might overlook it.

He waited without speaking as Krithannia's cheeks flushed like Tamuril's, though not in arousal or shame. I wondered what she saw that I didn't.

"Perhaps begin with the night the Witch Hunters murdered you."

The Guild Mistress was certainly well-informed. I tossed a glare at Mourn across the table. He smiled back, leaving me to wonder how he'd communicated so much detail so fast. Gavin stared at the Naulor for quite a while.

Then he spoke.

"My Vis became aware in the Nexus. What modest preparations I'd made assured I did not arrive centered in a wasteland of hungry ghosts, but on a border where I could be found by a psychopomp who'd even heard of this world. I knew what I needed to do, and it guided me to an oasis to wait. I waited for a long time."

Scores of tiny bumps spread out over my arms listening to him. None of us made a peep; I doubted any of us blinked.

"She sent tutors to me in the form of crows," Gavin said. "I had to feed them, somehow, for them to feed me in return."

He glanced down at his right arm.

"She?" Krithannia invited respectfully.

"The Grey Maiden. Nyx. I never saw her as an eidolon. Never heard her. Not as I've seen her as I've slept."

The Naulor waited as she had with me, motioning for him to continue. The Deathwalker considered the cup of water he'd poured, of which he'd only taken a sip.

"Eventually," he said, "I deduced that my Vitas *was* the pool by which I waited, and through the crows on both sides of the veil, I could affect my original body. I *had* performed the ritual properly for I could touch the 'water' and see flashes of my home world.

"I knew I was to return through it, to entwine my Vis with this altered Vitas once I'd learned enough, but no matter how much I fed the crows of my flesh so they would regurgitate what they knew into the pool, no matter how it turned black, and blacker..." He paused, studying his palms. "The pool repelled me. My Vitas and my Vis would not reunite. The silver dagger of the *Dyos Guerrimos* kept them severed despite my efforts. Despite seeing and hearing the crows above the shed where my body lay."

My fingers fiddled with the tips of my gloves; I noticed and made myself stop. Krithannia noticed this as well and offered us a small smile. "Until you received a little earned luck from an ally who had not given up on you."

My scholar won't know how to respond to that.

Sure enough, Gavin looked away from all of us, at a point on the far wall. "Indeed, Sirana removed the silver dagger before my Vitas or my body could be corrupted by the Ma'ab or the Deathless. Although she was ignorant of the cause or the outcome, I owe this opportunity to her. I would see her well through what I must do, that we may return to the Ley Tower to complete her mission as well."

Huh, bua…

Now Gavin and Mourn shared a look, and my face flushed hot with a stab of pain in my skull. I hoped it wouldn't get worse. I was glad I didn't blush like a Naulor, though I could sweat like one.

Krithannia looked intrigued with Gavin's offer. "And what is it you both must do?"

I breathed slowly, willing my trembling stomach to calm down. Gavin didn't show his teeth when he smiled and spoke for us.

"To remove Sarilis and whatever influence has been keeping him entrenched there. My Lady has made it clear to me this crossroad must remain open and neutral, and the sacred pool at Manalar is due a change of hands. It would seem another Seer agrees with both visions, given I did not arrive in Yong-wen alone."

Krithannia turned that over, interlacing her elegant fingers in front of her lips. "Hm." She refocused on the shard. "And I understand this soul shard is attuned to the Bishops of Manalar, specifically, and will not harm other magics."

"It is. Correct."

"That is an incredible first task, Deathwalker."

He shook his head, dismissing the praise. "Only one of many, Guild Mistress, and each with many facets."

"True." The black-haired Elf looked to the side as well, in deep thought once again. It took her time to come out of it. She blinked at me, at the food, at Gavin. "Hm. So, the path is clear for you, and the Guild has means to infiltrate the Temple if the need is dire, though do not think even we are without risk of failure. Tell me, what known obstacles lie in your way?"

"The Ma'ab army," Gavin began. "Possibly the Deathless."

He fell quiet and glanced my way. The Naulor lifted her brows expectantly at me.

I sighed. "Soul Drinker."

And this fucking geas.

Gavin twisted his neck to look at me. "You must know now, Sirana, I have carried this dagger so it could not prey upon you at your most vulnerable. But, in doing so, I have been listening to the void of souls inside for some time, and the demon becomes ever more agitated while it cannot dig hooks into me. I understand the strain on the bearer, but for the sake of living and dead, I cannot carry both the soul shard and this relic close to the pool. The consequences—"

My mouth opened as my gut tightened in fear. "I-I was not expecting you to carry it for me the entire journey, Gavin. I will bear it again."

Gavin was satisfied; it was Mourn who asked, "When?"

"Do you wish it to be here at the table?" I retorted.

"I do not wish for fast actions from you. I ask what you need for this transfer to be successful."

"Your word of protection from others at Manalar," I answered, "however long it lasts."

The hybrid smirked wryly, but I continued.

"I cannot bear the dagger and be prepared for the Deathless or Witch Hunters every moment I am awake. Sometimes, I am neither awake nor in Reverie."

"A great concern," the Dragonchild said. "The demon would prefer that I *not* protect you. One of those times you are neither awake nor asleep, you may attempt to stab me from behind."

But I can't do that, ever! I can't!!

I burst out laughing, my head tilted up. I knew my voice sounded hysterical; otherwise, it hurt too much. Mourn and Krithannia watched me warily, neither moving nor talking.

Gavin tapped the table with his fingers; whether he meant it or not, it gained their attention. He said, "She, ah, has tried and failed already."

"What?" Mourn asked. "When?"

"Inside the circle of protection against the warp-rotted."

Golden eyes blinked in disbelief; the mercenary looked at me. I put my head and arms on the table, squeezing my eyes shut, trying to breathe and stay awake. I listened to them.

"She tried mere moments after striking a deal?"

"Moments after she traded the blue stone to you out of fear and confusion," the death mage replied. "I do not believe it was her but the demon who tried to puppet her to throw itself at you."

I groaned to hear that; my jaw hurt from gritting it in shame that he had to speak for me. Maybe they still would not accept Gavin's explanation.

"For whatever reason," he continued, "their wills clashed, and this attempt failed before the dagger left her hand. Since she has had the stone back, I have witnessed vast improvement."

"What improvement?" Krithannia asked, her voice calm and interested.

"There was a 'magical squall' in the Archipelago," Gavin said. "That is what you call it, yes?"

"Yes, I have experienced those. Go on."

"I have not experienced such turbulence in my visions of the dead since boyhood, and I have never before seen places and souls I recognized as 'home' but outside my own time. I was lost and could get no bearing until Sirana offered her soul as a lodestar. Her... thoughts cut through the storm. They were a line to *her* life and time, a preserver I could cling to until it passed. Her will is extraordinarily strong even as she doubts. I do not think another could, or should, carry the relic long term."

"Yet she would take it with you inside the temple sanctum?"

I lifted my head, snarling, "I want the Guild's help finding Jael! Unless she is in the sanctum, I do not need follow Gavin *everywhere*."

"Jael?" asked my grey scholar. "The third of you, of the Blood Sisters?"

"Yes, my sister," I croaked. "She seeks someone specific at Manalar, no doubt influential in the coming siege. I do not know why or what she was to do. She couldn't tell me, but I know her. It was only from watching hints in her face when my elder was teaching us of the Surface."

Krithannia's eyebrows remained expressive, a delicate lift. Her voice was gentle. "Why couldn't she tell you her mission, Sirana?"

"*Nau'chinder*," I answered hoarsely, feeling a tic spasm in my face.

Mourn rumbled in thought, and Krithannia had understood as well.

"Forbidden," she repeated for Gavin's benefit. "Very well." The Naulor considered her next words with care. "When you are ready, Sirana, if you can… show me that you can hold the Soul Blade, be the bearer. Then allow me to set a magical peace knot upon it, and I shall help you locate your sister."

Ah, on the condition…

I frowned. "How does one set a 'magical' peace knot?"

"I inscribe an interlinking rune on the hilt and scabbard. You need never draw it."

Gavin shifted similarly to how he'd reacted to Sarilis's spoken plans about his vials, and I sensed a warning at the back of my mind as well.

I met her eyes. "The thing is *covered* in runes. How powerful of a caster are you? Can you be certain yours will keep blade and sheath together and override the others, or might they interact and conflict?"

Any reasonable mage-scholar *would* look concerned, I thought. Fortunately, the Naulor did. She looked to Mourn. "You have seen it. Your salt ring worked to quiet it."

He nodded confirmation.

"Are the sigils *not* Infernal or Abyssal?"

"Infernal and Abyssal are both present, yes."

"We can work together on the spell, then."

The Dragonchild considered but shook his head. "There are some sigils I do not recognize. I agree with Sirana's caution in adding magic to the relic, even temporary spells. It would take study to find something the demon couldn't overcome while not risking the structure of what is already in place. Time we may not have."

"What else do you suggest?"

"I can draw and sheath it again," I said. "I know I can, especially if Jael's life and freedom depend on it. You do not need the peace knot."

Mourn turned to me slowly. His gold eyes were set in a challenge. "I think that must be proven once again before I can negotiate any further with you, Baenar."

Now, then. I drew in a huge breath, let it out. *Of course, it must be.*

After all he'd done for me, had seen around me; a pregnant Dark Elf with "unusually" vivid dreams, acting on the edge of insanity, unpredictable at times. I had come as close as I could in telling him my geas was partly about *him*. He must have caught it.

I didn't feel insane, though, and I'd done enough thus far that Gavin saw me as an anchor. *A lodestar.* Experience and wisdom were gained only by doing, and Jael needed me to try.

I withdrew the *Ridhian* from my pouch and leaned to my left, setting the red gem in front of the mercenary. He looked down at it but did not jump on it; he offered a questioning look.

"Can you break its attunement from me?" I asked. "Or rather, from Soul Drinker. I am sure it lied about that. I do not want the foul Ma'ab thing anymore, and the relic will *not* use it against me when we speak."

Mourn considered this. "I can. It is fairly easy."

"Please, do it now."

Without hesitation he reached out and closed the pendant in his fist, whispering something in Draconic. I swore my ears popped, and Krithannia smiled.

"Done," he said, leaving the ruby on the table for now.

I squeezed my thighs together. "And where can I relieve my bladder?"

Krithannia blinked twice but pointed at a smaller door. "That closet."

"Thank you." I stood up. "Gavin, please have Soul Drinker's bundle on the table when I return. I really should take a piss, first."

The Deathwalker's expression looking up at me made me smile and Mourn audibly chuckled.

"I will go next," he said, "and will watch over you. Show us what you did at Brom's Inn where none of us could witness it."

"Deal. Be right back."

No demons but us.

CHAPTER 16

I HAD THAT SHORT TIME SQUATTING IN PRIVATE TO CENTER MY mind and body at once. This was the first time since the struggle at the inn's kitchen that I thought about my "tether" settled low in my gut. An unseen presence not always felt but which needed me to return sane. The "lifeline," as Gavin put it, that would help pull me out when I was ready.

I saw again Innathi's mature, joyful face as she assured me that I would dream my baby's face at some point. She assumed it was a Daughter, of course, as most Davrin of importance did. We Nobles "always" wanted our first to be a cait, knowing half the time this did not happen. I'd always thought it a strange omission, an unspoken pressure to willfully ignore the reasonable possibility until it stared one in the face, be it in Reverie or in holding a tiny, newborn body.

Some matas seemed to adjust to the First Son well enough, and others chose to be resentful of the time and energy spent to have him. Some blamed him for having to "begin again."

As if he could help being born male.

But then, it all had to do with ever-evolving power and status, not the baby. The pregnant caits who were soldiers, servants, and merchants verbalized caring far less if their first was cait or bua, so long as they were not sickly or deformed. None of them could invest further if the child would never be able to care for themselves. The Priestesses were aware of this and very persuasive as their agents sought to collect them.

A shiver passed through me as I finished my time in the privy, resetting my leathers but removing my belt and cloak. Had that conversation with Innathi been what I thought it was? Was this the Dark Queen of the Desert from millennia ago, or was it only the demon in the dagger using another form to trick me, to urge me to carry it to Sivaraus?

I must find out if I could. *Here and now.*

I returned to the office, holding my belt and cloak for Gavin to take. "If you please. I don't see where these would help."

My spiders moved inside their pouch. *I'm sorry, no.*

Subtly, Krithannia nodded in agreement, and Gavin accepted and took them over to a small couch by the shaded window where both our packs rested. I noticed the table had been cleared of food and drink, and the wrap holding the red rune dagger rested there as I'd asked.

Mourn passed behind me on his way to the closet, and I grinned, wondering if he was silent in *all* things if he wished to be.

Irrelevant, of course.

"This room has been sealed," Krithannia said, "and I have cast a defensive shield upon Gavin and me. Mourn can cast for himself and will be watching for the demon turning on you and your child. We will take all precautions to turn the blade should it gain control."

"And if it does?" I asked.

"We must discuss the peace knot again or find a place it may be secured but not scried by the Deathless sorcerer or the Ma'ab Ascended."

"The threats I heard from the void," Gavin offered helpfully, "should we try to isolate it in a vault or similar, suggested it had unpleasant retaliation prepared against living, dead, and not yet born. I do not know the extent of its truth, but it will not go quietly. I believe there is a cost."

"My first choice is to face it," I said. "Abyssal lies have a cadence to them I can hear. I know the demon is not as certain as it sounds." I shrugged. "However, if I am wrong about its true strength beneath the lies, well... I am glad you are here to do what you must. It might not matter to me, then."

I bore in mind this was no different from confronting Jilrina and Kaltra, or later on, Wilsira and Kerse. As with those I once knew in Sivaraus, all of them dead, I may have begun this confrontation alone and beaten, but it hadn't ended that way. Soul Drinker feared Mourn and could not overwhelm Gavin, so it tried to coax me away from them, insisting I should distrust them when their actions only spoke of helping me live.

The demon had *wanted* me to throw away Shyntre's pendant, and that had decided a crucial contest I realized too late it was winning. No wonder I was so ill for days after my allies had wrested it from my grip.

Here in Yong-wen, I remembered D'Shea's laughter in her quarters when she discovered that she—even she—could not see who I thought of while wearing the saphgar stone. Neither could Cris-ri-phon see my Valsharess's face in my memory when he wanted it most.

Mourn emerged from the closet, signaling he was ready; with a tiny smile, I reflected that I hadn't heard any base function from the half-blood this time. Finding no words beyond those spoken, I stepped to unwrap the bundle, hearing the joyful whispers before the runes flared like fresh blood.

I lifted it with both hands.

★Yessss! Sirana! At last!★

~Hello, Soul Drinker. I have questions.~

★Goood. Drawww meee...★

THE RUSH OF ENERGY AND CHAOS I EXPECTED DID NOT MATERIALIZE as before. I did not stand upon ever-eroding stone beneath a surreal night sky, with a churning, blue well of light falling into a single point behind me.

A heavy, smothering silence surrounded me in a void. The darkness was total; my eyes could detect no Radiants as in the Deepearth. I reminded myself I wasn't using my real eyes or ears.

Her will is extraordinarily strong even as she doubts. I do not think another could, or should, carry the relic long term.

"Let me see," I said.

The darkness thinned and drifted like fog as Soul Drinker responded, **Are you sure?**

Ancient stone spread out before me without color, I recognized the same sense of being underground, of the massive, awe-inspiring presence of the stone and earth cradling me. Although, despite a shadow of Kain's comfort and expertise perking up in interest, I had no sense of its true age.

Have care. Thiss is not the Deepearth, Sirana.

The enormous room was a hollowed-out part of a mountain several times larger than the Valsharess's richly decorated throne room high in the Palace, although the only indication of a similar center of rule here was the stone seat atop a rise of stairs to my right. The base of the throne had been neither set upon nor fixed to the platform but flowed into it, carved from the stone itself. All else of value had been stripped long ago.

The floor had once been polished and flat, perhaps covered in rugs, but scores of scuffs and scorch marks scarred the fine gloss now. The walls had been dressed by stonecutters to rise as straight-lined sentinels toward a ceiling which disappeared like the Great Cavern. Even these great walls showed their age in cracks left untended after many quakes and tremors.

Broken stairs led to my left away from the throne, but these were nothing like the shallow, consecutive steps leading to the platform. Steep and tall, the path lifted the climber into empty air without railings to hold on to, reaching a dizzying, uncertain height.

I didn't make out where this path led before something cooed and sniggered, its voice caressing the throne. I watched as a deep, impenetrable shadow swirled around the base of the throne before pouring into the hard, bare seat. It attempted to form a torso, four arms, and a head with a set of deep red eyes. It found no need for legs at present.

Ssiranna. Warrior. My bearer. You've felt how powerful I am, and I know you're afraid of me. So long I've waited after you pawned me to the Deathwalker to spend time cuddling with the Dragonchild. And now you've stripped the Ridhian from me before finally answering my call? Tsk. You're not treating me fairly after what I've done for you. We must renegotiate my providing any further aid.

"Where is Innathi?" I asked. "I made the agreement with her about receiving aid. Or was that just you in Davrin form, and there never was a Desert Queen?"

The demon chortled, the edges of its form curling into wisps which broke off before sweeping in to reblend in its core. *Oh, there was, and still is after all this time. I may have provided hints, for I know what she wants. I always have since the day she drew the blade.*

"Where is she?"

Such a poor question displays your ignorance of what you try to wield yet can hardly bear instead.

"How do I speak with her again?*

Ahhh… there we are. Simple enough. You must get past me.

It raised its incorporeal limbs above its "head," indicating the featureless space behind the throne. I saw neither door nor wall.

I am the keeper of every soul ever taken, crowed the demon, *every morsel of Vis and Vitas given birth, yet to be sundered and *drained from their meat. As one, we crave this, and the bearer must be loyal and serve this need. Or we turn on the bearer and find another.* ★

"Why did you try to claim Morixxyleth the moment he turned his back?" I asked. "That was truly a stupid impulse. Gavin and I would have been overwhelmed, and you not only would have no chance to find the Davrin, but the cannibals might have taken you to the heart of the warp rot."

The floating eyes flared, a rope of runes appearing briefly across its chest like the tracks of a scurrying mouse. The demon hissed, ★*I could puppet your corpse. I would have won.* ★

"Hah. You would have been dragged shrieking into something more primal than you. Ignoring what may have happened to the land, the black blade would have been torn apart and transformed, and you with it. You lost contact with me when I got too close. I'd even been holding the dagger, and that severance scared you. I *felt* it. Like all denizens of the Abyss, you can't keep to a strategy or a bargain to save your existence, so why should I renegotiate anything with you? You'll just change it again."

★*Chillld,* ★ it cooed. ★*What else can you do? You must deal with me, or I will make your life pure...unending... torment. I will suck down your unborn's soul like the genital slime that it is. I shall trap your Vis with the Queen of long ago, feast on your Vitas, and you will regret your choice for eternity like all the others.* ★

"That is no choice. I know your sort too well, from my earliest memories in the nursery. It never helped me to accept a threat in hopes of avoiding it."

★*Yesss, but the pain gets worse, until one of us dies. Isn't that how your compulsions work? And unlike these others, I* can't *die. But you can, yet never find peace.* ★ It adopted a hairstyle my eldest sister once favored, growing ears shaped like hers. ★*How you hate feeling so helpless, hmm? You remember.* ★

I smiled, resting my hands on my hips. I could feel the custom fit of my red uniform muting its jabs. Shyntre's pendant soon hung visible from my neck, glowing as the only light in the throne room.

"The Soul Blade is well made," I said. "So many layers of magic. Abyssal, Infernal, and others. And so old."

Nice bluff, warrior. You repeat what you've been told.

"Mm-hm. I heard that and wondered. Do you even *know* who set the rules for you anymore? Or how you got here? Can you leave if you wish? Surely you didn't choose this begging dependence. I wager it was someone more powerful putting a leash on you. A curse works both ways."

The four-armed creature launched off the throne, flying straight at me like a phantom cat, screeching, claws outstretched. I reacted with the speed of thought, of my memory, mimicking my wizard when his magic had shielded me from harm while I'd lain bleeding out.

Except, I had no magic.

Soul Drinker struck a dome of raw, compressed visions, sounds, and sensations as if this moment were as solid as stone. To push through would be to feel everything that I had, Kerse with Kain and me. It recoiled in momentary disgust, its eyes changing from that deep red to a familiar, sickly yellow, then to crimson again. A low, rising cackle swelled in the chamber along with its spreading shadow losing any appearance of a body.

Is that all you have, Ssirana? Soon, I shall sup on that agony built by the Spider Queen.

I backed up before its shade could engulf me. "What happens if I trade the rune blade to a Dragonchild who collects such things?"

...Nnnot wise, Elf.

"But he must be paid, and I understand To'vah blood actually keep their bargains. What would happen to you if I did this? Or do you still want Ishuna?"

Soul Drinker hovered as if playing this through for the first time. Turning, drifting around me, it laughed in cunning delight, moody and piercing. *Yesss... Hmm. ...Yes, I dare you. Give me to either one, Child, either one...*

As the demon's thoughts took full form, I dropped my shield of memories and plunged forward into a different collection altogether.

Desperately, I sought the sense in it.

MOTHER. FATHER.

Do you know, sometimes, they are One? The Same.

~One.~

I hadn't thought of Ullipmious in months and months. I didn't *want* to recall the emaciated Ornilleth prisoner covered in offal, who'd coaxed a demonblood to help it escape in exchange for a pair of wings. Its thoughts had reached as deeply as Kerse's cock had inside me, though it barely remembered being *One,* clinging to a fractured, separate visage of its Elder Mind. As frightening of a memory as Kain and I had been, bound in lust. As painful as Kerse and I, bound in ritual.

*The dissolution and transformation of the Self always begins with the Parent following a Birth. The Parent rises above all Creation in that moment, rises above itself, for the caretaker will both consume and set free this new Self, this **Rebirth** of Itself.*

I listened. I felt. I heard my sister, the Priestesses, and the Valsharess in the claim. I wondered about Ullipmious, if that fractured mind had survived?

~And if the new Self must stay to feed the void of the elder,~ I answered, ~the caretaker becomes the defiler.~

The one who claimed to be Soul Drinker agreed. *The Destroyer! Yesss, that is crucial! That **is** our hunger, we all defile what we make.*

~It doesn't have to be this way.~

Yesss, it does.

~Not here! Not my home.~

*It will **always** be. You cannot stop us when we always want you. Always, all of you! We want you!*

I snarled. ~How did you get here? Show me.~

The flicker of memory was unintended; so quick, it only took a blink to know. It had been a Parent, once. A refugee and stowaway newly arrived in the cradle of this world, writhing in this throne room, wherever it was, and on the cusp of agonizing birth.

My home had given it strength to *know* its creation as a new mind. It knew a new soul separate from the Abyss. And hated it.

~Why?~

Because its Child, its new Self, rejected becoming its Parent, refused to dissolve into the Abyss. It did not stay to feed the Void, no matter how the Parent had beaten it down to stay. This could not happen before, had it birthed where it conceived.

The Child had done something familiar to escape.

And left its Parent behind. Trapped.

Here.

How daarrre youuu...

Soul Drinker pitched me out, threw me like I was the dagger, spinning at vertiginous speed until my mind struck something I could not break. I collapsed onto a barren floor as if I had a body but the instants immediately after were different. The sharp ache was all over, one sensation engulfing me. I could pinpoint no bruises, scrapes, or breaks because they hadn't stopped yet to be assessed.

It was just *pain*. Continually being struck by something I couldn't see.

I couldn't stand.

Red slut, it hissed above me. *You were a fool to challenge me a second time. How easy you made it. You lost our contest of wills; each bearer only gets one chance.*

As it spoke, flint-like shards appeared in the walls of the throne room, glossy, reflective, showing me my face at different, searing moments of my short life. My back, my neck, my head all set afire by countless, heated needles.

*Those shards piercing your mind? Oh, yes, they are only too easy to push in **deeper**. Again, and again, until they pin you down. You and your fractions are mine, Sirana.*

Soul Drinker watched in endless delight, squealing in glee, spinning in place to witness it all. Every humiliation at home, every violation following everywhere I'd ever crawled and tried to be. Within the prison and these glassy shards, my face contorted in ways I'd never seen before but had delighted others for a century.

I would entertain the Abyss for eternity.

Your soul serves me. Give up and spread yourself before me.

~No...~

A Tragar strode up and kicked me, turning me over with his toe. His belt buckle clinked.

You will give me to the Dragonchild. Coax him to take it for payment, for that satisfies your Slut Queen's geas, and may be my way to escape. The pain will stop if you go.

I scrambled on heels and elbows away from the prong-tipped, saw-edged cock revealed. ~No!~

You'll scream for a while longer, Sirana, and do what we want anyway. You cannot stand. You can only lie there. You are broken for the last time. I'll feast on what's inside, nice and slow, and you will wake again. Promise.

My spine bowed like forge-bright wire threaded through the center, and I kicked at Lana's demonic Vungren with my heel.

Hehehehe!

The demonic, white-bearded Dwarf grabbed at my boot, teeth both square and sharp. He had yellow eyes, sick and putrid. Not pure and golden.

~Gaelan! Jael!~

Ohh, they are dead, sweet slit.

~No, they're not!~

Yes, they are! You are too late!

My Sisters *were* alive to hear me. Somewhere. I scrabbled along the floor.

Hold still. Look at me. Don't think about them. Think about me, and what is about to happen to you. Again. And again.

He presented his cock in one stubby hand, and I averted my eyes.

~Jael...~

I *must* find her. She was why I was here. In my mind's eye, I saw Shyntre's map as he'd shown it in the Wizard's Tower. I added to it all the vast land and waters I'd crossed so as not to lose the scent of her.

I closed my eyes. ~Where to next?~

Quiet.

~They are dead. They can no longer control you.~

I saw Kerse's new wings in my memory. He'd never tried them before we stopped him, never left the ground before he killed himself, trying to kill us. The gate to the Abyss hadn't opened yet, and the weight of the world surrounded us all. If I could have sprouted his wings, I might have found Gaelan faster.

Now I was here, yet I was not really lying upon a hard stone altar, waiting helplessly to be raped again. The weight which had helped them all to hurt me was missing. Or it was never present. I'd forgotten.

I opened my eyes. The red-eyed Tragar gave ground as I rose above its own height. ~If I cannot stand, Soul Drinker...~

The squat creature toppled backward, landing in a pile of shadow before flowing up to rejoin with the demon of the Soul Dagger as I brought myself to its level.

~Then I will fly.~

Blood red eyes narrowed like scalpel-thin cuts, condensing its delight.

Eeeeheeee!

Spindly, clawed hands lashed out at me again, seeking the wounds from my own shards burrowed in. I reached forward, braced for the moment I seized an essence I'd finally become brave or numb enough to touch.

Ohhhh, thisss will be fuuun...

Clasped together, my hands matching its grip, the demon pricked my palms a thousand times at once, and I screamed but did not release it. Immediately, a thin, gossamer thread of fluid seeped from between each of our pressed palms, crystallizing as each drop struck the throne room.

Soul Drinker glanced down and hissed. *What is...?*

~Hey. Look at me.~

It did, and I could face this familiar presence once again and not be afraid.

~Just greedy and hungry,~ I thought while pushing us toward the stairs to the throne. ~Desperate and bored. Grappling for any prey that stumbles by the mouth of your den. You can't wait for something better. Curious, do you mimic Braqth on purpose?~

Enormous eyes flared like lava. It boasted, pushing back at me, *I was on this world long before her!*

The crystal built itself up beneath us, nipping at wisps of darkness and turning it ice blue. I floated us toward the barren chair in the center of the platform.

~Getting here first proves you're caught with no way out, or you'd have done it by now without me. I won't be helping you, demon. Someone put you here for a reason. I only want to talk to Innathi, and I must get past you, correct?~

I pressed the curling shadow in its throne where it stopped, and climbed into its lap, straddling the seat with our hands mutually encased in crystal. The black throne began to shimmer from liquid quartz pouring out over the sides, and Soul Drinker tried to yank its hands away.

You'll never find her without me! it cried in panic. *Only I can show you the way to the Elsewhere!*

~Another lie. I can hear your suppressed thoughts inside the throne, you know. I can hear your heart, now.~

I wasn't bluffing. Something akin to a heart raced in the center of its mass as crystal climbed up like a slow, stone wave.

~I have found it best simply to silence defilers like you in one's own mind. You who delight in betraying the sovereignty of any new mind born into this world.~

Soon, we submerged into the stressed fractures and creaking shifts of the smallest particles, settling into a tight, rigid pattern.

~Careful. Bend, don't break.~

Finally, its voice was gone from my head.

Good. *This is enough.*

I leaned back, passing through many facets only to fall off the throne, my mind numb, staring at the vanishing ceiling. Then a sliver of deep gold light appeared in the void behind the demon entombed in crystal, and I turned my eyes toward it. Sand shifted in a breeze beyond.

Encouraged, if achy and weary, I stood up again, my red armor bright and my pendant shining blue in the light. I approached the crack in the stone with care, peeked in…

And stepped through.

THE "ELSEWHERE" WAS MUCH… FIRMER THAN IT HAD BEEN before in that brief time I'd shared a stone raft floating on waves of sand with an ancient queen. Back then, the stars had been blinking and spying upon us, and a blue whorl lighting up the night sky like a collapsing moon trying to suck me in like a hooked fish.

The tall, iron-red dunes moved slowly as if in memory of a stout wind. The sky was that of a soon-ending day, shifting from blue to pink to purple and deepest indigo. The Sun itself was absent from any point above the horizon. I didn't know where the light which cast all the shadows came from, though they grew longer as I stood.

Like night is coming.

I could have chosen any dune to climb but selected the one behind me so I could see how far away the night might be. My slow-sinking boots stopped in place when, at the top, I saw a twisting canyon not far in the distance. From here, the bands of colors signaled to me where I was.

Koorul.

I loped toward it, becoming accustomed to working the sand before I remembered that I didn't have to. This was not a real place. This could not be but another dream, or a trance. I was communing with the blade that killed and kept the Queen of the Desert. Here, I would find her.

The waterfall deep in this sacred place is where it started.

The distance seemed to fold in on itself as if I dragged the horizon closer to me from sheer will. The canyon walls reached toward the sky, growing higher as I approached their every shade of swirling fire struck through with thin, dark veins of purple and blue.

I kept going, plunging deep into the canyon on a fleet thought, where it cooled and darkened gradually. My nose detected moisture, the drifting vapor leading me through the labyrinth until my ears picked up the echo of rushing water. I ran up one final hill, was greeted by the small, sparkling river, and curved down into the ravine.

Innathi was waiting there, standing barefoot in the flowing water, wearing the same flowing, sleeveless gown of startling white. Her dark arms and wrists were decorated with gold bands and bracelets; her hair was piled up and accented by fine, gold chains; rings of several metals and gems adorned her fingers.

Hearing my gait, she turned with a welcoming smile, her arms lifting, opening. *"Cris-ri-phon!"*

We paused in place, and I waited to see if she knew me at all. If she knew she was dead. Her scarlet eyes glimmered as she appraised me, realizing her mistake. Her gaze rested on the nearest cliff wall before returning to me.

"Ah. It is you, khalithan. It has been so long, I thought you'd died."

I smirked. *"The gatekeeper is a selfish and obstinate one, your Majesty."*

Innathi's expression brightened. *"Do you mean you got past the Black Heart?"*

I opened my palms. *"I am here, aren't I?"*

Her lovely, mature face smiled skeptically. *"Sometimes it lets the bearer glimpse the souls beyond in exchange for something."*

"So I discovered, and in the most difficult way. I can assure you, your Majesty, that it didn't want me to catch another glimpse of this 'Elsewhere,' much less stand here in private council with you."

Innathi gazed up at the darkening sky, and I joined her. Unlike before, the stars were still-points of pure light, not a wink among them. I hadn't seen a true Sun set here.

"Hm," she said, bowing her chin to grant my words an intrigued smile. *"Not just the bearer, then? Are you the wielder in truth, now, khali?"*

"I am. I escaped the Deathless, and the relic is mine now, for better or worse."

She turned toward me in the clear river, splashing water, the gown's hem soaking up the precious liquid. Her luminous eyes were wider, slowly growing excited like when we first met, again able to imagine looking forward.

"Can you take me to wherever the Davrin have fled?"

"I can, your Grace."

"Can you evade the Deathless in doing so?"

"I have means, yes. Obtaining it is where I've been for so long."

"Yes. You are determined with the will to travel far. I can see it in your wilder eyes." Innathi lifted her chin. *"We may not be able to aid you in*

body as the Black Heart controls that schism of this relic, but we can aid in knowledge of your past."

"*We?*" I asked, then blinked as I spotted other forms in the mist of the waterfall.

"*Oh, yes. There were other wielders both before and after me.*" The Davrin Queen glanced behind her. "*We are still here in one form or another, though none kept and wielded the Soul Blade for as long as I did.*"

I believed her and could see what she meant. None of the misty figures drifting stepless toward us as the canyon grew darker were as vivid and crisp to me as Innathi was. I did not know whether that reflected the strength of her will or mine in what was most familiar. I easily counted a score of Humans, half as many Dwarves, but only a few Elves whose shade of skin in life I could not determine.

There were also a handful of creatures I did not recognize in any form, some of them larger in stature than a Ma'ab man, though I suppressed my immediate assumption that this size made them all male. I watched them approach, trying to see them as Gavin might. Other than the Queen, however, I could not rightly say much about them than a vaguely recollected identity which must be their own. Perhaps I did not wish to see them any clearer.

So many… over how long? Yet all of these, in the end, failed to control Soul Drinker. All of these.

How many had escaped? Had anyone?

Warily, I asked, "*Where are those killed by the dagger, if these are the wielders?*"

Innathi's brow lifted with interest, and she smiled how I'd imagine a Valsharess might while scarlet eyes pointedly looked left, then right, then up. "*They are all around you, khali. This is a familiar form to take, what you expect to see, but you commune with all of us.*"

I was glad that I had taken a piss before this.

Where to begin? How had she died? That seemed obvious. What happened, either at the start or the end? There was too much before and in between to explain yet. I could not stay until I starved, again. I needed to find my tether and pull my way home.

As I thought about leaving, the misted figures dissolved into the sparkling river, and Innathi pulled up her gown and stepped out of it, leaving footprints and drag marks upon the red stone. I did not know how close she might come to me, or what she might say next.

I asked, *"Do you know, from your time of rule, a Davrin bua with pure gold eyes?"*

Innathi stopped, and her smile faded until her face was almost blank, her gaze growing distant even as she watched me. *"Not during my reign, no."*

I waited, willing her to add whatever it was. *"But, Majesty? You do now?"*

Her chin lowered, eyes piercing me as she stared up from beneath her brow. *"My Husband confessed it to me, the last time I saw him. I could not imagine him ever neglecting something of that import, but you somehow wrenched this secret from him."*

I held my breath. *"Wrenched what?"*

"That my younger sister had given birth to a son in hiding, a bua I never knew existed." The Desert Queen contemplated. *"He was kept well-hidden for centuries, he was fully grown when my General stumbled on the remote prison holding him. Cris-ri-phon failed to free the bua before he was moved elsewhere."* She smirked briefly. *"He also said the bua possessed most unusual eyes for the pure Davrin he saw. Something his Mother did to him. It is not a natural color among us."*

I swallowed. *"Could the unusual eyes have anything to do with the To'vah?"*

Her eyes flew up to me, her head tilted. *"You know this word links to the color?"*

"Recently. It's important to know what it means to you, Majesty."

"It… it means…ah," Innathi stepped farther away from the water, her feet dried to leave no marks. She pressed fingers to her brow. *"My Queen-Mother Alyarra warned me not to call upon them, even*

during a crisis, for they manipulate whole reigns to their design. It is always a struggle for a Queendom when a To'vah becomes known from an alliance of any sort, for they shall be fervently worshipped by the ignorant and superstitious. Their strength is alluring to many, and they are too eager to accept gifts of metal and magic."

I chewed on my cheek rather than draw upon any of my memories right then. *"They? Who **are** they, Majesty?"*

"The Dragons, khali." The Davrin Queen peered above us at the strengthening stars as if she expected to see one flying the night sky overhead. *"The most intrinsic magic users in our world."*

"Intrinsic to what, Majesty?"

She blinked. *"To all of it."*

"I don't understand."

"As I learned it from the best tutors we had to offer, Sirana, the To'vah are thought to have created the Word, the first language of magic. And if they did, then all spoken focus for mages of the younger races branch off from theirs, including mine."

I waited, keeping my mind blank. *"Do the Dragons all possess eyes like the gold you wear, Majesty?"*

Innathi sighed. *"That is what they liked to show, as the stories went. I did not meet one in my time, but there is clear evidence that my sister did while I was unaware."*

She watched me swallow. *"And... what is your sister's name, Majesty?"*

The mature Davrin's face first softened then reversed its course. *"Her name was Ishuna. She... struggled with hallucinations and terrors in Reverie since she was young, embarrassing our Queen-Mother before Her Court at times."* Innathi lifted her chin imperiously. *"I found a better way, though only after our Queen-Mother died. My sister returned from exile and became a Seer for my Court, respected in V'Gedra as she'd never been. Our people bowed to her in fear and awe, and I played her mystique to our Queendom's advantage.*

"With the Zauyrian Godblood allied with us as well, we had the farthest reach in the dunes and beyond them, leading toward Manalar. It was

only that the three of us stood together that we could repel the Naulor Queen's increasingly vicious attacks over three hundred years."

She paused. "Then something went wrong. V'Gedra fell quickly. I have been told it is no more."

Cautiously, my eyebrow lifted. "You were…told?"

The Desert Queen chuckled; it held a bitter tang. "I was the first of us to die, khalithan. My assassins came for me in my birthing chambers as I worked to bear my twelfth child. A most cowardly and repugnant tactic, especially as they let my Husband find my body."

I pursed my mouth. "Did you know them?"

Scarlet eyes darkened. "Not by name. A sisterhood who did not approve of my union, one of many that rose and fell in my reign. These must have had help from within my Court." She paused. "Or closer to me, so my General has suggested."

"He blames Ishuna, since she has become the Valsharess."

Innathi did not speak to this but I watched a burgeon of emotions churn beneath the surface. Then, "I wonder, now. They wore red, like you."

I feared to imagine. But Fadele wasn't that old, I didn't think, but… did I know about how the Red Sisters started? Was it with the murder of a birthing Queen? I hoped not.

"We are the Vloszia Dalnanin, your Majesty," I said, "and I do not know how we came to be."

Innathi accepted this honesty. "Hm. A question, if I may? Do you yet know the face of your child, my warrior?"

A chill seeped into my core as I saw the light in her eyes, and I shook my head, hardly thought about the next words to tumble out of my mouth.

"The Black Heart starved it out of me as we fought for control, Majesty. I will never know."

Her face crumpled in compassion. "Oh! Oh… I am sorry, Red Sister. There is no treasure of greater reward, no way of being complete than to have children!"

If one could gain a House and lose a Queendom by them, I was forced to agree. I knew others who wouldn't believe so, no matter what.

"I must go," I said, backing up from the small canyon river and the vibrant Queen standing on its bank. *"We shall commune again."*

"Yes. We shall."

~*Wake up. Take me back.*~

Home.

SOMEONE HELD ME CLOSE, THEIR ARM TIGHT AROUND MY shoulders. A non-threatening hand cupped my abdomen, and another squeezed my wrist. Someone was whispering in my ear.

"Iyllinath prughethenna vuls..."

My body quaked as I opened eyes in confusion to yet another hand holding a cloth to my nose. I stared at a metallic, To'vah gaze.

Mourn gripped my wrist. The unsheathed, red runed dagger quivered in my cramping hand, its tip pointed at his throat.

Ohhh, shit.

My eyes slid to look right; I kept still lest the Dragonchild take it as a threat. It was the Naulor who held me upright, Krithannia's hand which cradled my womb with a warm, comforting hand. She chanted soft and soothing.

"Hm," Gavin grunted, checking the flow of blood from my nose. "You are awake. Who are you? May we have your name?"

Fair turnabout.

I croaked, "Sirana Thalluensareci. And you'll burn that cloth, won't you, Gavin?"

"Hm. If you wish."

"You will *not* keep it."

"Very well. I believe it has stopped." He wiped more blood away, giving the bridge of my nose a firmer scrub before setting it down by my knee.

Krithannia had stopped chanting and listened to us, though she held me as Mourn clutched my arm with the naked blade. The Naulor's arm left my shoulder, and she leaned down to press her ear awkwardly to my gut, right into my bladder.

I grunted. "What—?"

"Shhh."

Mourn's face had not shifted from his "focused hunter" look up until that point. He finally cracked a ridiculously small smile as I stayed quiet until Krithannia straightened up, sighing in relief.

"All is well," she said, shifting behind me and closer to Gavin.

No doubt the Naulor meant *just* my pregnancy because all was not well where Mourn was concerned. I was trapped in the position of having tried to stab him at some point in my trance, and he kept staring at me. We were located near a curtained window rather far from the table where I'd picked up the relic, and my spiders were scrambling to get out of their pouch.

"I won, *Melthra'vlos du Vuthra'tern.*" I held his gaze; no matter what, I would not blink. "Let me up, Mourn, and I will prove it."

Tilting an Elven ear toward me, the half-blood gently took my free elbow and helped me to my feet. Pain darted behind and through my knees from the long time kneeling on wooden boards, and tiny, unseen pins pricked the bottoms of my feet as I resettled and grounded myself inside my real boots.

Neither of us had blinked yet.

Slowly, I uncurled my fingers, one at a time so I wouldn't drop the weight of the relic. Nothing, no voices at all, as I turned the hilt to clasp it with the point aimed at the window. I turned it again, the tip shifting toward me.

Silence.

"Where is the sheath?" I asked.

"Here."

Gavin handed it out where I could see and reach for it. I thanked him and took it, tugging lightly at my other arm. Mourn still wouldn't let it go.

So be it.

I brought the sheath up to the blade, had only brief trouble aiming, and slid the dagger home. I paused, drew the sheath off again, and heard whispers this time, but it wasn't the Black Heart. I donned the sheath without trouble and Mourn loosened his grip with a nod. My arm dropped like the dagger weighed ten times its size, and the blood rushed to my fingertips.

Oh, thank Goddess…

I laughed in astonishment at the immensity of what had been lifted from me. I released my spiders to crawl over me and inspect me to their satisfaction. Mourn's gaze was on them as they crossed my belly, my heart, around my neck and shoulders. He made a gesture I recognized.

★Introduce us.★

I blinked once but did not hesitate, gathering them into one palm and holding out my hand. Mourn surprised me by lightly touching his claws into my palm, where my guardians inspected him immediately.

~Guardian, like you,~ I told them. ~Morixxyleth.~

They believed me; my babies rested on his hand where he could have crushed them if ambush had been his intent. Them and me, both.

The Dragonchild studied them, observed me, his pupils shifting first thin then widening. His tail hushed a slow curve along the floor, and he grunted, nodding his satisfaction.

"Well done," he said. "You won a battle few have, Sirana."

I grinned broadly, breathing in slow and deep as I grew light-headed from the surge of something pure. I wasn't sure what it was, but I had hope, now.

Attaching the relic to my belt, I next removed one of my ordinary matte daggers, lifting it up where all could see it and separated the new weapon from its case. My allies watched with curiosity and a sliver of caution as I reversed the grip and pointed it at Mourn's chest. Made the motion to stab him.

My arm stopped.

Only because my motive was so weak did the real pain and nausea not overwhelm me. Nonetheless, I dropped the blade, clutching my middle and backing away from him, letting them all watch as my brow began to sweat. In time, I straightened, taking a deep breath, and comforting my guardians.

*~I **cannot** harm you. No matter what.~*

Whether he could have heard me or not, Mourn understood what I was showing him. I saw the look of concern shared between him and Krithannia, though it was the Guild Mistress who shrugged first.

"The Queen has seen you, my friend," she said. "But we knew Sivaraus would not remain ignorant of you forever. There is time yet. We shall make use of it."

The Dragon's son nodded in agreement, returning his focus to me. His expression became serious. "Then I have decided, Sirana."

I swallowed my sore throat with a nod, waiting.

"I will make a bargain with you as well as the Deathwalker," he said, nodding to Gavin. "I believe we can find terms to defend your body as you've asked, and to retrieve your sister, if she lives."

Oh, Goddess, yes.

"Thank you, Mourn. I-I hope we come to an agreement. I... I need to sit down."

Gavin turned out a chair for me, and I collapsed into it, my heart pounding. If that surge of hope earlier had been just a guttering candle fighting persistent gusts of air, now it had become like a roaring campfire ready to ignite a whole company of torches.

I wished Jael could see the signal and know to wait for me.

We're coming, Sister.

CHAPTER 17

Each time Lead Qivni shared the debriefing room with the Prime, she breathed easier with Elder Rausery present. If spoken or signaled, this thought would come as no surprise to any Red Sister, least of all the Prime herself as she smirked and winked at the Lead's quickly taken position to the right and behind her Elder.

The Lead knew she had done well with her preferred Elder gone to the Surface, not for the first time bearing the smaller abuses either alone or alongside the Elder Sorceress while they accomplished their cyclic tasks. But it was always good when Rausery returned.

Especially when their Eldest had that look on her face.

"Wait…" said the Prime slowly. "She declared what?"

"Elder D'Shea will be working directly with the Confessor—"

"Who?" she growled.

"Our liaison. Priestess. Lelinahdara."

"And?"

"And the Headmaster to uncover the secrets of Wilsira's Royal Consort legacy," Rausery repeated.

Ancient eyes narrowed, the creases making themselves known. "For how long will they need D'Shea?"

"For an unset amount of time. Probably until something useful breaks through."

The Prime slammed her fist on the mapping table. "*Goddess-damned fucking breeders!* How in the fuck can that be more important than preparing for mindflayers?!"

"The Valsharess did not say, Prime."

The subtle reminder couldn't retain the furious resentment all that much. "I am sick to offal-spewing *death* of the number of resources the Priestesses get even after their most pompous wailer choked in her own webbing. They don't matter. The Consorts and their fungus are gone and dead!"

"Except one."

"Should have gutted him the moment I became aware of him in solitary."

Indeed, Qivni *still* wondered exactly how the Elder Sorceress had managed to delay that until he could be moved elsewhere. Not even she knew where D'Shea had taken him. The Lead kept her expression stern and her back straight, while Rausery grinned with genuine pleasure that translated in her tone.

"He's that rare kind of healer, Prime," she said. "Worth a hundred wizards in the Tower. Forbidden to kill. D'Shea knew it when Jaunda reported with Sirana."

The Prime spit onto the floor hearing the novice's name. "So why isn't he being prodded in the Palace and sucked dry by the Priestesses right now?"

"Because Wilsira *had* been keeping his talent secret except to her best allies among the Matrons. D'Shea won him for the Sisterhood for now, specifically for Jaunda while on her mission, which will help us planning for the mindflayers. The Queen also wants to know how Wilsira made the healer."

The Prime snorted. "What, she wants to make more?"

Rausery shrugged. "I don't know. Too early to say. But D'Shea was directly involved in Wilsira's machinations with creating the

Consorts in the first place, remember? It'll go quicker with her on it, and that's good for the Sisterhood not being left out of this."

Their Eldest was quiet, resting with her knuckles upon the table, as she recollected something in the last two centuries. She grunted. "Oh, yeah. Shyntre. Fuck. That bua *acts* like he was born in the Drider Pit."

"The Forming Pit."

"Same thing. Just another in a long line of Queen's pets. They can never be normal, but he's like a frantic *jabrau* about living in the Palace."

Rausery hummed noncommittally.

"So, where is the fuckin' healer–Consort right now?"

"D'Shea hasn't told me."

"Find out, then. Report back."

"But the mindflayers are priority, right?"

"Right."

"Got it. Anything else, Prime?"

"Yeah. The Sisters are waiting to have some discipline slapped into them after that pile-up on the Consort in solitary. Don't think D'Shea has managed to purge whatever the fuck made them lose their minds over one slutty bua."

"On it, Prime."

"Get to it." The Prime flicked her faded eyes to Qivni, who paused her breath, then looked down at the table. "Next time you see Corpora Thena, Lead, send her to me."

That order was both a relief and a concern.

"Yes, Prime."

Qivni had been glad to stay in the room with Rausery, but she was more so to be leaving with her. She had been under enough strain with no release that her thoughts had been wandering too often to a place she did *not* want them to go.

Rausery signed as they walked through the curving, sloping halls of the Cloister. ★Thoughts on the lingering effects the Prime has noticed?"

Qivni grimaced. ★There is a reason I did not take my turn with him, Elder.★

★But you didn't stop the others.★

★It was beyond my authority in this case. The Prime encouraged it at first. She thought it would help blow off the last Purge from their minds.★

★But it had the opposite effect, sounds like.★

★Agreed, Elder. It has. They mention him to each other without need, wonder where the Elder Sorceress took him. I do not know yet if any caught from him, but they should be tested soon.★

Her Elder's eyes widened. ★You mean some took his cock up their twats and made him cum?★

★I overheard three bragging, Elder, yes. The Prime is ignoring the possibility. I can name them.★

★Tell me.★

Qivni did, and Rausery narrowed her eyes in thought. ★What did D'Shea say on letting it happen so freely?★

★She was handling another issue and did not get a say before enough Sisters had sampled him without any order. Only convincing the Prime herself would have interrupted it.★

★Which the Sorceress did.★

★Indeed, I remain impressed with her persuasion talents despite how opinionated and stubborn she can be.★

Rausery's umber red eyes sometimes twinkled when she smiled; Qivni could never show it, but she enjoyed prompting that look. It happened more often when the former Sanctuary servant found something to admire in those most effective using their status without provoking constant fights to prove it. It happened when Qivni chose this way as a Lead.

A pity how something about Sirana had set her teeth on edge. The cait was a sneaky one, definitely of D'Shea's preferred ilk, not always provoking a fight. However, her long-term effectiveness and self-discipline remained untested.

And may never be, now.

Her Elder stopped in the hall, listening to activity ahead, and jerked her chin toward a storage room as she opened it up. Qivni followed, moving aside so it could be closed quickly; the Lead set a silence-lock spell on the door without being told. Her Elder stepped close, lightly placing her hands on her shoulders. Qivni felt her heart quicken as they met eyes.

Rausery murmured, "So, what's *your* reason you didn't enter solitary, Qiv? Won't tell. Promise."

Her well-practiced expression almost cracked. Almost.

"You know why I was sent to you from the Sanctuary," she whispered. "Why I had to undergo the Prime's trials. You *know.*"

The General nodded, her hands sliding from Qivni's shoulders to her neck, so close to cradling her jaw. "I remember. Is Auslan like that first batch of Wilsira's that she had to destroy? Can you tell?"

"N-no, Elder, I don't think he is," she answered. "He is far less bold. But because of the natural born strength of his magic, I believe he may be as…"

"As what?"

Qivni swallowed. "As addicting. Like many Priestesses' spells."

Rausery rolled that around in her mind. "Is that to say… he's potentially as powerful as a Priestess?"

Qivni snapped her mouth closed, pursing her lips. She would *never* say such a thing out loud. Regardless, her Elder knew her too well. Rausery smirked, letting it rest so she could lean forward to kiss the Lead with an unsparing tenderness that weakened Qivni's knees. Every time.

Oh, please…

"Describe that first time, Qiv," her Elder whispered with forbidden softness, tugging gently at the leather ties beneath her belt. "It's been a long time. I want to listen to you describe it again."

This. This was where her thoughts had been drifting far too often with that Consort here, and even after he was taken away.

She wants me to say it.

The Lead shivered with shame and a horrifyingly swift arousal as she removed her own belt, hanging it up while Rausery watched. Her Elder's hands returned to Qivni's hips, loosening the leather knots atop the crisscrossing thongs there.

"I-I was working too hard in the new quarters created for them," she whispered, her chin down. "I...fell asleep on their floor, in the laundry room. Th-they found me..."

Rausery dropped smoothly to one knee, pulling her subordinate's leathers down, quickly removing her gloves so she could caress the bare skin with attentive admiration. Qivni's skin pebbled as her superior stared at her white thatch. Rausery leaned to nestle her nose into it, breathing in then out. She licked her. Kissed and sucked. Qivni's sex tingled, swelled.

"Keep going, Qiv."

Oh, Goddess...

"There were eight," she gasped, reaching to grab the edge of a shelf, her other hand braced against the stone wall.

Rausery stroked her slit firmly with her tongue, sucked on her.

"Oh! They s-smuggled me into one of their bedrooms. I woke there, disoriented. M-my small clothes, gone. Bent over the bed with my robes pulled up—"

Rausery growled quietly, rising to shove a few bags out of the way on the stout sorting table. Taking Qivni by the shoulders, she turned her to face it, pushing her down onto it.

"Like this, Lead?"

Qivni did not fight; she mewled as the General held her neck with one hand and tugged her leathers down farther with the other.

Then Rausery massaged her hips and buttocks with both hands; she kneeled, spread her open...

And feasted on her again.

"*Gener*—! Ah!"

A chuckle. "Been a while, eh, Qiv? Mmm, me, too."

Rausery moved her face eagerly against her Lead's slick crotch, resting one warm hand on the small of her back; a reminder without pressure to stay in place.

"Go on," the Elder murmured. "Who started it? Who went first?"

Qivni blinked, trying to remember as she felt a slippery probe dip in deep then rise and swirl in circles around her netherhole. "*Ohh!* Uh-uh...K-Kino. H-He told the others I was shaped like 'Mother.'"

"One of the Priestesses."

"Yeah...the others had never seen us naked before. Th-then he showed them how..."

"How to what?"

Qivni stared at the wall, holding onto the table with both hands as Rausery stood up behind her. She heard the familiar sounds of a Feldeu being inserted at the base end, the magical word following, and the head of the pleasure tool settling between her labia. *At last.*

"How. To. What?" her Elder repeated slowly.

She quivered, whispered, "He sh-showed them how to f-fuck...!"

"Like this?"

Qivni gasped as the Feldeu speared her sex. Her Elder took her full length without hesitation, and her body clutched the phallus in complete welcome. *"Yes!"*

It's been so long...

Rausery rumbled, "You held still for it, hm? All eight buas in the same eve?"

Qivni's face burned as her cunt greedily accepted the strong pounding like a punishment she deserved. She was close, so close. "I-I have said, Elder, the strong ones are addictive."

"The strong what?"

"C-Consorts!"

"What else? Were they done after a shot a piece in your sloppy hole?"

The Lead hid her eyes. "....n-no, Elder..."

"Twice each?"

Qivni bit her lip.

"More? Wow, you enjoyed a gang fuck *long* before the Sisterhood got you, huh? You were meant for us."

Rausery fucked her. Qivni moaned.

"Bet you didn't make a peep, Lead. Lest someone find out how you *really* want to be treated by a pile of willful buas, as their sexy piece of raw gooey ass and sweaty thighs, dripping on the carpet."

Oh, Goddess!

Blood roaring in her ears, Qivni climaxed on her Elder's Feldeu, writhing, mouth pressed and whimpering into her arm. Rausery let her finish, not yet done herself when she pulled out of a flexing, hungry sex. She pried her subordinate's buttocks apart, nudging the tool at her dark star.

"What else did they do?" Rausery panted, her palms sweaty. She already knew. "Who started it?"

The Feldeu pressed in.

"K-Kino, again," Qivni confessed as her asshole yielded to her superior. "He watched a-a Sathoet take his M-Mother like, *ungh!* This. H-he wanted to...to tr-*aaiiee!*"

Immediately, Rausery clapped her hand across her mouth as the buas once had to keep the mountings going. The Elder muffled Qivni's second climax as the slick pole stretched her netherhole open. She thrashed and trembled as her Elder took her deeper still, sliding in all the way by the time Qivni was in her afterglow, breathing heavily through her nose, desperate for air.

Rausery held her pinned and penetrated, slowly withdrew her hand from her mouth. She whispered in her ear, "Did this Sathoet have a name?"

"Kerse," she confessed, again.

"Ah, right."

Rausery fucked her ass. Qivni felt her cunt drooling down her thigh.

"Kino was Wilsira's first experiment," her Elder said. "She taught him before the others. Let him observe her and her son."

Qivni lay passively, belly atop the table, the old memories of all those Consorts filling every moment that wasn't Rausery's voice or her wonderful cock.

"Kino broke in your slit and your pucker without asking, didn't he?"

The younger Davrin's cheeks were hot as lava while tears pricked her eyes. "Uh-yes! A-and all the others followed him. And I didn't *stop* them…"

"Because you *wanted* them. All of them."

"Th-they were dangerous!" she cried. "I-I couldn't close my legs, I was compelled to hold them open while even one bua was hard! That's why I was caught!"

"Ha! Maybe some magic, Qiv, but I bet you looked so sexy. You knew what you wanted then. No wonder you took the Prime with such ease."

"It *wasn't* easy!"

Rausery leaned down again, bit the back of her neck, making her gasp and clench down on the Feldeu lodged in her ass. Her Elder kissed the bite to soothe it. "Mmm! So fucking hot."

She drew out, thrust back in.

"Anything else?"

Qivni braced herself, tilting her hips, gratefully taking every thrust her Elder gave her. She tried to think. It was difficult.

"Let me help, Qiv. Why do you think Wilsira made you take that new Consort with the knot up your ass?"

The Lead cried out in shock at this most recent humiliation, seeing it clear as if she'd been sober. Shyntre was practically fisting her to keep Wilsira's toy bua from taking her slit as he tried to do. How drunken she felt when he touched her, when that strange phallus leaked on her skin or inside her.

That massive bulb, far too big for a bua his size…

Qivni remembered how it squeezed in and swelled inside her body, locking them together. How she'd struggled to dislodge it, and couldn't. And the novice Sirana had witnessed her Collector squealing beneath the bua, her asshole being bred by a mindless, demon-touched beast. The shame had been unbearable until all witnessed it about to happen *again*, and Lelinahdara and D'Shea had attacked with their proof of demonic taint.

At long last, Wilsira and all the demon-tainted were dead. The Conceiver couldn't torment her former servant anymore.

"She was too…" Qivni grunted, "prideful…"

Rausery plucked something smooth from her belt to press to her compliant partner's clit. The Lead cooed, shivered, swiveled her hips as Rausery closed in on her own peak. Qivni remembered something else, too, stared into space at it while rising a third time.

We didn't check, I don't think…

But held her peace until the Elder achieved her own pleasure first. Once she did, Qivni succumbed to that swell of smaller waves sweeping through her again, leaving her exhausted.

The Lead was happily sore as her superior pulled the Feldeu out of her with a care she never experienced with anyone else. Then Rausery embraced her, lying on top of her while Qivni lay relaxing on the table. Her Elder's heart always raced like hers right afterward, belying her outward calm with a deep excitement.

This part had always sparked a strange urge in Qivni to weep. She'd never understood why, but she always resisted showing it.

She licked her lips. "Um, Elder...?"

"Mm?" Rausery sounded drowsy.

The corner of Qivni's mouth twitched.

"When I served in the Sanctuary," she said, "the Conceiver kept parchments with odd symbols beneath a piece of stone under each Consort's bed. I never read them. I do not know if she did this with the last ones, but..."

"Hmm," Rausery hummed, nibbling appreciatively at Qivni's earlobe before pushing herself off and regaining her feet. "Worth a try. Thanks, Qiv." She slapped her Lead's bare, sweaty ass, making her peep. "For all of it. I mean it."

The Lead exhaled slowly. The unwelcome tension of Rausery's absence drained from her as she took the cloth her Elder offered, bracing to stand up as well. While she wiped her copious lubricant from her crotch and inner thighs, Qivni felt the heat in her face.

Thanks, Qiv. For all of it.

"For whatever reason, Elder," she replied, "you have never spit to hear me speak of my final service at the Sanctuary. For that, I thank *you*. For everything."

Rausery straightened her own uniform after setting the magical cock aside for cleaning. "We all have our ways that we bend, Lead. What I've seen, it's never in the same direction. If it were, we'd be mindflayers."

Qivni looked down, hating herself for the urge to bring it up after hearing something so intimate. "Like Reishel?"

Her Elder paused but met her eyes with neither hesitation nor aggression. "Yeah. Like Reishel. We'll do everything we can to keep that from happening to Sivaraus." Rausery winked. "Right, Lead?"

The Collector for the Sisterhood didn't quite smile, but she bowed her head with a purposeful and regained poise. "Yes, General. We will. I am here to serve the greater good for the Davrin and the Valsharess."

"So am I. Let's go. Lots of work after that break." Rausery exhaled, with an alluring nod and smirk. "But worth it."

Now, Qivni did smile as she released her privacy spell upon the door.

D'SHEA HAD MOSTLY NUMBED HERSELF TO THE SANCTUARY surroundings, to the lingering scents of Wilsira's proven methods, so she could focus on work, on accurately translating the Conceiver's cypher. Every so often, she would glance up at either the Confessor or the Headmaster, aware again of the age difference and reflecting how she stood right in between them in centuries.

Phaelous had always been there, for as long as D'Shea could remember. In contrast, young Tarra merely represented everything after Matron Siranet's death and Shyntre's tumultuous birth.

Has it really been so long? And I am free again.

Just not as she had been before.

The compulsion and the struggle to become an Elder in the Sisterhood had suppressed and blacked out much of that time, but memories drifted forward with Wilsira dead at last. They were so clear, she could hear conversations, threats; she could smell incense and soaps and bodies. In many ways, the Sorceress had long understood young Sirana and what she'd endured. Fortunately for Siranet's granddaughter, the torment didn't last beyond half a century.

We deserve to breathe. To know who we are, eventually.

Now, however, D'Shea wondered if this disturbing clarity from the past had happened in the young Noble's head after Jilrina died, when the newly freed cait had been sent to the Thalluen suites in the Palace to live alone. It might explain some of what Jaunda had described in her reports, or why Sirana had become bua-crazy after the ritual orgy, looking for affable cocks to share the massive, empty suites.

Some of that behavior had spilled over while wearing her reds, although D'Shea would never have predicted her son and Sirana would start acting like her and Phaelous in her four-hundreds.

And, like us, gained the Valsharess's attention for it.

The Elder Sorceress allowed her eyes to land on Shyntre's sire. The ancient Headmaster had found several starting points to test Wilsira's scripts and had been methodically going through them without speaking. He possessed more of those fine creases on his brow, around his eyes and the corners of his mouth, but his eyes remained brilliant with intelligence after all this time.

Meanwhile the younger Confessor fussed and poked around the Conceiver's old suites, checking for secrets and insights in between the studious requirements. Tarra would be magically exhausted by the end of the cycle, no doubt, but D'Shea was content to let her.

Despite herself, D'Shea kept thinking about Phaelous and Tarra, albeit in different times than the present. On the desk before her, certain marks in Wilsira's charts reminded her of the Forming Pit. She felt the impulse to tell them.

I will never go down there again.

The inevitability of being proven wrong in that ill-boding thought loomed.

"Tarra?" D'Shea called, waiting until the Priestess came to the door frame to meet her gaze. "How many unborn quickened by Consorts remain?"

Lelinahdara quirked an eyebrow but knew them off the top of her head. "All have either been expunged or cleared by the Priesthood, except for two."

Phaelous's stylus stilled as he looked up to listen. D'Shea motioned she was listening.

"The Noble Curgia Itlaunaduv carries a mage more powerful than her; we can tell this, if not the sex. The Valsharess has deemed her baby untainted, though the mata is unhealthily obsessed with the Consort she caught from, mourning his loss far beyond good form. She remains in the dungeon because of that and will give birth there."

D'Shea nodded placidly, appearing only mildly interested, although it hadn't been lost on her that both Curgia and Sirana had conceived by the same, strange healer who had stopped the bleeding from their cunts and revived the fertility of their wombs. Sirana hadn't had the time to become fixated on him like Itlaunaduv, before being expelled from the Deepearth, but a few of her behaviors after her healing could have implied it might go that way.

Then there are the Red Sisters who raped him and wonder aloud, quad-spans later, where he's disappeared to.

Auslan didn't seem aware of the strength of his magic. Or he was aware enough to suppress it, but the recent stress and abuse had made it difficult to control.

Or he enters that stage few male mages of his ilk are allowed to if he's bred, and there is simply no hiding it anymore.

Shyntre was only half a century behind him. How would he change?

"The other unborn, you know quite well," Tarra continued, breaking into the Elder's thoughts, "is down in the Forming Pit. That one is for certain tainted, though the auras are entwined. To expunge it now would kill the surrogate and, for some reason, the Queen has spared her. She will give birth and the baby sacrificed to the Abyss."

D'Shea closed her eyes briefly as nausea slapped at her middle.

"Bathila will need to be fed and cleaned soon," Phaelous said.

The Priestess glowered at the reminder. "I may as well move into these suites for how often I must come here to clean buckets like a common drub."

D'Shea replied dryly, "May you have pleasant dreams if you do, Tarra."

The Confessor darted a look at her. Phaelous had barely moved after speaking.

"Care to join me, you two?" the Confessor invited, her odd eyes glinting as she approached D'Shea's table. She took up a scroll with entries like an incomprehensible ledger, glancing over it though she'd looked at it several times. "I'm sure Varessa has noticed similarities here to the runes down there."

D'Shea wanted to tell her where to shove that scroll, though she'd long developed better impulse control than that. She glanced at Phaelous, who made motions like he was preparing for a break.

Sigh.

D'Shea stood up. "If you clearly need the help."

Tarra smirked. "Don't try that cool arrogance act, Varessa. We were both there, remember?"

"Barely," she said, carefully piling three scrolls to roll up together. "But some things grow clearer."

"Oh? What things?"

D'Shea caught Phaelous watching her but swiftly focused on the emerald-eyed Confessor. "How opportunistic you were, pretending to care for my child's health when you really wanted the secrets of what Wilsira was doing. A pity I couldn't speak on it, then, I might have spilled it all. I'm not inclined now, my opinion firmer than ever that Priestesses can't handle such knowledge with any wisdom."

Phaelous busily shuffled parchment, and Tarra frowned, weighing her bluff. She shrugged, invited them toward the jump circle in Wilsira's chambers.

"Come along, then. Just keep in mind, Varessa, it's not you in the cage this time."

Although Tarra's jab before they'd entered the Forming Pit had been blunt as a club, that didn't make it ineffectual. D'Shea followed the protected path between the red runes in the stone like the other two mages, observed with her usual poise and confidence, but refused to get closer to Bathila at first.

Phaelous was of greater help than D'Shea had expected him to be, pinning up his sleeves to reach for the sponge and water bucket. Tarra noticed and allowed him to handle the filthy work, though she also seemed challenged to do as well with the feeding.

D'Shea concentrated frequently on slowing her heart rate so they wouldn't hear it. Voices sounded in her head—questions, taunts, threats, promises—and she remembered the way Shyntre had moved inside her, as if his tiny body was frantic, scared. She'd seen his face in her dreams by then.

The Sorceress *hadn't* spent span after span in the cage down here like this poor commoner, only the few cycles before her contractions began and her son was soon to arrive, but…

I remember both these Davrin with me, afterward.

She almost wished Phaelous had cleaned and comforted her as gently then as he did Bathila, who couldn't hear him and did not appreciate it.

But I'd rather it never had happened. He betrayed me and his son. I don't know why I trusted him. I should have known better. Siranet was smart to leave males out of her inner circle.

Ironically, D'Shea had been quietly mourning and missing the Matron's companionship for decades when the Headmaster had become too interesting to ignore.

And she had let him in.

The pregnant Davrin was left in her cage with enough to eat, a fresh pelvic wrap, bedding, and blanket, while the three mages stood together in the Pit, studying the inert markings carved on every surface. Tarra looked at the altar; Phaelous and D'Shea ignored it.

Then the Confessor pulled out a scroll and a light stone, temporarily blinding them all before comparing and pointing out a few specific runes.

"These," she said simply.

Phaelous leaned to see. "Those aren't Abyssal, Priestess."

"I know. What are they, Headmaster?"

D'Shea didn't have to look to know what they talked about. "Elemental, my dear Tarra."

An eyebrow arched. "Don't you mean Arcane, my dear Varessa?"

"No. There is a deliberate collaboration and intelligence applied to the Arcane studies that you do not see in the Divine. Elemental is neither of those."

"Yet our crafters regularly collaborate with stone, fire, and water. You and I have done the same creating the spyways in the Sanctuary. The wizards in the Tower are devoted to the Arcane studies. Are not 'elemental' spells within the definition of Arcane, Sorceress?"

"Some like to insist so, Priestess. I have changed my mind."

Tarra was wise enough to stop there, looking at Phaelous, who was watching D'Shea.

"When?" asked the Headmaster simply.

The one word seemed to prick a waterskin as her chest filled with a flood of old emotion. D'Shea tossed a poisonous look at him.

"When our son was born. I only was forced to forget." Her voice rumbled. "It wasn't myself alone that Wilsira wanted to finish and strengthen her Forming Pit. It was Shyntre. He is not a wizard like the other buas in your Tower, Phaelous. He is something else, and I believe you've been given *ample* opportunity to notice, yes?"

Her former lover nodded. "I have noticed he accomplishes changes in the fundamentals of stone and fire which he is unable to teach or describe to others. Nor is he able to write it in a language of magic. His jewelry was always one of a kind, sometimes with unexpected qualities, and could not be duplicated."

D'Shea heard the clear message he conveyed in front of Tarra without specifics. Whether he intended it or not, Phaelous had just given her an idea.

Meanwhile, the Priestess was turning this over, comparing the scroll with the walls. "If Shyntre has an 'elemental' talent in which he is illiterate, which I find laughable for one of the highest-tutored buas in Sivaraus, then how are *these* runes known to be of that talent?"

"They appeared mid-ritual," D'Shea said curtly, her arms folded over a subtly quivering middle. "No one wrote them first, but Wilsira copied them."

"Ah-ha," the Priestess breathed, giving them closer, serious inspection. "Has he been down here since his birth?"

"No," D'Shea barked, forbidding rather than answering.

Tarra blinked at her, and Phaelous agreed in tone while confirming, "No, he has not been here since then."

"I see. Well, let us see what the Valsharess thinks, hm?"

The Sorceress Elder stewed in silent fury, kicking herself for the slip of temper, while Lelinahdara made copious notes of which ones were "Elemental" runes, at least according to Phaelous. D'Shea did not help but was privately chagrinned how accurate the old male was.

"Time to go for now," the Priestess said, "until the next infantile feeding and cleaning. Though I thank you both for your presence. Finally, a breakthrough!"

Back in Wilsira's chambers, they secured their materials, preparing to leave as all three of them had duties awaiting them elsewhere. The Headmaster said nothing at all until he invited to cut her jump circles in half by going through the Tower. D'Shea recoiled from the blatant attempt to get her into his private space.

"I can manage alone, Headmaster. A few extra jumps do not tire me anymore."

"Of course, Elder, apology for any insult. If you choose to jump by way of the Twelfth Well, you might retain that endurance. But it is your right as you please."

This was his version of being stubborn.

D'Shea sighed, rolled her eyes, glancing around them. Phaelous hadn't blinked. He wanted something. Or, he wanted to tell her something. Unfortunately, she could not tell which, and they were being watched and listened to at all places within the Sanctuary.

Fine.

"No, Headmaster. Mind your circles."

She wouldn't know if he believed this key phrase here and now, as he had once, until she waited for him outside Sivaraus.

Just as *he* wouldn't know if she would be there once he retrieved whatever it was from the fifth library that he wanted to show her.

★YOU CHANGED CACHES AGAIN,★ PHAELOUS SIGNED AS HE looked about the private alcove where D'Shea had only brought Red Sisters in the last few decades, most recently Gaelan and Sirana. She sealed the alcove behind him, where no light or sound would escape.

★And I shall do so again after this meeting★ she signed. ★The time has come, anyway.★

He wasted no time, reaching into his robe's sleeve and the pocket she knew was there. She prepared, just in case. He noticed.

★Slow,★ he promised, gradually bringing out a scrap of parchment to hand to her without games.

D'Shea accepted, listened to the trickle of water in the darkness as neither of them made another motion until she cast a small light to read it. It was a chart, but not the original. Not even Phaelous could remove records from the library archives, nor could they be copied by magic *or* by hand using a single mage. It always required at least three, and one of them was the Valsharess.

What she held would be what Phaelous could memorize and transcribe in a way that did not recreate it. There would be deliberate inaccuracies and flaws that made it worthless if lost or stolen; subtle, disregarded as trash in all but the right set of hands.

Peering at it, D'Shea hazarded that he'd provided her with a key component of Wilsira's cypher, one he had been keeping from Lelinahdara. He'd been waiting for something—perhaps her attention or something else not yet occurred. She never knew *all* the ways in which the Headmaster's mind worked. It was why she'd had such difficulty ignoring him at one time in her life.

To the point I could not keep my legs closed.

She tucked the scrap away but kept the light out so she wouldn't miss a tic in his distinguished face. She used one hand to sign, ★How far back? Which mage?★

Phaelous smiled sadly to see how quickly she understood. He answered, ★Beliza D'Shea. I was only a century when she escaped the Palace but left four Daughters behind.★

Varessa D'Shea stared, her heartbeat slipping briefly out of her control. The Elder could *not*, to save her existence, imagine Phaelous once the same age as Sirana, yet here it was.

He was there.

The last sorceress of D'Shea had thought but never confirmed that her House's lack of property went at least as far as the current Headmaster's life. Swiftly growing unsettled and faster than she wished, D'Shea shifted the subject, promising herself she would probe into this next time she was in Wilsira's chambers.

★What is it about Bathila that troubles you?★ she signed instead.

Phaelous looked at the pouch where she had tucked his scribbles.

She held her breath, demanding, ★What? Who is she?★

His mouth tightened into a straight line. ★You said you expected to find Red Sisters entangled in the Conceiver's plan.★

★A given. But that one is not a Red Sister.★

★True, but I found a strong link to one.★

Only one?

★Who?★

★Rausery,★ he answered without resistance. ★Wilsira was *very* interested in her line, Varessa.★

D'Shea had a visible reaction in the light; it was pure disbelief. ★Her *line?* What line? She was an orphan running unfettered trade when the Prime pulled her off the street. Her Mother was a deep trader long dead by then, right?★

The Headmaster nodded patiently, offering nothing else to that story. ★This does not change that Wilsira was interested in the General as the head of a line. The Matriarch of the surrogates bearing the new sons of the Priestesses.★

★What? Rausery only had Tahna, who *should* have been a Red Sister like her Mother but was made to serve in the Sanctuary.★

★Rausery also had half-siblings or cousins she didn't name in her time under the Prime,★ Phaelous answered, ★but Tahna must have known who a few of them were, and they might have known each other. I've found notes of Wilsira tracking specific Davrin among the commoners and noting them as relatives to Rausery. I assume the Conceiver must have extracted them from Rausery's Daughter.★

Anger and confusion simmered together in a sickening boil, but D'Shea had her answer why Phaelous was willing to tend and observe the commoner inside her cage.

★Bathila is one of those cousins,★ she signed, ★bearing a tainted Consort that is not her child.★

★Bathila is distant in blood, but yes. Wilsira had already consumed the strength of those closer to the General, starting with Tahna, whom I believe experienced the Forming Pit about six decades before you did. She may have borne all the Consorts of that time, too close together, and that is what killed her.★

D'Shea's eyes widened. Her hands fumbled on her next question, and she leaned against the cave wall to get a stranglehold on the fear of the timing.

★That would have been the second generation of Consorts,★ she signed slowly, watching him. ★Those ones given away at the first worship ball. Well-trained and docile, unlike the initial group which never left the Sanctuary.★

The Headmaster bowed his head. *Exactly, my Elder. Whatever quality the Conceiver discovered in Tahna, it appeared to be critical to her process in trying again. The surrogate matters as much as the chosen Priestess and the sire; these three made the Consort and his magic whole. Tahna wasn't simply a vessel. None of them were. Or are. They are Mothers sharing the same sons with these Priestesses.*

That might be something Lelinahdara wouldn't believe even if explained in plain sign language like this. Tarra hadn't managed to convince Wilsira to give her a Consort of her own blood, but if she had, there would be no "shared" mother.

Yet a subtle lump rose in the Sorceress's throat which she tried to swallow down long enough to make her next mental leap.

Six decades before me, in the Forming Pit...

Auslan was about fifty turns older than D'Shea's own son.

The...healer, she signed hesitantly. *Whom we are researching?*

Phaelous tightened his mouth at the corners, looking to one side. *Probable. Not confirmed, but probable, given the timing.*

Probably Tahna's son.

And if so, Rausery's grandson. Him and many others the Sisterhood had just killed.

This has been your working theory, she signed.

Not confirmed, he repeated. *Not enough to give the Valsharess. Threads I am chasing through Wilsira's code.*

Too soon to reveal this, in any case, even if he were correct.

Understood. Will you tell Tarra?

Not if you do not wish it.

Hmm.

I do not wish it, Headmaster. Keep this closed for now.

I will, Elder. He bowed again, smooth and without a touch of stiffness or tension.

As if she did not still hate him.

They prepared to leave her cache, the last time she would be using this one for at least a century, when the Elder Sorceress paused with another thought.

As always, her Headmaster noticed. ★Yes, my Elder?★

She looked at him amid the Radiants, having doused the light. She could see him without the color, yet the golden flecks in the iris, possessed by both him and her son, somehow made themselves known within lightlessness.

★They know each other,★ she signed, ★do they not?★

The Headmaster made no assumptions. ★'They', Elder?★

★Shyntre and this surviving Consort.★

★I believe their time and training overlapped on the third floor, Elder.★

She eyed him skeptically. *Hm.* ★Perhaps I will ask if the healer possesses any insight of my son as a child. While he is able to answer my questions.★

Phaelous smiled a bit. ★I hope he remembers something worth sharing with you, my Elder.★

CHAPTER 18

THERE WAS A COMMOTION ON THE FAR SIDE OF HER PLANTATION. Although the Matron was too far to reach or see it before one of her Guard screamed, Rohenvi knew by the pitch that the time had come. Be it by accident, internal violence, or an attack on her land, she would normally be preparing for a death or several after things got under control.

Instead, she pushed instructions on a child.

"Cover Auslan in hood and robe and lead him to the empty healer's quarters, Natia. Do not let anyone see you."

Gaelan's Daughter nodded urgently and sped off toward the wall passage instead of his locked front door.

On her way outside, the Matron and a Guardsvrin carrying a stretcher were met by her Head Guard and two others who wordlessly flanked her, weapons drawn.

"Lutre," she demanded. "What is happening?"

"Uroan kicked Drani, Matron. We didn't detect what caused it but other animals and the Pytes are acting strange as well. We're securing the borders."

Could be another House causing trouble, could be Sathoet on the loose, could be a festering pincerworm nest...

It could be too many things. For now, her Heard Guardsvrin would focus on her job, and the Matron would focus on her House.

"Give me Drani. I'll take care of her. Bring any carcasses or prisoners to me later."

"Yes, Matron."

Two fellow Guards moved fast to roll their guardmate and tuck the stretcher beneath her. They lifted, and Rohenvi signed for them to follow her. After they had entered the mansion, cut left at the rear, and entered a smooth stone corridor, Roh knew Natia and the healer were waiting.

She halted them, wrapped blindfolds around the eyes of the two Guardsvrin, and continued. This was not the only unusual thing she had done lately but, so far, they were staying quiet, understanding and accepting that something they couldn't see threatened their House.

They obeyed because they could not imagine a good place to go if Thalluen fell, a strong possibility in their current disfavor with the Sanctuary. Rohenvi knew they felt this way because she had asked them shortly after Vekika was born. She listened and swore she would protect the place for all of them once again, even without her brother's many talents.

Even with Ruk back in my life, I do not know where I would go, either.

As the Matron, she would probably be dead or imprisoned if the House fell, anyway.

...I miss you, Azed.

Rohenvi came beside by the high-stilted bed and patted it with both palms. "Set her on this."

Between the bed and the wall, Auslan sat in a chair, covered with head down and hood up, his hands tucked inside sleeves too long for him. Natia sat beside him with huge eyes, staring at the injured Guardsvrin as they set the stretcher down.

Rohenvi saw the wound, now. The kick from a bulky hindquarter had been strong enough to shatter her ribs; the spurs on the heavy hooves had gashed her flank where a loop of intestine oozed out. Drani struggled to breathe; her lips were turning grey as blood spilled out. Natia peeped to see this then covered her mouth as if ashamed, and the Consort reached to pat her shoulder.

"Good, now please leave," the Matron told her guards. "Save the blindfolds for later. We'll see what we can do for Drani."

"Yes, Matron."

Rohenvi locked the door behind them, listened a moment with her ear to it, then braced a chair beneath the knob for good measure. She had turned around to speak when she saw Auslan cupping Drani's jaw, his eyes closed, and somehow pouring his first magic into her, to where the Guardsvrin's lips weren't such a frightful shade of death. He worked his way down, quickly forcing air into her blood without the use of one ruined lung, changing her coloring to normal before he repositioned his beautiful hands to cover the worst of the wound.

As Rohenvi and Natia watched in silence, the Davrin healer magically knitted shattered bones together, covered them again in remade flesh, stopped the bleeding inside and out. This process was neither instant nor without pain for them both. They mewled and groaned, sweated together, heating the room as if the Consort could feel every magical stitch.

Then Drani's left leg kicked in reflex, and Rohenvi recognized a revival over a death tremor. She stood in astonished silence while Natia cautiously reached for a pulse in the Guardsvrin's neck with two small fingers. Her shining garnet eyes—her sire's eyes—brightened first before the genuine smile touched her lips.

The cait remembered to whisper. "You did it, Auslan!"

"Yes." Rohenvi swallowed. "Thank you."

He grunted to acknowledge them, an unusually crude response for him, stepping backward to sit in his chair. He missed, collapsing on the floor beside it and against the wall.

"Oh! Careful! You okay?"

The Consort may have been embarrassed when Natia giggled nervously with her hand on his shoulder, like how he'd comforted her. He didn't speak but only pressed his drenched forehead to the cool stone, curling up and folding his arms in his lap to hide the tent at his crotch. The blood on his hands was drying and flaking off, and he trembled as if he might be in genuine fever, though Rohenvi wondered if he could be exaggerating.

After Rohenvi checked over the young Davrin for herself, ready to admit she was impressed at the strength of his magic, Auslan had neither spoken nor stopped shivering. He kept hiding what looked to be a painful erection.

The Matron frowned. *Hmm.*

"Will you stay with Drani for me, Natia?" she asked. "I will lead him back before he is seen."

"What?" Natia was disappointed. "But I can do it, Matron."

"No. I will."

"Aww." Her pout didn't last long before she remembered to acknowledge her elder. "Um, I will stay here with Drani, Matron."

"Good. Run to me if there's any problem. I won't be long."

Rohenvi was disturbed by the temperature of Auslan's skin as she helped him up, and how it smelled when wafts escaped his robe as he walked hunched over. The scent of pure, mature male at least a cycle old filled her nose. No strong soaps or perfumes, no wipe downs, or dabs of drying powders to please his matron.

He was just… a little dirty.

Argh, foul Priestess issue!

How could he know *exactly* what she enjoyed most and bring it out like this, without any effort?

Rohenvi took the secret passage into his room, though being in a close space with him was the last place she wanted to be. Pushing the switch, she shouldered the swivel panel open to drag them both into the room where he'd been staying for half a turn without complaint.

Auslan groaned again and took to his neatly made bed, burrowing his face in the pillow. She spotted his hips move against the mattress in need.

"What is wrong with you?" she demanded, her blood coursing in her veins. "You are not well but I don't recognize this ailment."

He stopped, didn't answer at first. Then he turned his head, his eyes closed. "I-I... I am not certain, my Matron..."

"Certain or not, guess. Tell me something."

He tried to wet his mouth, failed, looked for the pitcher and cup next to the bed; he hadn't knocked it over in his dreams this time. Rohenvi watched him struggle to one elbow to pour a cup and drink deeply, confirming that his erection hadn't gone away beneath his robe.

"Well?" she prompted again.

"I..." He laid down on his side, arm tucked under his head. "I think I..."

The Matron imagined weaving her fraying patience into a switch she was tempted to use. His hook and mannerisms were too familiar to her, and she hadn't wanted to ever be alone with a Consort again.

But I do not know what he might do if I ignore him. I cannot ignore him while he's in my care. The damned Priestesses have always known this!

When Auslan answered, it was with caution and a hint of shame. "I need to be touched, Matron."

I knew it.

Rohenvi shook her head. "No. No one here will couple with you. That was the code of conduct you agreed to." She swiped her hand at the look on his face. "You seemed eager for the peace! Do you not remember the span beneath the Red Sisters?"

He flinched. "I remember... but it...I have never gone so long without being touched before."

She grimaced then rolled her eyes. "Try being a Matron with much to lose. I must be picky about lovers. I have gone *decades* without being touched, Consort. One half a turn is not lethal to any Davrin."

"But I have been healing as well, each time without release afterward," he responded, as close as he'd yet come to protesting his situation. "Four times for Lead Jaunda, and for your Guardsvrin whose wounds were much worse than anything the Red Sister brought me. She nearly died."

"And I am grateful, healer. Truly." Rohenvi fiddled with a ring on her finger. "What is the one to do with the other? Healing and release."

Limpid, scarlet eyes watched her; they were tearing up. He whispered, "I think... that is how I heal myself... I have not healed since Elder D'Shea dragged me out of solitary. I feel pain."

She glanced down. "From a hard cock?"

Auslan shook his head, tucking a fist into his gut. "Here." Raising the fist to his chest. "Here..." He palmed his head. "I feel... a sickness."

He's lying. Acting. This isn't balanced. How dare he?

"Elder D'Shea warned me what may happen to your lovers when you lose control of your magic," the Matron hissed. "I will *not* allow it to knowingly happen to anyone of my House."

The healer stopped talking and looked away in acceptance. Rohenvi left then, or *escaped* was the better word, leaving him secure as she hurried to Natia and her Guard. Now she was terrified of leaving her granddaughter to Reverie alone in that room with him!

My little cait wouldn't understand the danger from someone so docile, she's never seen it before. It's wrong, what the Priestesses made him. What will I do? What will happen to him if he stays in there alone untended?

Would he feed himself? Die of thirst? Stay just ill enough from this dramatic longing to always be a disruption? Rohenvi did not have the time or focus to oversee him by herself for an unknown period, and Natia should not do it, either. Yet the Matron had no one she would trust to tend him, much less "touch" him as he claimed to need.

I know better. He is strange. He may not be pure Davrin.

She must try to reach the Elder Sorceress now, not wait until she understood the answers to these questions. For the sake of House Thalluen, contact must be indirect. As with those times she awaited her deep traveler, Rohenvi knew D'Shea may not answer for cycles or spans.

If whatever had happened outside didn't draw unpleasant attention here first.

RUK HAD BEEN HIDING ON THALLUEN LAND FOR OVER THREE marks, within a pockmark in the side of the rocky hill, before he broke the message pellet between callused fingers.

Eyin. Something's changed with Thalluen. I spotted a Drider. It spooked the livestock at the Fringeward boundary but did not attack before withdrawing.

It had not attacked but that was only a matter of time now. There were a great many Davrin at this House whom Ruk would like to save, but if given only a sliver of an opportunity, he knew the two he would carry out on his back if necessary.

Eventually, Eyin responded.

Check, Rausery knows. Word is Jaunda was interrogated by the Queen before heading off in the deep again. We must assume She knows about the healer.

Fuck. Roh had bought them only half a turn. *And for what?*

Elder D'Shea is involved, too, providing distraction at the top end.

Indeed, the stubborn Sorceress never seemed to stop doing that whenever things got interesting for Braqth's servants. It was like D'Shea knew she was bait they couldn't resist, and she wasn't afraid of dying.

Or she didn't let herself think about it.

Eyin wasn't finished. She must have used a second pellet. *I've sent two of ours after Jaunda, per Rausery's recommendation. We've got to pull something useful out of the sludge this time, and assume the Consort won't be around to heal her next time.*

Ruk frowned, wanting to ask who she'd sent down into that direction to help the Red Sister if it wasn't him. He decided it wasn't worth the extra pellet; he'd find out soon enough.

Eyin slipped in another thought before the spell cut off.

Time to follow up on that rumor about the Rin'oveaus—

Ruk smirked, observing the smaller, nonthreatening creatures which moved in the dark over the next short while. Not for the first time, he wondered if anyone he'd once known in Vuthra'tern was still alive, or if they'd all bred babies and killed each other by now. The Rin'oveaus *name* might have survived, but Ruk did not see how they could have bucked that same fate if they stayed.

Especially after raising that half-blood monster and teaching him how to kill Matrons.

SLOWLY, SO SLOWLY AND WITH AN EXHALATION OF RELIEF which made Her less of a statue, the Valsharess sat down upon Her throne inside the colorful, circular chamber where Wilsira had died not long ago. The Davrin Queen's distant eyes drifted among the blue and fire-red swirls of sky and sand blending together.

Shyntre could have sworn he heard the wind blow.

Trembling, he waited on the floor beside her having fasted long enough he had no waste to expel, though he couldn't say how many cycles that was. He had been hallucinating a lot since being forced to drink Auranka's milk, but he didn't remember any of his dreams. The Keeper was "eating" them, he presumed, as she'd boasted.

If that's what it takes to keep more buas from being thrown into the Pit with her, then she's welcome to them.

His head and joints ached fiercely. His eyes burned; they were so dry. He was uncomfortable but unafraid; they wouldn't leave him to die of something as unrewarding as negligence, as many times as he might have wished they would.

"A catastrophe diverted," murmured his Queen. "Its wound cauterized. One path reopened to possibility, one of many obstacles shifted to one side. Here We stand at the next."

Shyntre suppressed his sneer as he stared at the carpet. *Insane.*

"Your champion begins to learn herself, Mazdel."

Stop it. He closed his eyes. *I am not your son.*

She continued to mutter to Herself, fine robes shushing the one time She shifted. "Death closes with the Manalari pool, as it must to revive life, while the pull of serenity has drained life from the too-warm sea in what is not transition. We need a shield of the Flame, and someone to hold that shield between the Sun and the pillar in the sand…"

The Valsharess fell into contemplative silence again but for the occasional tap of Her fingernails on the arm of Her throne. Shyntre tried to ignore Her, counting the threads in a tapestry.

She turned Her head to him. "It is time for him to Awaken, We believe. He would not miss this."

Tap, tap.

The young mage waited tensely without looking up. He hoped She would return to talking to Herself.

No such mercy.

"Sirana ensnared his son and still carries yours."

Tap, tap.

Despite his better judgement, Shyntre finally looked.

His Queen smiled down at him, appearing lucid and aware, eyes like glittering topaz. "Your wild one will return in time, Mazdel. She cannot fail."

The Valsharess relaxed in Her seat.

Wild one? Return when? In time for what?

Did he want to know, or wish for her to return given what slavery awaited her? Maybe Sirana could stay up top, far away, and be better off. Her bua, too. What life could he have down here? What kind of life had any bua in Sivaraus?

"We only do not know yet who will stay with her when she has no choice left, Mazdel. We have always wondered…"

The Valsharess's voice drifted away again, the thought left dangling as Her gaze grew less sharp, but Shyntre felt ill regardless.

No choice left. Argh, damn it all…

How could he pretend there was no line hooked deep, ready to reel the Red Sister back when Braqth had had enough of the games? Of course, the Valsharess had usurped "his" champion to serve Her own Visions first.

Sirana wasn't free on the Surface. The only reason she was turned out of the Deepearth was because she'd caught, and the Valsharess had decided, for whatever reason, that She wanted this one. The only way Sirana *wouldn't* return was if she didn't survive. To see her again, pregnant or not, was both what Shyntre ached for and what he dreaded.

Royal purple and gold robes shushed again, and She reached down to cradle his face in one bejeweled hand. He tried hard not to flinch; his skin crawled all the same. His vision was blurred as he kept his lids lowered.

"Auranka has not seen either To'vah in your dreams. Not yet. The one of Ja'Prohn is toothless and has not tried to lure you out in a millennium. But the other of D'Shauranti? He is a trickster and only too pleased to encourage insurrection. We are ready for him now."

As She continued to speak like he should know what She was talking about, Shyntre gathered the writhing ball of panic and confusion inside his chest and waited.

He tried nodding. "Yes, my Queen."

She squeezed his chin. "You will tell Us if you meet a stranger, Mazdel, regardless of his shape. While awake or in Reverie. Tell Us."

"Yes, my Queen."

She released him, and the throne room fell silent.

She's paranoid. No one could reach him here while Auranka kept blanking out his Reverie and he could do nothing about it. Shyntre pushed that aside to clamp onto the names She had spoken.

He knew Ja'Prohn. That was his House, the male line of Headmasters and barely spoken of outside the Palace. Most commoners had never heard of it. Then, at first, he swore he didn't know who D'Shauranti had been, but heard Auranka's taunt to his real Mother in his memory.

"Ahhh, D'Shauranti, such fun your House has been, but your magic is almost gone. Do be careful, Varessa. Ja'Prohn tends to fail mustering the will to meet your passion the moment you turn your back…"

D'Shea was a House extinct, where a lone Red Sister had simply taken it as her name. Shyntre wasn't a cait, and the House had been broken down and dispersed before he was born anyway, so he wouldn't inherit it in any official capacity. He would stay House Ja'Prohn with Phaelous.

But had House D'Shea once been D'Shauranti? That seemed to be what the Drider Mistress had implied. If so, when did it change, and why? Had his Mother heard this name at all before Auranka had spewed it out? That could be why the Sorceress Elder held to D'Shea, as a lingering barb despite most forgetting what had happened as they always did?

Be careful. I doubt the Keeper was being careless after trading for her milk. Seems like blatant bait, glinting to distract us from web strands we can't see…

Yet it had stuck. Like always.

Shyntre avoided speaking first with the Valsharess. This was expected of any bua: *Don't speak unless spoken to.* Yet being passive with Her had seemed neither to help him nor satisfy Her any more than being aggressive had at the Wizard's Tower or in the Cloister. The Queen frequently said things as if pretending he was someone else.

Or maybe not pretending. Should I embrace it more? Would it satisfy Her?

Why did this thought terrify him, like he knew the answer and was going against some prevailing wisdom in trying?

Again.

"Mm," he began, sensing Her head move. "My Queen-Matron?"

He waited.

"Speak," She said, staring straight ahead and at the far wall, hands relaxed on the arms of Her throne.

"I... don't remember D'Shauranti. Or To'vah. It has been too long."

She tensed.

"What would you have me know about them to better serve Your Majesty?"

Her regal poise started to crumble before his eyes. Shyntre watched as a petrifying, naked horror and hatred overtook her face. She showed her white, perfect teeth, snapped them like an animal, the click resounding as the sole noise in the throne room. She swooped upon him, seized him like a hawk in Her claws as She revealed a strength that took his breath away.

Shyntre felt the wall against his back, pressed tight with his feet barely touching the floor. She crowded him, looming and suffocating. Both hands closed around his neck. He stupidly looked at Her eyes, Her rich fragrances clashing with the primal scent of fighting prey, desperate, angry—

Dangerous.

"Betrayers, all!" She hissed. "Once our best defenders! The singers and dancers, the loyal backbone of the Queen's Army! *You!* You are one of them!"

Shyntre hooked fingers against Hers, trying to pry them open to gain enough air. "M-mercy, V-Vahl...!"

"Your sire started it all when he made a bargain with that infernal for *petty* vengeance!"

"M-Mother, *stop!*"

Abruptly, She did, releasing him but also letting him fall to the carpet, shaking. Shyntre coughed, covered his throat as he pulled in deep breaths while he could. Her slippers shifted, and he braced for a kick.

It didn't come.

The young mage shook as heedless anger drained into the helpless, empty space inside him. He teetered on a snarl. "Oh? What about the To'vah? What did *they* do?"

He heard something, wagering his Queen ground Her teeth in a non-majestic way.

"He made it possible to keep you, Mazdel," She said. "For that, I *would* offer him gratitude. But he still deserved what came to him for how he did it."

I? Did She…? Fingernails digging into the plush padding, Shyntre took the risk. "Do you mean the trickster of House D'Shauranti, my Matron?"

"No. We mean the toothless of House Ja'Prohn."

Shyntre kept breathing, eyes down. Toothless certainly described his Headmaster, while his *real* Mother's blood seemed to have all the courage and grit.

Such fun your House has been, but your magic is almost gone…

He swallowed a lump in his throat. "What do you want from me, Your Majesty?"

"What you have always given Us, Royal Son."

The throne room fell quiet moments before a chime sounded, and the Valsharess looked toward the empty jump circle at the far end. Someone awaited an audience.

"Enter," said the Queen, who seemed not surprised when Elder D'Shea appeared alone in the room with them.

Shyntre, despite himself, very much was.

ELDER D'SHEA ARRIVED IN TIME TO WATCH THE VALSHARESS calmly take Her seat, but her son was cowering against the wall on the right, the image of a pincerworm that hadn't lashed out only because something else had bitten him first. He trembled from fear or from hunger and for certain hadn't slept well, if at all, since last she'd seen him.

At least he wasn't naked.

The Sorceress had done much to avoid laying eyes on Shyntre during his ill-requested time inside the Cloister training for the Surface, where he'd remained without a stitch of clothing and been treated worse than a new recruit. Not only would her compulsion make her show weakness in front of the others, but this old, swelling anger toward her superiors threatened to boil over, time and again.

We have no way out of the web, him and me.

Rausery had interrupted scenes like what lay before D'Shea now, albeit never by the Valsharess herself. The Elder General had mostly tried to avoid describing those confrontations in detail while D'Shea was around. Occasionally, the Prime would demand to know it all and require the Sorceress to stay and listen, a cruel smile on her lips as she listened to the "well deserved" abuse of a bua going where he "didn't belong."

"What else did he expect coming here?" the Prime crowed, laughing.

The only detail which prevented D'Shea from doing something truly regrettable back then was that the Prime herself seemed either disinclined or forbidden to touch Shyntre herself. The Elder Sorceress didn't know how her Queen and Auranka had been touching him since resuming his residence in the Palace after Sirana left, but the desperate fear in his eyes was the same as that last time he'd left it.

All too familiar.

"My Queen," she began with perfect poise. "I just came from the Thalluen plantation. I have learned the Consort-healer there has become ill."

The Valsharess waited, tapping Her finger.

"He is not responding to healing potions. They have a vastly reduced effect, somehow in conflict with his magic. It would take time and study to alter our common potions to suit his aura, but I believe he will only decline during that time. I w—"

"Ridiculous," interrupted the Queen in monotone. "The slut cleansed Sirana of Abyssal scars and primed her womb to conceive in the Tower by your son."

D'Shea's planned speech tripped and fell over a cliff. She blinked, staring with a genuine shock that brought a smile to the Valsharess's lips.

"We have touched the Red Sister," She said. "We know the Consort is not tainted. Your strongest healing potions *will* work."

Not yet speaking, D'Shea saw a sly tilt of the Queen's head.

"What?" She asked. "Did you not know your novice carried when she left?"

Not by Shyntre.

D'Shea glanced at her bua. His brow was pressed to the carpet, and his arms covered his head. Every line of his body language conveyed clear guilt.

Or *had* it been him?

No, impossible, I—

The Elder shook her head, trying to clear it. What conversations had her son been having with their Queen? *This is critical.*

She bowed. "Uhm. I did *not* know this, my Queen."

"We have Seen how her condition will aid the tapestry, Varessa. That is why We allowed her to go."

"Y-yes, Your Majesty."

The Valsharess had known Sirana was pregnant the entire time. *Of course, She did.* Thank the Goddess D'Shea had failed to convince Sirana to take one of her potions.

Her mind whirled in the quiet.

"Do you wish us to aid the healer, Your Majesty?"

She held her breath during a pause, then witnessed a nod.

"Yes, We do. We have witnessed in past centuries, this rare talent can aid those left catatonic by the Ornilleth. We will need him when the Elder Mind attacks."

D'Shea wished she had known this about Auslan after the last thrall battle. *We might have prevented all this penance and not lost six Sisters in the process.*

"Then I beseech to be heard about the potions not working, my Queen. If the Consort is this strong a mage but had been required to train his aura to share healing *only* through pleasure, then the lack of pleasure is draining his aura and interfering with our potions regardless of potency."

"How do you know he was trained in such a way, Elder?"

"I have discovered that the Conceiver had been selling his talent in exchange for magic and favors. Quickening wombs but also reducing wrinkles and erasing scars more quickly."

The Queen reacted to that. Her lip curled in disgust.

D'Shea continued, "The bua has told me he *has* taken healing potions before but only in service of his function. I believe the pleasure and healing are entwined too tightly, and he cannot undo it so easily after two centuries. He has been isolated from his function since the Purge, healing many Red Sisters for us, Jaunda especially, but not allowed any pleasure. It is making him ill."

Intense, tawny eyes narrowed at her, and D'Shea looked down, sensing the truth-aura swelling in the room, testing if the Elder was lying. D'Shea knew she was not. Meanwhile, Shyntre hid his own expression, not daring to show her a hint of what he thought.

"Hm," the Valsharess grunted.

D'Shea waited, sensing the opening before She acknowledged there was a problem with a gesture of Her hand.

"I have a proposal to fix this, my Queen."

"Speak it."

"He must be retrained to heal by touch without coupling." D'Shea straightened. "But I do not seek aid among the Red Sisters. Our own conditioning under the Prime, the pleasure in violence, is a conflict of interest in what we must accomplish, and many have failed the test of wills in the Cloister. He is potent, my Queen."

The Valsharess leaned forward. "What do you mean, D'Shea?"

The Elder ground her teeth having to say it. "One Red Sister has conceived since last he was in the Cloister and must be rehabilitated. It is why I removed him and instructed no one at House Thalluen was to touch him. We cannot put further Red Sisters at risk to catch while the Ornilleth remain a threat."

The Valsharess frowned in agreement. "Are you suggesting We execute this healer, Elder? Is he too unstable?"

Shyntre tensed so much that D'Shea worried he was about to snap his spine.

She rushed to say, "No, Your Majesty. This healer will be invaluable in the coming conflict, as You have said. But he must be prepared for that conflict the same as any fighter. I... I must request something extraordinary to see this happen, to break the Priestess's hold and repurpose it for war as I also uncover how the Consort was made."

The Valsharess hissed subtly. "What request?"

"I seek a bua, not a cait who may lose her mind in want to rut the Consort. I need a bua past the curiosity of coupling and with a powerful will to guide this Consort's aura in *unlearning* what Wilsira required of him. Lastly, given the urgency, I need a mage who has faced the magic of the Priestesses already and proven to withstand it."

The Queen was like a statue again. Then, hauntingly slow, She turned her head toward the young wizard on the floor, where his fingers arched like claws wanting to shred Her carpet.

She understands.

D'Shea licked her lips. "My Queen. Shyntre knows of this Consort from their shared time in the Sanctuary, and his will and aura are stronger. He has knowledge both of Sanctuary conditioning *and* of battle and resilience under pressure, the Elder General has seen to that. He has long despised the Priestesses while making it no secret. I have heard of none of them manipulating him for long."

Unexpectedly, the Valsharess chuckled. D'Shea felt a rush of chill she couldn't immediately explain; she didn't know if this was a good sign or not. Nonetheless, the Elder Sorceress took the risk and finished her speech.

"The Red Sisters are ill-equipped to retrain the healer to prepare Sivaraus for possible invasion, Your Majesty, and we cannot spare any more to pregnancy. The Sanctuary is in backbiting flux and are the ones who bent the healer this way in the first place. We need Phaelous's son to aid us in this task, if our Queen will grant us his help."

Mother and son waited in silence as the Valsharess pushed Herself up from the throne again, stepping beside him. Her tone was contemplative while She watched D'Shea's son. "Of course, you need him…"

Then the Valsharess slowly turned away from the Elder, stepping through the royal curtain through which Auranka and their Queen had arrived for the audience between Wilsira and Sirana over Kerse. D'Shea had never seen what lay behind it; she didn't know anyone who had.

The throne room fell into oppressive silence while the Elder Sister stood in place. She was ready to meet Shyntre's eyes if he looked up because she could now. He kept his eyes down, though it was clear to her he had not given up on whatever it was he held on to.

It was a long wait, but the Valsharess stepped through Her curtains again, alone, Her gaze distant and calm. Her aura tended to always remain hidden even from powerful mage-eyes like hers, and the Elder could not read what She had decided.

"Stand up," She commanded.

Shyntre pushed himself off the carpet to his unsteady feet; D'Shea could see the tremors, and he appeared dizzy. He made not one gesture or plea on behalf of himself, made no hint what outcome he might desire from his Mother's proposal, if any.

The Queen reached with one hand and caressed his face; he stood rock-still, his eyes locked on a neutral spot on Her robe. Then She stroked again with Her other hand, stepping close and cradling his face, pressing Her lips to his forehead. She brushed his cheeks with Her thumbs as if wiping away nonexistent tears.

D'Shea felt confusion, jealousy, and resentment, despite that she'd witnessed much harsher treatment than this. She showed none of it, trying to read her Queen's lips as She whispered to him, not bothering to cover Her mouth from sight.

"Tell Us who you are."

Shyntre hadn't blinked; D'Shea saw her son's throat flex in a swallow.

"Mazdel," he whispered. "The Royal Son."

"Royal, yes, remember. You will *not* sell yourself out there in the city. You are not a whore, do you understand? You are priceless to Us."

A hint of bafflement crossed his face as D'Shea stared in astonishment, remembering to close her mouth before either of them acknowledged her presence.

"Have no fear, for none in Sivaraus will harm you. You shall teach this bred Consort what you have learned, Mazdel. If he can be made worthy to strengthen Our people beyond using his cock to quicken, We will spare him the same fate as his brothers, and he shall not be sent to Auranka's Pit."

D'Shea would have said the Queen had plunged a dagger into his gut from the look of stunned betrayal on his face as they stared at one another.

He forced a nod. "I-I will, Queen-Mother. M-my vow."

Ohh, Goddess.

D'Shea moved her eyes to one side, waiting while this played through as it must as cold horror tightened low in her middle. Had she been sentenced as merely a surrogate as well?

*But he is **my** son.*

"Will you spare Matron Thalluen sanctions as well?" Shyntre said. "She was only doing as the Elder Sorceress commanded."

D'Shea blinked, cringing inside that he was trying to negotiate when they had so little to give.

The Valsharess chuckled and caressed his face again, planting another dry kiss on his brow. "Hm. Dream of Sirana for Us, in payment for her Mother. We would see her through your eyes."

Implying that he had not, thus far, whether he'd drunk the Drider Keeper's breast milk or not. As D'Shea had expected, her son realized he couldn't match the Queen's expectations. He nearly panicked.

The Sorceress spoke up. "My Queen amazes me with Her foresight. I had thought it too early to present this theory, but I believe us capable of reaching Sirana on the Surface through a shared bond."

The Valsharess whipped Her intense, topaz-yellow gaze at her, and abruptly D'Shea knew the weight she'd removed from her bua and taken onto herself.

"You do, Varessa? Why?"

The Sorceress smiled and bowed. "The saphgar stone, which the Sisterhood has been studying of late, Your Majesty."

She removed from her pouch the unfinished piece Phaelous had given her last turn and held it up. The Valsharess nodded, motioning to her.

"Under the Headmaster, Shyntre has proven the only mage in the Tower to alter its qualities to appear like the Tragar weapons, and Sirana has with her the piece he created. If he can create another stone like it, we may form a connection in Reverie. The vast distance may not matter."

The Elder witnessed an odd, scholarly expression on her Queen which was nonetheless encouraging. Not just a visionary and Davrin touched by the divine, the Valsharess was also knowledgeable of the arcane studied by Her wizards and sorceresses.

This was why She was their Queen.

"Good," She ruled. "We accept, Varessa. This in exchange for leniency on Matron Thalluen. In addition to rehabilitating a natural born healer, our son must make the effort to remind Sirana what awaits, lest she willfully forget what is at stake."

The Elder Sorceress bowed deeply. "Your Will be done, my Queen."

The Valsharess did not trust Shyntre to cross the circular room on his own as She steered him by his shoulders off the royal platform to stand before his birth Mother. He looked like a fly caught center-web and about to be spun into a meal. Gently, D'Shea took him by his arm.

The hand-off performed in silence.

"You have your objectives, Elder," She said. "Take him and leave the Palace immediately."

SHYNTRE WAS LIKE A BRISTLING BALL OF PINS THAT D'SHEA DARE not touch again as she escorted him quickly to the stables to claim a set of riding lizards. She had asked if he needed to pack anything from his rooms, and he'd met her gaze in silence, his eyes hot as coals.

She took it as a resounding negative.

He kept his mouth sealed as they rode without wasting time, as crowds parted for the Elder Sorceress and a powerful shield protected them from an ill-advised attack. His aura was simmering, sometimes flaring beyond good sense, and he could barely wait until they were out of the central market and in enough space and darkness to where his hands would be hard to read.

What the fuck are you doing?! he exploded. *Are you insane, too? How could you give away all that?!*

If D'Shea hadn't witnessed what she had moments ago, she might have struck him for taking that tone with her. As things were, she had no idea what he had been enduring since Sirana left, and only some of the two centuries he had lived without her. The Valsharess wished him to be someone other than who he was; She was convinced of it and that was outright terrifying.

Are you insane, too?

She brought her own temper to heel.

Did you not listen? she returned. *I am doing exactly what I told the Queen I would. It's not wise to lie to Her. He needs you, and I need you both.*

This had the same result as a strike. Her son flinched, and his eyes glistened with moisture. *What...? What did he tell you?*

D'Shea swept her senses around them before answering. The shield and alarm wards would allow them some ability to relax on the road, but she was not *completely* certain they wouldn't see Auranka over the next hill. She exhaled, taking the extra precaution of a shape-blurring spell before answering.

That you awakened his healing magic before his first worship ball. That his aura cannot overwhelm yours because you overwhelmed his first. That you know his name, and he has never forgotten you.

Shyntre withdrew, stunned and numb, and this response D'Shea did understand. She had seen it many times, as many in Sivaraus kept their true desires hidden. Lest someone more powerful decide to punish and play with them.

A few times, Shyntre considered bolting on his lizard, tempted to try escape; she could tell. Fortunately, some lingering practical sense pinned down the panic, and D'Shea waited, as Phaelous often did when she acted this way. The two traveled a long way before her son could communicate a hint of what agony roiled inside him.

Wait.

She had outlasted her share of nerves in plenty of interrogations. She could wait.

★Disgusted?★ he signed, showing his teeth like a trapped animal.

She smiled dryly. ★As if my opinion has ever mattered in your life? For what it is worth to you, I bed both caits and buas.★

★You are a Red Sister. It is expected.★

★I mostly prefer my own sex, probably for similar reasons as you.★

He wanted to scoff. ★Oh?★

She ticked off, ★No status games, no worthiness tests, no pregnancy.★

Shyntre didn't disagree.

Instead, he repeated, ★You are an Elder Red Sister. You have immense power and freedom.★

Now, D'Shea wanted to scoff. ★I am the last survivor of my House, as good as vanished. Power I may have, but no freedom such as you imagine it. I have seen so much which many Matrons and Nobles never do. I long ago accepted that desire between buas must be as commonly felt as between caits, and this is real and will always happen among Davrin, no matter the punishments, or they would not risk being caught so often.★

She could hear her son's heartbeat as she swept the ground again. Still no obstacles. Shyntre made a small noise, and she looked.

★What will you do, now,★ he signed, ★knowing this about me and the healer?★

D'Shea grinned. ★I have already done it, Shyntre. I came to retrieve you from the Palace and escort you to House Thalluen. Auslan must heal himself, and someone strong enough must touch him to begin the process.★

Her son didn't appreciate the rarity of being encouraged to bed another bua, odd as it must be for his own Mother to suggest it.

★Yes, to use him for war!★ Shyntre sniped back, rigid under any reassurance she could offer. ★As if he will be treated any better?★

D'Shea hid her sign behind her cloak. ★Listen, Shyntre. He *must* have another function if he is to survive even another decade. But first, I also want to reach Sirana. He has dreamt of her once or twice, but the visions make little sense. Color canyons and iron bars.★

Her bua's eyes widened; he gripped his saddle and reins. D'Shea noted it but as long as he didn't faint, she chose to ignore it for now.

★I believe Sirana tries to reach him from the Surface with psionics,★ she deflected, tidy and true. ★But Auslan must heal first, then we need an anchor and a focus to strengthen his reach. Which is *you*, my powerful and stubborn wizard.★

He glared at her, and she felt the impulse to laugh.

Instead, she added, ★It has worked with her before, son, I promise you. Or I would never have been freed from Wilsira's compulsion.★

Shyntre's mouth sagged. He didn't want to believe her.

He doesn't need to believe me now. I only need to get them in the same room together. Let it play out by their natures.

★If you get hungry on the way, Shyntre, let me know. I have some rations on me.★

This time, she didn't need to wait.

★I am starving.★

She passed over her waterskin and entire food pouch without playing games. He took both, capable of testing them for poison or drugs himself. She knew they were clean.

★Thank you.★ Her son paused. ★Mother.★

He does know who he is. He can tell me about this 'Mazdel' later.

The Elder Sorceress smiled with confidence and continued the journey to the one middling House which she could say had earned the closest thing to her loyalty outside the Sisterhood.

SHYNTRE HAD ARRIVED INSIDE THE PRIVATE PASSAGE WITH A bag over his head and his stomach no longer growling. Once it was removed in a small, trap-like entry way, he found the Matron Thalluen there with her child servant, who seemed to loath standing on the same side as D'Shea but also didn't beg to flee while Matron and Elder signed to each other.

The cait was in a strange sort of general distress but also perplexed as she looked up at him, asking in a whisper, "Are you a healer, too?"

For once, Shyntre tried to think what had been going on outside of his own misery in the Palace. He glanced at Sirana's Mother, who looked from D'Shea's hands to the small cait and to him.

He was honest as he could be. "I am here to help Auslan, if I can."

Rohenvi swallowed and dipped her chin to him. "Welcome. Ah, Shyntre. I-I never knew the Elder had a son. You look so much like the Headmaster."

Stung for a reason he couldn't fathom, Shyntre bowed his head as well. Sirana's Mother could recognize who his sire was without them standing in the same room? Why? Or was that common among Matrons who rarely came to Court, and he was ignoring "common sense," again?

This Matron never knew about me, though.

"He grew up tending Consorts in the Sanctuary but is not one himself," D'Shea explained. "He has knowledge and magic you will need to revive the healer. His arrival is known and blessed by the

Valsharess. We are to keep him here and out of public view until the right time."

"About how much longer?" Rohenvi asked. "Any estimate?"

D'Shea shook her head. "Not yet. Too many unknowns, but the Sisterhood is working on it. In the meantime, know that my son has a role in view of the Valsharess at Court, has been tutored at the Wizard's Tower in crafting gems and medicines, and has been tested as a battle mage. He is talented with fire and shield spells."

The two House females stared at him wide-eyed. His Mother continued, sounding almost boastful.

"Shyntre can defend himself if necessary and could aid you if this House is attacked, though he is unlikely to follow orders from someone he doesn't respect."

D'Shea tossed an arched eyebrow his way that made him want to smirk.

"Know also that many in high positions would recognize him as a protected male and know it is ill-advised to harm him or try to hold him for ransom. He is also a bold one, sometimes to his detriment, and frequently temperamental. He may act spoiled and young for his age."

"Hey," Shyntre protested, but the females ignored him.

"He's a favorite of the Queen?" the cait asked succinctly.

"Yes," replied the Elder with a pert smile.

"Well," the Matron breathed. "He sounds like what we need, Elder. I thank you for your keen eye to our situation."

"Always, Matron."

Now it was Shyntre's turn to arch an eyebrow at her.

"Should I bring him to Auslan now, Matron?"

The cait sounded eager.

"Indeed, I must leave this to you for now," said Elder D'Shea, straightening her hood as if she was about to turn toward the hidden door. "I shall return with further guidance."

Wait. She's not staying to watch?

"Stay well, Elder," said the Matron. "We will be here when you need them."

"That would be best."

Elder D'Shea left so fast after the introductions that Shyntre felt muzzy-headed when Sirana's Mother tried to coax him to follow her. The cait grabbed his hand and tugged.

"Natia," the Matron scolded. "Let him be. He can walk."

"Sorry, Matron."

What the fuck is happening?

The mage followed them through the in-wall passageway, each of them stepping in admirable silence. They had been practicing with Auslan here, or perhaps never stopped. Finally, they made it to a panel which held a switch that Matron Rohenvi flipped before pushing the wall to reveal the way in.

The warm scent of Auslan's sweat clubbed him in the face.

"Come on," Natia whispered, her small fingers itching to snatch his hand again.

Is she... worried about him?

He soon saw why, and it ripped his heart loose inside his chest.

Oh, Goddess. What have they done?

His brother hadn't been eating enough. Although he was covered neck to feet in the darkest, most modest clothing he had ever been provided, Shyntre could see in Auslan's face how much weight he'd lost since they'd seen each other last, on opposite sides of the bars in the Cloister. The Consort's eyes were closed, and he didn't stir as the three entered. The solid gold streak at his temple aged him another century, at least.

Natia was about to rush forward and wake him up, but Rohenvi snared her and wrapped both arms around her tightly, shushing her. The Matron looked at him.

"What do you need, mage?"

Uhhh...

"Water, both to drink and for bathing," he said. "A heating stone if you have it. Some food, enough for two to last a cycle. Fresh sheets and blankets."

Rohenvi nodded to all that without protest.

"Um, if I wrote down a list of components and wizard's tools," Shyntre continued, "would you try to get them for me, Matron?"

"You can write?" Natia blurted, being shushed again.

He arched a brow at her. "Most wizards can."

"Oh." She glanced at the healer. "He can't, but he's a mage, too."

He's not a wizard, he's a sex slave to aging Matrons.

Shyntre pursed his lips and shrugged instead.

"I will get you something to write it down," Rohenvi said, pulling the child along with her in a non-servant like way. "We will return with the other supplies. It may take a few trips, but I shall get it done with discretion."

The Matron was doing it herself? *This* was Sirana's Mother?

"Thank you—" he said too late for her to reply.

The mage sighed inside the quiet, sealed room. It was simply furnished, not large, and smelled like his brother had been here for quite some time. D'Shea had removed him from the Cloister only a span after Sirana had left because of the temptation and turmoil he caused, and by all signs had been here ever since.

It was more mercy than he might have ever expected from the ruthless Elder Sorceress by her reputation alone.

Knowing they wouldn't be alone for long, Shyntre sat down beside his brother, trying not to think about the next time Auranka would drop by to taunt him. He touched the damp, fevered brow with his fingertips, settled his palm, and immediately felt the grue-some injuries.

The healer's unseen aura was shot through with broken patterns and bonds that would be painstaking to repair. His Mother was cor-rect that this condition was past the point where they might repair themselves. So many frayed, dead ends and burnt points, caused by all these females feeding on his kindness, as they'd always done, but also—

Also.

My own. Reflecting back at me.

Until recently, they'd been only slow stretch marks and strains while Shyntre had been pretending he was someone else for a hundred and fifty years. But now, while the Spider Queen and her servants tormented him in the Palace, seeking *something* about what Sirana was doing on the Surface, about when she might come back, while Shyntre had blacked it all out of his memory and remembered nothing from one Reverie to the next...

Oh, no...

Ta'suil had felt some of it; he still remembered at least part of those visions being ripped out of him.

Again.

"Ta'suil," he whispered.

What have I done to you?

He squeezed his clothed shoulder, shook him. "Ta'suil!"

No response.

Shyntre touched skin again, tucking both hands against the Consort's too-lean face, his fingers sliding into oily, damp hair behind his ears.

Bruised eyelids fluttered.

Is he dreaming now? Will I make it worse, trying to wrench him out?

"Ta'suil."

Shyntre could not make his mouth form any other word. Nothing else seemed like it would help.

"Ta'suil."

The changes were small, but there.

Take it. You can have anything. All of it.

"Ta'suil."

Just open your eyes, damnit, come back! Don't give up, please. Don't let them do this again. Not again!

The healer was warm—too warm to be healthy—and breathing through his nose. Shyntre leaned down to press their lips together, knowing another kiss while he could. He held on to his brother, touching what naked skin there was to be seen.

It felt good. Better.

Take what you need.

"Ta'suil…"

Shyntre fell into it, whatever this was, gathering up the unconscious Consort to hold closer against him, pressing their cheeks together while he caught his breath, bare hand wrapped firmly around his nape.

What I need, too.

The Queen's pet kissed the Consort again, softly, along the edge of his mouth, his jaw, his neck. Breathed him in and pressed full on his mouth again.

A moan. His brother's.

Tired. Not in pain, I don't think.

He hoped.

"Ta'suil?"

Shyntre held his breath, stroking his brother's jaw with one thumb, until, at last those brilliant scarlet eyes opened. Looked at him.

Recognition.

Yes.

Ta'suil tried to smile, to lift his arms. He was heart-achingly weak. Shyntre couldn't aid with the smile except to offer one in return, though he helped the healer place his arms around his shoulders where he could cling the best he could. Ta'suil caressed his short-cut hair lightly with his fingertips, smiled in welcome. The young wizard exhaled, freed from the fear that he'd never see this light again.

The healer still loved him, despite everything.

Soon, Shyntre realized that he'd been so focused that he'd not noticed the Matron Thalluen had silently brought in everything but the bath water. There was a scrap of parchment, a stylus, and ink bottle set on the small table by the wall. Rohenvi had chosen not to say a thing about the blatant display she must have seen at least twice. Maybe the young cait, too. Nor had she withheld anything they needed in retaliation.

Still, his own Mother's hand sign returned to haunt him.

This is real and will always happen among Davrin, no matter the punishments, or they would not risk being caught so often.

Shit.

The healer touched his own flaming cheeks, as if testing him for fever. Shyntre blinked at him, refocusing on why he was here.

"You're awake?" he whispered.

That's the stupidest question ever.

The Consort wanted to laugh; his eyes crinkled at the corners instead. He claimed a trembling kiss of his own.

"As are you," Ta'suil whispered, "now."

CHAPTER 19

THE HIGH INQUISITOR'S BOOT HOVERED FOR A MOMENT BEFORE taking the first stone step leading to the undercroft of Mount Sonai. Vene Kegyek placed his palm upon the wall for balance as the voices of the damned greeted him even before passing through the gate. Little more than threatening whispers most times, occasionally they swelled to a wordless wail of regret such as he heard now.

You reap in death what you've sown in life.

The High Inquisitor was certain those voices which lingered in this labyrinthine combination of storage, dungeon, and crypt were of the time before the first Archbishop and the cleansing; when the holy mount had been overrun with greedy, Godless lords being ridden by sodomizing devils.

Before the Purification over three hundred years ago, when the last lord's family began falling under misfortune upon misfortune, be it disease, accident, violence, or poisoning. Before the Consecration of Iarmod Tefornin and the Revival of the *Pisc'sagrad*.

God's judgment resounded through the land through His Paladin.

Vene Kegyek was not from Manalar, nor could he pretend to be unless he gave up his Northern name. He had traveled here as a pilgrim decades before, hearing the call in this warm, Sun-blessed land. He had first heard the voices below within the Temple crypts then, once he'd proven worthy of entering. He'd ignored them for years; he certainly never mentioned their moans to a living soul.

Anyone who could hear the dead could be a Desecrator, or a Ma'ab spy, especially if they had been born in colder lands.

Noiri by birth, Vene had been blessed with rich red hair and fiery beard, unlike many of his Northern kin. Thus, he had been embraced by the warm-toned Paxian people of Manalar, though his skin did not brown beneath the sun like theirs.

I am one of them, now. With silver hair comes the accepted name.

The Archbishop Emil Keros had, indeed, approved of his highest interrogator, judge, and executioner being from outside the established family names.

"Easier politics," Keros had said with a confident smile. *"A stronger impression of impartiality."*

The Archbishop had never questioned how his High Inquisitor so often extracted verifiable truths from those under questioning shortly before they died. Every time Kegyek had, what he'd learned had never been wrong, and thus, the people had another name for their Inquisitor.

The Catechist of Truth.

*"We do wish you could spare just **one** of them after hearing their confessions, Vene. A public execution would set the right example."*

"Apologies, Archbishop. It is Musanlo's Will."

"For all time."

"Yes, Holiness."

Keros's smirk had been difficult to read, though not worrisome, especially since the blond man who would become Capitan of the Wall had arrived from the West.

While the Archbishop and High Inquisitor had moved together for the past two decades, Musanlo's Will seemed to pull and abrade them from within as a younger man arrived. Willven Isboern had become an immovable favorite among the commoners and defenders of the city only in the last five years.

This rise had begun quietly; Willven Isboern's popularity had raced up into the Bishops' faces only in the last year as rumors of returning war with the Ma'ab had begun to spread. Now, the Capitan was like a shooting star, drawing all eyes and shining new light of hope upon them.

A divine omen, they whispered among themselves. A defender sent by Musanlo just in time.

"No, let it run its course," said Emil in their private meeting this morning. *"Isboern pulls them together when they had been splintering, as we need this unified front to face the next attack from the North. Once the threat has passed, we may reevaluate his devotion, unless he becomes a fondly remembered hero. We will commission a statue in mourning."*

Meanwhile, the rest of the clergy and nobles were becoming agitated by the overconfident youth, complaining incessantly as supply routes and accustomed comforts were no longer guaranteed. Spies were everywhere, accusations were made daily, which was bad enough as a time sink, but the Capitan sometimes riled the masses up with promises of victory and a "better life" afterward, promising their "community-raised" wealth would be passed down to the poor and feckless.

"The nobles claim Isboern is causing the supply disruptions on purpose to turn the devoted against them, Your Holiness."

"Mm-hm. Yet you've seen the reports as I have, Inquisitor. War is coming. Will **they** *be fighting on the front lines and defending the walls, my Catechist? No, they will not. The nobles may sit with chafing pride for a while. This shift in attention is only temporary. This pilgrim is a born tactician with a cheaply bought ethic and impossible to remove now, but the survivors will be weary and grateful for order when it returns. Trust me, Vene."*

The Inquisitor did trust his Temple's highest bishop's plan, except for a new, poorly- timed wrinkle which threatened to set off a scorching blast within their ranks before the Ma'ab ever arrived.

"What of the black-skinned demon in the dungeon, Keros?"

Too many knew about her; many eyes had witnessed she was real, and mouths could not be sealed even under threat of caning. Word was spreading, as were the conspiracies and speculations.

Worse, too many saw Capitan Isboern as the holy warrior who had captured her and the one with the power to protect them from her trickery.

He is incorruptible, they said.

The *Dyos Guerrimos* had arrived too late to claim authority over her containment, but they refused to give up trying to wrest control of her from Isboern's loyal Templars.

"What of her?" Emil repeated. "We gain truth from her, Catechist, by whatever means. I have faith you can hear even a demon's confession. Do what you do best."

Vene had sighed. *"Yes, Archbishop."*

Why is this ridiculous infighting always over anything with tits?

The High Inquisitor reached the base floor of the cool undercroft and passed through the storage first. The door on the far wall was invisible to most, and a mage would have to know where to look and how to release the spell of protection without summoning every guard upstairs.

The High Inquisitor entered the hidden set of steps alone and unseen, sealing the door behind him before lighting a torch in utter blackness. The whispers of the crypts were louder while he did so, trying to distract him. To frighten him into leaving. After fifteen years since he'd attained access to this place, he'd never found a sure excuse to requisition an exorcism of the ghosts either bound or clinging to the Temple's underbelly.

At last, fire flared. Vene lifted his torch high.

Be gone, you haunting damned!

The light made it easier to ignore the voices as he turned left at the bottom of this second flight of stairs, for he must get nearer to the crypt before he could take the hall leading to the dungeon.

They grew louder.

Silence. I'll not listen to your lies.

The Inquisitor swept to the right as soon as he could, striding quickly down the ancient tunnel that could be a millennium old.

He hurried, listening to his bootsteps, eager to shed the sensation of cold mists touching his nape like a dead woman's fingers.

Stop. Malicious spirits, Musanlo compels you, stay in your consecrated graves!

Suddenly, an old figure stood in his path, and Vene brought himself up short, surrounded by his own gasp of fright. He stared at the apparition, able to see a hint of solid stone wall through it. Despite recognizing something akin to monk's robes adorning a blurry, elderly form, Vene could not decide if this was man or woman.

Do not speak to it. It can't hear you.

"Who are you?" he whispered despite his best advice.

The eyes were milky, the irises a smooth grey; its expression was one of mourning as a toothless maw opened.

Tried to speak.

"Shholvis'ya…rasshivag…"

That unwelcome, sibilant language again. Could he never escape it, even here? It was not Ma'ab, Noiri, or Manalari. In truth, Vene had heard it long before he had learned the Tongue of the South.

Deathless one returns?

"Musanlo put ye to rest," he rasped, gathering his courage as he grasped the sunburst pendant around his neck.

The High Inquisitor walked forward, reciting the anti-possession prayer, reinforcing his will and focus. The ghost vanished before he could pass through it. There was no scent of the grave in his nostrils.

God be praised.

Vene continued to the dungeon, dismissing the hall leading to the bulk of the heretics and witches being held for trial. He went to the solitary wing, where currently they would hold only one prisoner. The guard seemed agitated when he answered the summons, sliding the metal panel to the side and looking through the small, iron bar window.

"High Inquisitor has arrived!" the guard announced.

He unlocked the heavy wooden door, letting the larger man inside before relocking it again. After armor clanked and scraped as men came to attention, the cramped room buzzed with life and voices.

Of course, someone had called in Isboern, first.

His torch was no longer the only source of light. Vene could see well, counting five Templars—including the one who opened the door—and three God Warriors, plus the Capitan. Tempers were simmering, tanned skin sweating, but they somehow hadn't erupted into violence, yet.

The Inquisitor smiled enough to unsettle them, tucking his torch into an unused sconce, presenting freed hands. "I come to see the prisoner, and a brawl is about to happen among Musanlo's Best?"

The God Warriors dared to smile first.

"Inquisitor."

"Catechist Most Holy."

The third looked at Capitan Isboern. "Let's see you deny interrogation now, *God*blood."

Willven Isboern didn't appear worried. He never did. Despite every attempt to read that shining, resilient aura whenever he performed his "miracles," Vene had not yet uncovered what the Western mage feared most.

For he was a man like the rest of them.

"High Inquisitor Kegyek." Capitan Isboern saluted as was proper, hand fisted, touching first the brow then tapping above the heart. "Please remind the *Dyos Guerrimos* that the demon's deliberate and preplanned target was a Templar and thus under my jurisdiction."

Vene chuckled. "A Templar? Her target was *you*, or so I read under every eyewitness report."

"Such is the law."

A pity she didn't succeed.

"I come to bear witness," said Vene, correcting the neat crease at the hem of his long, black sleeve followed by a reverent touch of the gold sunburst pendant resting over his heart. "I need neither God Warrior nor Templar present, as you well know. Leave solitary until you are called again. I release the Capitan to his duties."

The two disparate defenders threw suspicious glares at each other. While the God Warriors were well-known farther outside the city's walls and endlessly useful and effective as the civil enforcers guarding their borders, they tended to be burdensome while inside the walls or anywhere near the Manalari army, as the Templars considered it interference if not a direct challenge to their territory.

Had Vene Kegyek been born here a hundred years ago, he would have advised the Archbishop of the time to blend the two together, by force if necessary, and let the next generation grow accustomed to a new set of rules. But that was impossible now, as part of their economy and defense had always been dependent on reining in the most zealous among them. Isboern's arrival had made that clear divide among their people all too apparent to neighboring lands, especially Augran and Taiding.

There is a Godless influence brewing, likely from Augran, and its agents have been here for a while, taking advantage.

Willven Isboern, however, for all his faults, was anything but Godless.

"I have time, High Inquisitor," he said. "I will stay and answer any questions you have about the capture. I offer to guard your mind and body from what surprises of the captive I know about, as she is not Human."

The damned youth knew he was not so prideful as the *Dyos Guerrimos.*

"Very well, Capitan. I accept."

The blond man turned to his Templars. "If you please, wait for me in the forechamber."

The Templars were not pleased but would obey, this was clear. Meanwhile the God Warriors began barking protests, using their typical lewd accusations about the demon being female as their sole justification to stay.

And it is up to me to quell them, as they will not listen to the Capitan. Sigh.

Vene slipped off his right glove and lifted a bare, pale hand, fingers curled in a gesture few here had seen before. Sets of Templar eyes widened, and the five fighters bumped fists with Isboern before filing toward the door without delay. The three Warriors checked each other, seeing which one of them might retreat first.

They will make me waste the spell on a show.

With any luck, the demon was watching through the crack in the door.

"*Ciolume fochere*," he chanted.

The heavy pull of his spiritual strength circled twice around his heart, making it jump and race inside him, before burning through his back and down his right arm.

"*Pi'glori ao'sul!*"

Blue sky fire erupted off his fingertips and swept the ceiling above the God Warriors, burning cobwebs and reaching down to make their hair stand up, sending tremors down their spines.

"*Agarde!*" one cried, saluting. "At your leisure, Inquisitor!"

Finally, they left. Whether they picked a fight with the Templars in the forechamber or not, Vene didn't care so long as they did not return. It was ill-advised anyway, as the Templars always outnumbered the God Warriors within and underneath the Temple itself.

"Ah," Vene sighed, closing both the door and the sliding metal over the window. He picked up his torch. "That is better, is it not?"

Isboern smiled, stood at ease, and saluted again. Unlike some mageborn officers of potent talent, the High Inquisitor never doubted his own safety around the Capitan of the Wall. The man's clear ambitions for rising in the leadership did not seem to include pompous threats or political sabotage of his rivals.

Not yet.

The Inquisitor approached the prisoner's door, listened to the silence inside, looked at the stout, Dwarven-made bolt-lock.

"Have you the key, Capitan?"

The younger man grinned with charming chagrin, glancing at the far corner of the room behind them near where Vene had been standing. Isboern murmured a prayer-spell as he outstretched his hand and, with enviously less effort, a piece of metal dragged in the dark corner then floated into view, gentle and direct, to settle in the Inquisitor's now-gloved hand.

The fine control in this display had never been lost on Vene, the few times he'd witnessed it before. Moving and blocking physical objects without touching them had been what got Willven Isboern noticed in the army in the first place.

The Western man seemed to have shields, ropes, and clubs none of them could see, plus a set of eyes in the back of his head. Isboern had yet to teach any of the Bishops these new spells he'd brought with him and had proven an exceedingly difficult man to kill.

Yet the people call him Godblood, not sorcerer, like so many others they've gleefully sent to the rack. Pfeh.

"Is she loose inside?" he asked, testing the key, preparing to slide the bolt.

"Chained on the far wall," said Isboern. "Two paces in length."

He jiggled the key into place one-handed, tightened his grip. "That's long enough to strangle herself, Capitan."

"She can't escape that way, Inquisitor."

"Oh? How do you know?"

Clunk.

"Because she has a mission to complete."

Vene pushed the door open as an outward display of confidence in the Capitan's assessment that attack wasn't imminent, or if it was, the self-appointed bodyguard would do his duty. The Inquisitor placed the torch in the door-side sconce to better light the cell, sniffing the air.

I cannot... place that scent. She is not Human, he said.

There was the same, mundane filth of the living to which he was accustomed among men and Dwarves—skin oil, sweat, urine, feces—but in these tight, breezeless quarters, they possessed an exotic quality. Foreign, even for a born foreigner like him.

The High Inquisitor looked for the demoness, and at first could not make her out among jumping shadows caused by his torch. Then he saw the white hair and red eyes as she lifted her head to glare at them over her shoulder. His mouth dropped in shock while annoyance and bafflement swept the Inquisitor.

Why was she positioned as if she loitered on a day bed being painted by an artist? He could see a clear hint how this creature with horn-shaped ears could tempt the holiest of Bishops.

Then she shifted, making it even clearer.

It was insultingly deliberate, that spreading of her legs, making it easy for him to see how her tuft of woman's hair matched the white on her head, and how her dark anus clenched and winked like any other. Despite his own preferences, his cock twitched under his robe.

She *was* real. Yet, she was unreal. He couldn't stop looking as she rested on her elbows, an evil smirk on her face. What was wrong with him? Did she hold him in a spell? And why was Isboern watching *him*, not her?

Did he not warn me to look away?

"Why is she naked, Capitan?" Vene asked with a snarl.

"She removed her own clothing the last time she washed," the younger man answered, pointing at a pile of black clothing. "She hasn't elected to don them again and we haven't opted to force-dress her."

Vene squinted, confused. "How long ago was this?"

"Two days."

"She possesses no maiden's modesty at all?"

"I don't think her origin has that concept."

Indeed, how silly of him to forget.

"A succubus, perhaps? Would she leech the living force from a man to enhance her magic and aid her escape?"

The Capitan smiled. "The God Warriors wanted to test that theory. I say if she's drained of magic, let her stay drained. Although I don't think they recognize what they see, anyway. She either has no mage's aura or has never let one be seen. Given I've watched her while she has slept—not faking, which she also does—and I've seen nothing. No hint of one."

"How could something that looks like this *not* have magic?"

"I don't know. You tell me, Inquisitor."

The two men stayed at the door and did not enter the room. The prisoner kept her anus on display, putting her head down while tensing up.

Then she farted, an abrupt blurt of sound in both his ears.

Vene blinked, turning his nose to the side, tightening it in disgust. "She is doing this on purpose."

Isboern chuckled, nodding, and genuinely amused. "Yes, sir, she is."

"You are not afraid of her. Tell me why."

"What I reported. Word came to me of a black creature stealthing toward the city on the backend. I took a contingent to seek this creature. We caught her and she stabbed me."

"You seem well."

"Thank you. I didn't see a flare of aura even under this basic threat of capture. I haven't seen one since. She eats and pisses and shits like any of us."

"And passes gas toward our noses."

"*And* she knows it's funny." Isboern grinned again as he shrugged. "She hasn't changed her shape, hasn't slipped her chains, hasn't altered her clothing, and if you would get any closer, you'll see she hasn't wounded herself pulling uselessly on them. She isn't in a panic. She still needs to accomplish something."

"Hm." Vene rubbed his clean-shaven jaw, intrigued despite himself. "It seems you have pulled some truths from her before I arrived, Capitan."

"A start, given she doesn't speak Manalari and her Trade is extremely confusing."

"Mimic without comprehension?"

"I think so. Although we got one word right."

"What word?"

"'Shield.'"

"Shield?"

"A relic, I think. She wants to find it, but neither she nor I know where it is."

The Inquisitor looked about him, mildly amused how bloodlessly this interrogation was going so far, and what he'd be reporting to the Archbishop at the end of the day. He felt calm. This made an odd sort of sense.

"Likely to steal it for the dark forces of the North," Vene murmured. "Which suggests *we* should find it first."

"My thoughts as well, Inquisitor."

"There are many shields at Manalar, Capitan, some reasonably enchanted."

"I doubt this is recent. Are there old legends of an exceptional one?"

Vene frowned in concentration, somehow staring at the creature's well-rounded backside but less offended doing so. He was over the surprise, and his interrogation practices rarely, if ever, required him to make use of another's nudity personally.

"I have heard some legends, yes," he said thoughtfully. "But they are prior to the Theocracy. All of those records were burned when Archbishop Tefornin cleansed *Pisc'sagrad*."

"Unfortunate. They might have provided some clues."

"I wager we possess greater libraries than you, Westerner."

The Capitan chuckled. "You'd win that wager, Catechist. Where else might we seek?"

"Hmm."

The demoness rolled over then, showing him her naked breasts and flat belly with her full, frosty pelt. She reached down and ruffled it, then stroked her woman's folds. The God Warriors would have gone mad to watch.

They would kill her for this display alone.

"I see why you do not want *Dyos Guerrimos* as her guards, Capitan."

"Hm, do you, sir?"

"Yes. She is attempting to be killed, since she cannot kill herself."

"Ah, you see it as well."

"Indeed. Best keep the Templars as the sole guards for now, until we learn more about this shield."

"Is that your recommendation to Archbishop Keros?"

Vene nodded smartly. "It is, Capitan."

"I'd request my Templars not be dragged into a long interrogation, if you please. We are preparing for the Ma'ab and running out of time."

"I need neither them nor God's Warriors to conduct my work."

"Of course, sir."

Vene forced himself to approach the demoness, then. He could not go to Keros saying he had stayed at the door the entire time. The creature's large, angled eyes fixed on him like two burning-red coals; she showed him her belly and—curse her stupidity—even opened her legs wider.

She seemed young.

The High Inquisitor smiled harshly down at her. "Do not act this way around the Archbishop when you meet him, demoness. He enjoys breaking libidinous girls of their wayward attempts to ruin good men."

She closed her legs and sat up, leaning against the wall with a scowl and a roll of her eyes.

Insolent bitch.

"Isboern… you said she doesn't speak Manalari."

"She doesn't understand a word. She *is* a good read of body and tone, though, and is trying to learn what riles you up, Inquisitor."

"Oh, I know this well, and we'll watch how she enjoys the tables turned." Vene squatted down beside her, showing his open disdain, presenting his chin within striking distance. "Won't you?"

She couldn't resist.

Her black leg swung up fast as a serpent despite the added weight, her face as venomous. Vene reached out, intending to snatch at her ankle at the right height. He was prepared to make her feel why *no one* had ever kept secrets from him when he wanted to know.

Her foot struck an obstacle unseen before her kick connected. She yelped, rolling away clutching her ankle which had fallen short of the Inquisitor's reach.

She feels true pain inside a living body. Good.

The High Inquisitor gradually lowered his hand as if in disappointment and looked up at the Capitan of the Wall. "Well done, bodyguard."

Now, to know for certain *which* body Isboern had been guarding was the real question. As always, the Westerner's blue and gold aura was nonthreatening; his matching blond and blue-eyed countenance were impossible to read.

He saluted as the High Inquisitor came to his feet. "Sir."

Stepping away from the creature, Vene added casually, "I never felt the spell go off, Isboern. How *do* you do it?"

That charm again. "With a lot of practice, sir."

Heh.

The riddle of the shield nudged for attention, and Vene made eye contact with the naked captive who would tear his throat out if she could.

He spoke in blunt Trade. "Shield?"

She blinked, an odd expression overtaking her face as she forced out, "Sh-shield…"

Her eyes darted to Isboern. The Godblood was telling the truth.

"I will report to the Archbishop," Vene repeated calmly, "and recommend keeping the God Warriors away until I find this relic."

"Yes, sir."

"There is much to be done, always, but I will research what old stories there may be, whether by mouth or book."

"Good, sir. I do think it should be looked into, given that she came here."

"Indeed. Continue your preparations and defenses, Capitan."

"Absolutely, sir. To be worthy of Musanlo."

The High Inquisitor waved his hand, retrieved his torch, and handed over the key. It was interesting how even Vene could not hear anything but a truth every time Willven Isboern said that. He was the only one who had when he first arrived, but now half the city mimicked him.

After some further minor annoyance expelling the God Warriors from the dungeon, Vene Kegyek retraced his steps through the undercroft, toward the crypts. His heart pulsed in his chest as he approached the point where he had seen that damned soul, but it did not appear again.

Deathless one returns.

He supposed it could be a reference to the Ma'ab liches sending their hungry deatheaters, but how would a spirit chained to a different time and death know about their army bearing down on the City of the Sun? Perhaps it alluded to something older. Something in the "before" times, like the shield sought by the black witch.

Vene Kegyek paused where the hall split. To go right would lead him to the crypts; to go left would rise him up into the sun. He raised his torch higher, trying to see down the darker hall without taking a step.

The whispers called to him.

"Be silent," he whispered back, baring his teeth at the chilling abyss. "Lies. Nothing but lies."

ACKNOWLEDGEMENTS

Many thanks, always, to my beta readers, who are the life pulse for each chapter and the compass for finding the way again.

Eris Adderly, Leonard, Dark Pulse, NecrosisBob, Axelotl, & welcoming *Pastor of Muppets* to the crew.

Much love to my Hubs, your delight in this tale will be the halcyon days of my youth.

Boundless appreciation to **Doc Kangey**, for his years-long dedication, design, and guidance to launch the Miurag Archive to my website. Check out our hard work and lore yet to come! miurag.etaski.com

Finally, to my top patrons who have backed us for every step along the way:

Sir Cumference, Baelus, Lesley P.L.A.Y., Jesse C., Does, John K., Roy & Stacy Meyer, Julie S., Paul B., Carla H., Briana R., Josanna, RainbowNight, Kalculyszero, NotSoWeird, Kelly D., Linda H., Raymond T., Lexanii, Zeroharas, Neil M., Fingon, & Johnathon Matlock.

ABOUT THE AUTHOR

Etaski has entertained herself with fantasy stories since the first day she sat on a school bus looking out the window. When handwritten letters were disappearing, she scribbled no less than five pages to be worth the postage. Her early stories were written by hand, and she had a writer's callus and three embarrassing novels before graduating high school.

She studied science, archaeology, history, and theater. Frank discussion of sexuality was rare growing up, so she wrote fantasies, theories, and observations within stories for deeper contemplation or just be entertained.

History speaks little on sexuality, yet biology demonstrates how it sways basic choices. Drama reveals our strongest bonds but may fade to black at its most intimate. In the Sister Seekers, the sex and the story are inseparable, and their discoveries will change the journey of Miurag without cutting away.

Please consider leaving a review of this book. It truly helps!

smarturl.it/etaskiamazon

www.goodreads.com/etaski

www.bookbub.com/authors/a-s-etaski

Sign up to Etaski's newsletter for Sister Seekers releases at:

www.etaski.com

NEW!

Read more about the setting of Sister Seekers at World Anvil!

miurag.etaski.com